The Mormon Secret

Lisa Puckrin

⚘ Creative Arts & Sciences House
West Melbourne, Florida USA

$ Creative Arts & Sciences House
   West Melbourne, Florida USA

ISBN 978-0-9829729-1-5

Current Printing: 2

Printed in the United States of America

Library of Congress Control Number: 2013954989

Acknowledgements

My husband, Glenn, for his belief in me and support taking care of the kids while I write. You are my soul mate and my best friend.

My kids, Gavin and Sienna, for their patience and understanding while I pursue my dream. I love you and thank God for the miracle of having you both each and every day.

My friends Claire Peterson and Jennilyn Walker. There's something to be said when a friendship spans decades.

My family, for providing a love of books and being enthusiastic readers who provide great feedback.

My editor, Rusty Allred, for making my book better, my prose tighter and reassuring me that there are others who feel as strongly as I do about grammar.

Our friend, Cody Hawkes, who designed the cover and brought the ideas in my head to life. You're an artistic genius.

For Glenn

Chapter 1

As Steve Call walked toward the southwest end of Brigham Young University's campus, he visibly relaxed. This was his favorite part of the nightly patrol. This end of campus had a creek, a small pond and lots of trees. He always ended his patrol here. He found the babbling of the creek and the sound of the crickets soothing and it helped relax him before bed. He didn't sleep well anymore.

He passed the Joseph Smith Memorial Building and glanced over at a couple sitting on one of the benches in front of the building. They were kissing, lost in each other. Looking at them brought a deep pang in his heart. He looked away and kept walking, lost in thought about his wife, Kari.

It was almost a year since the divorce. He often thought about her and his decisions while on patrol. He wondered how his life might have been different had he not joined the Army— if he had never been to Iraq. He joined the day after 9/11 in the height of the patriotic fervor. He felt he had a duty to go.

She had understood in the beginning. They were newlyweds and Kari was busy finishing her bachelor's degree. They both looked forward to his return with great anticipation. She e-mailed him regularly and they often had video calls. Her love kept him going through it all—first the brutal boot camp, and then the boredom and waiting and finally the terrible horror of seeing his friends die.

When he finally returned after his first tour, they were like newlyweds again. This line of thinking always brought a smile to Steve's lips, despite everything that had happened. He thought about how they had holed up in a hotel for a week, not even leaving the room. When he left for his second tour a year later, Kari had just discovered she was pregnant. He hated to leave her, but didn't have a choice. After a month, Kari started to feel very sick and her letters became despondent and eventually resentful that Steve was so far away.

He tried to support her as best he could from Iraq. His buddy even let him sneak in for extra video call time. He had his mom send her flowers. He did everything he possibly could. But by the time he arrived home, just in time for the baby's birth, Kari was deeply resentful and withdrawn. He thought he could get things back on track and made sure to help as much as possible with the baby. He was the first one up when Arianna cried. He would feed her a bottle and rock her back to sleep. Things started to get better for a few months and Kari seemed to be softening, but he got his next tour assignment when Ari was six months old.

He still remembered the finality in Kari's voice when he told her he had to leave again. "Don't bother coming back," she had said as she slammed the bedroom door. He had only been in Afghanistan for a few months when Kari e-mailed him to say she was pregnant again. Two weeks later she lost the baby. Things deteriorated. Kari stopped responding to Steve's e-mails and there were no more video calls. One day, Steve received an official-looking envelope—divorce papers.

Steve roughly shook his head. This line of thinking was too painful. He hadn't reupped when his time came. All he had left now was Ari, and he didn't want to be too far from her. Kari had remarried and moved to Provo, so Steve decided to finish his degree and work as a campus police officer.

As he neared the Maeser building, he suddenly stopped. His muscles tensed and he reflexively reached for his gun. Something was wrong. He glanced around—nothing. His body was reacting, even before his mind had figured out what was wrong. He mentally reviewed his patrol. Something had been wrong—the couple. His mind was just registering that the brief glimpse of the couple was disturbing him. He started walking back toward them, focusing on his mental review. The expensive clothes, the man's goatee, the *earpiece* in the woman's ear—they weren't students.

Steve broke into a run. He rounded the corner of the building, but the couple was gone. He instinctively approached the front door of the building, easing forward, listening for any sounds, rotating, covering his flank.

Nothing. He pulled on the doors, expecting them to still be locked. He had checked them earlier on his patrol. They easily swung open. He moved through the doors and did a quick glance around the corners. No one was in sight. He headed toward the common room. He glanced at the display cases and immediately saw their target. A section of the display glass had been removed. Steve approached the glass, glancing around to make sure the thieves weren't there.

Steve examined the display case, containing ancient Latin American artifacts. They had only taken one. It was a targeted theft. Steve's mind was spinning—why would anyone want to steal this artifact?

He quickly turned and headed toward the other door— scanning and listening. Nothing. He spent the next hour moving through the building methodically, searching the auditorium, the hallways, any open offices.

With each passing minute, he knew he had failed. By the end of his search, he was mentally exhausted. They were gone.

Chapter 2

RJ McAllister looked around the now empty board room at SalesPro's headquarters in Atlanta, Georgia. Cigarette smoke hung in thick clouds in the room and full ashtrays were scattered across the expensive, mahogany table. Imported crystal glasses were also strewn around the table, most empty. The late-night board meeting hadn't gone well. Profits were down last quarter—again.

RJ sighed, a luxury he hadn't allowed himself during the meeting, and pulled himself out of his soft, leather chair. He grunted, realizing he had probably put even more weight on his ample frame. He thought back to the days of his second wife—Heidi—a Swedish model. He had exercised daily with her and had been trim and strong. That was two wives ago and he no longer had time for frivolous things such as exercise—he had to pay for all of those high-maintenance ex-wives and their demanding children.

RJ walked over to the sidebar. He hadn't allowed himself a drink during the meeting, but he always drank heavily afterward. He chose straight bourbon and swallowed the first glass without hesitation. RJ heard the boardroom door open and then close behind him. He glanced over to see Preston, the company's chief financial officer, walking toward him. Preston was immaculately dressed as always. From his Armani suits to his Italian shoes, Preston was the picture of success and composure. Tall and thin with black hair graying at the temples, Preston was in his early 50s. RJ's hair was nearly gone at 60 and due to his weight, bad temper and inability to successfully deal with the press, Preston had become the public face of the company shortly after the departure of RJ's wife number three.

RJ downed his second glass, grabbed the bottle, and sank back into his chair. Preston came and sat down next to him, glancing at his smartphone to read his e-mails while he waited.

"Well, Preston, are you going to loosen your tie now?" RJ scowled. Preston's constant composure irritated him.

Preston, as usual, didn't react. They had worked together for over 10 years and he knew it was just RJ's way of venting his frustration. Preston finished reading an e-mail, put down his phone and looked RJ in the eye. "The board is calling for your head," he said directly.

RJ picked up his empty glass and violently threw it against the wall. It shattered and left bourbon dripping down the wall. He then picked up the bottle, took a long pull, and said through gritted teeth, "This is *my* company, Preston. Mine! I built it from the ground up. No one is going to take it away from me." He glanced around the room at the empty seats and added menacingly, "*No one.*"

"What are you going to do?" Preston asked calmly, thinking that because the company had gone public 10 years ago, the board could and, indeed, would remove RJ if things didn't change.

RJ inwardly laughed at Preston's question. It wasn't, "What are we going to do?" They had long ago assumed the roles they now occupied—Preston kept his hands clean and maintained the company image. RJ took care of the dirty work behind the scenes and it was usually *very* dirty. "I've already done it," RJ replied with a smirk.

Preston was tempted to ask for details, but he never did. It was better that he didn't know. Over the years, he had pieced together enough details of RJ's *handling* things to know that he didn't want to know more. He thought back to the early days when RJ had infiltrated their top competitor,

SalesTeam, with an ex-CIA agent. The man had proved genius and had quickly risen to VP. He regularly fed strategic information to RJ and kept SalesPro ahead of SalesTeam. Preston knew his services were expensive because he sent the wire transfers. Then one day, RJ just said the agent's contract was finished and Preston never heard from him again. He tried not to think that RJ most likely had him killed.

SalesTeam was headquartered in Salt Lake City, Utah and the founder was a Mormon. They had grown rapidly, despite all of RJ's tactics. He had tried bribery, slur campaigns, the infiltration and even regularly falsified numbers to make his own company look good, yet SalesTeam had continued to grow and was now eclipsing SalesPro. Just last quarter, they had lost one of their top clients, a $100M account, to SalesTeam and with the loss came their first-ever negative profit quarter.

The liquor had emboldened RJ and he added, "Let's just say I'm taking down those Mormons once and for all."

Chapter 3

The Joseph Smith Memorial Building's common room was now buzzing with activity. Steve's boss, the campus police chief, was directing efforts and the local Provo police had arrived as well. Curious students gathered around the building, but were kept out by the officers.

Steve watched in amusement as they searched for fingerprints on the doors and glass display cases. He knew they wouldn't find anything. Steve's boss caught the look on his face and walked over to join him at the back of the room.

"Waste of time, don't you think?" Steve asked his boss, Gary. Steve had shared his assessment earlier that the thieves were professionals.

Gary studied Steve's face and then replied honestly, "Yeah, probably. But we have to do it anyway, you know that." Gary had been the campus police chief for over 20 years. He was retired city police and had always liked Steve. He was one of the few on his team that had seen any real combat experience.

"We didn't find any door-lock tampering," Gary added, looking steadily at Steve.

Steve knew Gary thought he had forgot to checks the locks, but he had reviewed it in his mind numerous times. "They were locked," Steve said confidently and then concluded, "They must have had someone inside waiting. The doors had only been locked 30 minutes before."

Gary nodded in acceptance. He knew Steve was thorough.

Steve asked quietly, "Do we have security feed for the back of the building? They must have had a vehicle waiting on the road back there to get away so quickly."

Gary sighed and looked tired as he replied, "No, I've tried to get them to cover the entire campus for years, but they always say they don't have the budget. There are only a few covered areas—the bookstore, the art museum, the administration building—only the areas that have high value."

Just then the Provo police chief indicated for Gary to join him, so Steve turned and walked toward one of the hallways stretching south. He wanted some time alone to think, to try and recall more about the suspects.

He was lost in thought when he heard a door softly click around the corner. His body tensed and he pulled his gun. He edged forward toward the corner, gun leading the way. He heard someone walking toward him. His muscles were taut, his mind clear—all of his military training coming into effect. The intruder was rapidly approaching the corner. He realized he wouldn't have time to look and flattened himself against the wall waiting. As the intruder rounded the corner, he moved into position, raising his gun and shouted, "Stop."

He heard a gasp. It was a woman and her hands automatically shot up, dropping several textbooks, loose papers flying into the air. Steve studied her. She was in her early thirties with thick black hair pulled into a ponytail. She had no makeup and was wearing sweats. Steve circled her and looked for a weapon, frisking as he went. He pulled an MP3 player out of her pocket, the earphones trailing behind. He had just completed his search when he saw Gary walking toward him at a brisk pace with a panicked look.

"Dr. Worthington," Gary said in an anxious voice, "Our deepest apologies." He reached Steve and put his hand on his arm to lower his weapon. "Steve, this is Dr. Emma Worthington, our associate dean of religion."

Steve stepped away from Gary and raised his weapon again toward Dr. Worthington. He had been assessing her height and frame. She was roughly the same build as the woman he had seen outside the building earlier. Same black hair. Different clothes, but she could have changed. "What are you doing here so late?" Steve asked roughly.

Emma looked at Gary pleadingly, but answered nonetheless, "I was grading papers in my office."

Steve persisted, "I swept the building myself, checking every open office and calling for any staff to come out of the locked ones."

Emma confidently answered, "I lock my office door while in there late at night and I didn't hear you," pointing to her MP3 player that Steve was still holding. "I listen to my music while I grade papers. I *didn't* hear you."

Gary glared at Steve and said firmly, "Steve, I've known her since she was little. She's okay. Put your gun away." When Steve hesitated, Gary added, "That's an *order*." Steve reluctantly put his gun away, but went directly to her satchel and began to search it.

Emma lowered her arms and asked, "What in heaven's name is going on here, Gary?"

"We've had a break-in and a theft," Gary explained, rubbing his temples. This was definitely not how he had wanted to spend his Friday night. He was at dinner with his wife when he got the call from Steve.

"Who would want to break in here?" Emma asked and then added, "Maybe some students pulling a prank?"

"No, Steve saw them—they were professionals," Gary explained.

"So you saw them, but *didn't* stop them?" Emma asked Steve directly with her head cocked to one side.

"They were posing as students," Steve explained, handing her the satchel since he had found only books, papers and a cell phone. "I didn't realize until it was too late." Steve cursed himself for the hundredth time that evening. If he hadn't allowed himself his life reflections, he probably would have stopped them. He realized that civilian life was making him soft. A lack of concentration like that in combat would have cost him his life.

Gary started gathering up her papers, so Steve bent down to help. "What did they take?" Emma asked.

"One of the artifacts on display," Gary answered with a tired voice.

Emma considered that for a moment, and then replied softly, "Which one?"

Steve heard something in her voice and stood up, looking her in the eyes. "Third from the left," he answered, searching her face. Emma seemingly lost in thought, began to walk quickly toward the commons room. Steve and Gary followed behind. When she got to the room, she suddenly stopped.

Steve followed Emma's gaze to the empty space in the display case and then looked back at Emma. Her face had gone white. "What is it?" Steve asked intently, glancing from her to the display case.

"Our *worst* fears," Emma answered flatly and sighed. She then took her cell phone, dialed a number and waited for an answer. "Hi, Celia. It's Emma. How is Dr. Mangum tonight?"

Gary and Steve watched her closely, puzzled.

"That's good to hear," she answered and then got to the point. "May I please speak to him for a quick second?" She paused and then continued, "Hello, Roger. I'm sorry to bother you, but I knew you'd want to hear—the artifact has been stolen and they think it was professionals. . . Yes, third from the left. . . Mm, hmm. . . Ok, are you sure you feel up to it? We're on our way."

Emma snapped her phone closed and turned to Gary and Steve. "He wants to see us—right away. He has something to tell us."

Chapter 4

"Who are we going to see?" Steve asked as they rode in Gary's car.

"*Whom* are we going to see, you mean," Emma stated.

Steve looked at Gary, but Gary kept quiet. "You're correcting my grammar at a time like this?" Steve asked incredulously, shaking his head.

Emma ignored his remark and replied, "Dr. Roger Mangum is the dean of religion and my boss. He has Stage 4 cancer and is on medical leave. He put me in charge before he left and told me that, as dean, he had been entrusted to care for the artifacts and that the third one from the left was special. He told me it was our job to protect it and not mention it to anyone. He wanted me to know, in case he—" At this Emma broke off. All of the evening's stress had taken its toll on her and she suddenly realized she had failed in her duty to protect the artifact.

They arrived at the house and were let in by Dr. Mangum's wife. She led them to a small book-lined study where a man in his early 60's was sitting in a leather recliner. His face was withdrawn and pale and an oxygen tube ran from his nostrils to a nearby portable tank.

Emma walked over and hugged him, asking, "How are you tonight?"

"Fine, fine," he answered dismissively and then said, "Hello, Gary."

11

They shook hands and then Gary introduced Steve. Dr. Mangum examined Steve's face contemplatively and then, seeming satisfied, asked them to all take seats. His wife came in, went to his desk and opened a drawer. She removed a photocopy and handed it to her husband and then left the room and closed the door behind her.

"What I'm about to tell you is in the strictest of confidence," he began with a lilt of excitement in his voice. He reached over and handed the photocopy to Emma. "When I became the dean of religion at BYU, the previous dean came to my house one night. He told me that as dean it was our sacred duty to protect certain church artifacts. He told me that this one was special and we should guard it well. I asked him why it was with us and not in the church's secure vaults and he said sometimes the best place to hide things is in plain sight."

He took a deep breath and continued, "I was young then and curious about the artifact. I occasionally did research to try and discover more about it. But I never found anything in the church's history about it." The talking had dried out his voice and he took a sip of water.

Emma handed Gary the artifact copy and then Gary passed it to Steve. He studied the picture, trying to understand it. It looked about four inches in size, made of wood and had symbols on it—no wording.

The dean felt revived and added, "I came in on a holiday once to pick up some of my books and because the building was empty, I used my key and opened the artifact display case to get a better look at it. I wondered if there was something on the back. I looked, but there was nothing. I decided to make a copy of it, just in case." He paused again, seeming to struggle with whether or not to continue. He finally said, "It wasn't until I got back into my car that I realized something. The artifact was very unusual. The display card said it was found in South America in an Aztec village, but that was impossible."

"Why is that?" Emma asked, leaning forward.

"The artifact is made of oak," he added triumphantly. "Which is not found in South America." He paused for effect and they all considered his words, but he wasn't finished. "Emma, do you know where you can find a lot of oak trees?" he asked with a smile, knowing she could answer.

Emma looked at Dr. Mangum and then turned to Steve and Gary. "In the Sacred Grove," she answered.

"But there are oak trees all over America," Gary interjected, "How do you know it came from upstate New York and specifically the Sacred Grove?"

"Because someone wanted us to know it came from there," he added cryptically.

"What do you mean?" Emma asked, leaning forward in her chair.

"Emma, do you remember when I took a sabbatical about eight years ago and Sister Magnum and I went on a mission?" he asked with a twinkle in his eye.

"Yes, you served at the visitors' center at the Sacred Grove," she dutifully replied.

"Do you remember how I once told you I would take a walk every morning through the trees? After doing that, I got to know those old trees pretty well. One day, I wandered off the path a bit when I noticed something. There was a tree at the edge of the north clearing that had a notch cut out from it. The notch was four or five inches square. It appeared to be the very size of the artifact. I thought it was very strange that someone would have removed some of the tree like that." Silence filled the room as they all digested what the dean was saying. Steve looked at Emma and could see her mind was whirring, running through the possibilities. A ringing phone broke the silence and Sister Magnum opened the study door. "Honey, it's President Thompson for you," she said casually as though he received calls like that every day. President Thompson was the current president of the church. Both Gary and Steve instinctively stood up. Emma looked bewildered.

Dr. Magnum picked up the phone at his side, covered the mouthpiece for a minute, and then said, "Would all of you please step out for a minute?" They went into the hallway and then through to the living room. He called them back in a few minutes later.

"Steve and Emma, you are to meet with President Thompson tomorrow morning in his office on Temple Square at 8:00 a.m. sharp. A car and driver will pick you up at 6:45," he instructed. They both nodded mutely, stunned at the events unfolding. "Before you go," he added, looking sad now and weaker by the minute, "There's something else I need to tell you. Please, close the door for a minute," he indicated with his hand.

Gary closed the door and then sat down to listen. "My youngest daughter, Staci, is 19. Last year, she met a guy at church in her singles' ward who was visiting. He said he had just moved here from Georgia and was investigating the church. They dated for about six months and he seemed very near to converting. He was very enthusiastic and seemed madly in love with Staci. Then one day, he was just gone without a trace. They had come to visit me at work the night before at the JS Memorial Building. I showed him around, telling him more about the church and the artifacts on display. After that, I left him and Staci alone. She later told me that she had disclosed to him that I had a deep interest in the wood artifact and was researching the origins."

His eyes filled with tears and his face was twisted with emotion. "She had no idea she disclosed a church secret. She thought I was just curious about the piece because she had seen research on my desk here at home and in my office. She, of course, felt terrible later when she realized he had just been using her for information. I consulted with President Thompson and asked if he wanted to have the artifact removed, but he felt it was still secure and so we just decided to heighten security on it. That's when we hired you, Steve. We knew with your military background you would be more than capable of protecting it. Gary here assigned you to the south end of campus on the weekends since we figured that would be the time of greatest risk."

Steve felt the guilt return and flood his chest. All along he had been protecting an important church artifact and he never knew. And he had failed. He resolved to not let personal things distract him anymore. He would find a way to get it back, no matter what it took.

As they said goodbye to the dean and walked out to Gary's car, they didn't see a man, dressed in black, watching from the shadows.

Chapter 5

"Yeah, I've got it," the man answered into his Bluetooth earpiece as he followed Gary's car from a distance.

"Did you have any complications?" RJ asked.

"No," the man answered with a laugh. "There wasn't even an alarm or security cameras to knock out. Easiest job I've had in years."

RJ laughed. "Those Mormons are trusting—too trusting! It's their greatest weakness and we'll use it to our full advantage. What about the girl—did you take care of her?"

The man thought for a second about the professional girl he had used for the job. He liked her. She was *very* friendly with him. He was supposed to dispose of her afterward, but he decided to keep her around as company for awhile. She was back at the hotel waiting for him now. "I did some research on the campus officer, Call. He's divorced and lonely. She might come in handy."

RJ laughed on the other end of the line. "Just don't let her get in the way." Normally, RJ wouldn't allow this kind of distraction, but this guy was the best he'd used in years and he needed the best on this job. Besides, he was worried deep down. He had a thick file on Steve Call sitting on his desk. It highlighted his several tours of duty and that he was Special Forces. He might be problematic.

He also had a file on Emma Worthington. It wasn't as thick. She was pretty boring, actually. Grew up in the Provo area, received her bachelor's, master's and then her doctorate, all from BYU. A few minor boyfriends through the years, but as she got older, it happened less and less. She threw herself into her career and despite all of the odds, advanced in a male-dominated profession as a single woman. RJ was counting on her extensive Mormon history knowledge to help him find what he was looking for.

"Call me tomorrow with an update to tell me if they've taken the bait," RJ said as he hung up the office phone.

Chapter 6

Steve shifted in the leather seat uncomfortably. He didn't like being chauffeured. He looked at the two security guards in the front seat with their earpiece wires stretching behind their ears. He already knew he could take them both out in seconds. He'd developed the ability in the Army to quickly size up an opponent and know if he could win. He heard them talking about the Utah Jazz win last night and knew they weren't paying attention to the car that was following them. He had noticed it shortly after they had picked him up. Someone was way ahead of them. He didn't like feeling outmaneuvered without even knowing who the enemy was.

He looked over at Emma. Last night she had looked tired, irritated and unattractive. Today, she was dressed up and had done her hair and makeup and he realized she was pretty. He glanced away, determined not to get distracted again.

She didn't notice. She was lost in study of the photocopy and was searching through a history book, looking for clues. She looked agitated and nervous. He had to admit, he was nervous himself. He had never met an apostle before, let alone a prophet of God. He was worried that President Thompson would see right down into his soul. Divorced. Angry. Killed a lot of people in battle.

They finally arrived in downtown Salt Lake City. The driver turned at Main Street and entered the underground parking garage. Steve glanced behind them as they descended, but the blue car didn't follow them. They parked and then were taken into a garage office. Here they had to go through metal detectors and get frisked. They searched Emma's bag and then let them through. The same driver led them to a golf cart and drove them through an underground passageway. Steve started to feel lost as they made several turns. A few minutes later, they came to a stop at a door. Security guards, posted at the entrance, greeted them as they passed. They were led into an elevator and the driver scanned his badge and selected the button. When the doors opened, Steve had no idea where they were. He glanced at Emma, but she seemed calm and confident.

She caught his glance, and, reading his confusion explained, "We're in the Church Administration building, where the First Presidency has their offices." They walked a few short steps across the marble floors and then the driver indicated for them to sit and wait in two plush, burgundy chairs.

They waited about 10 minutes and then heard voices. Steve recognized President Thompson's melodic voice and instinctively stood up. He looked much the same on TV and Steve recognized the governor of Utah shaking his hand.

"Good to see you, as always," the governor said to President Thompson with a smile. The driver then escorted the governor to the same elevator they had come up in. Emma had stood as well and they turned to meet President Thompson. He greeted them both with a warm smile and invited them to come into his office. It was tastefully decorated.

"Well, good morning, and thank you both for coming to see me today," President Thompson said with a smile as he lowered himself down into his chair. Steve looked at the prophet warily, wondering if he was assessing him, but he only found kindness and a bit of sadness in his eyes.

"Roger has brought me up to speed on the break-in last night," President Thompson started.

"It was my fault, sir," Steve spoke up as he sat upright in his chair. "I was on patrol that night. I failed in my duty to protect the university and the church's property."

President Thompson just smiled and replied, "No, no, if it's anyone's fault it's mine." Emma had been studying her

19

hands, feeling at fault as well, but looked up in surprise. He continued, "I should have put it into our church vault years ago. I honestly didn't think anyone would ever try to steal it. To be honest, I don't even know what the symbols on the artifact mean. Roger has told me his theory that the wood came from the Sacred Grove."

He paused then and reached into his desk. He pulled out a small box and opened the lid. Inside was a scrolled parchment. He put on protective gloves and then gently unrolled the parchment. "I was given this box by President Anderson before he passed away. He told me that it had been handed down by all of the prophets over time, no one knowing when it originated. The instructions were to only open it if the artifact was ever stolen."

He indicated for Steve and Emma to come and look at the parchment with him. "I opened it late last night when I heard of the theft. But I'm afraid I'm no further ahead with what this all means."

Emma looked at the document. It had a scrawled handwriting in ink with only a few lines. Emma read aloud:

There once was a man who lived near a mighty river in the East.

One day, he saw smoke afar off. He didn't worry.

Then the strong breeze shifted north and the destroyer was born.

Soon his house was ablaze.

He tried to squelch the destroyer, but he couldn't.

He was sorrowful and died.

His friends buried them near the mighty river.

Both Steve and Emma turned to look at President Thompson. "That's it, I'm afraid. It's obviously a parable, but as to the meaning, I am not clear. I prayed about it this morning, but felt strongly that it was your mission to figure this out."

Emma turned back to study the document. "The first part is Joseph's handwriting," Emma said. "But I don't recognize the second one."

President Thompson looked closer at the document and said, "You know, I believe that's Brigham Young's." Emma studied it again and nodded her assent. President Thompson looked lost in thought for a moment. "I have just remembered something that John Taylor supposedly said. He stated that Brigham had once told him there was a secret and it was about Joseph. But that's all he said."

President Thompson stood up and walked over to the window. He looked out and said, "Someone knows about this secret. That is why they have stolen the artifact. You must find out what the secret is before they do." He turned back toward them and his smile was gone. He looked at them both intently and said, "We are *all* relying on you. The brethren and I will pray for you. You will have the church's full resources at your disposal to find this secret." He then looked directly at Steve and said, "Be careful." He then handed them both a photocopy of the parchment. "Don't let this get into the wrong hands."

The man waited at the parking entrance and was rewarded for his patience. Within an hour, the same black Town Car emerged and headed toward the freeway. The man chuckled at the ease of the job—clearly these Mormons either didn't know he was watching them or were incapable of using any stealth. He thought about his Cayman Islands bank account which was growing larger by the week. When he finished this job, he would have enough to disappear. He might even take this new woman with him.

He followed them back to Provo and watched as they each came out of their apartment with luggage—the girl with a suitcase and the guy with a military bag. Soon they were on the freeway headed to the airport. He hit the speed dial on his phone and RJ picked up on the first ring. "They met with some church official. I couldn't follow them; there was too much security. They're on their way to the airport now. They've definitely taken the bait."

Chapter 7

Emma absentmindedly bit the nail on her index finger. She hated flying and hadn't attempted it in years. As a historian, she had always wanted to go and see a lot of the church history sites, but it was too far to drive; her fear of flying had kept her in Utah. She pulled her finger away from her mouth and made herself stop exhibiting her fears. This was how she had gotten to where she was—acting strong and confident even when inside she was terrified.

She looked over at Steve. He was glancing casually behind them. "What are you looking at?" she asked.

"Nothing," he replied. She could see the tight lines in his jaw though and knew he was tense about something. They had decided to go to the Sacred Grove in Palmyra, New York to look for clues. It was the only clue they had at this point until she figured out the parable.

They were close to the airport and were surprised when the driver pulled into a different area. "Where are we going?" Steve asked the driver.

"To the private airport," he answered, "We're already a day behind the thieves. A wealthy church member has indefinitely loaned his private jet to the First Presidency for official business and President Thompson wants you to use it."

They pulled up next to an impressive-looking white jet with the pilot and flight attendant waiting at the top of the stairs for them. Steve got their bags out of the trunk and headed toward the plane. Another car then pulled up next to them and a security guard jumped out. He ran toward Steve and handed him a thick envelope. "This is from President Thompson. There are secure cell phones in here as well as plenty of cash for your trip. Remember, just in case, don't use any personal credit cards; that will make you easy to trace." Steve nodded and took the envelope. He gave him their personal cell phones to ensure their location wasn't tracked. He was on the first step before he realized Emma wasn't behind him. He turned and looked back and saw she was frozen on the spot, staring at the jet.

"Are you coming?" he asked, surprised to see a frightened look on her face.

She seemed to muster some internal courage and propelled herself forward, "Of course I am," she replied confidently. The flight attendant helped them stow their bags and they settled into the luxurious leather seats. They soon were ready for take-off. Steve chose a seat by the window facing the airport and looked out. The blue car was nowhere in sight. Using the private jet had likely thrown off their tail.

Emma sat facing him, but away from the window in the aisle seat. She pulled her seatbelt tight and clutched the armrests for security. Steve noticed her knuckles turning white and remarked, "Not a fan of flying, huh?"

Emma thought about replying with a smart remark, but just then the pilot edged the plane forward and she lost her gusto. As they taxied onto the runway and the pilot revved the engines, she felt her face going white. Her stomach churned and she began to think she might throw up. She looked up at Steve and expected to see a mocking smile, but instead found concern on his face. He undid his seatbelt and came over to sit beside her. He gently asked, "Are you all right?"

She didn't have time to answer as she was pushed back into her seat as the plane surged forward. They ascended rapidly; the higher they got, the greener Emma's face became. When they finally leveled off and the pilot turned off the fasten seatbelt sign, Emma rapidly undid her seatbelt and headed for the small bathroom in the back.

Steve looked sympathetically toward the bathroom. Emma didn't come out for 15 minutes and he started to worry about her. He finally went over and knocked on the door. "Emma, are you all right?"

"Yes," came a weak voice. "I'll be out in a minute."

When she finally came out, the color was returning to her pale face. She looked away, embarrassed. Steve decided to change the subject. "Come sit down for a minute. I want to go through some things with you."

Emma nodded mutely and sat down in her chair, rapidly buckling her seatbelt. Steve waited until she was ready and then said, "Emma, I didn't want to alarm you before, but I think we both need to be open and honest with each other. Someone has been following us for the past 24 hours. I think President Thompson is right. I think the stakes are really high. These are definitely professionals that we're up against. Now, I can protect us, but I need you to do whatever I say, exactly when I say it—can you do that?"

The frightened look was back in her eyes, but her voice didn't betray it. "Yes, I will," she said confidently.

"And I don't think we should talk about any of this when anyone else is around," he added. "We can't trust anyone but each other."

"Agreed," she said.

"Now, the private jet gives us a huge advantage," he explained. "We've lost our tail for now. If he's good, he'll figure out where we've gone though. Before we land, I want you to go into the bathroom and change your clothes and hairstyle. I will do the same and wear a cap. I brought you a backpack. We're going to ditch your suitcase and get more mobile in case we need to move quickly."

He opened up the packet from President Thompson's security guard and gave her one of the phones. "These are clean—I mean secure. Keep it in your backpack, but keep it turned off to save power. We'll only use them if we get separated." He also handed her a wad of money. "Put some of this in each of your shoes and in your backpack. Don't use any of your debit or credit cards no matter what."

Emma nodded again and he could see fear in her eyes. He decided to venture into her terrain to make her feel more comfortable. "Any ideas on the parable?"

She pulled out the paper and began to study the photocopy again. "I have a couple of thoughts," she began. "Either the poem is about Joseph and Brigham, or just Joseph and Brigham finished it after Joseph was murdered." Steve nodded his encouragement, so Emma continued. "There are only two geographic mentions—north and east, so I'd say we're right in heading to the New England area. Other than that, I'm not sure. We could take the parable for face value and assume that it's talking about Joseph and the adversity he faced in his life. In the end, it overcame him and he died. But first of all, parables are meant to have hidden meanings, so it can't be that obvious. And secondly, in the last line it says, 'they were buried.' It's not just referring to Joseph. Of course, Joseph and his brother Hyrum were buried together in Nauvoo and Nauvoo is near a mighty river, so that might be something."

Emma sighed and looked up at Steve. "But I'm not sure how this all ties into the artifact. Hopefully, we'll find some answers at the Sacred Grove." She began to write some notes into her notepad, so Steve leaned back into the comfortable leather seat and tried to relax for a bit. He hadn't slept well last night given everything that happened. He finally drifted off to sleep.

Emma took the chance while Steve was asleep to examine his sleeping face. He had a lot of sorrow and sometimes anger in his eyes and she wondered what he had been through. He had sandy blonde hair and a handsome face. She noticed a three-inch scar on the left side of his neck and wondered if he had been hurt in battle. He hadn't mentioned a wife, but they hadn't really talked about their personal lives. She thought back to their first meeting and how he had held a gun to her head.

She inwardly laughed and thought to herself that she was glad he was on her side. She wondered who was looking for the secret and to what lengths they might go to get it. This worried her, so she pushed it from her mind. Steve's steady breathing and the hum of the engines made her feel sleepy as well. She had tossed and turned in her sleep last night. She finally drifted off as well.

About an hour later, she heard a distant shout and then another more loudly this time and she forced her eyes open. She looked over at Steve and he was sweating and writhing in his chair. Realizing he was having a nightmare, she reached over to gently wake him. When he felt her touch, his eyes sprang open and he reached over, grabbed her hand and twisted it painfully.

"Steve, it's me, Emma," she cried out. The flight attendant heard the commotion and came to see what happened. Steve shook his head. His eyes came into focus and he immediately let go of her arm.

"I . . . I'm sorry, Emma," he breathed, his pulse still racing. "I'm sorry." Seeing everything was all right, the flight attendant left. Steve wiped the sweat from his face and took a few deep breaths. "Did I hurt you?" he asked softly.

"N-n-no, I'm fine," Emma replied a little shaken. "Are *you* okay?" She looked at him with deep concern on her face.

Steve continued to try and compose himself and then replied honestly, "I don't sleep well. I have a lot of nightmares . . . reliving the worst of my Army days."

"It's very common for soldiers to have post-traumatic stress syndrome," Emma added. "I think it's your mind trying to deal with what you've been through."

Steve shook his head in frustration and said, "I know, but it was bad enough living through it the first time. To see the replay in my head each night is so much worse."

"Maybe it would help if you talked about it," Emma suggested softly.

Steve looked at Emma. He could tell she had been very sheltered growing up and she had an innocence about her. How could he tell her about seeing his best friends being shot next to him and having their blood splash onto his face? Or being near a suicide bomber when he detonated and having the bomber's flesh and body parts splat all over him? Or watching women and children be used as human shields? It was unthinkable, unbearable.

"Maybe another time," Steve replied, picking up a nearby magazine. It was *Fortune* and he wasn't interested in it. He just flipped through the pages until Emma returned to her research.

They prepared to descend a while later and both Emma and Steve changed their clothes. Emma transferred her belongings into the backpack and they were soon on the ground.

Chapter 8

RJ slammed his fist down on his desk in frustration. His man had just called to say he'd lost them. His man had not even considered that the Mormons would use a private jet. *He* didn't even have a private jet. He picked up the phone and dialed his son's number. Riley was his eldest child from his first wife and was about the only child still speaking to him. Riley was named after his dad, Riley James, and they were a lot alike.

Riley's good looks and superb acting ability made him very useful. He had done a brilliant job posing as an eager "investigator" in the Mormon religion and was the one to uncover the artifact secret from Staci, the dean's daughter.

RJ glanced at the clock. It was nearly noon. Was his lazy son still in bed after a late-night party? Finally, the line picked up and he heard a woman's voice on the phone. She was giggling and said, "Hello?" RJ glanced at the number he had dialed. Yes, it was the right number.

"Let me talk to my son, NOW!" RJ barked.

A second later his son's voice came on the line sounding annoyed. "What is it, Dad? I'm . . . in the middle of something." He heard more giggling.

"I'm changing my will," he said coldly. He planned to leave everything to Riley and it was always his leverage to get Riley to do what he wanted.

He heard shuffling in the background and a door clicking. "All right, all right, you've got my attention," Riley said. "Now, what do you want?"

"Tell me everything you've learned about the Mormons," he demanded and then clarified, "About their history."

"Well, they believe Joseph Smith saw God and Jesus in a grove of trees in Palmyra, New York," Riley began. "They call it their Sacred Grove or something like that. And God told him not to join any of the organized religions at the time, but to wait and Jesus would bring back his original church on the earth again." RJ jotted down Palmyra, New York on a piece of paper. Riley continued, "After that, he was supposedly visited by an angel called Moroni and he told Joseph that he would lead him to some gold plates that contained a history of people who lived here in America. They believe that Joseph did receive the gold plates from the angel at a place called Hill Cumorah. It's near Palmyra."

RJ wrote down Cumorah. "What else?" RJ prompted impatiently.

"Joseph Smith formed a church and they moved around a lot after that. They were in Ohio, Missouri, Illinois. People didn't like them because of their beliefs and they finally got Joseph Smith and his brother and killed them. They are buried in Nauvoo, Illinois."

"I need actual cities and all of them," RJ said, "NOW!"

Riley took a deep breath. This meant the end of his morning with the beautiful girl in his bedroom. "I'll have to go through my notes and then e-mail it all to you."

"Do it," RJ commanded. "And don't leave out anything." He hung up and then quickly dialed his contact's number. "Head to Palmyra, New York. Send the girl to Nauvoo, Illinois. Call in some more help. We're going to have to cover all of their historical sites until we pick them back up again."

Chapter 9

Emma was feeling much better now that they were on the ground and she was excited to see the Sacred Grove. She felt like a kid going to Disneyland. Steve was all business. He hadn't wanted to use a rental car or taxi that could be traced. In the end, he had called President Thompson's office and arranged to have a local ward bishop pick them up at the airport.

The bishop, infused with excitement at receiving a call from President Thompson's office, was anxious to help. He talked nonstop from the time he picked them up. Steve caught Emma's eye and gave a frustrated look. Emma tried not to laugh. "Bishop," Steve said, "I was wondering if we could borrow your car for the rest of the day. We can drop you home so you don't have to hang around with us all day. We will drop it back to you when we're ready to go to the airport." They were posing as distant family members of President Thompson's who had come to visit the Sacred Grove as tourists.

The bishop looked deflated and said, "I can do that, but are you sure you wouldn't prefer a tour guide?"

"That's very kind of you to offer," Emma replied, "But I have a doctorate in church history so I think we'll be okay on our own."

The bishop was stumped by that and drove toward his house. He lived only a few miles from Palmyra. "Take all the time that you need!" he offered as Steve took the wheel.

"We sure appreciate it," Steve said and waved as they pulled out.

He had given them directions, but in the end it was easy to find. There were signs all over the place. "Ironic, isn't it?" Emma asked.

"What is?" Steve asked, turning a corner.

"Palmyra hated and persecuted Joseph, even drove him out. Now they have tourist direction signs all over the place and they probably benefit quite a bit financially from all of the tourism to this area by members of the church," she laughed.

"Yeah, I see what you mean," he agreed, nodding his head.

Steve pulled into the visitors' center parking lot. There was only one other car in the lot and they assumed it belonged to the missionary couple who ran the visitors' center. They decided not to go in and instead headed into the Sacred Grove. They followed the winding path through the forest and Steve used the compass on his watch to lead them toward the north clearing.

They were both quiet as they walked through, Emma lost in thought and emotion and Steve listening for any sounds behind them. He was sure they had lost their tail, but he wasn't taking anything for granted. The area was quite large and it took them longer than they expected to reach the north clearing.

When they finally did, Steve and Emma split up and began searching all of the trees for the notch. They searched for about 30 minutes with no luck. Finally, they met back together, disappointed.

"Any ideas?" Steve asked Emma.

Emma thought for a minute and then said, "We're probably looking too low. He wouldn't have left it at eye level. Let's look higher up." Steve nodded and they split up again. This time, Emma found it within a few minutes. It was five feet above them and difficult to examine. They were quietly

31

discussing it when Steve tensed up and put a finger to his lips to indicate quiet.

At first it was a shuffling sound and then they heard a twig snap. Steve pushed Emma behind him and they used one of the large trees to block them from view. Whomever it was had left the paved trail and was now searching for them in the trees.

Emma's heart pounded in her chest and she reached out to grab Steve's arm. He shrugged her off though, wanting to keep both of his hands free to protect her. The sound stopped and then started again. The searcher clearly had lost them and was trying to regroup. Emma watched Steve withdraw a large knife from under his shirt and her eyes went wide. She clamped her hand over her mouth to ensure she wouldn't cry out.

The sound was getting closer and Emma saw Steve's arm muscles flexing with tenseness. She had never noticed before how built he was. Just then the sound stopped again and they heard a tentative voice call out, "Umm, hello? Are you there?" The voice sounded unsure and a bit worried. Steve didn't respond and Emma kept her hand over her mouth.

"I-I'm Brother Ellis and I run the visitors' center here," the man called out. "I'm afraid you aren't allowed to leave the trail. You know, protect the trees and all." The man sounded harmless and so Steve put away his knife and sneaked a glance. There was an elderly man in a suit with a missionary tag looking anxiously at him. Steve turned and nodded to Emma that it was all right and they stepped out from behind the tree.

"Sorry about that," Steve said in a friendly voice. "I'm fascinated by these beautiful trees and wanted to get a closer look at one of them." They walked toward the missionary who smiled back at them.

"No harm done," he replied in a kind voice. "Where you folks from?" he asked with a smile.

"California," Steve replied, protecting their cover. "My wife here has always wanted to see the Sacred Grove and we've finally made it out." Emma managed to maintain her composure although she didn't like lying to the nice man. She knew it was for the best in case anyone came looking for them later.

They small talked for a few minutes and then, anxious to get another look at the tree, Emma said, "Brother Ellis, would you mind if we had some time alone? I'd like to meditate and pray before we leave."

A smile played at Steve's lips as he listened to Emma. He was anxious to get back to examining the tree also. He glanced around and the area still seemed quiet, but they didn't know how much time they had until their tail picked them back up again.

"Not at all, not at all," the kind man replied. "Just be sure to stay on the path."

"No problem," Steve added and then shook his hand. He and Emma went over to a nearby bench and bowed their heads. They waited until he was out of sight and then stood up. "How about you stand watch?" Steve suggested.

"No way," Emma said determinedly shaking her head. "I want to get a better look at that tree. Besides, I'll probably need you to lift me up so we can get a better look. It's pretty high up." They looked again and the missionary was clearly gone, so they headed back to the tree. Steve kneeled down and Emma got on his shoulders. He easily lifted her up to the notch. The groove was about five inches square.

Steve held Emma's legs tight, keeping her balanced. He heard her sharp intake of breath and asked, "What is it? What do you see?"

Emma examined the small etching in front of her and tried to think how best to describe it. "It's a rough compass," she started, "With two intersecting arrows. The symbols from the artifact are on here—but they are now broken out into geographic regions. North points to the sharp wavy lines, east to the three straight lines, west to the rectangle and south to the soft wavy lines. Does that cell phone they gave us have a camera on it?"

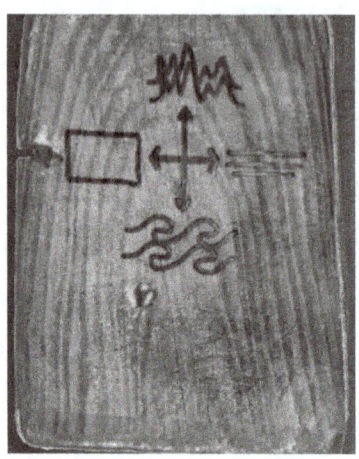

"Yes," Steve said and gently lowered her down. He pulled one of the cell phones from his backpack and powered it on. Once it was ready, he handed it to Emma and then hoisted her back up again. She took several pictures and then Steve slowly edged around the tree, so Emma could look for any more clues, but there was nothing more.

Emma handed the phone to Steve so he could have a look. He studied the picture and agreed with Emma's assessment—it was some type of a compass. Steve looked at Emma, but she was lost in thought. She went and sat down on the bench and pulled out her copy of the parable. She held it in one hand and the cell phone with the picture in the other.

Steve decided to sweep the area while he waited and look for any signs of their tail. He headed for higher ground, while still keeping Emma in his sights. She was muttering to herself, reading the parable. He heard voices then and stiffened. He tried to catch Emma's eye and indicate for her to hide, but she was consumed with trying to figure out the parable. He silently moved to a better vantage point to get a look. The first person he saw was a three-year-old kid, happily running through the trees. An older girl around 10-years-old came running after him, telling him to stay on the path. He was blissfully ignoring her. Steve smiled and twisted so he could see the others. There were two parents coming up at the rear with a few more kids. Steve noted their long shorts and modest clothes and assessed they were just Mormon tourists.

He stayed hidden—the fewer people that saw them, the better. They were heading straight for Emma and he hoped she would hear them in time. He silently followed them, moving from tree to tree. He could see Emma again, but she was still lost in her study. She had all of the documents laid out on the bench. The family was only about ten feet away now. Steve decided to intervene and stepped out from his hiding place.

"Hello, there," he said in a booming voice as he walked toward them. "How are you guys today?" Emma, hearing his voice, looked up and seeing the family, gathered up all of the documents and stuffed them into her backpack. The family turned and looked at Steve. The father answered, "Fine, how are you?"

"Great, sure a peaceful place, isn't it?" Steve answered.

"Yep," the father answered politely.

"Well, honey, we best be heading home," Steve said as he turned to Emma. "The babysitter has to be home by dark."

The father was interested though and said, "Oh, do you guys live around here?"

"Yeah," Steve answered. "We live near Niagara Falls. We try to come visit the Sacred Grove at least once a year to reconnect."

"It must be great to live so close," the father answered. "We're from Provo, Utah, and this is our first trip out."

Steve shifted uncomfortably wondering if he might recognize Emma. "Well, we'd better hit the road," he said walking over to Emma and putting his arm around her. "Nice to meet you," he said to the father as they walked away.

"You, too," the father replied and then heard his wife calling for the kids to come back on the path. He went to help.

Once he was out of sight, Emma shrugged off Steve's arm around her shoulders and said, "What are you doing?"

"Trying to get you away from there as quickly as possible," Steve said clearly annoyed. "And they almost saw all of the papers, Emma. You've got to be more careful."

Emma's eyes narrowed, "I was trying to figure all of this out," she said through gritted teeth.

Steve stopped, turned, and put his hands on Emma's shoulders as he looked her square in the eye. "Emma, these people that are after us, they won't hesitate to use anyone, hurt anyone, to get what they want. We need to try and stay away from people as much as possible. People are naturally friendly, especially Mormons, and if our tail asks, they'll be helpful and tell everything they can. We've apparently lost our tail for a few hours, but it won't be long before he finds us again. I've seen too many people get hurt just because they think they never will."

Emma looked into Steve's eyes and saw a lot of pain in them. She wondered what he had been through in the Iraq and Afghanistan wars. Judging by the haunting look in his eyes, it had been awful. Emma finally nodded her head and said, "I'll be more careful. But we need to find a safe place for me to think. I need some time to figure this all out. I feel it's just at the edge of my mind, but I can't get through it with all of these interruptions."

Steve dropped his arms and nodded his head. They walked back toward the car. Before they left the trees, Steve checked the parking lot to see if it was safe. There were only three cars now—the missionary couple's, theirs and a minivan that he assumed belonged to the family. He indicated to Emma that it was safe and they headed quickly to the car.

Steve drove into Palmyra, went through a drive-through to get them some food, and then drove out into the country, memorizing the path so he could get back. He finally found a secluded road and pulled onto it, out of sight from the main road. He was confident they hadn't been followed. He started to eat his food, but Emma was anxious to study the parable again. She spread out all of her papers and turned the cell phone on again to get a better look at the compass image.

Steve looked at the picture of the artifact and offered, "What if they're topographical references. The sharp wavy lines are mountains, the straight lines are flats, the waves are gentle hills..."

"Could be," Emma murmured absently. She was reading the parable for the hundredth time and then started rapidly making notes.

Steve sat up and leaned toward her, trying to read her handwriting, but couldn't. He finished eating while occasionally glancing in the rearview mirror, just in case. Emma kept writing animatedly and finally finished. She looked up at Steve triumphantly and had a light and excitement in her eyes. "I think I've figured it out!" she said excitedly.

Steve moved closer, but still couldn't read her handwriting. "I was thinking that the clues had to be something universal and constant," she explained, "Something timeless. Then it hit me. The parable mentions some very basic elements without naming them by name. The river is water, the smoke is fire, the breeze is wind and the ground is earth. These symbols represent the four elements! Water, fire, wind and earth!"

Steve looked at Emma and her face was glowing with excitement. She looked so pretty when she smiled like that. Pushing the thought immediately from his mind, he reached over to the compass picture.

"So the wavy lines are water, the rectangle is earth, the jagged lines are fire and that leaves the straight lines for wind," he offered, trying not to look at her face.

"That's my assessment as well," she said happily. She sounded so positive and happy that he risked another glance. He missed that kind of enthusiasm. He knew he was jaded from both his marriage and his war experiences. It was refreshing to see someone so optimistic and positive. She was smiling at him and he gently smiled back. He knew she wasn't married and hadn't been—Gary had told him that before they left. He wondered why; she was pretty, smart and clearly talented.

Impulsively, Steve decided to risk it and reached over and placed his hand near hers—just close enough to touch, but not close enough to be threatening. Emma didn't notice; she was rambling on about the four elements. Steve wasn't listening as he felt drawn toward her. All of the sudden he wanted to be close to her—to hold her and protect her. It had been so long since he'd been near a woman. He hadn't allowed himself to get close to anyone after the divorce. He didn't want to hurt anyone ever again like he had his wife.

But there was something so young and hopeful about Emma. She wasn't scarred and broken like he was. It seemed an eternity and to take all of his strength, but he moved his hand slightly closer and gently touched her hand with his thumb.

Emma stopped midsentence and looked over at him in surprise, jerking her hand away. It was unbearable for Steve to watch all of the excitement and enthusiasm drain from her face and have it replaced by fear and mistrust. He had blown it.

"What are you doing?" she demanded, sliding further away from him.

Steve couldn't meet her eyes now, but he didn't move his hand. He left it where it was on the seat even though she had pulled away. "Trying to hold your hand," he said softly, studying his shoes.

"Oh," Emma replied in surprise, her voice full of surprise and mistrust. "I—I thought you were married."

Steve felt the pain of the past sneak back into his heart. "I was, once," he replied sadly nodding. "I've been divorced for a year now."

"Oh," Emma said, not sure what else to say. She thought back to why she had assumed he was married. In her experience, nearly every guy she met was—especially the handsome, respectable ones that were her age or older.

"I have a daughter," Steve added. "Arianna. She's four-years-old." Steve pulled out his wallet and gently lifted out a small picture and handed it to Emma.

Emma studied the small girl, dressed in a bright red, white and navy outfit. She must have had her mother's blonde hair, but Emma recognized Steve's eyes. She was beautiful and looked very happy.

"I took that on the 4th of July," Steve said sadly. "I only get to see her every other weekend and some holidays."

"That must be hard," Emma offered gently.

Steve didn't trust his emotions to speak, so he just nodded. He swallowed hard.

"What happened?" Emma asked softly.

Steve sighed. How could he possibly explain everything that happened between him and Kari? He finally said, "It was my fault. I was away too much with my service in the military. I thought it was important, but in the end, it destroyed my marriage. All I have left now is Ari." He looked at the picture, trying to memorize Ari's face. He could still smell the soft sweetness of her hair and the strawberry lip gloss that she loved to wear.

"She's beautiful," Emma said.

Steve put the picture back into his wallet and with it, his emotions. "So what's next with the parable?"

Emma regretted pulling her hand away. Steve was clearly in a lot of pain from the past and she wanted to help him. But the moment was gone now and she turned back to her papers.

She read through the parable again:

There once was a man who lived near a mighty river in the east.

One day, he saw smoke afar off. He didn't worry.

Then the strong breeze shifted north and the destroyer was born.

Soon his house was ablaze.

He tried to squelch the destroyer, but he couldn't.

He was sorrowful and died.

His friends buried them near the mighty river.

"Well," Emma said, "Let's take it line by line. 'There once was a man who lived near a mighty river in the east.' Let's assume the man is Joseph and he lived near a mighty river. That could be when they were in Nauvoo, although, it also adds 'in the east.' Given that Joseph grew up here, Illinois would be 'in the west' to him. He moved around a lot and was near several smaller rivers, but a 'mighty one?' The compass image has water on the south, yet the parable specifically mentions east. I still need to think about that some more."

She looked up at Steve and he nodded his head in agreement. He didn't know a lot about church history and wouldn't be much help there. She continued, "The next line says 'One day, he saw smoke afar off. He didn't worry.' This goes into the part about fire. Smoke is the first sign of fire, the start. He was not concerned or alarmed at that point. 'Then the strong breeze shifted north and the destroyer was born.' This part is puzzling to me. Who is the destroyer? Satan? Satan was never born on this earth. But it clearly mentions north and the compass also shows fire to the north."

Steve looked at Emma and noticed she was biting the nail on her index finger. He could tell she was agitated—it was bothering her that she couldn't figure out the parable. "'Soon his house was ablaze. He tried to squelch the destroyer, but he couldn't.' This seems to be the clearest reference to Joseph himself. Especially toward the end, he faced constant adversity and persecution. In the end he was murdered. That's where Joseph's handwriting ends and Brigham's begins.

He was sorrowful and died.

His friends buried them near the mighty river.

"It still bothers me that it's only talking about one person all along, but multiple people are buried. It could be, like I said earlier, a reference to Joseph and Hyrum being murdered together and then buried together in Nauvoo. It certainly fits with the 'mighty river.' When the Saints left Nauvoo, they had to cross the Mississippi river and were leaving their beautiful Nauvoo homes—it was one of the better times for the Saints in Nauvoo. They had become stronger and prosperous there."

Steve had been keeping track—that covered all of the elements except for one. "What about wind?"

Emma looked back over the parable and then pointed to *Then the strong breeze shifted north and the destroyer was born.* Joseph described it as a strong breeze. "Hmm," Emma thought, reaching over and starting to eat her food. They ate in silence for a few minutes. Emma was halfway through her burger when she sighed, "I just don't know, Steve. They were trying to keep the meaning hidden—maybe they did too good of a job."

Steve looked over at her. Her forehead was wrinkled in frustration. Steve could tell she was the type of person who never gave up. "You'll figure it out," he replied with an encouraging smile.

She looked at him gratefully and smiled. "I was named after Emma Smith, Joseph's wife," she offered.

"Oh, really?" Steve said interested and pleased that she was opening up a little. "That's cool."

Emma half laughed and said, "Yeah, I'm pretty feisty about it. Whenever I hear anyone in the church say something judgmental about Emma, I defend her."

"What do people say about her?" Steve asked, trying to remember his church history.

"Oh, you know, about how she didn't come west to Salt Lake with Brigham and the Saints," Emma explained. "People say she abandoned her faith. But I think she was incredible. Did you know her second husband had an affair and Emma was so Christlike that she offered to have the woman and her illegitimate child come and live with them? She treated the child like it was her own."

"Wow, that's pretty impressive," Steve agreed nodding his head.

Emma looked out the car window and added, "She went through so much. Standing at Joseph's side through everything, having so many of her children die, living in constant poverty and fear. Oftentimes, when Joseph was unjustly jailed, Emma was alone and had to be both the father and the mother to their children. I have no doubt she's at Joseph's side now and always will be."

Steve sat silently, watching Emma as she was lost in thought. She finally said, "I've read a lot about them. They were very much in love. Emma left her home and family to be with Joseph when most people thought he was delusional. Her

41

parents were strongly against their marriage. It's one of the greatest love stories in church history."

Steve could hear the wistfulness in her voice. He thought back to Kari again. He had thought he had the kind of love with her—the kind of love that would survive the absences and loneliness. He was wrong. His mind then drifted back to the war. For some reason, he was thinking about a particular mission. They were unfamiliar with the terrain and were using a map to try and assess where the enemy would be hiding.

"A map," Steve said suddenly, "We need a map."

Emma looked over at him in surprise. "How will a map help?" she asked.

"When I was in Afghanistan, we would heavily rely on maps to help us understand situations," he explained. "Maps would show us where good hiding places were in the mountains. Good vantage points. Maps would show us where the roads led and we could anticipate dangerous locations. The compass on the tree can help us. They gave us distinct geographical directions on where we would find the locations of the symbols."

Steve put his seatbelt back on and started the car. They drove back into Palmyra and found a convenience store that had a local and national map. They got back into the car and unfolded the local map first. He marked a star by the Sacred Grove first and said, "This is our center point." Now, wind is east. What is east of here?"

"The Palmyra temple," Emma replied. They had passed it as they turned toward the Sacred Grove. "But that wouldn't be it," she added, thinking aloud. "It would have had to be a landmark present during Joseph's time."

Emma traced her finger slightly east and then a bit south and stopped. "Hill Cumorah is technically east of here. Not by much, but it is east." They both looked at each other intently. Steve started the car, "Let's go."

Chapter 10

The man was in a bad mood. He had been forced to fly coach to New York since it was last minute and all first-class seats were taken. He had to take the only thing left—a middle seat between a chatty lady and a man who smelled like he hadn't showered for a couple of days. He spent the whole flight planning how he would take out his frustration on the Mormon professor and ex-soldier.

He had underestimated the ex-soldier. When he arrived at the airport, he checked all of the car rentals and taxis with no luck. He had shelled out several hundred dollars in bribes for employees to check their systems, but nothing. Not a trace.

He got himself a fast rental car and headed to Palmyra. His mood worsened with each passing hour. He was annoyed that he'd had to send the girl to Illinois. She was pleasing company and he liked the idea of having backup. Not that he needed it, but if this Steve guy turned out to be as much of a threat as RJ thought, he might need her help.

He finally arrived at what the Mormons called their "Sacred Grove" where they believed Joseph Smith saw God. The man shook his head—what a load of nonsense. It was just another strange cult and the sooner he finished this job, the better.

He went into the visitors' center and flashed his fake FBI badge. It had come in really handy over the years. He showed the elderly couple a picture he had taken yesterday of Emma and Steve. The man looked at his wife and he knew from the expression on his face that he had found them. The elderly man said they had been there about three hours ago.

He decided to ask around town and see if he could pick up their trail. After about thirty minutes, he knew they had picked up a local map at the convenience store. He asked the young clerk if there were any other Mormon historical sites in the area and she gave him directions to Hill Cumorah. When he got back into his car, he loaded his gun and called in a report to RJ that he had found them.

Chapter 11

"Do you hear that?" Steve asked Emma. Emma paused and listened, but she could only hear the chirping of birds in the nearby trees and kids playing lower down on the hill. They had walked up the switchbacked trail to the top of Hill Cumorah. They were sitting on the grass at the top and were waiting to examine the monument; another family was there and they didn't want anyone to see what they were looking for.

"Hear what?" she asked, straining to hear anything unusual.

"That humming noise," Steve said.

Now that he mentioned it, Emma could hear a faint noise, but it was distant. The family finally moved away from the monument and headed back down the hill. Steve and Emma looked all around the monument. It had a description of how Joseph was guided to the hill by a visitation from an angel called Moroni to find and then translate ancient gold records of the American inhabitants.

"Joseph wrote a history of the church. In it, he says the plates were on the west side of the hill, not far from the top," Emma explained. "He described that the plates were under a large rock in a makeshift stone box."

She and Steve looked down the hill toward the west side. It was smooth and covered with grass while the east side was dense with trees.

"It looks like they have cleared a lot of the trees and smoothed out the landscape over the years. Maybe the clue is gone. A lot of Palmyra residents were trying to get the plates during Joseph's time. They wanted them because they thought they were pure solid gold. There's actually some discussion on that. Some historians say they were just metal, gold-colored plates. Others think they were overlaid with gold and some say pure gold. I tend to lean toward that they were pure gold or overlaid, because the angel Moroni warned Joseph not to try and use them for personal profit."

Emma glanced over the surrounding area—they could see quite well from on top of the hill. Being here, finally, at these church history sites made everything connect. She could see the young boy Joseph walking down the road, searching for the hill Moroni had described. She wondered if his heart had pounded in his chest as he climbed up the hill and found the large stone, knowing the plates were underneath. How exciting it must have been, as a teenager, to lift up that stone and see an ancient record inside, with the Urim and Thummim interpreters waiting inside for thousands of years.

"It's so interesting to look back and see how the Lord guided Joseph to this hill," Emma mused. "He grew up in Sharon, Vermont. When his mom and dad got married, his mom received a family inheritance. It was actually quite a bit of money. They unfortunately decided to 'invest it' and gave the money to a boat captain to buy supplies for them in another country. They felt they could trust the boat captain, but he ran off with all of their money."

"That's terrible," Steve replied, imagining the trusting young couple.

"Yes, but all part of God's plan," Emma added with a smile. "They became farmers. But when Joseph was around 10, they had several bad crop years. It got so bad, that Joseph's dad decided if they had one more bad year, they would move. And of course, they did and came here to the Palmyra area."

But Steve wasn't listening. "That humming noise is bothering me," Steve said, looking around.

"Why?" Emma asked, looking around.

"It's not logical," he explained. "The visitors' center is way over there—where is that sound coming from?" Steve dropped down flat and put his ear to the ground. The humming noise was louder. "It's coming from right below us." Steve looked up at Emma and saw a strange look on her face. "What is it?" he asked.

Emma looked around to make sure no one was in earshot. Steve stood up and met her gaze. "In the *Journal of Discourses*, Brigham Young documented a story from Oliver Cowdery. In the story, it says when Joseph took the plates back to Hill Cumorah, Oliver was with him. As they approached the hill, it opened and they went into a cave which had a very large room. He said it had so many plates in it that it would take several wagonloads to haul them. The sword of Laban was also there sitting on top of the records. A lot of people have come here, searching for the door, but no one has found it."

"Do you believe it?" Steve asked intently.

"Well, the *Journal of Discourses* isn't an official church publication. There's even some doubt as to the accuracy of the transcriptions and it wasn't a first-hand account. But, there's one thing that sticks in my mind—the article repeatedly said it was something Brigham Young didn't want to forget and wanted future generations to know." Emma suddenly felt silly and smiled. "It's probably just an urban legend."

Steve thought about the sound, "Is it?" he asked Emma seriously, raising his eyebrows. "It sounds like some serious power is being pushed toward this hill. Maybe something to do with a room within the hill?"

Emma looked like a young kid again, "Let's look for it," she said imagining what kind of artifacts she might be able to discover and examine.

They looked for several hours, for clues in the trees as well as for a hidden door. The man watched them from the trees, staying well away from them, using binoculars to monitor their progress. He was half tempted to just shoot them both, but he needed them to find the secret if he was going to get paid. Patience, he reminded himself. Plenty of time to kill them later.

Emma's excitement was waning with each passing hour and she finally started to feel foolish, "Maybe it is just a legend after all," she offered to Steve.

"It's been almost two hundred years since Joseph's time," Steve answered disappointed as well. "Grass grows over things, topography changes. It might be there, but we're missing it." He looked around and felt the hairs on the back of his neck raise up again. He had known for about an hour that they were being watched, but he hadn't been able to figure out where the intruder was. He was keeping his distance for some reason, but Steve knew that might change when their tail figured out they couldn't find what they were looking for.

"Let's go into the visitors' center," Steve suggested. He felt he could protect Emma better in there and their tail would be less likely to approach them with so many other visitors around.

Emma looked tired and discouraged. It had been a long day. It was now late afternoon and the visitors' center was closing in 15 minutes. Several families were milling around the displays. Kids were tired and grouchy and families started to head out. Steve finally got the couple running the visitors' center by themselves. He drew a picture of the three straight lines on a piece of paper.

"Have you ever seen these marks anywhere on the hill or nearby?" Steve asked the couple.

They both shook their heads. Emma said, "Have you ever seen a hidden or secret door anywhere on the hill?" She felt foolish even asking, but they didn't have any other clues to go on at this point.

They both laughed and the elderly sister missionary said, "So many people ask us that and lots look for it, but no, we've never seen anything and no one else has either that we know of."

Steve glanced toward the door, but so far, their tail hadn't entered. "Have you ever found anything unusual at all here?"

The missionary couple thought for a minute and then the sister said, "There is a cleaning closet that I've never been into. I asked the previous missionary couple about it and they said they have never been in there either."

"Do you have a key for the door?" Emma asked intently.

"No, that's one of the strange things about the closet," she continued. "It doesn't have a door handle. It has a keypad on the outside. I looked in all of the center's documentation to see if the code was written down somewhere, but there's nothing. Why would a cleaning closet need a keypad?" she asked innocently.

"May we see the door?" Steve asked. The elderly couple led them around a corner and down a long hall. If Steve's bearings were right, they were headed straight toward Hill Cumorah. He looked behind him again, but still didn't see anyone. The visitors' center was quiet now.

They arrived at the door with the keypad. A plaque at the side said, "Cleaning Closet." Emma studied the keypad. There was no way to know how many numbers were required for the code.

"I've punched in some numbers, just for fun," the elderly missionary said. "But who knows, it could be anything. I never could get it open."

The elderly sister missionary looked at her watch, "Honey, it's time to lock up the visitors' center."

"Yup, so it is," her husband replied with a smile. "We'll leave you two here to try and figure out the code. I must admit, I'm curious to see those priceless cleaning supplies."

Steve and Emma watched them disappear around the corridor. "Any ideas?" Steve asked Emma hopefully.

"If I knew how many digits, it would really help," Emma replied, biting on her nail again as she thought. "Let's try an obvious one—the day Joseph received the gold plates." She punched in the eight-digit date code. They waited—nothing happened. Steve pushed on the door, but it was still locked. "All right, maybe the date of the church organization," she punched in the code. Nothing. Emma proceeded to try several other historical dates to no avail.

She thought back to the parable and a specific word came to mind—born. She punched in Joseph Smiths' birthdate: 12231805. They heard a clicking noise and this time when Steve pushed on the door, it swung open.

The cleaning closet turned out to be a dimly lit hallway leading further into the hill. Steve and Emma looked at each other smiling. Steve pulled out a flashlight he had in his backpack and they headed down the hallway.

Emma's pulse raced in anticipation of what they might find. She envisioned a room, full of scrolls, gold plates and ancient artifacts. She nearly ran down the hallway. Steve looked behind them to see if the missionary couple was following, but he didn't see anyone.

The hallway twisted gently to the left and then they saw it. Ahead was an old, wooden door. Carved into the door were the three straight lines. Steve and Emma instinctively ran to the door. Steve reached the door handle first and thinking it would be locked, he gave it a firm twist. The door easily opened and Steve hesitated for a minute, fully realizing what they were about to see. He looked at Emma. She had a nervous, yet excited look on her face as well. She met his steady gaze and smiled, "Let's go," she said.

Steve swung the door open and they looked in. The room was dark. The dim light from the hallway was enough to light their first few steps, but after that, it was black. Steve felt along the walls for a light switch, using his flashlight to guide him. Not finding one, he swung the light around the room.

He heard Emma gasp. He swung around the room again to confirm what they had seen. He finally swung the light toward the wall and saw the light switch on the other side of the room. He walked over and switched it on.

Both of them blinked to adjust their eyes to the light. Emma looked at Steve and said, "I don't understand..." Steve could hear the disappointment in her voice—the room was empty. Steve assessed the room—it felt very cavernous and was roughly hewn out of the hillside.

There were some rough, wooden shelves built into the right and left walls. They were about 10 feet long and had six shelves per side, 12 total. There was a large table in the middle of the room with a chair. Emma assessed that they both came from Joseph Smith's time and were maybe even made by him or Brigham Young, who was a carpenter.

Emma glanced frantically around the room again now that her eyes had adjusted. There had to be something here. But the room was basic—it was easy to see at another glance that the room was indeed empty.

Chapter 12

The man was in a terrible mood. The statue of Christ in the foyer of the visitors' center had unnerved him. It was as though the statue saw right down into his soul and knew all of the murders he had committed. Normally, it didn't bother him. It was just a job for him and his upbringing had hardened him to any normal feelings toward guilt and decency.

He hated this job—hated religion in general. He had slipped in unnoticed. He waited until the old couple locked the visitors' center and then had easily tied them up in one of the offices. He had wanted to just kill them, but RJ had said to keep the body count zero—he didn't want to attract attention.

There was something about the old man that reminded him about his grandpa. He thought back to summers when he used to go fishing with his grandpa at the nearby lake. It was his respite from his drunken, abusive father and his broken, scared mother.

The memories only made him angrier and he let the rage fuel him. The keypad door was still open and he quietly edged his way down the hallway toward the open door. He silently pulled out his gun. This hallway was leading him to a remote room. Maybe he could still kill the soldier and professor and no one would know for years.

As he came around the bend, he saw them both standing in the middle of the room. He could tell from their body language that they hadn't found what they were looking for. He hadn't anticipated that this job was going to be some type of elongated treasure hunt. His typical jobs were to go in and kill someone and get out. He was becoming impatient.

He flattened himself against the wall and listened. ". . . isn't here, Emma. Maybe someone got here before we did. Maybe the clue trail is broken. Joseph and Brigham left those clues a long time ago." He assessed his options. He could follow them around for a few more days playing wait and see or he could get things moving with his own methods.

He moved silently into the room and pointed the gun directly at Emma. Steve heard him seconds before and reached for his knife, but he froze when he realized that he had a direct line of sight to Emma with the gun. Steve could see the look in the man's eyes—he would kill her and not even think twice.

The man could see the look of fear all over the professor's face, but the soldier was calm and cool—watching his every move. "Throw it over here, soldier," he said gruffly.

Steve slowly reached in and pulled out his knife. The long blade glistened in the dim light. He threw it halfway toward the intruder. Steve glanced at Emma. Her face had gone completely white and she had instinctively put her hands in the air. Steve assessed his options. He had the man on size and if he could get close enough, he thought he could incapacitate him. But there was a good chance Emma might get hurt in the attempt and he couldn't risk that.

"Now," the killer asked, "Where is it?"

"W-w-e don't know," Emma answered weakly.

The man, for emphasis, drew out his silencer and screwed it onto his gun. It usually frightened people to realize that he was ready to kill them. It typically helped him get what he wanted, even though he still shot them in the end.

"We don't know," Steve added in a clear, strong voice, "We followed the clues here to this room and it was empty when we got here."

The man walked closer toward Emma. He could see the fear increasing on her face—it reminded him of his mother.

Hatred coursed through his body and he started to long for the moment when he would kill her.

"I *don't* think you're trying hard enough," the man spat. He was now within close enough range that instant death would be certain. He hesitated. He still needed that final payment from RJ. He doubted he would get it if he killed the girl. RJ thought they needed her to get to the "Mormon secret." The man had no idea what it actually was, but it must have been valuable since RJ was willing to pay so much for it.

The soft swooshing sound came unexpectedly and Steve looked over at Emma. Her face was twisted in pain and surprise. She fell to the ground clutching her side. Blood oozed out from her clutched hand.

"Next time, I won't be so generous," the man said as he backed out of the room. "*Find it*," he said and then was gone.

Steve rushed over to Emma, pulling off his shirt as he knelt beside her. She had passed out from the pain. He stemmed the blood flow with his shirt, trying to assess the injury. He relaxed when he realized the man had been telling the truth—he had only shot Emma in the arm as a warning. A few inches over and she would now be dead.

He heard a heavy thud sound and realized the man had closed the keypad door and had locked them in. He turned back to Emma and probed her wound with his fingers. He felt an exit wound at the back of her arm and relaxed. The bullet had gone clean through. He looked at the wall near where Emma had stood and saw the bullet lodged in the wall. He tied his shirt around her arm and pulled out his backpack. He powered on the cell phone and looked at the bar signal strength. Nothing. He knew it was a long shot because they were deep within the hill. He turned off the cell phone and pulled out one of his spare t-shirts. He began to rip it into long strips that he could use as makeshift bandages for Emma's wound.

Emma made a moaning sound and he looked at her. She was regaining consciousness. She clutched her arm and opened her eyes suddenly. She tried to sit up quickly, remembering that she had been shot.

Steve went over to her side and said, "Emma, it's okay. He's gone." Emma looked extremely pale so he put his arm around her back in case she fainted.

Emma looked wildly around the room and then finally relaxed. "W-what happened?"

Steve looked under his shirt that he had tied around her arm and saw that the blood was starting to flow quicker now that she was sitting up. He decided to replace it with the makeshift bandages he had created. "He shot you as a warning," Steve explained while he worked. "He said we need to find it."

"I can't believe someone would shoot me over whatever this is," Emma said weakly. Steve noticed Emma started to shiver and he started to worry about shock. He made her a pillow from her jacket and pulled out his old army blanket he had brought with him. He helped her lie down and wrapped her up tightly.

"These people are definitely serious," he said. "Whatever it is we're looking for must be extremely powerful information." Steve pulled the blood-stained t-shirt off of Emma's arm and began to layer the bandages on top of it. He then pulled one around her arm and tied it off securely.

Emma looked at the blood-soaked t-shirt and started to cry. Steve watched her awkwardly and finally reached over and gently stroked her black hair. Emma reached up and impulsively took his hand and held it tightly as if grasping for a lifeline. "I—I didn't know it was going to be like this," Emma said through her tears.

Steve smiled sadly and applied pressure to the wound. The blood flow was slowing. "It's my fault," he answered softly. "I should have protected you better. I misjudged the guy. I thought he would only shoot you if I attacked him. I was wrong. I've met his type before. They *live* to kill. They thrive on it. They are the most unpredictable and the hardest to anticipate."

Emma looked up at Steve with tears continuing to stream down her face. "I'm sure you saw lots of horrible things on your deployments," she said softly.

"Yes," Steve answered nearly in a whisper. "Things no one should ever have to see." He thought back to a day when a woman and a child had approached their convoy. The woman was frantically speaking to them, urging them to come closer. His sergeant got out of the Humvee and approached them, trying to assess the situation. Seconds later the woman and child exploded, killing his sergeant and spattering the vehicle with their blood. Steve had only been there for a month. He watched the blood streak down his window and thought of his sergeant. He had a wife and two children at home. Tears had sprung to his eyes and he fought off throwing up. How could anyone use a woman and a child as a trap and kill them? It was unfathomable. Emma saw the haunted look in Steve's eyes and squeezed his hand. It brought Steve back to the present and he looked at Emma. "Now that I know what we're up against, Emma, I *won't* let you get hurt again," he said firmly. "When we get out of here, I'm going to call President Thompson and have them send the jet for you."

"No, Steve," Emma answered firmly. "I'm in this all the way." Steve was about to protest so Emma added with a smile, "Besides, you need me to help you figure out the clues."

Steve admired her courage but shook his head, "Emma, you can help me figure out the clues via cell phone safely from Utah."

Emma dropped her smile and looked intently at Steve, "Do you really think now I'd be safe back in Utah? That's where this all started, remember?"

Steve looked down at his hand holding Emma's. He could feel a warmth transferring from her small, white hand into his. Her hand was so soft. It had been so long since he had held a woman's hand. He hadn't gotten close to anyone since his divorce. Emma looked so fragile, but he could see a determination and strength in her eyes. She was aptly named for Emma Smith, he thought with admiration.

He felt a longing inside him that he had pushed deep down inside years ago. A longing to be close to someone, to love someone. He felt vulnerable and yet powerful all at the same time. He wanted to kiss Emma, but he hesitated. He looked into her eyes, trying to see if she felt the same. He saw a warmness there, but still wasn't sure.

She seemed to understand what he was thinking and she nervously gazed down at his lips momentarily. She finally said, "Steve, I'd rather be here with you than anywhere else." That was enough for Steve. He slowly leaned down toward her and softly kissed her lips. He felt his body tremble—it had been so long since he had allowed himself this closeness. He longed for more, but pulled back, searching Emma's face for a reaction.

She opened her eyes, looking surprised that he had only kissed her once and so gently. She smiled encouragingly and used her free hand to reach up and pull him back toward her. She was cold from the shock and his breath was warm. As he kissed her softly again, she could feel the longing in his kiss, but she knew he was holding back, restraining himself.

He made himself pull back. He smiled at her and then walked over to his backpack. He pulled out a gun and loaded it although he was careful to leave on the safety. He knew he had been too soft—that's why he was distracted when the artifact was stolen and why Emma had been shot.

"What are you doing?" Emma asked softly, watching him carefully.

"All of this so far has been my fault. The artifact was stolen on my watch. You were shot while I stood here and did nothing. It's . . . it's because of things that happened in Iraq and Afghanistan," Steve started to explain.

"Go on," Emma prompted gently.

Steve looked down at her lying on the floor and said bluntly, "I killed people, Emma. A lot of people. And not just men. They trained me—conditioned me. I thought I could do it without feeling anything, but every time I did, I felt I lost a bit of myself . . . of my soul. I still dream about them nearly every night." A single tear ran down Steve's cheek, but he didn't brush it away. Instead, he let it fall onto the ground.

"You're not responsible for that, Steve," Emma said firmly. "You were a soldier in a war."

"It's easy to say that," Steve said shaking his head gently. "Bishops and stake presidents have told me that. But I can't get it into my heart—into my nightmares. So that's why I've only been carrying my knife this time. I knew that these people were professionals, but I thought they would keep their distance until we found the secret. I . . . don't want to kill anyone ever again, Emma. So I carry my knife—I know with it, I can frighten and injure, but it's easier not to kill. I'm afraid of killing again. I carried a gun on duty on BYU, but I knew I wouldn't ever have to use it. But tonight, I could see it in that man's eyes—I've seen it in war. He would have killed you. No, Emma, he *wanted* to kill you. And I won't let that happen. Even if I have to kill him."

Steve put on a gun holster around his chest and then put on a spare t-shirt. His face had turned hard and serious.

"Steve, what we're searching for . . . this secret, it might be the most dangerous thing the church has ever faced. Do you remember in the Book of Mormon what God told Nephi about Laban?" she leaned up onto her elbow, wanting to help him understand.

Steve thought back to the story and nodded, "Yes, that God told him it was all right to kill Laban, that it was better than a nation suffering in disbelief."

"Yes, and this is the same thing," Emma said, "As well as you're protecting our very lives—both of ours."

Steve thought about that for a minute and then said, "Emma, have you ever thought that maybe this secret shouldn't be found? Maybe we're leading them straight to it."

"Yes, I've thought about that as well," Emma said with a sigh, leaning back down onto the jacket as her pillow. "But what choice do we have? What if we stop and they find it first somehow? Or what if we stop and they hurt others to get what they want?"

"Well, we're nowhere anyway," Steve said in frustration. "There's nothing here." Steve glanced around again at the room. He walked over to the shelves and felt on the top and underside of the shelves. When he caught Emma looking at him questioningly, he said, "I'm looking for a clue or maybe something to open another secret room." They both laughed. Steve searched the room, but found nothing. He then came over and checked Emma's dressing. The blood was turning darker and seemed to have stopped for the time being. Still, he wanted to get her out of here and to a hospital.

"You know, I've just thought of something that I should have realized before," Emma mused. "The three straight lines—the wind—it's Moroni blowing his trumpet. That's the strong breeze in the parable."

"Any thoughts on the rest of the parable?" Steve asked hopefully.

"No, not yet," Emma said frustrated.

"Well, we need to figure out a way to get out of here. While you were passed out I tried the cell, but no reception. I'm going to try the door," Steve said as he walked briskly toward the hallway. He unsheathed his gun—he thought the man was gone, but he wasn't taking any chances anymore.

Steve slowly walked down the hallway, a few steps at a time, stopping and listening. It was silent. He finally reached the door and saw that there wasn't a handle on the inside. He pushed on the door firmly, but it didn't budge.

It was then that he thought about the missionary couple. His heart sank with dread, wondering what might have become of them. He hoped that since the killer had left Emma alive that he left them alive also. But they were an older couple and even the stress might be too much for them.

Steve pounded on the door as loudly as he could just in case. Nothing. He was just turning away when he heard a noise. He raised his gun, flattened against the wall and waited.

"Hello? Is there someone in there?" he heard a voice call. He thought the voice sounded familiar, but he couldn't place it.

It wasn't the killer though, so he answered back, "Yes, we're trapped in here. Who are you?"

"It's Bishop Michaels," the man called out. Steve recognized the bishop's voice. He had forgotten all about him. They still had his car. "I was worried when you two didn't come back and so I drove around town in my wife's car looking for you," he began. "I saw my car here at the visitors' center and was worried."

"Is the keypad still on the outside of the door?" Steve called, wondering if the killer had removed it.

"Yes," the bishop responded.

"Punch in 12-23-1805," Steve shouted. He heard the keypad beeping and then the door clicked. Steve gave it a firm shove and almost knocked over the bishop. Steve felt the fresh air and inhaled deeply. He hadn't realized how stuffy the secret room was. "Thank you, Bishop," he said gratefully. "Now, did you find a missionary couple anywhere on your way in?"

"No," the bishop said puzzled. "I had to get the stake president to give me a key and when I came in, everything was quiet."

Steve felt alarm growing within his stomach, wondering if they were dead. "Go call 911 and then look in every room for them. Tell 911 that we need an ambulance for a gunshot wound."

The bishop's eyes became bigger, but he hurried off in search of a phone. Steve decided to go back and get Emma. She was sitting up when he got back into the room and as he picked up his knife, he noticed her bandage was seeping bright red blood again. "Emma, can you stand if I help you? The bishop is here and is calling 911. We've got the door open. I know there's nothing in this room, but still, someone wanted it to be a secret all of these years, so I don't think we should let the paramedics in here."

Emma nodded and put her arm around Steve's neck. He put his strong arm around her shoulders and lifted. Her face went white, so he decided to just pick her up. She was light to carry and she smiled at him gratefully. They were just outside of the keypad door when Steve spied a couch. He laid Emma on it and then said, "I'll go back for our backpacks."

He ran down the hallway and into the room and grabbed both packs. He was almost out the door when something registered in his mind. He stopped suddenly and turned around. He blinked to make sure he was seeing correctly.

On the rough wooden table was a rolled-up scroll. He glanced around the room, but no one was there. He opened the scroll, looked at the parchment and smiled. He carefully placed it into his backpack and smiled. "Thanks," he said to the unseen visitor who had delivered the scroll.

He ran out to the visitors' center and firmly shut the door as the bishop came running toward him. "I found the couple," he said breathlessly. "They're in the center's office tied up. I was able to remove the duct tape gags, but can't get the ropes undone. They're alive."

Steve pulled out his knife and the bishop's eyes when big again. "I'll go help them," he said and then noticed emergency lights flashing on the front door. "You go let in the paramedics and tell them Emma has a gunshot wound in her arm, but it cleanly exited." He glanced over at Emma and noticed that she had gone unconscious again. He ran to the direction the bishop pointed for the office while the bishop ran to the front door.

Steve's heart broke when he entered the office. Both of the missionary couple were tied to chairs. They looked extremely frightened and he worried for their health. They looked relieved as they recognized Steve. He cut the ropes as gently as he could. He heard the paramedics in the foyer and went out and directed them to come and help the couple. He made it back to Emma, just as they were putting her onto the stretcher. She reached out for his hand and they waited for a second.

"You okay?" Steve asked. Emma nodded bravely. He leaned over pretending to kiss her cheek and whispered, "Moroni left us something. I found it when I went back for the packs." He pulled back and studied Emma's face. Her eyes danced with excitement and she longed to ask, but surrounded by paramedics, she kept silent.

The police wanted to question Steve, but he wouldn't let the ambulance leave without him so he could go with Emma. Finally, the police agreed to travel in the ambulance with them. As they were leaving the visitors' center, the bishop came up to Steve and curiously asked, "So, what's behind that door anyway?"

"Nothing, actually," Steve replied honestly. "Just a very large janitorial closet." He smiled and hopped into the ambulance. "Is the couple okay?"

The bishop smiled and said, "Yes, they're taking them in just to check them over since the husband has a heart condition, but they'll be fine."

Steve leaned over and handed the bishop his car keys. He then stretched out his hand to shake the bishop's hand. "Thank you," he said earnestly. "You saved our lives."

The bishop studied Steve's face and finally said, "Someday, you'll have to come back and tell me what this is all about."

Steve smiled and said sedately, "If we live through this, I will."

Chapter 13

A few days later, Emma was well enough to leave the hospital. Steve had stayed by her side, only leaving to sleep at a local motel. He was watching carefully now and he couldn't see the man. He still had a feeling he was out there, but he was keeping his distance this time.

Saying they were on vacation and a madman had come into the visitors' center and threatened to kill them, Steve and Emma had given a description of the man to the local police who were searching everywhere for him.

Steve had rented a car—there was no reason to pretend now; the killer knew they were there. He picked Emma up and then headed toward the freeway. "Where are we going?" Emma asked glancing at the freeway signs.

"Oh, just doing a little sightseeing," he said and then added, "But don't worry—no flying required."

Emma smiled at him gratefully and reached over and held his hand. She felt comforted holding Steve's strong hand. It was just then that she remembered. "Steve, what did Moroni leave us?" They had decided not to talk about in the hospital in case anyone was listening. Emma leaned forward in anticipation. "And did you see him or anyone else?"

"No," Steve answered, "The scroll was just sitting there when I got back into the room. I don't know if it was Moroni or Joseph or someone else."

63

"Where is it now?" Emma asked, pulling on Steve's arm anxiously.

"Reach back into my pack," Steve answered with a smile. Emma pulled out the rolled parchment. She laid it on her lap and gently unrolled it.

Steve glanced over at Emma and saw her looking at it in surprise. "Not what you thought it would be?" Steve said with a smile.

"No, not really," Emma said puzzled. The parchment had a child's drawing of a waterfall.

"Look at it closer, Emma," Steve prompted, glancing at the rearview mirror. The car was still following them.

Emma leaned closer to the picture and studied it. It was a simple sketch. It had a large waterfall, falling quite far with little squiggles coming away from the water. The picture had a smiling sun looking down on the water. Emma's eyes traveled down to the water in the picture and noticed two very small initials. J.S. She smiled and looked up at Steve. "Joseph drew this?"

"I think so," Steve said with a smile. "'There once was a man who lived near a mighty river in the east,'" Steve quoted. "There's a very mighty river not too far from here. And it has a huge waterfall."

Emma thought for a minute and then her face lit up, "Niagara! Steve, you figured it out!"

"Well, now, I'm not too sure about that," Steve added. "For one thing, it doesn't really make sense. Niagara Falls isn't a church historical site. Why would Joseph leave a clue there?"

"How far is Niagara from Palmyra?" Emma asked, lost in thought.

"About 100 miles," Steve answered.

Emma's brow wrinkled. "It's pretty far, for them back then I mean. It would have meant several days to get there. But think about it. They had probably met people who had been there or had been there themselves. Can you image what

64

it was like to first see Niagara Falls? I mean, it's spectacular today, but it would have been even more awe-inspiring then. Rough and untouched. It wasn't until the late 1800s that they figured out how to divert part of the Niagara River to generate hydro-electric power."

"Maybe Joseph went there with his family and he drew this picture to remember it," Steve suggested. "The little squiggles are probably the mist coming up from the spray. My parents took us there on vacation when I was little. I don't remember much about it except how wet my face got from the mist and spray."

Steve was lost in thought while they drove. He was trying to remember details of his visit as a child, but he couldn't recall much. He wondered where they would go to when they arrived at Niagara. The area was large, encompassing both the U.S. and Canada sides. Neither he nor Emma had brought their passports, so he hoped they would find the clue on the U.S. side.

After two hours of driving, Steve exited the freeway and said to Emma, "Our friend is still behind us. I think we should act very casually, like we're on vacation. Since it's during the day, it will be crowded and he won't try anything with other people around. If we find anything, let's wait and discuss it when we're alone."

"Agreed," Emma replied.

They parked and walked down toward the Falls. Steve took Emma's hand in an effort to look like a vacationing couple and also to help calm her. She had looked edgy once they left the car—even looking over her shoulder once. Steve thought how she must be nervous to be out in the open again with the man who shot her still on the loose.

It was mid-morning and there were throngs of people at the lookout point. Tourists of all nationalities were smiling and taking pictures. Steve relaxed. It would be hard for the hit-man to do anything here. He glanced over his shoulder and saw the man sitting on a park bench up on the hill, watching them through binoculars. Steve was tempted to call the police, but he knew if they arrested him, whoever it was behind all of this would just send someone else. At least they knew what he looked like and could watch out for him.

Steve turned his cell phone on and started taking pictures of Emma with it. He looked all around the rock and cement, looking for a clue. Emma was trying to appear casual as she looked as well. With so many people around, it was easy to get lost in the crowd and look.

They didn't find anything after an hour of looking and finally Steve reached over and hugged Emma so he could get close enough to whisper. She felt warm and safe in his arms and momentarily forgot all about looking for the clue.

Steve moved his mouth next to her ear and said, "What do you think?"

Emma tried to clear her head from the growing attraction she felt for Steve. She dragged her mind back to the task at hand. "I'm sure this look-out wasn't here in Joseph's time," Emma said. We should look more along the river and in the park, places that haven't really changed that much." They spent the rest of the day searching, but found nothing. Even their tail began to look bored. Emma was tired and a bit weak still after her surgery so they headed to a nearby hotel. Steve arranged for two adjoining rooms. When Emma raised her eyebrows at him, he replied, "For safety."

They ordered pizza and ate in Emma's room together. They talked about the parable and tried to figure out where the clue might be. The conversation lagged and Steve glanced up nervously at Emma. He had been wondering this past week and he finally had to ask. "Emma, have you ever been married before?"

Emma immediately dropped her eyes down to the table and shook her head. "Why do you ask?" she said, finally meeting his gaze.

"Well, for one thing, I can't figure out why not," Steve replied. "You're pretty, smart, talented and strong in the church. It's hard to believe that someone hasn't snatched you up before."

Emma blushed at Steve's words, paused for a moment and said, "I was almost engaged once. It was years ago. I was only 19. He wasn't a member of our Church. You can imagine how that went down with my family. I guess deep down I hoped he might convert, but he told me he had no interest in it at all—just in me."

Steve looked at Emma and could see the pain on her face as she remembered. "It was actually a very hard decision. He and I were really good together; we really loved each other. But I imagined my future of going to church by myself, raising my children in the gospel by myself. And it wouldn't have been fair to him—I would have always been hoping he would change."

Emma smiled and said looking at Steve, "I was so young then. I thought I would have plenty of chances to get married to an LDS guy. But the years went by—it got harder and harder to meet nice, single guys. Soon I graduated and decided to do my master's. I thought it would happen then. But it didn't. It was then I realized I probably wouldn't ever be married. I became quite bitter about it and threw myself into my career. That was difficult as well, being in a male-dominated profession where most of my colleagues thought I should be home having babies. But Dr. Mangum was like a father to me. He helped me, guided me. Even protected and defended me when professionally attacked. He saw something in me that I didn't even see in myself back then. He made quite a stir when he named me associate dean."

Steve liked learning more about her and stuffed another slice of pizza in his mouth, content to listen. Emma smiled and continued, "Truth be told, I don't even know how I'd feel to be married and give up my career to stay home and raise kids. I love my job. I honestly don't know if I *could* give it up. I would feel so empty without it."

It was getting late, so they finally got ready for bed. Steve insisted they leave the adjoined door open, just in case their tail decided to come for a visit.

The next morning they headed back to Niagara and Emma teased Steve, "You're a snorer."

"Am I?" Steve asked surprised. "Usually I don't sleep soundly enough. I must have been pretty tired." Steve realized he hadn't had any nightmares the night before. Maybe being near Emma is a calming influence, he thought to himself. "I liked your sexy flannel jammies," Steve jibbed back.

Emma smiled and reached over to hold his hand. They arrived at Niagara and sat in the car in the parking lot.

"Okay, so, what's the plan?" Emma asked Steve.

"Maybe we should ask around—ask the guides. It worked for us at the visitors' center," Steve replied.

As they walked toward the nearest guide, Steve glanced around. He hadn't seen their tail yet and wondered where he went. They waited while the guide finished his tour and then approached him. He was in his 60s, portly and friendly. He was wearing a national park green t-shirt and shorts with a button that said, "I love Niagara."

They chatted for a minute about Niagara and then Steve got to the point. "Have you ever seen a marking like this anywhere on the grounds?" Steve knelt down and drew the three wavy lines in the nearby dirt.

The guide knelt down and studied the lines seriously. After thinking for a minute, he shook his head. "Nope, but I've only been here for a few years now. While Ed, over there, he's been here for 20. If anyone would know, he would."

Emma and Steve looked over at the man the guide was pointing to. He looked about 70 or 80, had white hair, and used a cane to walk. They moved closer and listened to him talk. It quickly became apparent to Steve and Emma that he was an expert on Niagara Falls. He was talking about the war of 1812 and how Fort Niagara had played an important role in the war. They waited patiently, enjoying his stories. Steve glanced around—still no sign of their tail.

When Ed finally finished, the other guide approached him. "Say, Ed, these folks are looking for a marking. Kind of looks like an Indian marking. Three wavy lines." The guide drew it in the air with his finger. "Ever seen anything like that around?"

Emma leaned forward, holding her breath. "Hmm," Ed replied as he thought. "Nope, not that I've ever seen."

Emma exhaled and Steve took a deep breath in disappointment. They had scoured everywhere yesterday, looking for the clue. Steve started to wonder if it was on the Canada side and realized they would have to send for their passports.

"Yeah, the only marking I've ever seen 'round Niagara is a sun," he added.

Emma's head turned quickly toward Ed. "A sun?" she asked excitedly, thinking of the sun in Joseph's drawing.

"Can you draw it for us?" Steve added stepping closer.

"Sure," Ed replied and pulled out a notepad and pen from his pocket. He sketched for a minute with shaky hands and then turned the pad toward them.

Steve smiled. He didn't need to be an expert in church history to recognize the symbol. It was on several of the modern-day temples. The drawing was a half sun, with rays coming from it and an eye in the middle.

Emma squeezed Steve's hand. This was definitely it.

Chapter 14

Preston leaned back in his soft, leather chair. The office was quiet. Preston liked coming in the office on Sundays. It was the one day RJ never came because he usually drank heavily on Saturday nights and needed a day to sober up before Monday's chaos ensued.

He looked out the window. It was a beautiful day in Atlanta. His office felt stuffy and he hated how the modern buildings had the windows sealed shut. He could see the trees swaying gently outside and the breeze would feel good.

Preston was lost in thought. The board had given RJ 90 days to turn things around. RJ assured them he would do it. Preston knew he would—but at what cost? He took off his jacket and undid his tie. He only allowed himself this luxury on Sundays when RJ wasn't around.

He was thinking of her now. He opened his filing cabinet and fingered through thick financial statements. It was in Dec. He always kept her picture secretly in the Dec. statement—it was the month she had died.

He glanced around, but the office was still empty. He pulled out the faded picture and smiled. Warm memories flooded his mind of better times with her. He studied her face for the thousandth time. It was kind and loving.

He put the picture carefully back in place and locked the drawer. He finally decided to get out of the office and headed toward his Porsche, the only car in the parking lot. It was parked in his designated parking spot, perfectly even between the two lines, right next to RJ's spot.

Preston drove on and on—lost in thought of the woman. He just drove without thinking, but after an hour, he realized where he was headed. He finally, almost two hours later, pulled up at the old cemetery. There were a couple of other families there, so he waited. When the cemetery was deserted, he got out of the car and walked up to the headstone. He saw fresh flowers on the headstone and realized his sisters had been there earlier that week. They lived close by and visited regularly.

Looking around again to make sure he was alone, he knelt down next to the headstone and bowed his head in prayer. He said in a whisper, "I miss you, Mama. Help me know what to do."

Chapter 15

Ed had driven them up to Fort Niagara in one of the National Park Service's trucks. Emma had clung to Steve's hand as Ed swerved all over the road. In his old age, he struggled to keep the truck on the right side of the road.

They finally arrived at the fort. Tours were going through there as well, but one had just finished. They walked around the back of the fort and Ed showed them the sun, roughly etched by a knife into the fort's sturdy logs at eye level.

"We say on the tour that the symbol means vigilance—keeping a vigilant watch out for the enemy. In this case, it was the French." Ed went on to describe some of the key battles of the War of 1812 that had taken place at Fort Niagara. Steve tried to picture it as it would have been back then.

After about 20 minutes, Ed finished and walked over to say hi to one of his fellow tour guides assembling a group. Emma turned to Steve and said, "Wow, I never knew what that symbol meant before, but it takes on a whole new meaning now. Watching out for the enemy. I wonder if it was there before and Joseph used that symbol or if Joseph carved it on the fort."

"We'll probably never know, but let's look for the water symbol," Steve answered. He glanced around again, but still didn't feel like they were being watched. He wondered what had happened to their tail. They looked around the fort, especially on the rocks. But after looking for nearly an hour, they gave up and went inside, looking for Ed. He was talking with some tourists so they looked around inside the fort.

They were inside a small room—the commander's private room. Emma was examining several of the artifacts on display when Steve interjected, "If I've got my bearings right, this room is right inside of where the sun marking was."

"Really?" Emma asked in surprise, thinking of the placement.

"Yes, it would be that wall right there," Steve said, indicating behind the commander's desk. There was a large bear-skin rug on the wall. Steve glanced around and then stepped over the rope line protecting the artifacts. He lifted up the dusty bear-skin rug and came face-to-face with the three wavy lines. They were roughly carved into the hewn logs.

He heard Emma inhale sharply. In a second she had swept under the rope and was at his side. Steve held up the rug while Emma examined the marks with her fingers. She felt above and beneath them, between the logs.

"Steve," she said animatedly. "Feel this." Emma guided his hand with hers toward the spot between logs right underneath the wavy lines. "Do you feel this little notch?" Emma asked excitedly.

Steve could feel a line running along the bottom of the log. In the middle, he found the notch. Realizing suddenly what it was, he tried to use his finger to pry deeper into the notch, but the wood was old and stubborn. Steve pulled out his knife and used it as leverage to pop open some space in between the wood. In a second he had it. The little wood door underneath swung open and dust cascaded to the floor.

Steve smiled and looked at Emma. She was smiling as well and her entire face was lit from within. Steve paused for a moment, studying her face, thinking she was so beautiful this way.

But Emma couldn't wait and reached her small hand up into the underside of the log. She could feel something soft and long inside. She tried to pull it out, but the opening was smaller than the item. She worked it back and forth until she

73

managed to get the end of it closer to the opening. She finally pulled it free.

Steve examined the find. It looked like something long and slender, wrapped in a tanned deerskin. Emma had just started to unwrap it when they heard voices coming closer. Steve quickly turned and closed the log and replaced the bear rug while Emma stuffed the item into her backpack.

They were just back on the other side of the rope when Ed and the other tour guide came into view.

"Here ya two are," Ed said with a smile. "Thought the Injuns had got ya. Any luck on finding your symbol?"

"Nah," Steve said casually glancing sideways at Emma, "It's probably just a wild goose chase anyway. We're ready to head back to the Falls if you are."

"Actually, I need to use the ladies' room before we go," Emma requested. She had a mischievous look on her face and Steve knew she just couldn't wait until they got back to the Falls to see what was underneath the deerskin covering.

Steve small-talked with Ed and the other guide for a few minutes. Finally, Emma came back into the fort with a huge smile on her face. She was springing along as she walked, her feet barely touching the ground. Steve knew—whatever it was—was *exactly* what they had come looking for.

The man felt horrible as he lay in his hotel bed. He hadn't been this sick in years. He either had a vicious case of the stomach flu or possibly even food poisoning. He had been throwing up since 5:00 a.m. RJ had called for a report and the man had just lied and said they were still at Niagara looking around and he was just keeping an eye on them. As he talked with RJ, he could feel it starting again and said they were moving and he had to follow them as he quickly hung up.

He wasn't worried though about the soldier and professor finding anything. They looked clueless yesterday, searching every inch of the falls and finding nothing. He was sure they were just doing more of the same today.

Regardless, he was getting bored. All of this waiting around wasn't his style. Once he started to feel better, he texted the girl and told her to come to Niagara. Once he felt better, he was going to need her around to keep this job interesting.

Chapter 16

Emma waited until they were back in their rental car and moving toward the freeway before she pulled out the deerskin wrap. She gingerly eased the deerskin open. Steve glanced over. With the deerskin now lying flat, Steve could see a small piece of parchment about 14 inches wide and five inches long. It was smooth at the top, but ragged at the bottom, as if the rest of it had been torn away. On the parchment were rows of hieroglyphics written with ink, forming a paragraph.

"What is it?" Steve asked curiously as he glanced back and forth at the parchment and the road.

"It looks like Reformed Egyptian characters," Emma replied excitedly. "The same language that Mormon used on the gold plates."

"Can you translate it?" Steve asked.

"No," Emma said in a deflated voice. "I never learned it. I never thought I'd need to know it." She sighed. "But, Dr. Mangum does or at least he did. He studied it when he was younger. I bet he could piece enough of it together for us. Maybe we can find somewhere to scan it and e-mail it to him."

"E-mail is too dangerous," Steve said as he thought out loud. "Whoever is trailing us could easily hack into it. They might be watching his mail at home and at the university as well. But we do need to make some copies of it. For whatever reason, our tail hasn't been around today, so we need to take advantage of that and get this into other people's hands as backup." Steve took the next exit and they wound their way into a small town, stopping at an insurance agency.

"Shouldn't we look for a convenience store or a Kinko's or something?" Emma asked confused as she glanced over at the insurance agency door.

"Too obvious," Steve replied. "It would be the first place our tail would look if he's out there." Steve powered on his cell phone and made a call to President Thompson's office. He spoke with the prophet's assistant and wrote down a number. "Please have President Thompson call me as soon as he can," he added before he hung up.

"So what are we going to do?" Emma asked.

"I've got a plan," Steve said with a smile. "C'mon."

They walked into the insurance agency and a woman in her late 40s with big, bleached blonde hair and long, fake nails typed on the keyboard in front of her. She stopped typing, looked up with a bright smile and said, "Hello! How can I help you two?"

"I'm Ryan and this is my sister Samantha. We're on vacation and it's our dad's birthday today. We totally forgot and we feel terrible. We were hoping we could use your machine and send him a fax."

The lady looked up at Steve and smiled. "Why of course, I'd love to help you out. What do you need faxed?"

Emma looked around the room and saw a copy machine in the corner. "We just need to make one copy. We wrote out his birthday message on a larger paper and need to copy it down to a smaller size so we can fax it. We'd be happy to pay for the copies and the fax," Emma offered.

The lady smiled and said, "Sure, it's no problem. Go ahead and help yourself." The phone rang then and she turned to answer it. Steve and Emma walked over to the copy machine and Emma efficiently resized the copy and hit print. Steve then handed her the number and she quickly faxed a copy to President Thompson's office. They heard the confirmation beep from the fax that it had transmitted successfully and they both visibly relaxed. Emma saw an insurance envelope sitting on a nearby counter and had another idea.

She heard the insurance lady ending her call, so she turned around and said, "You know, we feel so bad about forgetting our dad's birthday that we'd like to send him this letter as well describing our trip. We want him to be surprised, so we were thinking we could send it in one of your State Farm envelopes. Is that okay?"

"That's a great idea—he'll think it's a bill and never expect that it's a letter from his kids!" she gushed. Emma folded the photocopy into thirds and wrote on the outside— "Happy Birthday. Having a great trip. Love, Us." She then handed it to the lady and she put it in a State Farm envelope. "What's his address?"

Emma knew it by heart and gave her Dr. Mangum's address. They thanked the lady profusely and she promised to get it out with the mail the next day.

Steve was watching out the window, checking for their tail, but he was still nowhere in sight. As they got back into the car, Steve turned to Emma. "I feel good about this—I feel like we're finally getting to the clues and ahead of our tail. I think we should push on to the next clue quickly before he finds us again."

"I agree," Emma concurred. "It's a lot more nerve-wracking knowing he's watching us. The further ahead we can stay, the better."

"So where to next then?" Steve asked, starting the car.

Emma pulled out her notes and looked at the compass. "Well, so far, we've found the 'east' wind at Hill Cumorah and the 'west' water at Niagara. It's making it easier to know that we've got to go north or south." She pulled out her copy of the parable again.

One day, he saw smoke afar off. He didn't worry.

Then the strong breeze shifted north and the destroyer was born.

"So fire is somewhere north of here," Emma continued lost in thought.

Steve pulled out the local map and looked. "Not much north of here on a local level."

"Somewhere that Joseph wasn't worried," Emma muttered, still thinking.

Steve folded the local map and pulled out the regional map. He found Palmyra on it and then traced his finger north. "Not much directly north other than Lake Ontario," he commented. He started to move his finger to the right and upward. "If we stay inside the U.S., the next state is Vermont."

Emma turned her head sharply toward him. "Vermont! Joseph was born in Vermont! A place where Joseph wasn't worried. It would have to be before Palmyra. Before the First Vision. It was when he was younger, growing up in Vermont! He didn't move to New York until he was 10!" she exclaimed. She looked back down at the parable. "Joseph must be the destroyer who was born! Wow, that really threw me off. The play on words with destroyer. I thought it was Satan. But destroyer has a dual meaning. Joseph destroyed all past ideas of God and the trinity. He destroyed the idea that God no longer speaks to men here on earth. He destroyed the notion that God is just a spirit and doesn't have a body."

Steve loved to see her like this—her face full of excitement and enthusiasm. It made him want to kiss her. But he had to take advantage of this lead. The further they got away from their tail, the better. He put the car in drive and did a U-turn and headed toward the interstate.

"Vermont," Emma said, shaking her head. "I should have figured that out a lot time ago. He was born in Sharon, Vermont."

"Remember, they didn't want just anyone to be able to figure out the parable. They wanted it to be difficult," Steve assured her and then glanced over at Emma. "They wanted it to be someone special."

Emma smiled gratefully and reached over for Steve's free hand.

Chapter 17

The man knew he was in trouble. He had searched everywhere, but they were gone. He had checked at the hotel and found they left that morning and had taken everything with them. He drove to Niagara the next day and asked around. He found one guide who had met them. He told the man he had taken them up to the fort and described the sun/eye symbol. The man drove up to the fort and spent the whole day searching for clues, but came up with nothing. No one knew where they had gone.

He decided the sun/eye symbol was his best lead. When he got back to his hotel, he Googled it. The image came up on several of the Mormon temples, but nowhere was it more prominent than Nauvoo, Illinois. He checked out and drove toward the airport. They already had a day on him, but given their history, it would take them that long to figure out what they were looking for and where. He could still catch up.

He hit number one on his speed dial. The girl picked up.

"I'm almost there," she said in a sultry voice. "I'm only 30 minutes away."

He hit his fist on the steering wheel, audibly cursing his bad decision of sending for her. In his frantic search for the professor and soldier, he had completely forgotten that he had told her to leave Nauvoo and come to Palmyra.

"What's wrong?" she asked calmly. That's one of the things he liked about her—she was very cool under pressure.

"Turn around and head back to the airport," he barked into the cell phone. "I'll meet you there soon. Buy us two tickets on the next flight out toward Nauvoo—no matter what it costs. They're on the move."

She hung up her phone and got off the next exit. Turning back toward the freeway, she hit number one on her speed dial. "Yeah, it's me. No, he's lost them," she reported. She heard RJ shouting down the phone, using every obscenity he knew. She waited until his fury was spent and then asked, "What do you want me to do?" She listened for a minute and then replied, "I understand."

She took a deep breath as she drove toward the airport. This was finally her chance. She knew when he approached her that this was her big break. She had been waiting patiently for him to mess up and for RJ to turn the project over to her.

She knew she wasn't as experienced as he was, but she was much smarter. He was a hired thug—little more. Yes, he was an expert marksman and loved to kill, but this job was different. It required patience. Intelligence. He didn't possess any of that. This would be the opportunity she had been waiting for.

When she finally met him at the airport, he was in a foul mood. He had messed up and they both knew it, although he lied to her and tried to pass it off as something else. She pretended to console him—acting was another talent she possessed.

They finally arrived in Illinois and drove rapidly to Nauvoo. They split up—she waited at the Mormon temple site while he checked all of the local hotels. After two days, she knew he had definitely lost them.

Killing him ended up being very easy. He got roaring drunk in frustration and didn't even notice when she slipped something into his drink. That's the way she liked it—subtle, yet sure. It was her turn finally now.

When he stopped breathing, she sent a text to RJ, "It's done."

RJ replied with, "It's in your account." She knew the money would be there, but that's not the only reason she was doing it. RJ was known throughout her industry to provide regular work and to pay handsomely. Enough that all of his past "special employees" had retired nicely in some remote region in the world. That had perpetuated the myth that he killed them all, but insiders knew better.

She opened her laptop and powered it on. She hadn't wasted her time waiting in Nauvoo. She had asked endless questions of the missionary couple who led the tours around the Mormon Temple. She had learned everything there was to know about the Mormons. She had a list of places that were "sacred" to the Mormons. She knew they would be headed to one of them.

They weren't in Palmyra or Nauvoo. She looked down her list—it was pretty long. The Mormons had moved around a lot until they settled in Utah. She looked at the map and thought about it logically. She had no way to know where they were, but she reasonably assumed that they would go to the nearest site to Palmyra. There were two. Joseph Smith's birthplace in Vermont or Harmony, Pennsylvania where Joseph had received the priesthood authority from John the Baptist and Peter, James and John. She researched them both online. Both had recognized sites and plaques by the Mormon church. As she considered her options, she suddenly knew what to do to find them.

Chapter 18

Emma smiled as she got ready. She and Steve were at a motel just outside Sharon, Vermont. As before, they had stayed in separate rooms, but had adjoining doors which Steve insisted they leave open just in case.

She hoped that his nightmares were becoming more infrequent and that is was due to her, that maybe she was a soothing influence on him. The tortured look in his eye had faded and he seemed more relaxed.

Emma had never felt like this before. Steve was strong and brave, yet kind and gentle. She thought back to their first kiss in the secret room in Hill Cumorah. It had created a deep warmness within her and she had been longing for him to kiss her again. Part of her wondered why he hadn't yet. Maybe it was because they were in danger at Hill Cumorah and thought they wouldn't get out alive.

Emma began to brush her hair, lost in thought, wondering how Steve felt about her. She heard a noise and looked up. Steve was standing behind her, watching her face in the mirror. He was dressed and had his army backpack in his hand. He met her gaze and smiled at her. She smiled back and then, on an impulse, she turned around quickly, wrapped her arms around Steve's neck and pulled him close to her in a kiss.

Steve, in surprise, dropped his backpack, and put his arms around her. She kissed him again and again, hungry for more. It had been hard to be so close to him every day—to spend every minute together. To feel attracted to him and yet to not be close like this. For a brief minute, she didn't care anymore about the secret or the next clue. She just wanted to be close to him.

She felt warm in his arms. She could feel his heart pounding in his chest. She tried to pull him even closer to her. He responded by lifting her off the ground in his strong arms.

He was fighting within himself. It felt incredible to finally be like this with Emma. He had realized the past few days that he was falling in love with her. He hadn't allowed himself to get physical with her because he wanted to keep a clear head to protect her. But he hadn't expected this—for Emma to be like this, pulling him closer, encouraging him. It made it so hard and part of him wanted to abandon caution.

It had been so long. His body was shaking now, but he couldn't make himself stop. Not yet. He kissed her again and again, at first hard, longing kisses, but as his conscience nagged at the back of his head, he slowed and the kisses became gentler, softer. Every inch of his body wanted her, but due to his religious beliefs and his disciplined, military training, he would make himself stop.

He slowly pulled back and set Emma down gently. She wasn't ready to stop and tried to encourage him by kissing him again. He moved his lips away from hers toward her ear. "Emma," he whispered, "You're making it really hard for me to be a good Mormon boy." He heard her sigh, resigned that they needed to stop. He wrapped his arms around her shoulders and pulled her in close and held her for several minutes. Neither of them said anything. He gently kissed the top of her head and stroked her hair.

"I . . . I was wondering this morning why you hadn't kissed me again," Emma said softly. "I was worried that you had regretted it or something," she admitted openly. "Or that you weren't attracted to me."

"Well, I think you can dismiss that idea," Steve said with a laugh. When she didn't respond, Steve gently pushed her backward so she would meet his eyes. "Emma, I think you are beautiful, smart, brave and . . . I think I'm falling in love with you. But I'm scared, Emma."

Emma looked up at Steve with concerned-filled eyes. "Why are you scared?" she asked softly.

He sighed and stepped away. He walked over and sat down on the bed. He noticed Emma had neatly made the bed out of habit, despite the fact that a maid would come in and clean as soon as they left. Steve had left his in a jumbled heap. He ran his fingers through his hair and took a deep breath. It was so painful to think of Kari and the past.

Emma walked over and sat beside him, reaching over and putting her hand on his shoulder. She waited patiently, thinking about his first wife and what she must have been like, what they were like together.

"Emma, I loved Kari—deeply. I thought we were so great together. I thought we were strong enough together to survive being apart. I was wrong. It was just too hard for her to have me gone so much and looking back, I understand that. But I hurt her, Emma. She turned from being my best friend and a loving wife into an angry, resentful person. That was my fault. I . . . I am worried I'll never be a good husband. That I'll hurt someone else."

Emma waited silently, gently moving her hand to lightly rub his back. She could hear the emotion in his voice—see the pain in his eyes. "And then there's Ari," he continued and his voice caught. "What kind of a dad am I? I was gone a lot. She hardly knew me when I came home, always going to Kari for comfort. And she will always be hurt by the fact that her parents are divorced."

The tears started to well up in his eyes and a single tear ran down his left cheek. He was staring at the carpet, his hands tightly clasped together. "I . . . miss her, Emma. I didn't ever want it to be like this. I only get to see her every other weekend and some holidays. I love her—" His voice broke and he began sobbing. Emma leaned her head over onto his shoulder, wrapping her right hand around his back and held him tightly. He sobbed and sobbed, his body shaking with emotion. He felt exposed as he cried like this, but he hadn't really had anyone to talk to during and after the divorce. He had packed up all of his emotion deep down inside and was letting it all out now.

"I miss Ari so much, Emma. I feel so guilty. Another man, Kari's new husband, is there with Ari every day. He is the one kissing her goodnight each night. He is the one who is seeing her beautiful smile first thing in the morning. I worry that—" he broke off, unable to continue.

Emma knew what he was going to say and finished softly, "You worry that Ari will love him more."

Steve couldn't speak, just nodding his head.

"You gave up your military career to be back near her," Emma reasoned. "You moved to be near her in Provo so you could be with her every other weekend. She may not understand all of that now, but she will when she's older."

Steve listened and then added, "The judge offered me every Wednesday night as well, but I felt it was too much back and forth for Ari, so I said I would just take the every other weekend. I was thinking how hard it would be for her, to sleep in one bed one night and then another the next night. It just seemed too hard for her."

Emma could see how much Steve loved Ari. She knew that kind of love would mean his relationship with Ari would always somehow work out. Emma also thought that he was young enough to remarry and still have other children. Perhaps that would ease the pain a bit. She began to wonder if she and Steve would marry, but she pushed the thought to the back of her mind. It was too soon to tell. Steve had a lot of baggage and would need to work through a lot of that before he could ever move on.

There was one question Emma just had to ask, "Steve, do you still love Kari?"

Steve turned to look at Emma and she studied his tear-stained face. He finally dropped her gaze back down to the carpet and Emma knew then that part of the answer was yes. "I don't love who Kari is anymore. She hates me and is deeply resentful. It was so hard for me, being overseas, fighting, watching my friends die and not having her support. She never wanted to hear about what I'd been through when I came home—so I never was able to talk about it with anyone. I signed the divorce papers because I knew we could never recover from her anger and bitterness and my loneliness. But I truly believe, if I wouldn't have joined the military, Kari and I would still be married and would happily be raising Ari together. So I guess I still love my memories of Kari, how things were at the start. But I know it's just a memory. It will never be like that again."

He paused, wiping the tears away from his face. "I'm glad she met Brian. He's a good guy. And I honestly believe that he loves Ari. I'm glad she's happy now and that Ari has someone there with her every day—even though I wish it was me."

Emma got down on her knees in front of Steve and moved into his arms. She held him tightly and he wrapped his arms around her as well. He was emotionally exhausted. They held one another until Emma's knees became sore and she stood up. She started to pack up her things and they checked out of the motel. Steve scanned the parking lot, but still no sign of their tail. As they got into the rental car and Steve was about to turn the key, he paused. "Emma, when this is all over, will you go on a date with me?" he asked hopefully, but a bit nervously.

"Yes," Emma said with a broad smile spreading across her face.

Chapter 19

She was waiting for them as they pulled into the parking lot. They looked relaxed and happy, holding hands as they walked toward the visitors' center. She smiled to herself—that would be an advantage for her. She pretended to take pictures of the trees and the area. They walked right past her and didn't take notice.

She never left anything to chance. She had hired a hacker to get into all of the major car rental agencies' databases and find out who they were using. All of the cars had an embedded GPS which was traceable. They used it to recover lost or stolen cars. Within a few hours, she knew exactly where they were. She had arrived at the visitors' center in Sharon, Vermont, as soon as it opened that morning. She walked around confidently; she had changed her appearance the day before and was now a blonde with glasses. She picked out modest clothes and even added a CTR ring which was fashionable among LDS youth.

She stayed close to a group of youth as they walked toward the visitors' center to give the impression that she was with them. She listened as they went from room to room, learning more about Joseph Smith's early years and his family.

She watched the professor and soldier from the back of the room. They were at the front of the group and she noticed how they were scanning the visitors' center's walls and artifacts—they were looking for something.

Toward the end of the presentation, the elderly missionary man was talking about the hearth on the floor. He described how it was the only original artifact left from Joseph Smith's birthplace home. They knelt down and examined the hearth closely from all sides. But after about 10 minutes, they looked discouraged and left the room with the rest of the tour.

After the tour, they talked at length with the guide. They drew something on a piece of paper; she saw the guide shake his head. They searched outside for a while, but the morning wore on and they became more and more frustrated. They finally left and she turned the opposite way on the freeway. She didn't need to follow them—she knew her hacker could trace them online. She went to grab a bite to eat and to think.

As she ate, she wrote down observations she had made that morning about the professor and the soldier. Despite the day being hot and them having a hotel room, they carried heavy backpacks with them. That might be so they could move quickly, she thought to herself, or because they have something valuable on them.

They must have already found something, she thought to herself. She didn't like all of this following around—she wanted to get ahead of them. She knew exactly what she needed to do.

Chapter 20

Steve turned to face Emma with his determined jaw set. "No, Emma, you're not coming and that's that."

"Steve, we're in this together. I'm coming with you," Emma tried to sound as determined as Steve, but her statement ended as more of a plea.

"Emma, we've been through all of this already. It's too dangerous! I'm going to break into the site and search in the dark for clues. If I can't find anything outside, I'm going into the visitors' center. I checked out the locks today and they're easy to jimmy," Steve explained.

"Why don't we ask President Thompson to just have someone let us in," Emma asked rationally, raising her eyebrows in frustration.

"Because, I have a feeling I'm going to have to destroy church property to get to the clue," Steve said in a resigned voice. He hadn't told Emma this before—he knew she wouldn't like it.

"You're going to *what?*" Emma shouted.

"I think it's the hearth," Steve said. "The missionary said that the hearth was the original one in Joseph's house and it was moved into the visitors' center when it was built. So it's either underneath the hearth or back in the original spot where the house was. Either way, I'm going to be destroying church property by either breaking up the hearth or digging on a sacred site."

Emma had a wild look in her eyes. Steve knew she was losing it now. "And what if you're wrong? And you destroy this historical property? We couldn't find the symbol, Steve. We couldn't find the jagged lines indicating fire."

"I know, I know," Steve admitted, "But it's got to be the hearth. It's only natural with the symbol meaning fire."

Emma sighed—she couldn't argue with that. They both thought it had to do with the hearth. "But why can't I come then?" she tried one more time. "I can hold the flashlight for you."

Steve looked at Emma and she could now see worry in his eyes. "Steve, what is it you're not telling me?" she asked sharply.

Steve walked over and glanced out the curtains on an angle so he couldn't be seen. The parking lot below was quiet. "I had a feeling today . . . a feeling that we were being watched again."

Shock went through Emma's body. She had taken the past few days for granted—it had felt so nice to not be afraid anymore. Somewhere in her mind she had hoped that their tail was gone for good. "Did you see him?" she whispered, her face going white.

"No," Steve admitted. "I looked everywhere, but couldn't see him."

"Maybe you're just being paranoid," Emma suggested.

"If there's one thing I learned in the military, it's when I know I'm being watched. It's like a sixth sense you develop," Steve explained. "Someone is here watching us again."

Emma shuddered and she briefly thought back to her encounter at Hill Cumorah with their tail and how he shot her. "Maybe I will stay here," she acquiesced.

"Good," Steve replied. "Now, stay in the room, keep the curtains closed and don't let anyone in, not even the hotel staff." Emma watched as he strapped on his gun and put his knife behind his belt underneath his shirt. He checked his pack to make sure he had everything he would need. He had come prepared for something just like this and was ready. "Power on your cell phone and only call me if it's an emergency. I'll have mine on vibrate."

Steve put his pack on and slung it over his shoulder. He walked over to the window and checked the parking lot one more time. Still quiet. When he was ready to go, he came over to Emma. His face was firm and determined—his eyes clear and strong. Emma wondered if this was how he looked right before he went into battle.

"Steve, I love you," she said impulsively, worried about him. She put both of her hands on his strong arms, as if to assure herself that he could take care of himself. She leaned up on her tiptoes and kissed him gently. He kissed her back softly, but just briefly. He was all business now. "Remember what I said, Emma. Be careful," he instructed.

She nodded her head and tears sprang to her eyes out of worry—not for herself, but for him. He saw them and the determined look on his face softened for a minute and he kissed her again. "Don't worry," he whispered in her ear as he held her tight. "I always come home."

He left then and walked past the elevators to take the stairs. He went down the three flights rapidly and then stopped to listen at the door. He heard a family passing, so he waited. When he was satisfied that the back hallway was quiet, he entered. He would have to pass through about 10 feet of the hotel hallway before he could get out the back door. He had parked back there where it was quieter.

He moved quickly through the hallway and out to his car, starting up quickly and driving away. He drove the speed limit, not wanting to attract attention. He watched his rearview mirror for a tail, but there was nothing.

He drove near the visitors' center where a large gate was closed, blocking the road. He didn't turn in, but instead continued further down the road. After about a quarter mile, he found a spot. It was off the road and was covered by a lot of trees. He pulled the car off the road and into the trees as much as he could.

Glancing around him again, he checked for someone following, but there was still no one. He locked the car and headed up the hillside. He had night vision goggles with him and put them on. He moved comfortably through the trees, pausing every few minutes to listen for any activity around him.

Steve knew he was getting close and came to a fence. Because the church didn't have anything of much value in the visitors' center, it was just a normal fence. Steve easily scaled it and headed toward the house site. It was covered by trees and he felt secure, so he took off his goggles and pulled out his flashlight. The site where Joseph's house had stood was small. Steve thought about all of those children in such a small house. The house was long gone, but the location was marked.

Steve kept his light low to the ground so that someone would have to be very close to see it. He silently searched the ground with his light, looking for the symbol. He and Emma had searched as closely as they could without attracting attention. He used his hand to gently sweep the area, feeling for anything unusual. He worked methodically across the house site.

When he was halfway, he heard a twig snap about 30 feet to his left. He quickly switched off his light and held still. He listened for further sounds for a full 10 minutes, counting in his head. When his pulse returned to normal, he switched on the light and resumed his work.

After an hour of searching, he determined that there was nothing on the house site. He put on his night vision goggles again and headed toward the visitors' center.

Chapter 21

Emma nervously bit her index finger nail. She hated being here alone in the hotel. She watched the news for a while, but after that there wasn't anything good to watch. She tried to read her scriptures for comfort, but she couldn't concentrate on the words.

She thought about Steve and prayed he would be all right. She wondered if this was how his ex-wife, Kari, must have felt each time he was deployed.

She thought about trying to decipher more of the parable, but her mind was too anxious. There was no way she could concentrate now. She glanced over at the nightstand alarm clock, willing it to go faster; yet each number moved so slowly that Emma wanted to throw the clock out the window.

In her highly nervous state, she nearly leapt off of the bed when she heard the shrill, piercing alarm. She glanced around in confusion, covering her ears to protect them from the sound.

The fire alarm. Emma stood up, wondering what to do. Steve had told her to stay in her room. But what if it was a real fire? She would have to leave. But what if it was just a drill or some kids pulling a prank?

She walked quickly over to the window, trying to decide what to do. She glanced out the window carefully as she had seen Steve do so she could see, but not be seen. She saw a few guests filtering out into the parking lot.

Still unsure, she waited. She heard her room phone ring, but she didn't pick it up. A minute later, a hotel employee came knocking on all of the doors, telling everyone to head down the stairs and exit the building immediately.

It wasn't until Emma saw smoke coming out of a window on the ground floor and a fire truck arriving that she finally moved. She grabbed her backpack and headed out her door. The corridor was empty. Her heart raced as she moved toward the stairwell door. It was empty as well.

She moved down as quickly as she could, picking up speed when she heard footsteps above her on the stairs. She finally got out into the parking lot and relaxed when she saw all of the other guests. She stood close to a family with several kids who were running around the parking lot, enjoying the excitement. They squealed with delight when they saw another fire truck arrive.

She watched as the firemen rushed inside the lobby. She clutched her backpack tightly, not getting too close to any of the guests other than the family. The mother tried to start a conversation with Emma, but she just nodded mutely and finally the woman gave up. Emma studied the faces of all of the guests. Most were business travelers and families on vacation. The families looked tired and the business travelers looked annoyed.

She didn't see anyone who looked like their tail and she relaxed slightly. I'm getting so jumpy, she thought to herself.

After an hour, the fireman finally climbed back into their trucks and headed off. The hotel staff said there had been a small fire in one room only and it had been extinguished. They instructed all of the guests to return to their rooms.

Emma rode up the elevator with the family. She noticed they got off on her floor. The children bolted for a room toward the end of the hall. Emma put the key card in her door, waited for the green light and gently pushed it open. She paused in the hallway, looking into her room. Everything seemed as she left it so she went in and lowered her pack onto the ground.

She lay down on the bed and was just starting to massage her pounding head when she heard a sound.

The woman moved quickly around the corner and pointed her gun directly at Emma. "Hello, Professor Worthington," she said with a smirk. "I think I'll call you Emma since we're going to get to be such good friends."

Emma's eyes darted toward the room phone, but the girl followed her gaze. "Now, I wouldn't do that if I were you," she said menacingly. "I'd hate to have to kill you before you get to solve this little Mormon mystery for me." To emphasize her point, she cocked her gun and walked closer.

Emma's mind was racing, trying to figure out a way to get help. It would take too long to get into her pack and dial Steve's cell phone. The hotel phone was too far across the room. Think, Emma, think, she demanded of herself. But nothing came to mind. She instead studied her attacker. She was in her late 20s, pretty, with bleached blonde hair and glasses. But she had a look in her eye that Emma knew meant she would kill her if she had to.

The girl motioned for Emma to move off of the bed and over to the chair near the small table. She kept an eye on Emma while she reached over with her free hand to grab Emma's pack. She dumped the contents on the bed and her eyes widened when she saw the deerskin wrap with the parchment inside.

"All right, Emma, now why don't you start at the beginning and tell me what this is all about," the girl prompted.

Emma kept her mouth closed in a determined silence.

"Oh, so you want to die, is that it?" the girl asked questioningly. "Well, Emma, even if you don't value your own life, I know someone's that you do."

Emma's eyes filled with panic and the girl knew she had her leverage. "Yes, so many choices. There's your lover boy, the soldier. There's your mentor, Dr. Mangum. So easy to make that one look natural with his cancer and all. Oh, and I almost forgot, there's the soldier's little girl. Arianna, isn't it?" she asked.

Emma considered her options. She knew Steve could take care of himself, but what about Dr. Mangum? Or Arianna? "What do you want?" Emma asked in a clipped voice.

"Like I said, start at the beginning and tell me everything," the girl replied, keeping the gun pointed at Emma.

Emma began to recount their journey, starting with the artifact being stolen and then through their journey. She focused on the places, but didn't include anything about the symbols or the parable or what they had found at each location.

The girl listened until Emma finished and then picked up her cell phone. She dialed a number and then said, "Go ahead and kill him," and then hung up. "Such a shame, Emma, that you'll have to deal with that the rest of your life—killing your mentor and all. You see, I have a friend who was recently hired by the home hospice that is caring for your dear doctor. He is bringing Dr. Mangum's medications to his house now. Did I mention I specialize in rare and untraceable poisons? They will, of course, assume that the cancer finally got him. But we'll know differently, won't we Emma?"

Tears came to Emma's eyes, but she remained silent. She hoped Dr. Mangum was okay. She hoped it was all a bluff. There was no way for her to know. She said a silent prayer for him.

"You see, Emma, you haven't told me anything I don't already know and nothing of importance," she scowled, "So we're right back to where we started. We have lover boy and the cute little girl, Arianna left. Which one is next?"

If it would just have been Steve, Emma could have done it, knowing that Steve could and would put up a fight. But given that it was Steve's daughter, Emma just couldn't do that to him—Steve would never recover from losing Ari.

"All right," Emma said defeated.

"Let's start with some of these things in your backpack," the girl prompted. "Tell me about this little story here and this parchment with the symbols on it."

Emma recounted what they knew, leaving out only that they had sent a copy to church headquarters and to Dr. Mangum. She talked about how they were looking for the fire symbol and how Steve had gone to look for it.

"And the last clue, the rectangular shape," the girl asked.

"I don't know, I haven't gotten that far yet," Emma answered honestly. When the girl raised her eyebrows, Emma added, "It's true. We've been taking it one step at a time."

"And the symbols on this parchment, what do they mean?" she asked again.

"I don't know that either," Emma answered. "It's in a dead language and very few people in the world know it." Emma had a thought come into her head. "If fact, you might want to spare Dr. Mangum as he's one of them."

"Hmm, I'll think about that," she replied, gauging Emma's words. "In the meantime, roll up your sleeve."

When Emma hesitated, the girl said, "I can either shoot you or you can roll up your sleeve—your choice." Emma finally complied and rolled up her left sleeve. The girl pulled out a hypodermic needle and quickly injected it into Emma's arm. As Emma started to black out, she wondered if she was dying or just going to sleep. Either way, her last thought was of Steve.

Chapter 22

Steve easily picked the lock on the back door of the visitors' center. In Iraq, one of his bunkmates was an expert at it and had taught Steve. He was from New Jersey and Steve wondered if he had acquired his skill on the streets. Regardless, it had come in handy a few times over the years.

Steve relocked the door and moved toward the location of the hearth near the front of the visitors' center. He first headed to a front window, flattening himself against the wall next to the window. He watched outside for a few minutes, but everything was quiet. He saw a small light in the bushes nearby and took another look. He then saw another and another. He realized they were fireflies. It had been years since he had seen them.

He finally moved back toward the hearth and turned his flashlight on, again, keeping it low to the ground. He searched slowly for the jagged fire symbol. Nothing. He turned off his light, thinking. There was no clue outside nor here on the actual hearth. Maybe they had it wrong. Maybe this wasn't the right site. Steve considered his options. He could unearth the stone and still look for the clue or he and Emma could continue to consider other possible sites.

He looked back at the stone and felt its size again with his fingers. If he tried to unearth it, there was a good chance it would crack. What if they were wrong? Could he live with himself for destroying the only remaining relic of Joseph's birth home?

Steve stood up and glanced out the window again—still quiet. He decided he'd better call Emma and ask her opinion. He pulled out his cell phone. He quickly dialed Emma's number and waited. It rang once. Twice. Three times. No answer. It finally went to a generic voice mail message and Steve pulled back the phone in surprise. He hung up and dialed again. Still, no answer.

He wondered if Emma was in the bathroom or maybe asleep. He glanced at his watch—it was only 11:30. He waited five minutes and then called again. Nothing. A sick feeling started to creep into his stomach. Steve started to pace up and down the room, trying to figure out what was going on. He knew her phone was on—it was ringing and not going straight to voicemail. He stopped in the middle of the room and dialed information. He gave them instructions and then waited.

The hotel lobby clerk answered with a friendly, "Hello, this is Monica."

"Hi Monica, I'm a guest in room 634. I'm trying to reach my girlfriend, Emma, in 636, but she isn't picking up her cell. Will you please try and call her room for me?" Steve asked politely, trying not to sound anxious.

"Sure, hold please," Monica said. Steve felt like it was an eternity as he waited. She finally came back on the line. "I'm sorry, there's no answer," she said.

"Is there any way you could go up there and check on her? I'm worried she has fallen or is hurt or something. I just left her a few hours ago and she was staying in all night," Steve explained.

"Well, maybe she was fed up with our fire earlier this evening. The guests had to wait out in the parking lot for nearly an hour," Monica offered.

"Fire? What fire? Where was it?" Steve drilled.

"Oh, it wasn't anywhere near her," Monica assured. "It was on the first floor. I heard one of the firemen talking to his captain and they said it turned out to just be a prank."

"You mean there wasn't an actual fire?" Steve asked.

"Well, there was smoke, but no fire," Monica explained. "Turns out it was a couple of smoke bombs. Must have been some kids messing around."

Steve considered the events. Emma was up in her room and wouldn't have left given Steve's strict instructions. However, seeing smoke might have prompted Emma to leave her room thinking it was an actual fire. Steve knew one thing for sure now—their tail was back and Emma was in danger.

"Is there anything else, sir?" Monica asked politely.

"No. . ." Steve answered as he hung up his phone. He had left Emma at the hotel to protect her and it now looked like the worst possible thing he could have done. Steve shoved his phone into his bag. He had to get back and search for Emma. Nothing else mattered now.

He walked quickly toward the back door, checking outside to make sure it was clear. He moved swiftly through the trees, using a zig zag pattern that had become a habit during his training. He was within sight of the road and his rental car when he heard a gun cocking.

"Where are you going, soldier?" the woman asked in a clear, strong voice behind him. Steve froze and slowly put his hands in the air.

"Who are you?" Steve asked without turning around.

"Look for yourself, Steve" she responded with a laugh. "You and I, we're old friends."

Steve turned slowly and tried to see through the dark. She was half behind a tree, protecting herself, but her face and her arm with the gun were visible. Steve didn't recognize the blonde-haired lady with glasses.

"Of course, I'm not a natural blonde," she explained. "I have black hair and a penchant for making out on campus."

Finally, Steve thought, he was face-to-face with the other accomplice to the robbery. She was a talker—maybe he could pick up some clues. "Where's your make-out partner then?" he asked. "I haven't seen him around for a couple of days."

"He, um, got *sick*," she said playfully. Steve could see with the moonlight that she was smiling.

Steve sized her up as he did all opponents. He knew if he could get close enough to her, he could quickly incapacitate her. He subtly reached for his gun, thinking she wouldn't be able to see in the darkness.

"Naughty, naughty," she continued playfully. "Now, throw that gun over here before you get yourself shot." When Steve hesitated, she added, "Or before your girlfriend gets shot. I see that I'm not the only one who's been playing around on this little adventure."

"Where is Emma?" Steve asked menacingly through gritted teeth.

"Hmm, now, is she resting or dead? Let me think. . ." she continued. "I think better when I know you're not going to go for your gun."

Steve took out his gun slowly and threw it over by the girl. She came out from behind the tree and picked it up, tucking it in her belt.

"Now, what did you find here on good old Joe's pilgrimage site?" she inquired, still pointing the gun at Steve.

"I'm not telling you anything until I know Emma is safe," Steve replied stubbornly.

"Sorry, lover boy, but I've got the gun and the girl, so we're playing this my way. But I will tell you one thing—she's alive. Whether she's safe or not is *entirely* up to you," she taunted.

Steve had been stalling, formulating a plan in his mind. He decided to take the bait. "All right, I know where it is, and I'll take you to it."

"Now, that's better," she replied, pleased with his cooperation. He went ahead first, leading her to the site. He led her the long way, knowing that she wouldn't be familiar with the terrain. He started with a short, slow gait, keeping her close to him. The moon was bright, but he could tell clouds would soon cover it.

Just as the clouds began to overshadow the moon, he quickly lengthened his stride to create distance between them. A second later, everything went dark and he dodged behind a nearby tree, crouching down, pulling out his knife simultaneously. He heard her stop.

"Now, Steve, you don't want to do this," she said. "You don't want anything to happen to Emma now do you? Or how about your little Arianna? She's awfully cute."

Steve froze momentarily, but knew what he had to do. He had to shift the power—it was the only way to save Emma and heaven help him if it was true—Ari. He blocked everything else out of his mind and focused on the sound of her voice. She was moving slowly toward him.

Years of training had enabled him to see, by sound, exactly where she was. He waited patiently as she moved away from him a few steps and then back toward him again. He could tell from the sounds that she was shuffling her feet—a common mistake when you can't see. He counted in his head her footsteps and then, when he knew she was one step away, lunged out from behind the tree in a crouching position and tackled her at the waist, pushing her up into the air and off balance. He landed on top of her and used his weight to disable any movement. With his free hand he reached up, grabbed the hand where she had the gun and twisted it tightly around her back. He heard the gun go off, but as he twisted harder, he heard her cry out. He knew he was about to break her arm when she finally dropped the gun.

Steve brought his knife up to the back of her head, deftly turned it around in his hand and used the back of the handle to hit her on the head sharply. He knew the exact part of the skull to hit, ensuring unconsciousness. Her body went slack and her head fell to the ground. He pulled his gun out of her belt and put it back into his holster. He took the magazine out of her gun and threw it deep into the forest. He then pulled some rope out of his backpack and quickly tied her hands behind her back and her feet together. He slung her over his shoulder, moving toward the visitors' center.

He glanced at his watch. He still had plenty of time. He didn't have anything for a gag, so he decided to lock up his assailant in the visitors' center while he went back to her car to search for Emma.

He found a small closet and laid her in it then tied her to a water pipe. He wanted plenty of time to search for Emma.

The moon had reemerged as Steve ran through the forest toward his car. He assumed she had parked nearby. He deftly scaled the fence and searched for her car. He found it within five minutes, parked further down the road in another layby. He switched on his flashlight, searching the backseat for Emma. Nothing. He then forced open the truck, bracing himself for what he might find. Still nothing. He searched the car for anything that would lead him to Emma. There was nothing. The car was a rental and she had kept it free of anything personal.

Steve ran back to his rental car and decided to head back to the hotel to search for Emma. He thought about calling the police, but didn't want to have them become suspicious since the police had a file on their attack at Hill Cumorah.

He sped through the streets, hoping to avoid any cops. He finally reached the hotel and came to a screeching halt. He ran into the lobby and toward the elevator. It was taking too long, so he sprinted toward the stairs.

When Steve arrived at his room, he threw open the door, hoping to somehow find Emma in it. But everything was exactly as he had left it. He went through the adjoining door into Emma's room. Everything was quiet. He searched the room for Emma's bag, but it was gone. He sat on the bed, out of breath, thinking. His mind whirred—how would he ever find Emma?

He could torture the girl, get her to talk. Steve dropped his head into his hands. Could he do it? His mind turned to Emma. Was she still alive? He thought that she was. They needed Emma and had demonstrated that by not killing her earlier in the trip. No, she wouldn't be dead. They still had two clues to find and Emma was everyone's best chance. So she was hidden somewhere, probably unconscious. But where?

Steve's heart and mind were racing. He knew he had to get the girl to talk. He would have to do whatever it took to save Emma. And what about Ari? Was she bluffing on that?

He had to know. He powered on his cell phone and dialed Kari's number. He looked at his watch—2:00 a.m. It was midnight back in Utah. Kari was a night owl and he hoped she was still up.

The phone rang and rang. It was just about to go to voice mail when Steve heard a sleepy, "Hello?"

He recognized Kari's voice. "Kari, it's me, Steve. Kari, I'm sorry to call so late, but this is urgent. I need you to wake up and go see if Ari is all right."

"Steve?" she asked confused, still dazed.

"Kari, this is important. I need to know if Ari is all right. Please, Kari, go check and make sure," Steve pleaded.

"Steve, what's going on? What have you done?" Kari's voice was clearer now and becoming edgy.

"Just go look, Kari," Steve said sternly.

She knew that tone of voice and he could hear her walking with the cordless phone toward Arianna's room. He heard her walking back and then she said, "Steve, she's fine. She's sleeping soundly."

"Kari, I don't have much time, but listen very carefully. I'm doing a special job for the church. We're up against some very bad people. They have already kidnapped someone working with me. The kidnapper mentioned Ari, Kari. Don't let her out of your sight. Watch for anyone suspicious around the neighborhood. Don't open the door to any strangers. I'm going to call President Thompson's office in the morning and have them arrange to take you to somewhere safe until this is all over," Steve explained in a panic, his words jumbling together.

"President Thompson?" Kari asked.

"Yes, I'm sorry, Kari, I can't tell you anything else. Just please, please, Kari, take care of Arianna. Don't trust anyone except the church bodyguards," Steve urged.

"Steve, *what* have you gotten us into? How could you do this to us?" Kari cried. "I thought that part of my life was over. I don't want to be on an emotional rollercoaster anymore. That's why I divorced you. I will *never forgive* you for this, Steve."

He could hear her voice shaking and knew she was crying. He felt a deep pain in his heart, knowing he had hurt her again. He could barely talk, his tongue thick with emotion and he fought back the tears. "I'm sorry, Kari. I'm sorry for everything," he whispered.

He hung up then. He ran his fingers through his hair, saying a silent prayer that they would be all right and that he would somehow find Emma.

Steve blinked—he was getting tired. He walked into the bathroom and ran some cold water in the sink. Cupping his hands, he filled them with water and splashed it on his face. He quickly dried it, grabbed his pack and headed back down the stairs. He would have to get the girl to talk.

He drove back to the visitors' center site and retraced his path through the forest. He bent down to pick the lock and stopped. The lock was shattered by bullet holes. He glanced around listening, but everything was quiet.

Pulling his gun, Steve eased the door open. Listening, he moved slowly into the visitors' center. His heart pounding, Steve expected someone to attack him any moment, but the room was quiet. He moved from room to room, checking them all. Once he was satisfied that they were secure, he moved toward the closet.

He quickly opened the door and thrust his gun in, pointing at the floor where he had left the girl. She was still there, still tied up as he left her, but either asleep or unconscious. Steve prodded her with his foot, pushing her back, still keeping the gun focused on her. As she rolled back onto her arms, he saw a small pool of blood underneath her. Steve knelt down and examined her wound. She had been shot in the chest.

Steve glanced around the room again, looking for the intruder, but the room was still. Keeping his gun in one hand, he reached down with his free hand and felt for a pulse. At first he couldn't find one, but as he patiently waited and pressed harder into her neck, he felt a very faint pulse.

He needed her to survive so he could find Emma. He quickly pulled a spare t-shirt out of his pack and applied pressure to her open wound. He held it there until the bleeding slowed. While he waited, he considered his options. He had to get her to a hospital. But he needed to be careful not to implicate himself or the church in her attack.

He finally untied her and moved her gently from the closet. He cleaned up the pooled blood, leaving no trace. He then picked her up, pressing her wound close to him so the t-shirt would continue to stem the blood flow. She was light; he had carried much heavier men across battlefields before. He went out through the main entrance. He wouldn't be able to scale the fence with her in his arms.

It was a long walk to her car from the main entrance and as he walked, he heard her start to groan in pain. She was regaining consciousness. After about 10 minutes, she opened her eyes and looked up at him in fear. "Where are you taking me?" she whispered weakly.

"To your car and then I'll call for an ambulance," Steve explained. He looked down at her face. She looked so young and vulnerable now. He wondered how she got into this line of business. As he walked, he also wondered who had shot her and if the killer was still around.

She looked up in confusion at him, trying to comprehend his kindness. "You're not going to kill me?" she asked in a whisper.

"No," Steve answered honestly. "Where is Emma?" he pressed. But just then, he had to shift her slightly in his arms and the pressure loosened. He saw her face go pale and she passed out.

After what felt like an eternity, he arrived at her car. He placed her in it, called 911 with an anonymous tip. He waited, applying firm pressure on her wound until he heard an ambulance in the distance. Knowing the paramedics could take it from there, he quickly changed out of his blood-soaked t-shirt and drove back to the hotel.

Chapter 23

RJ paced his office, his blood boiling. He finally sat down in his leather office chair and pounded his fist on the desk, rattling everything on it. He thought back to his conversation earlier that morning. He had been shocked to hear his voice again.

"Tried to have me *killed*, did you RJ?" the voice was low and menacing. "You should have sent someone other than a baby to do it. I've been killing people since she was in diapers. I knew she would try it and I knew how. I just pretended to get drunk and switched the glasses when she wasn't looking. Maybe I should come out and pay *you* a visit instead of continuing your little treasure hunt out here."

"Have you taken care of her?" he asked, ignoring the threat.

"Yes, and right on Mormon property, too," he added with a chuckle. "The Mormons will be up to their eyeballs trying to explain a dead body in their visitors' center. But RJ, this little . . . *lapse in trust* . . . it's going to cost you."

RJ sighed. This was adding up fast. "How much?" he asked bluntly.

"Double," the man spat.

RJ thought for a second. Bringing someone new in would be time-consuming albeit a lot cheaper. But time was a luxury that he didn't have right now with the board breathing down his neck and his 90-day turnaround time quickly passing.

"Agreed," said RJ reluctantly.

"I want half now," the man continued, "as, let's say, a *restoration* of trust."

RJ considered. His ready cash was long gone—he would have to take it from the business. "All right, but I'd better start seeing some results," RJ added. "And soon."

He hung up and then walked over to Preston's office. Preston was looking through a thick financial statement, lost in thought. RJ glanced at Preston's desk. Unlike his, it was immaculate. All of the papers were neatly arranged and the cherry wood desk accessories all perfectly aligned. Every time RJ came into Preston's office, he wanted to sweep everything off his desk and make a mess. Preston's neatness and order irked RJ. That same methodology spread into Preston's life. He had only been married once and he was still married. He had three children, who had all gone to Ivy League schools and were successful. He invested his money wisely and probably had a small fortune, whereas RJ was constantly on the verge of bankruptcy.

RJ walked in and closed the door. Preston heard him and looked up. RJ only closed the door when he wanted money.

"How much?" Preston asked, coming straight to the point. He picked up his expensive fountain pen and poised it over his blank legal notepad.

"Double," RJ stated as he walked over to Preston's window and looked out, keeping his back to Preston.

"Double?" Preston challenged. "You know we don't have that much available in the company funds anymore."

RJ turned around and pointed his thick finger at Preston. "No, but *you* do," he stated looking intently at Preston.

Preston kept his emotions in check, his face blank, while inside his mind was in turmoil. The only reason he'd stayed with the company and RJ all of these years was because he had made a small fortune. He'd been able to take care of his wife and kids in comfort and style. His lavish house and cars were all paid off. He had significant investments, all steadily making him large profits that would enable him to retire soon.

"Look, Preston, I've put in my own money on this, you know I have," RJ reasoned, "In fact, I've put in everything I have. It's time you ponied up."

Preston considered his words. He didn't doubt RJ. He probably had put in everything he had—although that was quite limited these days with all of his ex-wives and his wild, wasteful son, Riley.

"Maybe you should cancel the whole operation," Preston suggested in vain. He knew RJ wouldn't go for that. Once RJ decided to do something, he was like a pit bull.

"We're in too deeply already," RJ countered. Preston didn't like how he used the word "we." "Preston, we are running out of time!" RJ shouted, raising his voice and slamming his fist down on Preston's desk, rattling the perfectly placed items. "We either destroy the Mormons or we're out—*both* of us."

Preston thought for a minute and then wrote down the sum on his pad. "I'll get it," he agreed reluctantly.

"Good," RJ said satisfied. "And wire it to the same location as the others." He then walked over to the door, opened it roughly and flung it back as he walked out. The door reverberated for a few seconds and Preston stood up, walked over to the door and steadied it. He then decided to close it so he could think uninterrupted.

He spent the rest of the day looking through the company's books, trying to see where he could get the money without touching his own. His conscience nagged at him, pulling him to his filing drawer.

He was too disciplined to take out her picture during normal work hours. Preston was always very careful—there was a lot at stake here. But he could still see his mother's picture in his mind and it kept invading his thoughts.

He finally gave in and thought about her. A smile came to his lips when he did. She was warm and loving, doting on him in every way possible, despite being tired from working two jobs.

That led Preston to think about their home. He had grown up in a small town in Georgia. His dad abandoned them when Preston was a baby and had left his mom to provide for Preston and his two sisters. He was the youngest, and his sisters had raised him. But each night, he would look forward to when his mom would come home from her first job and before she left for her second job.

Looking back, she must have been exhausted, but she always had a warm smile for Preston and his sisters. She would praise her daughters for taking such good care of Preston and would check their homework while the eldest made dinner. She loved to sing and would often hum around the house. One of her favorites was *Amazing Grace*. When she sang, the melodic notes would fill the house and Preston's heart would lift.

His favorite memory when he was little was when he had chicken pox. His mom had taken a whole week off of her day job to tend to Preston while his sisters were at school. He treasured the long days spent being nursed by his mother. It was a rare time, just the two of them. They only owned a few books, but she read them over and over again to Preston. She would stroke his head gently until he fell asleep each night.

As he got older, he became more aware of their situation. They had little to no money, living in a rented trailer home in a rundown trailer park. His sisters left one by one and went to Atlanta to find work. They would send money home each week to help their mother. As a teenager, Preston became embarrassed by his circumstances and hung out most days with a wealthy friend from school. He liked how his friend's family lived. He liked their large, rambling house, exotic foreign cars and plush, luxurious furniture. It was then and there that he decided he would never be poor again.

He managed to get a scholarship to go to college and dedicated himself to his studies. He also worked a campus part-time job as an assistant for a business professor. He saved every penny he could to go toward business school. Given all of that, he had little time for a social life. Yet, during his senior year he had met Beth in the library while he was studying. She was kind and loving and reminded him of his mother.

It was a few months before his graduation when he had an early morning call from his oldest sister. His mother had died of a heart attack sometime during the night.

Beth went with him to the funeral. Afterward, at the graveside, Preston was amazed to see so many mourners. He didn't realize his mother knew so many people. Each came up to Preston and his sisters, telling their individual story of kindness they had received from his mother. A loaf of bread here. Helping with a sick child there. Helping a friend pay her rent when she lost her job.

Preston stood in awe as he listened to their stories. He couldn't believe how much his mother had accomplished with her life despite her limited means and available time. All past embarrassment gone, his boyhood love and devotion to his mother returned. As they lowered her casket into the ground, Preston made a vow to his mother that he would live a good life in her memory.

He married Beth and made it through business school. He steadily worked his way up in his career, achieving promotion after promotion due to his integrity and hard work.

He had hesitated taking the job as CFO with SalesPro. A colleague knew of RJ's growing reputation and advised Preston against it. But Preston's children were fast approaching college age and he wanted the best for them—graduation from Ivy League schools. He knew from there they would be set for life.

They were good kids—Beth saw to that. Preston worked long hours, but still tried to follow his mother's example and show love and kindness to his children when at home. He took them on family vacations to Italy, France, England and Ireland.

But somewhere in the past decade, he had grown to know the depth of RJ's seedy tactics. And it had disturbed him these past few years. He had begun preparing financially for an early retirement. He and Beth would travel more and he would play golf. They would move away from Atlanta and live quietly in the country.

But he wasn't ready—not quite yet. His company stock had dipped dramatically lately and that had thrown off his plans. He knew deep down he had to help RJ out of this mess. RJ had been good to Preston, offering him the CFO position when no one else would have at such a young age. Somehow, he would have to find a way to help RJ and not break his promise to his mother.

Chapter 24

Emma tried to open her eyes, but they felt heavy. Her arms and legs were sore. She felt as though there was a deep fog smothering her mind, but it was starting to lift.

She tried to remember where she was or what had happened, but couldn't. Her throat was dry and her tongue felt thick. She tried to move her arms, but they were tied together behind her. She realized her feet were tied as well.

She finally managed to force her eyes open, only to realize she was blindfolded and gagged with duct tape. Panic filled her heart and she remembered the girl in her room. She froze and listened, trying to find out if the girl was nearby. After several minutes, she relaxed, not hearing anything.

She tried to squirm out of her bonds, but they were too tight. Her senses were returning and she realized desperately that she smelled smoke. Her mind raced, wondering if she would be burned to death in this room, wherever she was. But she didn't feel any heat and the smoke was faint.

Emma heard a buzzing noise and tried to focus on what it was. The sound became louder and she realized it was a vacuum. A few minutes later, she heard doors opening and closing, and people walking past the door. She realized she was probably in a hotel room somewhere. She tried to scream for help, but the gag muffled it to a mere whisper.

Her head was resting on a pillow, so she pushed it away with her head and rubbed the edges of her gag back and forth on the bed. The effort made her face slightly sweaty and the gag moved further. She doubled her efforts and flipped over to the other side and began working on that edge. She had to stop and rest a few times since the effort put a strain on her hands behind her back.

She finally felt the corner of her lip becoming free. She tried to sit up, but it took a few tries. She finally made it to a sitting position by leaning forward away from her tied up hands and swinging her legs down to the floor. Managing to stand up, Emma swayed slightly, but stayed on her feet. Her head spun for a moment, but she forced herself to concentrate. Where was a phone typically in a hotel room? She wondered if her kidnapper had removed it. There was only one way to find out.

She turned around and used her hands to feel the nightstand next to the bed. She knocked over a lamp and heard it crash. She could also feel a pad of paper and a pen, but no phone. She hopped along the bed, balancing against it. She thought about the hotels they had stayed at so far. Most had a desk or small table near the window. She moved away from the sound of the vacuum and hopped until she ran into something. As she fell, she hit her head on the object.

Feeling dizzy for a moment, Emma tried to stay focused. She finally inched her way back to the bed and used it as leverage to help her stand up again. She remembered that she had fallen on the ninth hop, so this time, she only hopped seven and then turned around, using her hands to feel.

It *was* a desk. She felt alongside it, hopping gently, using the desk to steady herself. She then sat on the desk and tried to reach back as far as she could. She felt a hotel book and then, finally, a phone cord. She grabbed onto it and pulled, hearing the receiver fall onto the desk. She couldn't reach the keypad with her hands, so she turned around and used her chin.

It took several tries, but she finally hit where she thought "0" was and was relieved to hear a voice come on the line.

"Hello, how may I assist you?" she heard a friendly voice say.

Emma leaned as close as she could and said into the handset, "What hotel is this?"

"I'm sorry, I can't quite hear you," the receptionist replied.

Emma realized the gag was mainly still over her lips and said louder, "What hotel is this?"

The woman paused and Emma almost wondered if she hadn't heard her, then she answered, "Which hotel? It's the Hampton Inn in White River Junction.

The Hampton Inn. She was still in the hotel. "What room am I in?" she asked.

The receptionist paused again, wondering why she didn't know any of these salient details. She wondered if the guest had a hangover from too much drinking the night before. "Room 103," she said puzzled.

Steve was in the hotel—at least she hoped so. "Please put me through to room . . ." She paused, trying to remember, "Room 634."

"Just one moment, please," the lady said and Emma almost fainted when she heard Steve's voice come on the line, "Hello?"

"Steve, Steve—" she started to cry and couldn't continue.

"Emma, where are you?" Steve asked.

"I'm here, in the hotel, room 103," Emma said. "Steve, I'm tied up and blindfolded. Please hurry; she might come back any minute."

"She's not coming back," Steve replied. "Don't worry. I'll explain everything when I get there. Just hang on."

Steve grabbed his gun and put it in the holster just in case. He also grabbed his knife and tucked it in his belt under his shirt. He ran down the stairs, taking them two at a time. He raced past the other rooms on her floor, almost knocking over an elderly couple in the process. He finally got to room 103 and stopped. How would he get in? He heard a vacuum

116

running across the hall and stepped into the room. He saw a young Hispanic woman cleaning—she looked up in surprise when she saw him.

"I went to the gym and forgot my key—can you please let me in?" he asked. She smiled and nodded, walking over to 103 with him. She put the card key in the lock and it finally turned green. "Thank you," he said breathlessly and quickly eased into the door.

He stopped when he saw Emma. She was lying on the floor, facing away from him, tied up and her wrists were starting to bleed. He pulled out his gun and checked the bathroom, but it was clear. He locked the door and then ran over to Emma.

"Emma, it's me, hold really still while I cut these ropes," Steve said as he pulled out his knife. He gently sliced the ropes, careful not to cut Emma. He turned her around and gathered her up in his arms. Walking over to the bed he gently set her down and took off her blindfold. Tears were streaming down her face and Steve wrapped his arms around her.

"Oh, Emma, thank God you are safe," Steve said, tears welling up in his eyes as well. He kissed the top of her head and held her tightly while she recounted what had happened the previous night.

Steve listened and then walked over to the bathroom and soaked a washcloth with cold water. He brought it back and gently placed it on Emma's bleeding wrists. He then caught Emma up with everything that had happened to him and her abductor at the site.

"Do you think she'll be okay?" Emma asked about her kidnapper.

Steve smiled at Emma's compassion despite her ordeal and answered, "Yes, she will probably be in the hospital for a while, but I think she'll pull through." Steve looked around the room and saw Emma's backpack sitting on a nearby chair. He relaxed, realizing they still had all of the clues.

"What about the symbol?" Emma asked, leaning forward.

Steve sighed and turned the washcloth over to the other side and placed it on Emma's other wrist. "I couldn't find it, Emma. I could have missed something in the dark on the house site, but we looked during the day as well and couldn't see anything. I think we're right about it being the hearth, but I don't know why there's not a visible sign for the fire. Maybe it's been destroyed. I think the only thing left is to unearth the hearth and see if there's anything underneath."

Emma's face flexed in concern. Steve knew she wouldn't like the idea of potentially damaging a church artifact. "Steve, I want to get out of this room," Emma said, standing up. She felt weak as she stood up and she unsteadily grabbed Steve's arm. Steve nodded his head and protectively put his arm around Emma. He grabbed her backpack with his other hand and guided her out of the room.

He sat by the ICU nurses' station, pretending to read a magazine, but was intently listening. He had wanted her to suffer, to slowly bleed to death. That's why he hadn't shot her right through the heart in the first place. But he didn't count on the soldier coming back and saving her life. These Mormons were so unpredictable. Who would have thought the soldier would save the very person who was trying to kill them and had kidnapped his girlfriend? His ears perked up as he heard one of the nurses asking another nurse how her patient was doing. She answered that it looked like she would pull through, but she would have a long recovery. He momentarily thought about slipping in and finishing the job, but decided against it. Finding this clue had taken way too long already and he didn't want to have the police breathing down his neck, slowing things down more.

Chapter 25

Riley slowly put the top down on the luxury convertible he had rented. He was annoyed his dad had pulled him away from his latest fling and sent him on this job. But Riley knew he couldn't refuse if he wanted to inherit his dad's fortune one day.

And that one day would come sooner rather than later, Riley thought with a smile. His dad was drinking heavily these days and the weight was piling on from his luxurious meals. He knew his blood pressure was up as well.

He just had to continue to play the dutiful son and he would be set for life. Riley drove out into the hot, dry Western air, turned the radio on full blast and sped toward the freeway. He had programmed the address into the car's GPS.

As he drove, he glanced over at the huge mountains, looming over him. They almost looked unreal. It felt strange to be back. He never thought he would return to Utah after he left with the knowledge of the artifact and the Mormons' secret.

He had wanted to bring his girlfriend of the week, but his dad only bought one plane ticket to reinforce that he needed to focus on the job at hand. Besides, this was a messy job, and he was sure his girlfriend would protest.

Riley drove up and over the point of the mountain and descended into Utah Valley. He saw a billboard at the side of the road that showed a happy, smiling family with the caption "Taking time for what matters most."

He scowled and laughed bitterly. His dad practically ignored him as he grew up. He was either at the office late or sequestered in his home office until after Riley went to bed. When he was young, his mother tried to console him by saying that his dad was an important man and he needed to focus on his business. But Riley couldn't understand why his dad never came to his soccer, baseball and then football games.

In fact, his dad hadn't really taken any interest in him at all until he was a junior in high school. That's when the lectures started about how one day Riley would take over the family business and he needed to get good grades so he could go on to college.

It was the only time RJ even really spoke to Riley, so Riley intentionally started doing poorly at school. Looking back, Riley could see that it had been a desperate plea for attention, and it had accomplished that, but it only amounted to more lectures and being told constantly that he was a disappointment.

Despite his poor grades, RJ had somehow fixed it for Riley to go to a local university. Riley played more than he studied and RJ's impatience grew. They had finally had it out when Riley was 21. That was the first time RJ had played the "inheritance card."

Riley had been home for Christmas break. "You're a worthless slacker," RJ had spat, his face turning red with a purple tinge. "When I was your age, I was already planning to build my own business."

Riley looked up from his car magazine with a minimal amount of interest. "Good for you, Dad."

RJ had walked over, grabbed the magazine and flung it across the room. "Listen here, boy. You'd better straighten up and fast. You like the easy life? You like living off of my money? Well, that's it. You're done as of right now."

Riley didn't look at his dad, but considered his options. He loathed the idea of having to get a job. He was comfortable as he was. He glanced up at his dad and could see the determination in his eyes. It was then they had finally come to an understanding.

"Look, Dad. I'm never going to be like you—an office type. But I'll help you with your business. I know I owe you that. I'll help you in other ways," Riley offered.

RJ considered Riley's words and finally smiled, realizing the potential he had. His son would never talk. He could be trusted due to his financial reliance. He was a good-looking kid and knew how to work things to his advantage.

It was only a few months later when RJ divorced Riley's mom. He had only been keeping her around as assurance for Riley's loyalty, but he knew he had that now. He quickly moved on to his second wife, a sexy model who was nearly half his age.

At first Riley resented all of the subsequent wives and ensuing children. But they didn't last long and RJ never had any interest in them. RJ divorced their moms while the children were young and they became bitter against him.

That was fine with RJ and Riley. Riley had proven himself very valuable over the years. Most of his jobs involved very pleasant things such as sleeping with women to get them to talk. His first job had been to seduce the secretary of a competitor in New York and learn all of their business secrets. He had wined and dined her in a lavish manner and she quickly fell in love with him. She loved to complain about work and it was an easy job.

Seducing the Mormon girl had been much more complicated since they didn't believe in premarital sex. He had loved acting in high school since it felt like an escape for him. He had leveraged those acting skills to pretend to be interested in converting to the Mormon church. It was easy from there as she was intent on converting him. She was very sweet and there were times that he felt slightly sorry for her, but he was becoming restless after months of denying himself a physical relationship and wanted to move on. He had even broken up with her once, stating that she wasn't open enough with him.

It worked and soon after that she started to open up about her dad's work and the deeper intricacies of the Mormon church. That was when he realized they had a secret. He didn't know what it was, but it had something to do with the artifact.

Those jobs had been easy. He shifted uncomfortably in his seat, thinking of his next job. It was unlike his dad to ask him to do something like this. He typically asked his hired guns to do it. When Riley had questioned it, his dad had just barked that they were busy elsewhere.

As he got off the freeway and wound his way to the house, he started to feel a sick feeling in his stomach. When he finally pulled up near the house, he paused, putting up the top on the convertible to shield him from view. He watched the house for over an hour, watching for any activity.

Finally, a UPS truck pulled up in front of the house and the driver ran to the door, dropped the package, and rang the doorbell. Riley sat forward in his seat, waiting to see who would answer the door. The driver ran back to his truck and drove away. Riley waited. The package just sat expectantly on the porch. He glanced at his watch and noted five and then 10 minutes passing. Nothing.

The neighborhood was quiet, so he decided to risk it. With his sunglasses on, he walked quickly up to the front door and rang the doorbell, prepared with a story in case anyone opened the door.

Nothing. He tried to look through a window, but couldn't see much. He walked around the house, trying to get through a gate, but found it locked.

He finally went back to his car and decided to wait it out. He glanced at his watch again. It was 3:00 in the afternoon. They would probably be home around dinnertime. He would wait.

Chapter 26

Emma crept behind Steve, following in his footsteps. He had his night vision goggles on and they had agreed to not talk as they crossed through the dark woods so that Steve could listen for anyone nearby.

Emma's heart raced. Someone had shot the girl. Someone was still after them.

They finally arrived at the visitors' center and Steve noted that the lock had been replaced with a better lock. It took him longer this time to jimmy it, but he finally got in and locked the door behind them. They kept the flashlight off and Steve used his night vision goggles to guide them through the visitors' center.

When they arrived at the hearth, Steve looked at Emma for reassurance. They had talked at length earlier in the day about any other options, but couldn't come up with anything. Steve had gone to a hardware store to purchase some supplies to unearth the hearth. He worked quickly, while Emma kept watch, alternating between the front and the back windows.

Steve took his time, being careful to not damage the hearth more than absolutely necessary. He started by weakening the mortar around the edges with a hammer and chisel. He carefully worked his way around the large stone. When he finally had the mortar removed, he used several levers to try to lift the stone all at once.

"Steve," Emma whispered from the back room window.

Steve froze, "Yes?" he answered.

"I . . . I think I saw something," she whispered.

Steve pulled his knife and walked quickly to the other room. He came up behind Emma and looked out the window. "Where?" he asked intently.

Emma pointed to a group of trees to the right about 20 yards from the visitors' center. "There," she answered, "behind those trees." Steve fixed his gaze on the trees, watching. After several minutes, he asked, "Are you sure?"

"I saw something, a movement," Emma explained. "But I'm really nervous and who knows, it could be my mind playing tricks on me," she added with a laugh.

Steve leaned over and kissed her on the top of her head. "You've been through a lot, Emma. Let me know if you see it again."

As Emma watched Steve walk back over to the other room, she smiled. She loved how he believed her. She watched the trees, but still couldn't see anything else. She heard Steve resume his work in the other room.

After about 15 minutes, he called to Emma. She ran into the room. "Emma, I need you to help me lift this up. I want to try to raise it together so it doesn't crack." Emma kneeled down and put her hands on the other two levers. Steve grasped his tightly, looked up at Emma, smiled at her for encouragement and then nodded.

They both pushed down on the levers and the stone started to rise. They got to where the stone was about two inches above the ground. "Now, Emma, push down a bit more and hold it—I'm going to try to grab the stone with my hands. Whatever you do, don't let go," Steve said with another smile.

Emma could feel the weight of the stone when Steve let go, but she pushed as hard as she could. Steve's strong hands clasped on to the stone and then he lifted it up. Emma gasped as the stone's underside became visible in the moonlight from the window. On the lower right-hand corner was the three jagged lines—the fire symbol. "It was just upside down!" Emma said with a laugh.

"All right, Emma, I've got it," Steve said as he balanced the stone on its edge. "Now, switch on your flashlight and see if you can find anything."

Emma eagerly switched on her flashlight and examined the stone. Underneath was empty. She guided her flashlight along the hearth to the edges and slid around for a better look. She rubbed her free hand over the edges, feeling for anything out of the ordinary. When she got to the last edge, she stopped.

"Steve, do you feel that?" Emma asked, guiding one of Steve's hands over to the side of the hearth. On the side, there was a small slit.

"Yeah, I feel it," Steve replied. "It's pretty small." The slit was about three inches wide and less than an inch high.

Emma slid closer and shined her flashlight directly into the slit. She looked up at Steve with wide eyes and a playful smile. "There's something in there!" she exclaimed.

"Can you get your finger in there?" Steve asked.

"No, it's too narrow," she said. "Wait, I've got an idea." Emma rushed over to her backpack sitting on the floor. She rummaged through the contents and finally pulled out a small item and came back to the hearth.

She held up the flashlight again and inserted her pencil, eraser side first, into the slit. She worked for several minutes, trying to grasp the item in the slit. She finally got it and gently eased it out, smiling up at Steve. It was longer than she thought. It was a folded piece of parchment, the same color and length as the one they had found at Fort Niagara.

Emma gingerly opened the parchment. The top and bottom edges were ragged, matching the other piece of parchment. Just as the other piece, the parchment contained Reformed Egyptian hieroglyphics.

Emma went over to her backpack, pulled out the other piece of parchment and matched them up. The first one was

125

the top and this piece appeared to be the middle as there were still ragged edges on the bottom of it. Emma heard Steve lowering down the hearth and putting away his tools. Emma studied the characters, wishing for the hundredth time that she had studied the ancient language.

"Looks like we've got one more," Steve said as he came up behind Emma and looked at the matching parchment pieces.

"Yes, the rectangle," Emma nodded. "The earth symbol." She sighed and turned to look at Steve. "I wish we knew what it said. Whatever it is, Joseph was very, very careful. It wasn't enough to hide the pieces in different places—he also put them in a language that very few could translate."

"I'm kinda glad we don't know," Steve said. "I mean, what could it say that would make Joseph so worried? Maybe it's better not to know."

Emma laughed. "I'm too curious for that," she replied. "As a historian, I've just got to know!"

"We'll find a way to get it faxed to President Thompson's office and mailed to Dr. Mangum tomorrow morning," Steve said. "For now, let's head back to the hotel and get some sleep."

Emma wrapped up both of the parchment pieces and gently put them in her backpack. They both put their packs on and Steve went over to the back window. He watched for a few minutes and then said, "Ok, I'll go first. Stay close, Emma."

Steve opened the door, listened for a minute and then stepped out. Emma followed him. They had only gone a few steps when they heard a voice from the darkness, "Stop right there."

Steve didn't hesitate this time. He reached out and shoved Emma behind a tree and to the ground. He dove behind a nearby tree in the direction of the attacker and paused, listening for a sound. He heard the attacker move toward where Emma was hiding. Steve rushed the attacker, sweeping his arm up quickly, knocking the gun up and out of his hands. He succeeded in knocking the attacker to the ground, but as the man fell, he rolled and was up quickly. Steve waited, knowing the man would attack. A few seconds later he felt a fist impacting on his stomach. He tightened his stomach to shield the impact and then seized the man's arm and twisted it violently. He heard a reluctant cry, but the man managed to twist free.

Steve stopped again, listening. He heard a few twigs snapping and realized with fear that the man was moving closer to Emma. He glanced up at the sky, wishing the moon would reappear so that he could see better. He was just about to dive forward, hoping to catch the attacker when he heard a click. Steve rapidly blinked at the sudden appearance of a bright light. He could distinctly see his attacker now. Emma had switched on a flashlight and had pointed it at the man. The attacker had instinctively turned his face away from the light and was facing Steve.

Steve took advantage of the situation and stepped forward, swinging his right arm in a strong arc. It caught the attacker on the chin and launched him up into the air. Emma kept the flashlight on him as he fell to the ground. Steve leapt onto him, but it was unnecessary. The man was out cold.

"Emma, hand me some rope," Steve said. Emma rummaged through Steve's backpack until she found a long rope and tossed it over to him. Steve cut the rope and quickly tied the man's hands together behind his back. He then tied his feet as well.

Emma stood up and shined the flashlight on the man's face. "Our old friend is back," she commented sadly.

Steve looked at the man's face and nodded. "Good thinking with the flashlight, Emma. It was just the distraction I needed."

Emma smiled and then stepped into Steve's arms. Steve was tense from the adrenaline and she could hear his heart still pounding. "Good job, yourself," Emma whispered. After a moment, Steve's body relaxed and he held Emma tightly. He then kissed her softly on the top of her head, but only briefly. He was still all business. He let Emma go and then resumed his work. He cut some additional rope and tied the man's hands onto a nearby tree trunk.

"The security guard should find him in the morning," Steve explained. "They'll think he broke in and I'm sure they'll lock him up for a bit." Steve then took the flashlight from Emma and swept the area. "Here it is," he said as he reached down to pick up the man's gun and stuffed it into his backpack. "I'm not taking any chances this time."

Steve headed back through the forest, switching off the flashlight. He had memorized his path through the forest and didn't need the light. He held Emma's hand and kept her close, still listening for any other sounds in the forest in case the man had back-up.

Emma could feel the tenseness in Steve's hand and couldn't help imagining someone was going to leap out of the darkness at them at any moment. They walked quickly and Emma gave an audible sigh of relief when they got to the car.

Steve stopped abruptly and Emma nearly ran into him. "What's wrong?" she asked quietly, glancing around frantically.

"He didn't take any chances either," Steve said in a flat voice. Emma followed Steve's gaze and with some moonlight could see that their two side tires were flat. Steve walked forward, knelt down and felt the tires. He could feel a knife gash in both of them at the top. Steve sighed. "If it would have been just one, we could have used the spare." He looked back at Emma. She tried to smile an encouraging smile back at him, but it was weak at best.

"Let's go see if his car is around here somewhere," Steve suggested reaching out for Emma's hand. Emma took his hand and they set off down the road. They walked for a half-mile in both directions, but couldn't find a car.

Emma's legs were getting tired and after the adrenaline rush in the forest, she began to feel exhausted. She looked up and down the empty road longingly, hoping someone would come by and give them a ride to the hotel.

Steve followed her gaze and put his arm around her. "I know, we could use a guardian angel right about now. It's getting really late and we need to get some sleep. Are you much of a camper?"

Emma screwed up her face and looked at Steve in the moonlight. Steve laughed. "All right, all right, but we'll have to. We can't risk sleeping in the car in case our friend has some back-up that comes looking for him. They'll search the main road first and see our car. We'll need to walk for a while into the woods, Emma. We've got to put some distance between us and the visitors' center. Are you up for it?"

Emma's tired body screamed no, but she put on a brave smile and nodded, reaching for Steve's hand. They headed back up the slight incline into the woods and Steve turned a southern direction, away from the visitors' center. They were only a few steps into the trees when Emma heard a sound.

"Steve, it's a car!" Emma shouted, pulling Steve back toward the road.

Steve clamped on to Emma's hand and pulled her deeper into the trees and put his hand over her mouth. "Shhh," he whispered and pulled both of them behind the largest nearby tree. Steve and Emma watched silently as the car slowed and pulled up behind their car. The driver paused and finally got out.

Emma gasped slightly, but it was muffled due to Steve's hand. Emma looked at Steve with wide eyes. They watched as the man came into the moonlight and they both recognized their attacker. Emma looked into Steve's eyes with a puzzled expression.

He circled the car, checked the doors and then turned on a flashlight and directed the beam into the woods. Emma's heart started to race and she realized tears were streaming down her face in frustration. They had just gotten away from him—how did he get free? Was there someone else?

The man finally headed back into the woods toward the visitors' center. They could hear his feet crunching through the dry brush on the forest floor. Once the sound of his

129

movement became inaudible, Steve grabbed Emma's hand, pulled her toward the road and said, "Emma, we've got to run. We can't run through the forest in case he hears us. We're going to run fast along the road for several hundred yards and then re-enter the forest further down."

Without waiting for a reply, Steve pulled Emma forward into a run. They stayed on the edge of the road, ready to dart into the trees if someone else came along the road. The road remained quiet and they ran in silence.

Just when Emma felt she couldn't run any more, Steve pulled her into the trees. He stopped once they got into the trees and were shielded from the road. "Take your shoes off, Emma," Steve requested as he bent down to take his own off. Steve slipped both of their shoes into his backpack and then put on his night vision goggles. "Follow me, in my footsteps," Steve whispered.

Emma clutched Steve's hand and followed him closely. She moved slowly at first—the moon had gone behind the clouds and she felt afraid as she walked through the unknown terrain. But Steve squeezed her hand encouragingly and she felt more confident, knowing he could see the ground and would protect her from any harm.

They walked for what felt like hours and then Steve finally stopped and knelt down. Emma could hear him rustling in his backpack. The moon reappeared and Emma could see he was spreading out a camouflage Army blanket. "Emma, come lie here and put your pack at your feet." Steve had pulled out some of his clothing and made a makeshift pillow for Emma. She lay down and then Steve cuddled up next to her. He pulled the blanket over both of them so that it covered everything except their faces.

Emma's heart beat rapidly as she realized they were going to sleep like this together. Thoughts whirred through her mind, but her fear of their attacker somewhere in the woods searching for them outweighed everything else. She snuggled closer to Steve and he reacted by putting his arm around her.

"Try and get some sleep," Steve whispered in her ear. "I'll keep watch."

Sleep was the last thing on Emma's mind. She felt comforted being so close to Steve, but her fear and also the excitement of being this close to a man who loved her and was protecting her was very intoxicating. She thought of turning toward him and kissing him, but changed her mind. They were in a dangerous situation and the best thing she could do was try to get some sleep.

The crickets nearby, satisfied that they wouldn't be disturbed anymore, began their serenade. The sound relaxed Emma and she felt herself drifting off to sleep. Her last thought was how ironic it was that she was in so much danger and yet so happy at the same time.

Chapter 27

RJ began pacing his office again. Riley was giving him a report.

"I told you, Dad," Riley repeated, "I waited all night and nothing. I came back before sunup this morning and still nothing. They're on to you, Dad, and they're gone." Riley was relieved and tired. He never wanted to be involved in kidnapping the soldier's little girl in the first place. He wanted to get back home and resume his latest fling.

"I have another job for you," RJ said gruffly.

"Please tell me it's not in *Utah*," Riley moaned.

"You'll feel right at home," RJ barked. "I want you to dig around and find out how sick that dean of religion is, you know, the dad of the girl you dated to get the info. He could be our other leverage point since *you've* lost the soldier's girl."

Riley shifted uncomfortably in the seat of his rental car. Staci had been a sweet kid and very sincere. It had been an easy job, but he still felt a twinge of guilt when he thought about her. She was so naïve and gullible. Most of the people his dad had him get involved with were the same ilk of his dad—but these Mormons were different. They had an openness and an honesty that were both disconcerting and yet impressive at the same time.

Riley hesitated for a minute, trying to think of an excuse. "Did you *hear me*, boy?" RJ shouted into the phone.

"I heard you, Dad," Riley replied. "Half of Utah heard you."

"Just get on it and I want a report by end of day tomorrow," RJ commanded.

Riley hit the red phone button on his expensive phone and threw it across onto the leather passenger seat in frustration. He slammed his rental car into gear and sped off back to his hotel. He would treat himself to a massage or something in the spa before continuing his dad's dirty work.

As he drove, he thought about his dad's control. He hated being subject to his dad's angry whims. But what could he do? Get a real job? Riley laughed inwardly. For one thing, he hated actual work. Secondly, it would seriously cramp his social life and that was unacceptable.

By the time he got to the hotel, he had decided the quickest way to get back to his latest fling was to do exactly what his dad wanted. He checked out at the front desk, his resolve slightly weakening when the receptionist smiled very meaningfully at him. But Riley put his sunglasses on and walked out the door. Besides, she was probably a Mormon and they were all talk with no action unless you were willing to marry them. And that wasn't Riley's game at all.

He drove straight to Staci's parents' house. He didn't even need the GPS—he remembered the way exactly and had been there many times while pretending to date Staci. As he neared their street, he closed the convertible roof to avoid recognition. He came around the corner and instantly slowed. The street in front of the house was crowded with cars on both sides of the street.

Riley looked around at the neighborhood. Was someone having a party? But Dr. Magnum's driveway was crammed with cars. Riley drove past slowly and then continued on down the road. He had to park farther away than he would have liked, due to the limited availability on the street. He turned off his car and waited. He examined the cars, looking for Staci's pink VW bug. He saw it parked at the very front of the driveway. He sunk further down in his seat, just in case Staci appeared and reached into the backseat for a baseball cap.

He waited nearly an hour and then saw someone in his rearview mirror from further down the street walking in his direction on the sidewalk. It was a lady in her 50s with silver hair carrying a covered plate in her hands. She continued walking and glanced at Riley as she passed. He instinctively picked up his cell phone and began to pretend to talk so he wouldn't look as suspicious sitting in a car on the street.

The lady walked up to Dr. Magnum's front door and rang the doorbell. Riley saw the door open and tried to squint to see who was at the door, but he was too far away. He had met several of Staci's brothers. One of them was a former BYU football player and he didn't relish running into the huge lineman. The woman didn't go in; she just talked at the door for a few minutes, hugged the person at the door and handed them the plate she had carried.

She then headed back toward Riley. He continued his pretend conversation, but Riley noticed she had tears streaming down her face as she passed. Riley dialed his dad's number and his dad answered on the first ring. "Well?" his dad demanded.

"We're too late," Riley answered. "He's already dead."

RJ swore on the other end of the phone and Riley could hear a crashing noise. He could picture his dad in his office throwing something against the wall. When RJ finally calmed down enough to speak, he said, "Stick around for a few days. Look for an opportunity to get in the house. See if he's got any clues in his home office and let me know."

Riley headed back to the hotel to check in again. He wouldn't be able to get into the house today with all of the family there. He picked up a local paper in the lobby and went straight to the obituaries. He examined all of the pictures of the old people and a few small children. Nothing. It was probably too soon. He would check each day for the funeral time and get into the house then—it would be the perfect time when he was sure no one would be around, not even the neighbors.

He looked up at the lavish reception desk and saw the same woman smiling at him. He decided to have some fun while he waited. He walked up to the brunette with blue eyes and said in his Southern accent, glancing at her nametag, "Hello, Tasha."

"Hello, Mr. McAlister," she said with a coy smile and a quick glance around to see if her manager was nearby. "So, you've come back to stay with us again?"

"Yes," Riley answered smiling back at her and leaning closer. "I found your hotel too alluring to leave." Riley noticed she smiled back and leaned closer as well. There was no blush, no embarrassment. This girl was a player and he'd bet money she wasn't a Mormon after all. But he decided to make sure, with the picture of Staci in the back of his mind. "I'm wondering how good your room service is here?" he ventured. "Are any of your staff available for late-night . . . service?"

She didn't even hesitate and reached over to brush her hand across his. "I'm off at 10. I'll see to your needs personally, Mr. McAllister."

Riley smiled and headed up to his room. Maybe Utah wasn't so bad after all.

Chapter 28

Emma woke up feeling warm and confused. Dazed, she didn't remember where she was for a minute or whose arm was lying across her chest. She sat up with a start and then let out her breath. Steve was lying next to her, still asleep. She glanced around the woods, remembering their hit man was back and looking for them. The sun was just streaming through the trees, but the birds sang happily and everything felt peaceful.

Her muscles ached with the movement and she stood up and stretched, breathing in the fresh morning air. Steve, missing her warmth, rolled over and looked at Emma.

"Good morning," he said with an impish smile.

"Good morning," she replied back. Still glancing around the forest she added, "Think our friend is gone?"

Steve sat up and took a look around. "He must be," Steve answered as he nodded toward their backpacks at their feet. "If he found us, he would have taken the clues."

Emma frowned and walked over to the backpacks. She opened hers and felt down inside. Then she turned and nodded at Steve. "They're still here," she offered with a sigh of relief.

"I think it's time we call in reinforcements," Steve said as he reached into his pack for the cell phone. He looked at his clock—it was still very early back in Utah, but he would try

136

anyway. The phone line rang for a few minutes and then he heard a sleepy voice on the phone. "Hello?"

"Hi, this is Steve," Steve said, feeling guilty that he had just woken someone up.

"Hi Steve, this is Marcy, President Thompson's assistant. I had my desk phone forwarded to my cell just in case you guys needed something in off-hours," she explained with a yawn.

"I'm so sorry to have woken you up," Steve apologized, "but we could use some help."

Steve heard Marcy sitting up and rummaging for a pen. "Anything," she offered with determination in her voice.

"First of all, are my ex-wife and daughter safe?" Steve asked.

"Yes, they have been moved to a secure location," Marcy replied.

"That's a relief. Thank you. We could use a ride from a local bishop and we need access to a secure fax machine," Steve requested.

"Sure, no problem," Marcy replied and Steve envisioned her writing it all down.

"And we need a car—something that can't be traced back to us or the church," Steve continued.

"Ok, I'll need probably 30 to 60 minutes and I'll have it all arranged for you. I'll call you back when everything is ready," she said in a clear, strong voice. Steve was impressed with her efficiency and positive attitude.

"Ok, thanks," he said and was almost ready to hang up when he heard Marcy interject. "Oh, I almost forgot something."

Steve put the phone back to his ear and said, "I'm still here."

"It's actually a message for Dr. Worthington," Marcy said. "But it might be best if you deliver it. President Thompson asked me to let her know that Dr. Magnum passed away yesterday. I know he was like a father to her. Please let her know of the First Presidency's deepest condolences."

Emma was watching Steve as he talked and noticed his face went white. Her brow creased in concern and she walked back closer to Steve.

"Yes, I will," Steve replied and then added, "Thank you for letting us know."

She had barely ended the call when Emma anxiously asked, "What is it, Steve? I can tell something is wrong."

Steve looked up at Emma with compassion and said, "Emma, come and sit by me." He patted the spot next to him on the blanket.

Emma sank next to Steve and then asked again, "What happened?"

Steve took a deep breath and said, "President Thompson wanted you to know that Dr. Magnum passed away yesterday." Steve watched Emma's face carefully and then reached over and held her hand.

Emma looked away from Steve when she felt tears springing to her eyes. She blinked rapidly, trying to control her emotions, but finally gave in and started to cry. Steve reached over and put his arm around her and held her. She cried for several minutes and then she suddenly lifted her head and angrily asked, "Did *they* kill him?"

Steve thought about that for a minute and then replied, "She didn't say, but I doubt it. Didn't you say Dr. Magnum is one of the very few people who can translate the Reformed Egyptian hieroglyphics? They would have wanted to keep him alive for that."

Emma nodded and reached into her backpack for a pack of travel tissues. She wiped her eyes and stared off into the woods.

"I'm so sorry, Emma," Steve offered gently. "I could tell you were close."

That started more tears and Emma continued to frantically wipe them away. "He's been in Stage 4 for a while," she admitted, "But I somehow always thought he would beat it, you know? I remember the day he told me. He was in shock—they diagnosed him with breast cancer. I remember him telling me he didn't even know men could get breast cancer. He had found the lump almost a year earlier, but had dismissed it because he was a guy. It wasn't until he felt it continuing to grow larger that he finally asked his doctor about it. By then, it was too late. It had already spread to his lymph nodes. From then on, it was just a battle for time."

Steve remained quiet and just let Emma sit quietly or talk, whatever she needed.

"He always believed in me," Emma added after a few minutes. "I first met him when I was a freshman. He was teaching a church history class. I was enthralled. I spent a ton of time on a project assignment and he asked me to wait after class one day. He told me he thought my project was fantastic and spent over an hour discussing it with me. He encouraged me to become a scholar right then and there. I took every class I could from him over the years, but I still didn't think I'd become a professor one day. I thought I would be a mom and a housewife."

Steve watched as Emma raised her chin slightly in defiance and then continued. "I dated a couple of guys, but it just never went anywhere. I watched each of my roommates get married year after year. I started over with new roommates, but soon they were engaged, too. I remember that a few weeks before graduation, I was sitting in the Joseph Smith Memorial Building. It was getting late and the room was empty. Dr. Mangum was leaving for the evening and noticed me. I was lost in thought, feeling sorry for myself, wondering what I would do with my life since it didn't look like I'd be following the typical get-married-and-have-kids model. He came and sat down beside me. He looked tired and withdrawn. When I realized he was sitting beside me, I quickly smiled as brightly as I could and tried to look like I hadn't been crying."

"Dr. Mangum knew me quite well by then, though. He just smiled and said, 'So what's your plan?' My smile disappeared and I felt my bottom lip quiver. He reached over, put his hand on my shoulder and said, 'You've always got to have a plan, Emma. Life rarely turns out the way we think it will. Take your namesake for example. She probably never envisioned that she would meet a man like Joseph and have to leave her family to be with him. That she would be hated and persecuted for marrying him and sharing his beliefs. How she would never get comfortable in a home before she was driven out again. How she lost so many of her children. And after enduring her husband being murdered, she even had a disappointing second marriage with her husband having an affair. Emma probably had so many Plan Bs that she got through the whole alphabet.'"

"I let what he was saying sink in and realized my life would never be as tough as Emma Smith's. But I could have faith that God had a plan for me. That I could choose my own path for happiness and not have to rely on getting married and having children to be happy. I looked up at Dr. Mangum with hope filling my heart and said, 'My Plan B is graduate school and on to a PhD after that.' He smiled at me and suggested slyly, 'I could use a graduate student as an assistant.' I knew right then and there I was destined to be a teacher and a scholar. Once I had given up on the idea of getting married, it made things a lot easier. I still dated, but only when I really wanted to, not out of desperation. But I was still human, and at least once a year, I would have a breakdown and Dr. Mangum was always there to help me through it. He was there for me, even when my own father wasn't."

Steve wondered about that, but didn't want to pry. Emma was already in a very fragile state. He waited, but she didn't continue. His cell phone started to vibrate and he picked it up. "Hello," he answered.

"Hi Steve, this is Marcy. We're all good to go. I've GPSed your location and a local bishop is on his way. Same story— you're extended family of President Thompson's and just need a lift to pick up a car. The rental car is in a fake name and all paid for. The bishop will also take you to the local meetinghouse and you can use the fax there," she concluded as if mentally checking off all of her tasks.

Steve was impressed at her efficiency. "Thank you so much, for everything," Steve said and then closed his phone and powered it off. He picked up Emma's pack and his and put them both over his shoulders. "Let's head for the road and we'll stay hidden until we see the car."

They walked in silence through the forest. Steve could tell Emma was still lost in thought about Dr. Mangum. As they reached the edge of the trees, Steve stopped Emma and crouched down behind a tree. Emma followed his example and they waited for the car. After 15 minutes, a car slowly came into sight, the driver looking regularly into the trees. "Wait here," Steve said as he stood up to flag down the car.

Emma nodded and watched Steve approach the car. The driver got out and came around quickly to shake Steve's hand. Emma's smiled. The bishop had dressed in his full suit and tie even though it was still very early in the morning. Calls from the First Presidency's office seemed to have that effect on people, she thought with a smile. Steve looked her way and smiled. She walked over to the car and shook hands with the bishop.

Emma was quiet as they drove to the meetinghouse. Steve small-talked with the bishop, occasionally glancing around to the backseat to check on Emma. They finally arrived at the church and the bishop unlocked the door. They followed him to the clerk's office. The bishop turned on the copy machine and fax to warm up. "What is it you need to fax?" he asked politely, looking at first Steve and then Emma.

"It's actually something very personal," Steve answered, glancing at Emma. "Would you mind giving us some privacy?"

The bishop hesitated for a minute and then smiled, "Well, I guess if I can trust anyone, it's President Thompson's family. I'll just be waiting in the foyer."

After he was out of sight, Steve closed the door and locked it just in case. Emma gently lifted out the parchment and then worked for a minute trying to make a copy of the oversized document. They finally captured it and sent the fax to President Thompson's office. Emma sighed with relief as they heard the confirmation beep.

"Well, that's two of the clues in President Thompson's hands," Emma said. "Maybe we should hide the originals here in the church somewhere. Just in case."

Steve thought about it for a minute and then replied, "M-m-m, I don't know. What if they're still following us somehow. What if someone here accidentally finds them?"

"True," Emma agreed. "I just hate worrying that if our tail finds us again, he might take them."

"At least President Thompson has them in his hands," Steve reassured. Steve studied Emma's face. She looked pale. "Let's get some breakfast in us and then we'll figure out our next move."

Emma nodded and they opened the office and called to the bishop. True to his word, he was still down the hall waiting. He came and locked up. Emma took a few minutes in the bathroom to wash her face and hands while Steve did the same. After that, they headed back to the car.

The bishop then took them to pick up the rental car and they headed out of town. Steve drove for about an hour and then they stopped at a roadside café for some breakfast. After they ordered their food, Emma sipped on her apple juice thoughtfully.

"Steve, I'd like to go to Dr. Mangum's funeral," she requested.

Steve looked up in surprise, but didn't say anything. He considered their options. It would be dangerous going back to the funeral—now that they had lost their tail, he would be looking for them to emerge at either one of the historical sites or back in Utah. On the other hand, Emma was clearly distracted since hearing about Dr. Mangum. Maybe they should go back so she could have some closure.

Emma read his thoughts, "I know it's probably not a good idea, Steve. But I still want to go. Perhaps we can have

President Thompson's security team keep an eye out for our tail while we're in Utah."

Steve thought back to the security guards who had picked them up. He knew they were no match for the assassin who was tailing them. He didn't want anyone else to get hurt. He was about to tell Emma no when he saw the desperate pleading in her eyes.

"Ok, we'll go in and out on the same day—we'll see if we can use the private jet again," Steve acquiesced. Emma's bright smile rewarded him, but the unsettled feeling in his stomach doubled.

Chapter 29

Preston leaned back in his chair thoughtfully. He glanced over his perfectly manicured lawn. His gardener, Juan, was expensive, but worth it. He loved sitting out here on his back patio and enjoying the beautiful flower gardens and expertly trimmed shrubbery. It brought him peace in what had lately become a troubled time.

He felt his life spinning out of control. But here, in his neat and clean house with his immaculate lawn, he had full control.

He could feel his wife's steady gaze on him and so he picked up his fork again and toyed with his quiche. Their French cook was excellent, but he had found his appetite waning the past few weeks.

"You might as well tell me what it is," his wife Beth said with a sigh. "Preston, I know something's wrong. Are there problems at work?"

Preston hesitated. He loved Beth so much. She had been an excellent wife and mother. She somehow hadn't let their wealth change her. She was still kind and compassionate, visiting their elderly neighbors regularly, volunteering for several causes like the Red Cross and the local Boys & Girls Club. He had never let Beth know the darker side of his work life—the side that RJ ruled in. Preston always tried to justify to himself that it was RJ who did these things, not him. But his partial participation still bothered him and he kept that from Beth.

But he had never lied to Beth. He just hadn't volunteered information on some of the things that happened at work. He wouldn't lie this time either. "Yes, our profits are down and the board of directors is calling for RJ's head," he said with an exhale. He finally gave up eating and pushed the quiche away.

"What does that mean for you, Preston?" Beth asked directly. She had always been no nonsense and Preston loved that about her. What you see is what you get with Beth, he thought to himself with a smile.

"I might be out, too," he said reluctantly, wondering how Beth would take it.

"Good, glad to hear it," she answered with a smile as she looked up. Their elderly maid, Sylvia, had arrived to clear their dishes. She had been with them for nearly nine years. She was much less a maid than a member of the family.

"M-m-m-" Sylvia said as she shook her silvery black head in disapproval. "Señor did not eat his breakfast today."

Preston smiled at her and said, "Gotta watch my waistline, Sylvia, if I'm going to keep beautiful Beth here." Sylvia smiled at both of them fondly and headed back into the kitchen with the dishes.

"You're glad to hear I might be out of a job?" Preston asked incredulously, yet smiling at Beth's unexpected answer.

"Yes, I am, honey," she answered, leaning across the table and taking Preston's hand in hers. "You are far too stressed out all of the time. It's time we start enjoying life. You've worked hard all of these years—let's enjoy life while we have time."

"I know, I know," Preston agreed, "But I just don't have enough saved yet. Our stocks took an unexpected nose-dive last quarter and a good portion of my investments are in our company stock. I need to get things righted so we can have enough to retire."

Beth squeezed his hand and said, "Preston, we have more than enough. We have *too* much." She gestured her arm toward the house. "Ten bedrooms and 10 baths. 10,000 square feet. I went into one of the guest rooms the other day and realized I hadn't even been in that room for almost a year, Preston. A year. We don't need all of this. We can sell the house and get something smaller. Let's travel and go lie on a beach somewhere together."

Preston looked at Beth and squeezed her hand, "I know, honey. I want that as much as you. I really do. I just can't leave when things are like this. I need to help RJ out of this mess."

"What mess?" Beth said, the smile gone from her face. She knew Preston well and knew that he wasn't telling her everything.

Preston considered his words carefully. "Do you remember that company I told you about that has been eclipsing us on sales recently?" he asked.

"Yes, the one with a similar name as yours," Beth said thoughtfully, thinking back to their earlier conversation, her brow knitted in concern.

"Well, I don't think I told you their headquarters is in Utah," Preston said, rushing to get it all out.

Beth stared at him, speechless.

"They were founded by a Mormon," he added, reading Beth's thoughts.

Beth contemplated Preston's revelation and then promoted, "And . . ."

Preston took a deep breath, knowing that he had to tell her. "And RJ has decided the only way left to beat them is to destroy them. To destroy the Mormon church."

Beth sat silently, searching Preston's expression. "But how can RJ destroy the Mormons?" she finally asked. "How can anyone? Their religion is worldwide and they have millions of members, right?"

Preston nodded his head. "He said he has found a way," he added, feeling his stomach churn, "To disprove the entire religion. To prove once and for all they're a bunch of deluded fanatics. No one will do business with them after that and it will not only destroy their religion but our largest competitor as well."

Beth replied, "Surely, no one can do that. What could he possibly have on them that would destroy the entire religion?"

"I don't know, but I do know RJ," Preston said, glancing across the manicured lawn again, wishing for the inner peace he so desired. "If he says he's got it, then he does," Preston explained, "or is in the process of getting it."

Beth studied Preston's face. "If he doesn't have it yet, or even if he does," she questioned leaning forward in her chair, "Then what are *you* going to do?"

Preston leaned back in his chair, subconsciously putting distance between Beth and himself. He brought his hands together and rested his index finger on his lip, the way he always did when considering an important decision. Beth made his choice sound so simple. Help RJ destroy the Mormons or stop him. It just wasn't that simple.

Beth could see his hesitation and so she finally stood up, came around the table and pulled up a chair next to Preston. She put her hand on Preston's arm, leaned over and looked straight into his eyes. "You know what your mother would want you to do," she offered.

Preston sighed and tears welled up in his eyes. He loved Beth so much. He leaned over and kissed her gently on the lips. He then pulled back and said, "I know, that's why I can't eat or sleep."

Chapter 30

The black hearse slowly wound its way through the graveyard. A long line of cars, all with their lights on, snaked along with it, coming to a gentle stop at a fresh gravesite. The velvet-covered chairs stood ready to comfort them while they laid their loved one to rest. Staci dabbed at her eyes with her wet tissue which was slowly disintegrating. She had nearly gone through an entire box at the viewing and funeral that morning. She thought she would be out of tears now, but somehow they were still coming.

She was holding her mother's hand. Her mother stared blankly out of the limousine window with her shoulders slumped. When her mother found her father dead a few days ago, the light simply went out of her. They had been in love their whole life and it showed.

Staci took a deep breath and squeezed her mother's hand. She answered back with a silent nod. They slid out of the limo and walked over to the gravesite. Staci sat by her mother and watched as her brothers carried her father's coffin to rest on the display stand.

Friends and family slowly descended from the cars and stood in a semicircle around the gravesite. Their heads all turned as a bulletproof car pulled up and came to a stop. Security guards leapt out and surrounded President Thompson as he walked over to the gravesite. As he was an old family friend, Staci's mom had asked him to dedicate the grave.

They all bowed their heads in prayer and listened to President Thompson's blessing of peace and protection on the gravesite until the resurrection. When Staci opened her eyes, she saw Dr. Worthington and the campus police officer standing at the edge of the crowd.

Guilt flooded her heart. She knew they were on a mission to protect the secret her dad was researching. It was her fault they were risking their lives. It was her fault that anyone outside of her family even knew about the artifact. She had trusted Riley, or whatever his real name was, and she was burned in the end. It was all a lie. He was just using her for information about the church.

It was the first time she had ever fallen that deeply in love and she had fallen hard. He was handsome, smart and he made her feel beautiful. Added to that was what seemed like his earnest investigation of the church. She thought she was helping someone come closer to Christ. She thought she was helping to save him.

She could taste her own bitter disappointment in her mouth. She felt like she had stressed and worried her dad when he was at his weakest point. She would never forgive herself for that.

Staci stared at her father's coffin. *"Help them,"* the thought came to her mind unbidden. Help whom? she thought to herself.

"Help them," it came again. She looked back at Dr. Worthington and the officer.

"How?" she asked in her mind.

"My papers," came the thought again. Staci thought of her father's home office. As his illness progressed, he did more and more work at home. His office desk was full of work papers. Staci grasped onto this thought firmly. If she helped them, it would help redeem her and her dad. Staci numbly talked briefly with family members at the grave site. She knew she wasn't paying attention to what they were saying, but it didn't matter.

As the family began to head back to their cars where they would proceed to the church for a family meal, Staci leaned over and whispered in her mother's ears, "Mom, I have to go back to the house for a minute. I will meet you at the church." Staci's mom, emotionally drained, absently nodded.

Staci walked over to her youngest brother. He wasn't married yet and had brought his own car. She asked him to drop her back to the house because she needed to pick up something. She then walked over to Dr. Worthington. "My father left something for you. Can you meet me at the church? I have to run home and pick it up." Emma agreed and looked at Steve curiously.

As Staci's brother drove toward their parents' house, Staci wracked her mind as to what she should look for. She then regretted not inviting Dr. Worthington to come and search herself. She was sure the professor would know better what to look for.

She walked up to the front door and realized she hadn't taken her key with her since her mom always had one. Pausing for a minute, she thought about where the spare key was hidden. She didn't even know if it was still there, but her mom used to hide one in the backyard under her favorite blue and yellow flowerpot.

Staci stepped down off of the porch and headed around to the side of the brick rambler. The lawn was thick and lush, but long—she would cut it tomorrow for her mom. As she came around the side of the house, she also noticed lots of weeds sprouting up between her mother's prize flowers. Her parents had loved working in the garden together and it was sad to see things neglected due to her father's illness. She paused for a minute and could almost see her dad bending over, pulling weeds while her mother gently planted more flowers. She felt angry somehow, seeing the weeds. They were like the cancer that had crept into her father's body and had choked out his life.

She defiantly leaned over and plucked out the largest weed she could find and flung it away from the weakening flowers. She pulled another few, but then felt pricks in her fingers. The weeds had prickly thorns and several were now lodged in Staci's right hand. She headed again toward the side gate, staring down at her palm and fingers, wincing as she tried to remove the thorn.

She was so engrossed that she didn't see the tall man coming toward her. He was running and they collided, knocking Staci to the ground. She heard him swear and looked up in shock. She knew that voice.

Riley had planned his arrival to sync with the start of the funeral at the church. He knew none of the family would be at the house and most of the neighborhood would be gone as well. He quickly moved to the side of the house and found the side gate unlocked. His dad was right—the Mormons were unsuspecting and naïve.

He tried the back door and was disappointed to find it locked. He thought about using his gun to blow the lock, but didn't want to alert anyone to his presence. It then dawned on him that he'd seen Staci use the hidden key once. He went to the same flower pot, hoping it was still there. He opened his bag and slipped on his gloves to protect his identity. He sighed with relief when he found the tarnished key still in its hiding place and quickly picked it up. He eased his way through the back door and moved quickly through the house. He remembered where Staci's father's study was. He would start there.

The house was quiet and Riley could hear the ticking of the grandfather clock in the living room. This would be his one chance to get what he needed. He hoped there was something useful, so he could head back to Georgia. Just being in Staci's parents' house again made him feel extremely uncomfortable.

He slid the study door open and stopped in surprise. Dr. Mangum was notoriously messy. Every time he had been to his office at the university or his home office, it was covered in papers and projected an aura of utter chaos. But now, the desk was completely tidy with no papers in sight.

Riley moved around the desk and pulled out the chair. He started with the top drawer and began methodically looking through all of the paperwork he found. The grandfather clock continued to tick loudly, reminding Riley he was on a limited timeline.

The desk was packed with papers. Riley read through each one and returned it to its place. He wanted to be able to leave quickly without detection if needed. Minutes turned into hours. Riley began glancing at his watch anxiously. He had found everything—life insurance policies, medical bills, household bills, research notes, correspondence, university documents. Everything *except* what he needed—information on the artifact. Staci had talked about her father's research. Maybe it was at his office at the university.

Riley glanced at his watch again. Over two hours had passed. He rifled through the bottom drawer, becoming increasingly frustrated. He finally slammed the file drawer shut and stood up to search the rest of the house when he paused. He thought he had heard something, but he wasn't sure what.

He moved over to the office window and gently separated the blinds. A car was in the driveway and Riley saw Staci walking toward the front door.

Riley swore and grabbed his bag. He would have to get out of the back door, replace the key, and hide at the side of the house until Staci left. He moved quickly, replacing the key and ran through the side gate when he plowed directly into Staci, knocking her to the ground.

Staci was only stunned for a second and then she leapt to her feet, swinging her open palm swiftly toward him, smacking him across the face. Riley felt the sharp sting on his cheek and saw the wild look in Staci's eyes.

Riley had forgotten how beautiful she was. She had always been pretty, but she looked more mature now, more streetwise, he thought ruefully. The fresh innocence and naïve look was gone. Now he only could see hatred and anger in her eyes.

"I deserved that," he said softly, looking at Staci intently. He deftly tried to shift his bag further behind him so she wouldn't notice.

"What are you doing here?" Staci demanded angrily, putting her hands on her hips.

Riley slipped back into his natural self, using lies to cover. "I heard about your dad. I came to see how you are doing." He stepped closer to her, using his most earnest smile.

But Staci had noticed the shoulder bag and spat, "No, you're not. You're here for more information. You're still *pillaging* my father and my family. *My father* has just been laid to rest in the ground and you're here looking for something of his to *steal*." Staci was processing as she talked out loud. She glanced toward the house, realizing that Riley had come for the same thing she had.

She reached over with a smooth movement and using all of her leverage, pushed Riley to the ground. He wasn't expecting it and easily fell off balance. Staci jumped to his side and ripped the shoulder bag away from him. She angrily opened it. Empty.

"I didn't find what I was looking for," Riley said with a sigh, slowly getting up from the ground and brushing off his trousers. He thought about his options—he could hurt Staci and make her help him. But that just wasn't him. He didn't like hurting women. He always used other, more persuasive methods to get what he wanted.

"Help me find what I'm looking for and I'll never come here again," he said softly, imploring her with his eyes. "I don't want to hurt you or your family. If I don't get what I need, my dad will send a professional. And it won't be a nice guy like me, Dolly."

It irked her down to the core that he would use her nickname like he used to. Her dad had said she looked like a china doll when she was born, so he had called her Dolly as a nickname.

"You can hurt me. You can kill me. You can send others after me. But I will *never, ever* help you again," she said, poking his chest roughly with her index finger and looking straight into his eyes.

They were so close that Riley could see the hurt in her eyes. She looked defiant and yet deeply wounded all at the same time. Riley suddenly wanted to kiss her.

Staci shoved his empty bag back into Riley's arms. "Now *leave*, before I call the police."

Riley looked at Stacy again, wishing things could be different. Wishing she would help him. She didn't know what RJ was like. He would stop at nothing to get what he wanted. He didn't want her to get hurt.

Riley walked past her, headed for the road. He hesitated and then turned around. "I'm sorry, Staci. I really am. I'm sorry about your dad. I'm sorry about lying to you. I'm sorry about everything."

"Go to hell," she replied and turned on her heel, slamming the gate as she passed through.

She went to the back door and in her flustered state, forgot that she didn't have a key. She went to the flower pot and relaxed when she saw the key. She let herself in and locked the door behind her. She went into her father's study and paused. She was proud that she hadn't cried in front of Riley. All of the hurt and disappointment returned, but instead of crushing her, it seemed to fire her with determination to set things right.

She had heard her mom in her dad's study yesterday. She thought she was just cleaning, but Staci only had to glance to realize even in her overwhelming grief, her mother had the presence of mind to protect her father's work. She had tidied the papers all away and Staci knew the ones she was looking for wouldn't be in the desk.

But where? Staci wandered around the house, trying to think. Where would her mother have put them? She moved from room to room. She checked some of the kitchen cupboards, but found nothing. Had her mother taken them to a safe deposit box? She dismissed the idea. Her mother hadn't left the house since her father died except to make funeral arrangements and Staci had been with her.

She felt drawn to their bedroom, without knowing why. Something tugged at the back of her mind. She remembered, as a small girl, telling her mom she needed her birth certificate for soccer registration. She was supposed to be cleaning her room, but she peeked through the door to see what her mom was doing. She had reached under her mattress and pulled out a manila envelope. Her mom had looked through the documents and had pulled out her birth certificate.

Staci moved to the same spot and reached between the mattress and the box spring. Nothing. She lifted up the heavy mattress, but it revealed nothing. She walked over to her father's side of the bed and tried the same thing. She blinked, making sure she wasn't imagining things. But the thick, manila envelope was still there. She lifted it out, glancing around to make sure she was alone even though she knew she was. She pulled out the first document on top, glanced at it and smiled. She was momentarily tempted to go through the papers, but in the end, she decided the less she knew, the better. She would get this in the right hands and that would be the end of it.

Staci went to the front door and was just about to open it when she stopped. There was a good chance Riley was out there waiting, watching. She decided to hide the envelope. She carefully tucked it down the back of her dress, using the top of her pantyhose to secure it. She would pass it at the church to Emma. She was sure her father wanted the documents to go to Emma and she would help him. She would do the right thing no matter what the cost.

Chapter 31

In typical generous style, the women of the local ward had put on an exceptional spread for Dr. Mangum's family. Three tables were filled with ham, funeral potatoes, salads and desserts. Family had flown in from all over the U.S. They all visited quietly together, hugging and reminiscing.

But Staci wasn't hungry. She felt the thick manila envelope pressing against her back; she needed to get it to Emma. She needed to make this right. While they ate, Emma was talking quietly to Steve about how she had passed the second clue to President Thompson at the cemetery. Staci walked over and stood next to them.

"Hi Dr. Worthington, do you have a minute?" Staci asked.

Emma smiled warmly and put down her fork and knife. "Of course."

Staci glanced around and then said quietly, "Why don't you come with me to the ladies' room."

Emma nodded and followed behind Staci. They walked through the family-filled gym to the hallway and turned the corner. It was dark, but Staci knew the way. Emma suddenly felt tense, like they were being watched. She glanced around, but didn't see anyone in the dark hallway. *I'm getting so jittery,* Emma thought to herself, trying to relax.

Emma could finally see as Staci switched on the bathroom light. They both went in and Emma watched as Staci checked each stall to make sure they were alone. Staci then lifted up her dress at the back and awkwardly tried to remove the envelope. She finally pulled it free and handed it to Emma.

"I had to hide this," she explained, smoothing down her dress. "I ran into Riley back at my parents' house. He was the guy I dated who pretended to be interested in the church. He had been in the house, searching it. But my mom had hidden the papers. During the gravesite dedication prayer, I felt my dad wants you to have it. I felt it very strongly."

Emma began to open the envelope, but they heard voices in the distance coming toward the bathroom and instead Emma copied Staci's hiding place and put the envelope behind her back, under her clothes.

Two elderly neighbors came into the bathroom and Emma and Staci said hi and then left. Emma walked awkwardly, trying to keep the envelope in place. "Thank you," she said to Staci as she hugged her goodbye. Emma didn't sit down by Steve, afraid the envelope would slip out. She just said, "Let's get going." Steve still had two brownies on his plate, but from the look in Emma's eyes, he quickly got up and stuffed one of them in his mouth.

They walked to the car; as soon as they both got in, Emma locked the doors. Steve started the car and drove. He saw a car pull out of the parking lot behind them and follow. Steve memorized the license plate and the make and model.

Emma leaned forward in her seat and awkwardly tried to pull the manila envelope out from her back. It was difficult in her sitting position and took several tries.

Steve watched the car behind them and decided to find out if they were being followed. He made several turns in succession and the car made each one as well.

Emma finally got the envelope free and began to straighten her dress with the envelope on her lap.

Steve turned another corner and stopped at a red light. He saw the car stop as well, but was surprised to see a man jump out and head toward them. "Emma, hide the envelope," he said urgently as he watched the man approaching the vehicle with a gun drawn. Steve looked up at the red light anxiously and looked both ways. There wasn't any traffic coming, so Steve hit the accelerator and ran the light.

Emma slipped the envelope under her legs on the seat and grabbed onto the car door handle. She could see the man with the gun in her side view mirror as he ran back to his car and jumped in. Her heart began to race and she looked over at Steve.

But Steve was focused on the road, his jaw set in determination to lose their tail. He turned quickly on a few streets, right and then left and then right, and then came to a long stretch of road. He headed toward Provo Canyon as fast as he could while still keeping them safe.

He took the canyon curves at a high speed, careful to stay in his own lane. He didn't see the car behind him anymore, but he wouldn't lose that advantage.

Emma clutched the door handle and her other hand went to her stomach. She started to feel sick as they wound through the curves quickly. Just when she felt as though she might throw up, Steve turned into a campground, maneuvered through it, and after finding a secluded spot where he could watch approaching cars, turned off the engine.

Emma took deep breaths and tried to calm down. Steve quietly watched the campground road, waiting for the other car to appear. Seconds turned into minutes and they waited. Steve glanced at the clock in the car. After 15 minutes, he took a deep breath, turned to Emma and said, "I think we lost him."

Emma's stomach was settling down, so she pulled the envelope out from under her legs. She turned it over and saw Dr. Mangum's scrawled writing on the front, *For Emma*. She ran her fingers over the handwriting, missing her mentor. But she saw Steve glance up toward the campground road and realized she needed to hurry in case their tail showed up again.

Emma turned over the envelope again, and gently slid out the documents. On top was a folded paper. Emma unfolded the paper and smoothed it out. The paper contained the Reformed Egyptian hieroglyphics that Joseph had used to hide the secret, the copy of the first clue that Steve and Emma had mailed to Dr. Mangum in an insurance envelope. Emma smiled. "He got it," she said to Steve. She saw small notes written next to each character. Her smile became even bigger. "And, he translated it," she said excitedly, looking at Steve.

He turned from watching the road and smiled back at Emma. He loved seeing this excited look on her face—it made her face glow. Steve thought how beautiful Emma was. Filled with hope. Filled with enthusiasm. He leaned over and spontaneously kissed her. She kissed him back, but then went back to the document, curious to see what it said.

"Let...all...the...Saints....of....the...most...high...God...listen....and...hear...His.......word...Let...not...their...hearts...be...hardened...but...open....to...the...will...of...the....Lord."

Emma's voice trailed off and Steve broke away his vigil of watching the road to look at Emma. "What does it say after that?" he asked anxiously.

"Nothing," Emma said dejectedly. "That's it. It's just a preamble."

"A preamble?" Steve asked, glancing at the paper.

"Yeah, in a lot of the Lord's revelations, he begins with a preamble. An introduction, usually to establish that it is from Him and to prepare the Saints for His message," Emma explained.

"Doesn't tell us much then," Steve said disappointed.

"Hmm," Emma mumbled, reading through the text again, lost in thought. Steve turned back to watch the road.

Emma's mind was whirring with thoughts. "It doesn't tell us much, but we can assume a couple of things," she began. "This is most likely a lost revelation from the Lord. The preamble identified it as such. It sounds like whatever is in the body of the revelation is something that will be hard for the Saints to hear, to bear. And it is clear that Joseph did not want this revelation to get out into the open. But he kept it; he didn't destroy it."

"It seems strange—why wouldn't he just destroy it if he felt that it could hurt the church?" Steve asked, glancing at Dr. Mangum's translation.

Emma thought for a minute and then answered, "Maybe because it was a revelation from God. He didn't feel right about just destroying it. There were a lot of hard things that the Lord revealed to Joseph. Think of the revelation on plural marriages. I'm sure it was very hard for Joseph and for Emma—as well as all others who were asked to live that law. But it was also very practical. There were a lot of men in the church who were killed by the mobs. The women needed protection and someone to provide for them."

"I'm glad we don't have to live it now," Steve said playfully. "Can't imagine having more than one wife to give me honey-do lists or get mad at me! And think of all of those anniversaries to remember!"

Emma punched Steve on the arm and thought again what it might be like to marry Steve. She didn't even dare hope. She wondered what their relationship would be like after this was all over.

Emma folded up the translation and looked through some of the other papers. A lot of them were photocopies from books Dr. Mangum had read. Emma scanned through them—it looked like some were on the subject they were searching for, but others were something entirely different.

Steve asked, "Any more ideas on where we should look for the earth symbol?"

Emma thought back to the parable's last two lines:

He was sorrowful and died.

His friends buried them near the mighty river.

"I think our best bet is Nauvoo. Joseph died in Nauvoo. He and Hyrum are both buried there. It's near a mighty river. I think we should go to Nauvoo," Emma decided.

"You know that means flying again," Steve said hesitantly. Even though Emma was getting better about flying, she still was very nervous on their way back to Salt Lake for the funeral.

Emma sighed and gave a weak smile, "Yeah, I know. Maybe the third time will be the charm."

Emma clung to Steve as the plane's engine's roared to life. She dug her nails into Steve's arm so deeply that he finally said, "Easy there, Emma. You're about to draw blood." Emma turned her head sharply and Steve could see the fear in her eyes.

"Sorry," she said as she released Steve's arm with a sheepish smile. Though Emma turned a bit green as the private jet took to the air she, managed to stay in her seat.

Steve decided to try to take her mind off of the flight. "Tell me about your life growing up."

Emma looked at Steve for a minute and hesitated. Her family life wasn't exactly ideal and few knew about her background. But if she was ever going to have a serious relationship with Steve, she knew she needed to open up.

"I grew up in a pretty normal household until I was eight, at least I thought it was normal at the time," Emma began. "I had an older brother, Tom. He was two years older than me. But I knew my parents fought a lot. They never did it in front of us, but late at night, when they thought we were asleep, they would close their bedroom door and argue."

She paused, reflecting and so Steve asked gently, "What would they fight about?"

"Not the stuff you would think like parenting skills or money," Emma explained. "They fought about living church standards. My dad was hard core, but my mother was always more . . ." Emma searched for the right word, "reluctant. She was a convert to the church and none of her family ever joined. She converted when she met my dad. Looking back, I think she just joined for him. If she did have a testimony, it wasn't strong enough to keep her faithful on her own."

"That's tough," Steve commented softly, watching Emma's face.

"Yeah, at first it was just subtle things," Emma continued. "I would notice my mom would find excuses more often than not to skip church. My dad called them her Mormon Migraines." Emma laughed and added, "Then, when my dad would leave for work, my mom would make herself a cup of coffee. She hid her coffeemaker in the basement in an old box. She made my brother and me promise not to tell. I remember another time they were going to a work party and they argued in their bedroom. It was one of the few times they argued during the day. My mother had bought a new dress for the party that day. But it was sleeveless and she had decided not to wear her garments to the party."

"I'm sure the rules were hard for her, as a convert," Steve said thoughtfully. I've always thought it must be harder for converts. For those of us who grow up in the church, it's just the way things are and it seems easier somehow."

"I'm sure it was, but my dad wasn't very understanding. They lived in Provo and my dad felt everyone would judge them if they knew she wasn't living the commandments. Looking back, as an adult, I think it was really hard for my mom. She was trying to do something she wasn't committed to, just for my dad and for us kids," Emma surmised.

"What ended up happening?" Steve asked, remembering that she said she *had* a brother.

Emma had a haunted look on her face. "My mom had been out with some college friends who were in town," she recalled. "Tom had been at a friend's house watching movies and my mom picked him up on her way home. I didn't know this until I was much older—my aunt ended up telling me—

but my mom had some wine with her college friends. It dulled her senses enough that she wasn't driving very carefully. It was winter and the roads were snowy and icy. She was going too fast and she ran into a snowplow. My brother was sitting on the side of the car that hit the plow. He didn't die instantly, but it damaged a lot of his internal organs. He died a couple of days later at Primary Children's Hospital."

"My dad of course blamed my mom," she continued. "The police report showed she had been drinking. Her blood alcohol level, though, was within the legal limit, so she just received a citation for reckless driving. After that, my mother became very depressed. My dad didn't speak to her much anymore and she was in a very dark place. I came home from school one day and found a note. She had left my dad, saying she knew he didn't love her anymore and could never forgive her."

Steve reached over and took Emma's hand. Tears had welled up in Emma's eyes. She had only told that story to one other person—Dr. Mangum. "My mom actually disappeared for several years. I used to cry myself to sleep at night, missing her. I felt somehow I was to blame for all of it. My dad was sullen and withdrawn. He made sure I had food to eat and clothes to wear, but wasn't able to help me much emotionally. My aunt Audrey helped look after me when I wasn't in school."

"Did you ever see her again?" Steve asked softly, stroking Emma's hand.

"On my 16th birthday, my mom showed up on our doorstep with a birthday present for me," Emma continued. "She looked like a completely different person. She had gone back to work and had landed a great job in New York where she grew up. She was stylish and happy, not at all like the depressed mom I remembered. She had remarried, but didn't have any more children. Losing Tom was too much for her."

Steve was listening intently. It all explained so much about the person Emma was today. Tough, independent because she had to be, closed off emotionally—until now. "How did you feel when you saw her again?" Steve asked softly.

Emma was far away, reliving the past. "Much like you'd expect. Angry. Happy. Nervous. Distrustful. That first visit, I felt like I didn't even know who she was. It didn't go very well. I'm sure she was nervous as well. I didn't see her until my birthday the following year. She had called a couple of times and we had talked about school and dating, but nothing too deep. For my 17th birthday, she flew me out to New York. I met her new husband. He is a stock broker and is 10 years older than her. He is funny and nice. They lived in a very upscale apartment and had a lavish lifestyle. My mother took me to her work in the fashion industry and I could see how happy she was."

"But it still didn't help me forgive her," Emma continued. "I felt like she had abandoned my dad, me, our faith and our life together. I could see she was happy now, but I just had a hard time feeling like it was okay. As I've gotten older, I think I understand her a bit better. She wasn't really converted and was uncomfortable living our lifestyle. She had loved her career and resented giving it up to be a stay-at-home mom. She preferred the city and found Provo to be boring and lonely, away from all of her friends. I think she really did love my dad though. She tried very hard to fit into his life, even though it was difficult for her."

"Did your dad ever remarry?" Steve asked, rubbing Emma's arm gently.

"No, I think he was really heartbroken after Mom left," Emma replied. "He's never been the same since. My mom and stepdad came when I graduated from BYU with my undergraduate degree. My dad was amazed at the change in my mom and I could see he was still in love with her, despite everything. But she had moved on with her life. He just couldn't."

She paused and then continued. "With Mom and Tom gone, my dad had such high expectations of me. He expected me to live every single commandment exactly. He pushed me pretty hard. But I truly believed the church was true and was willing to live the gospel, so I didn't mind. The hard part came when I was a senior at BYU. My dad, over the years, started to give me a hard time that I hadn't married yet. He told me I was too picky, that I needed to stop focusing on my career and find a husband. I think he was afraid I would turn into my mom in some ways. When I received my master's and began my career, he would lecture me that I was failing in my duty to become a wife and a mother. But the truth was, I *wanted* to meet someone. I was *praying* to meet someone. But I didn't."

"Until now," Steve prompted, squeezing her hand and smiling. But Emma was still feeling vulnerable—he could see it in her eyes. He leaned over and kissed her gently once and then twice, pulling away to see Emma's reaction. He could still see the hurt in her eyes though so he added, "I love you, Emma."

She smiled gratefully and leaned over to kiss him back. It felt so good to be loved. To be close to someone. She felt safe, here, on the private jet, away from all of the people chasing them, away from her troubled childhood.

They kissed for a few minutes and then leaned back for a nap for the rest of the flight.

Chapter 32

It couldn't be true, she thought to herself. She had a hazy recollection of the night she was shot. She remembered Carl coming back. The soldier had tied her up and she was helpless. She thought death would be instantaneous—Carl was an expert shot. She thought he would shoot her in the head or explode her heart. Instead, he had shot her so that she would slowly bleed to death.

And she would have if the soldier hadn't come back. That was the part she couldn't believe. She had abducted the soldier's girlfriend. *He didn't even know if the professor was alive when he carried me out and called the paramedics*, she mused. It bothered her.

What kind of people were these Mormons? The soldier had helped her, despite everything.

Her doctor came in and said she was healing nicely, but she would need to get some rest and would be in the hospital for over a week. It gave her a lot of time to think.

Carl treated her like a toy—a useful plaything. And then he tried to kill her. But then, she had tried to kill him. It was their nature, their business.

She had never known kindness growing up. Her father was a drunken louse who beat her and her mother. He was her first murder when she was old enough. She had used poison. No one suspected her because she was only 14.

When her mother repeated the pattern and married another louse who found her pretty at 16, Callie took off. She had starved and scraped to survive until she took her first professional job or two. They were small-time though. It wasn't until she moved to Atlanta that she met Riley in a bar one night. They had a fling and he got her some more work. But most people who hired professional killers had a hard time thinking of a woman to do it, so her work was usually stealing something or getting someone to talk.

She had been waiting patiently for her turn. She pretended to like Carl, only to keep him close so she could know when he messed up. She had told RJ she wanted the job, but he refused. But this wasn't Carl's kind of job. He didn't have the patience or the intelligence.

A nurse brought her lunch on a tray and while she ate she considered her options. She could kill Carl once and for all and retake leadership on the job. But that would prove difficult. Carl could outshoot her and outmatch her physically. Her strength had always been subtlety. She had done a few stranglings and suffocations. But she typically used the untraceable poison. It was easy and clean. She would have to get close to Carl again to use the poison and that was highly unlikely now.

But it bothered her that the soldier had helped her. No one had ever helped her. She had asked the nurse if she knew much about the Mormons. She had stated that they were devil worshipers and not Christians. That didn't make sense to Callie. The soldier's act of saving her was very Christian.

Callie had never been a church goer. She felt God had abandoned her to the world of men at such a young age. If God loved her, why didn't he protect or help her?

Maybe He had, she wondered. Maybe He had sent the soldier, Steve, back to save her.

She couldn't just give up this job—it was her chance to make a name for herself, to get bigger jobs. She needed the money as well. She had a good start with the money RJ had given her, but in this line of work, jobs came at infrequent intervals and she needed the money to stretch until her next assignment.

Deep down inside she felt it would be bad karma though. If there was a God up there, surely he wouldn't be happy about her hurting the soldier or the professor after He had saved her.

She tossed and turned in her sleep, weighing these things day after day. She could feel her body getting stronger with each passing day. She began to formulate a plan.

On the day she was dismissed from the hospital, she made her decision.

Nauvoo was a dream come true for Emma. She had always wanted to visit the quaint, well-preserved town. Besides Salt Lake City, Nauvoo was the other shining example of the Saints succeeding despite terrible odds. They carved the town out of the swamp land overlooking the Mississippi River. The Saints had finally built homes. While most were log cabins, many were solid brick homes.

They toured the visitors' center and then began visiting individual homes: Brigham Young's, Lucy Mack Smith's, Heber C. Kimball's, Sarah Granger Kimball's and Wilford Woodruff's. They went through the Seventies Hall, the bakery and the post office. They searched walls and artifacts for clues, but Nauvoo seemed overwhelming with over two dozen restored buildings.

They spent a lot of time looking around the Nauvoo temple grounds, but with little hope. The original Nauvoo temple had been destroyed. The temple now standing was very new. Steve and Emma discussed that maybe the clue had been on or near the original temple and was now lost.

They got excited when they learned there was a piece of the original temple preserved. They examined the sunstone through the protective glass, but couldn't see the earth symbol. Above the sunstone were two hands holding two trumpets.

Steve and Emma bought some bottled water and sat on a nearby bench across from the sunstone. "Well, that's pretty thick glass," Steve commended, "It will be tough to break."

Emma turned her head sharply, "Steve, you know how I feel about destroying church property."

"We're not going to destroy the sunstone, just the protective glass," Steve replied with a smile.

"I'm starting to think you're enjoying this—that maybe you have a destructive nature," Emma answered with a laugh in spite of herself.

"It's probably because I was too good of a kid growing up," Steve acknowledged with a shrug. "I never went through my rebellious, destructive phase."

"So you think the symbol might be on the bottom side of the sunstone?" Emma asked, still feeling uncomfortable about breaking the glass.

"It worked for us with the hearthstone," Steve replied.

Emma took a long drink, thinking. She finally said, "There's just something not right about this."

Steve took a drink as well and then asked, "What do you mean? This is where Joseph and Hyrum are buried, right?"

"Yeah, but I don't think it's the sunstone," Emma answered.

"That's just because you don't want me to break the glass on church property," Steve suggested with a nudge against Emma's arm.

"Well, that's part of it," Emma admitted, "But there's something else. First of all, they knew when they were building the temple that it would probably be destroyed. Maybe not at first, but the closer they were to finishing it, the worse the mob situation was becoming and the hostility toward Joseph. They

169

wouldn't have put this sunstone piece on until toward the end and by then they would have known they would leave Nauvoo. And once they abandoned the temple, they knew the mobs would destroy it. Would Joseph really leave an important clue where he knew it would be destroyed?"

"Joseph had a lot of things to worry about in his final days," Steve added, "Maybe he didn't think through all of the—"

"That's the other thing," Emma interjected. "I don't think Joseph left this clue. It was Brigham. It was his handwriting, not Joseph's in the parable. It was after Joseph had died."

"Where was Joseph buried?" Steve asked, glancing around the visitors' center grounds.

"That's complicated actually," Emma answered. "Joseph's family was afraid the mobs would desecrate Joseph's grave, so his family faked the burial in the city cemetery. The caskets just had sandbags in them. Joseph and Hyrum were secretly buried underneath the basement of the Nauvoo House."

"Maybe we should look there," Steve suggested, shifting uncomfortably in his seat. He didn't really enjoy the thought of trying to dig up hidden graves.

"Their bodies aren't there anymore," Emma said shaking her head. "After Emma died, the Smith family exhumed the bodies and re-interred them, along with Emma's under a shed on the property. For a long time, no one knew exactly where the bodies were. It wasn't until 1928, when Joseph's family was afraid the rising Mississippi River might destroy the graves, that they hired an excavation team to locate the bodies. They finally re-interred them in a permanent plot in the Smith Family Cemetery."

"So, it's doubtful that anything was hidden within Joseph's grave," Steve surmised.

"Yes, or if it was, it will be long gone by now with all of the moving," Emma agreed.

"Let's go have a look just in case," Steve suggested. They walked over to the cemetery and waited their turn to look at the graves. When it was finally their turn, they read the names carefully, Joseph in the middle with Emma on the right and Hyrum on the left. They walked around looking carefully, but the stone was smooth, only listing their names, titles, dates and places of birth and dates and places of death.

Steve and Emma finally gave up and went to dinner. Emma was quiet, lost in thought. Steve ate silently and took the opportunity to study the faces in the restaurant. As he glanced at the different patrons, he began to feel unsettled. There was a young man, in his later 20s in the corner booth. He was texting on his phone and then looking out the window. Steve mentally retraced today's steps. As he thought back through the day, he remembered seeing the young man in line to look at Joseph's grave. He also remembered seeing him at the visitors' center. Was he just being paranoid? There were a lot of tourists visiting Nauvoo and everyone was going to the same places. But there was something just not right about the guy. He was alone. Everyone else was with someone. He sat where he could have a good vantage point to watch Steve and Emma. He kept glancing at the window.

Just when Steve was about to say something to Emma about him, he quickly stood up, pulled out his wallet, threw some money on the table, and left without looking at Steve.

Chapter 33

"You're sure they didn't find anything?" Carl snarled at the young man in the dark, back parking lot of the restaurant.

"Positive," he answered nervously. "I followed them all over Nauvoo. I even got close enough to hear them talking. They were saying how they don't know if Nauvoo is the right place. They can't find what they're looking for."

"Close enough to hear them talk—you got too close!" Carl shouted, his face turning purple. "I was watching through the window—the soldier recognized you in the restaurant. He's seen your face one too many times. You're done here." He shoved the kid several feet away, almost knocking him off his feet.

The kid pulled a knife out of his back pocket and swished open the blade. "Not without my money," he said menacingly through gritted teeth.

Carl pulled out his gun and shot the boy without hesitation straight through the heart. The kid crumpled with a look of surprise on his face. "Amateurs," Carl said disgustedly as he walked past the kid, stuffing his gun back into jeans. He moved into the alley where he could see the restaurant door. Steve and Emma emerged 10 minutes later and Carl could tell from the look on their faces that the kid was telling the truth. He flattened himself against the wall and let them walk by. He waited until they turned the corner and then he briskly followed.

Carl watched them walk to a nearby park and sit on a bench. They were having an animated discussion. He watched the professor shrug off her pack and pull out a manila envelope. Carl squinted. He moved behind them, away from their field of vision and hid behind a bush. He was now close enough to hear what they were saying.

". . . we should keep looking," Steve said to Emma. "It's got to be here somewhere. There are thousands of artifacts. It's a church history goldmine. Joseph had to leave the last clue here somewhere."

"Steve, it just doesn't feel right," Emma countered. "Nauvoo is Joseph. We're quite sure that Brigham left the last clue. It wouldn't be here. Brigham would have taken it with him. He knew they were moving on. Joseph had the vision of the Saints going to the Rocky Mountains. Brigham knew that."

"So you think it's in Utah?" Steve asked.

"Possibly," Emma said weakly with a half-smile.

"You would think someone would have run across it by now," Steve replied. "If it was in Utah. Brigham is buried in Utah, in Salt Lake, right?"

"Yes," Emma answered. "But who is the 'they' in the parable? And there isn't a mighty river in Utah, not compared to the others the Saints lived near."

"So where do you think we should go?" Steve asked in a tired voice. This trip reminded him of the long reconnaissance missions that he and his team would take.

"I think we should go to bed and sleep on it," Emma replied, feeling tired herself. The humidity in Nauvoo and the hot sun were taking their toll on her.

Carl watched them walk toward the hotel. He circled the outside, checking to see how many rooms, where the security cameras were, how many cars were in the parking lot. He then went to get his car and parked around the back where he was sure there weren't any security cameras. He sat, waiting, anticipating his next move.

One by one he watched the lights go out in the hotel. He pulled on his black leather gloves and slowly screwed on his silencer. He was looking forward to this. Yes, RJ needed the professor, but Carl had decided they no longer needed the soldier. Things would move along a lot quicker if the professor was under pressure—he was sure of it.

He tucked away his gun and slowly moved toward the back door. He had stolen a master room key and quickly moved through the back door. He knew the night staff would be at the front desk, so he moved up the back stairs quickly. He had already acquired their room numbers. The soldier was in 405 and the professor in 407. He moved quickly along the hallway to room 405. Listening at the door, he couldn't hear anything. He glanced down both hallways, but everything was quiet.

Carl felt his blood start to race with excitement. No more talking. He would kill the soldier instantly. He couldn't wait to do it. He'd been planning it since the soldier took him out in the forest back in Vermont. No one humiliated him.

He blew the lock and quickly moved into the room, throwing on the lights and shooting several bullets into both of the queen-sized beds in the room. He could feel the thrill of the kill pulsing through his veins. He felt alive. He felt powerful and strong.

He blinked and then blinked again. The sheets were disheveled, but the hump underneath seemed too small. He eased forward, gun still pointing at the bed and threw back the sheets with his other hand. Pillows. Rage filled his body and he could taste the angry bile in his mouth. He moved to the adjoining door and shot out the lock, He kicked the door open and angrily shot into the adjoining room's beds. But the bed was perfectly made and he could see that it was empty.

They were gone.

Chapter 34

"I can't believe I didn't even think of Winter Quarters before!" Emma exclaimed in an excited voice as they drove to the airport. "Are you sure that's where it is?"

Steve had called for the private jet and they decided to move quickly now they knew they were being followed again by the guy in the restaurant. And there was something else. While they had sat in the park after dinner, Steve had felt the same familiar feeling of being watched that he had felt earlier on their journey. It felt ominous and threatening. But he didn't vocalize his concerns with Emma—it would only frighten her.

"It's just a thought, but while we were looking through Dr. Mangum's things again, I came across two photocopies of a burial names list. He had written Winter Quarters on the bottom. I wondered why there were two. And then I realized they weren't the same. One was in alphabetical order and it was an actual photograph of the stone where the names are listed. The other is a copy of a book where the names were handwritten. They weren't alphabetical."

Emma pulled the manila envelope out of her backpack and looked at the two documents which Steve had left on top. She studied the names. "Wow, it can't be that simple," she said. She looked at the paper in amazement. At the top of the list, the names were:

Ephraim Pierson
Alvy West

> Robert Haleman Pixton
> Thomas Callister
> Heber C. Grant

Emma underlined the first letter of each name. E...A...R...T...H

"Wow, that's got to be it," Emma exclaimed. "Brigham left a clear, strong clue."

"Yeah, but it was lost because they reordered the names alphabetically when they created the modern-day markers," Steve explained with a smile. "Thank heaven Dr. Mangum had done all of this research."

A sad smile came to Emma's lips. She missed him so much. "I'm sure he's up there trying to point us in the right direction," she laughed softly. "He probably went straight to Joseph in the next life and asked what it all meant."

"I'm sure our jet pilot isn't happy to be woken up in the middle of the night," Steve commented. "But we need to move quickly. This is it. The last clue. We need to get there before anyone else."

Emma used the ride to the airport to continue to look through Dr. Mangum's papers. He had a detailed page on all of the symbols of the Salt Lake Temple. Emma had heard him discuss it once when they went to Temple Square for a BYU faculty dinner at the Joseph Smith Memorial Building.

She noticed he had circled the North Star symbol, but there weren't any comments written in the margins. She continued through his other papers. There were so many things, but little made sense or explained a connection.

They finally arrived at the airport; the jet pilot arrived five minutes later. He managed a weak smile, but looked tired. Since they didn't have a prescheduled flight, they had to sit on the tarmac for a while before taking off.

Steve and Emma slept during the flight from Illinois to Omaha, Nebraska. They arrived just a few hours before dawn. After thanking the pilot, they rented a car.

"Do you want to check into a hotel and get a few more hours of sleep?" Steve asked as he backed the car out of its parking spot.

"No way! I'm too excited!" Emma exclaimed. Steve looked over at her and smiled. She looked like a kid on Christmas morning, eager with anticipation and excitement. "Unless you're tired," she added politely.

Steve thought about the ominous feeling he had back in Nauvoo. "No, I'm fine," he agreed. "Let's go straight to Winter Quarters."

Emma programmed the address into the GPS and they headed out. "I've never been to Nebraska before," Emma offered as she gazed out the window. The horizon was just starting to move from dark to dawn. Omaha was a relatively small city and they sped along the freeway. Looking west, Emma could see the land stretching out in front of her all the way to the horizon. To the east across the river into Iowa, the landscape was hilly, and lush with trees.

As they came around a bend, Emma noticed something on the GPS. "Steve, look!" she exclaimed. "Just over the Missouri River is Council Bluffs, Iowa! I've always wanted to go there. That's where Brigham Young was sustained as president of the church and Heber C. Kimball and Willard Richards as his counselors."

"Wow," Steve replied, glancing across the river. "Brigham Young wasn't sustained until they got here? Why so long after Joseph died? I always thought he was sustained in Nauvoo."

"I think it was mainly due to the fact that they were much too worried and focused on survival than to worry about formal sustainings," Emma mused. "Many believed Brigham was the clear successor. Before they left Nauvoo, Brigham spoke to the Saints and his face was transfigured into Joseph's and his voice sounded like Joseph's as well. Many took that as a sign that he was the successor."

"That would be wild to see," Steve said with a laugh.

"Yeah," Emma agreed and then added, "Kind of spooky, too. But they never had experienced a succession before. They actually established the succession pattern right here on the banks of the Missouri. It made it a lot easier as the years went on."

"That's definitely a mighty river," Steve commented, glancing again. "Nothing like our skinny rivers out West. It would definitely be nerve-wracking to cross, whether flowing or frozen."

They came up to their exit and Emma thoughtfully added, "Did you know that Council Bluffs had another name? The Saints called it Kanesville, after General Thomas Kane, who had proved himself an ally to the church and who was a personal friend of Brigham Young's. General Kane came all the way from Pennsylvania to attend Brigham's funeral. Kanesville was renamed Council Bluffs after the Saints left."

Steve smiled and sneaked a glance at Emma. "You sure know a lot about church history." Emma blushed and reached over to take Steve's hand. He squeezed hers in response and wondered yet again why someone hadn't snatched up Emma a long time ago. He loved her strength and intelligence, her childlike excitement and faith. Somewhere in Iraq and Afghanistan, he had lost some of that. He still believed in God and his testimony was intact, but he had a lot of scars from his military service and subsequent divorce.

Steve exited the freeway at Florence, Nebraska and they wound their way toward the cemetery. As they got out of the car, Emma grabbed the document with the alphabetized names and a cemetery map which Dr. Mangum had left in the pile of documents.

The gates were locked and it was still several hours before the visitors' center would open, but they preferred it that way. They both felt mounting excitement knowing this was the last clue, and, with any luck, they finally would have the entire revelation.

They walked along the edge of the fence into the countryside and found the fence shorter there. They finally came to a point where Steve felt they could get over. Steve hoisted Emma up by lifting her leg with his hands. She grabbed the top of the fence and pushed herself over, landing awkwardly on the other side, painfully twisting her ankle. She gasped and fell in a heap on the grass.

Alarmed, Steve threw their backpacks over and easily scaled the fence. His military training coming in handy, he gracefully landed next to Emma.

"You make it look way too easy," Emma said ruefully, rubbing her ankle.

"If you knew how many barricades and barbed wire fences I've had to get over, you would know I've had a lot of practice," Steve said smiling. He sat down next to Emma and reached over to touch her ankle. He gently moved his fingers up and down and then slowly rotated her foot while feeling the ankle.

Emma felt a rush of pleasure moving from her ankle up her leg. There was something intimate about having Steve gently touch her leg. She tried to remain composed, thinking how silly it was to have such a reaction.

Steve, focused on the task at hand, didn't notice her reaction. "It doesn't feel broken," he surmised, pulling back his hand. "Probably just a sprain." He helped Emma stand up, put his pack on his back, and carried Emma's as well. She tried to walk and painfully winced, so Steve put his arm around her, helping her take the weight off of her foot.

Emma smiled gratefully at him and hobbled along, enjoying the closeness. She leaned closer to him, wondering yet again what their relationship might be when all of this was over. She could picture them going out to dinner together, walking along campus at night, hiking in the mountains. She suddenly wanted to find the last clue and return to their normal lives so she could see if they might have a future together.

Steve took a deep breath, enjoying the closeness as well. His face close to Emma's head, he could smell the sweet perfume from her shampoo. "You know," he started with a smile, "you're much cuter than the last person I carried like this."

"Was it a girlfriend?" Emma asked playfully.

"No, it was a sweaty, smelly, wounded soldier who probably hadn't had a bath in over a week," Steve explained with a chuckle.

Emma acted hurt. "That's not much of a compliment then," she replied gazing coyly up at him.

"I said much cuter," Steve defended, pretending to be hurt and then added for emphasis, "*much* cuter." He added a sincere smile as they continued through the fields.

As they went deeper into the cemetery, they both felt a deep stillness come over them. Neither spoke. They followed a path to the visitors' center grounds and stopped in front of the statue of a couple burying their child. The husband had his arm around his wife, a blanket whipping with the wind, both of them gazing brokenheartedly at a shallow grave where they had just buried their baby.

"Almost half of the people who died along the trail were under two," Emma commented so softly that Steve almost didn't hear her. "Their little bodies just couldn't take the exposure to the cold and rain. Some of them didn't even have homes at Winter Quarters—they lived in hovels that were basically mud caves."

Feeling the anguish that he could see on the parents' faces, Steve thought back to when Kari had miscarried. Even though he had been away on his deployment, it still had devastated him when he heard. Sometimes on his walks around campus at night, he would think about the baby and wonder what it would have been like. Kari had told him that it was too early to tell the sex. But somehow Steve had always thought it was a boy. He didn't know why.

He tightened his grip around Emma's shoulders. He wondered if things worked out between them, if he might have more children. He hoped so. He desperately missed Ari and longed to have a large family one day. But doubt began to creep into his mind. He and Kari had been through difficulties, and they hadn't made it through. Would it be any different if he tried again?

They stood in silence before the statue for 10 or 15 minutes and then examined the stone plaques with the list of names. It brought them both back to the task at hand and Emma had Steve help her over to a nearby bench.

She looked at the names and began to search for them on the cemetery map photocopy. She identified each one, circling the name. She noticed the majority of them were in the first section of graves.

Steve looked over her shoulder, searching for some pattern or clue. "It looks significant that several of them are buried near each other," he began, looking up at Emma.

"Yes," she murmured absentmindedly.

"Do you think the last clue is hidden in one of the graves?" Steve asked hesitantly. He had done a lot of horrible things as a soldier, but grave digging wasn't one of them.

Emma didn't relish the thought either. "I don't know," she answered honestly. "Maybe we should go have a look at each of them."

As Steve helped her stand Emma noticed the pain was easing a bit. But she enjoyed having Steve's arm around her, so didn't offer the information. They walked toward where the graves were supposed to be, but the map was only an estimate; the graves weren't individually marked. The field yielded nothing but grass and a stillness in the air.

They began with the graves that were grouped together and then moved toward the one grave that was alone. Still finding nothing, they wandered around the cemetery, looking for clues.

After several hours, they headed back to the visitors' center. As they got closer, Steve's ominous feeling of dread returned and increased with each step.

Chapter 35

She knew he was here. She had used the usual source at the car rental agency to know he had come to Florence, Iowa. She had read up all about the Mormon settlement on both sides of the Missouri that had served as a resting/recovering place for the Mormons as they journeyed to the West.

It was fitting that what was most likely the last clue was here. While Emma had been unconscious in the hotel, she had taken photocopies of the parable and the first clue. She had found a professor back East who translated it roughly for her. But it didn't give her much to go on. She knew they had found another clue while she was recovering in the hospital. She needed it and whatever they found today to get her final payment.

And it was quite the final payment. But it wasn't just the money. She needed the success of this job to get her more high-profile jobs. Then she would be set. Like many in her industry, she would only need to do a couple of big jobs and then she could disappear to some island in the Pacific.

She would buy herself a beach house and lay on the beach every day. She would flirt with the locals and use them as disposable playthings, much as she had been used herself. She would never let anyone or anything control her again.

By the time she got there, the gate to the visitors' center was open and she watched the gray-haired couple go into the visitors' center. She moved quickly through the gate and into the trees. Moving to higher ground for a vantage point, she found the perfect spot and then pulled out her binoculars. It was easy to find Emma and Steve. They were sitting on a bench studying some papers.

She watched them for several minutes and then they headed into the visitors' center. She contemplated following them in. She had dramatically changed her appearance and she doubted they would recognize her. But it was early and the visitors' center was only occupied by the couple and Steve and Emma. It would be too hard to avoid scrutiny. She would stay here where she could see everything, including the parking lot. She would know if they left.

She checked her equipment while she waited. She had purchased a long-range rifle and had spent the past week practicing at least five hours a day. She felt very confident that she could take him out from a distance. And she would. There would be no hesitation. It had to be done.

The minutes turned into nearly an hour and she patiently waited. She spent the time scanning the area, becoming familiar with the terrain and landmarks. She found her mind drifting back to the night that she had been shot. She remembered going unconscious and her last thought was that she was going to die. And then somehow, the soldier had saved her and she woke up in the hospital, alive.

She pushed the thoughts from her mind. She needed to keep a clear head—needed to stay focused. This was it. She could feel it. She would have everything RJ wanted by the end of the day. And he would be dead.

Her senses heightened when she saw movement at the visitors' center door. She moved her binoculars toward the door and focused them. It was the elderly woman, leading Steve and Emma on what looked to be a tour. They walked out to a statue of a handcart being pulled by a family.

She quickly realized something was wrong with what she was seeing. She scanned Steve and Emma, trying to figure out what it was. It then came to her—they didn't have their backpacks on.

Her heart racing, she quickly packed her equipment in her own backpack. *They must have a policy against carrying backpacks,* she thought to herself. This was her chance. She would only have a few moments to get to the backpacks before Steve and Emma returned to the visitors' center.

She ran to the front door and then stopped. She slowed her pulse and casually walked in. She expected to be greeted by the elderly man she had seen coming in, but he was nowhere in sight. She moved rapidly around corners, looking for where the backpacks might be. As she came to the second hallway, she saw a wall full of lockers. It was easy to tell, even from a distance, where their backpacks were—only three bright orange keys had been removed.

She moved swiftly to the lockers and pulled out her tool set. With her heart racing, she deftly used one of her tools to spring the lock on the first locker. She sighed with disappointment, seeing the elderly lady's purse. She quickly closed it and tried the next one, which she had open in seconds.

Excitement coursed through her body as she saw Emma's backpack. She grabbed it, threw it over her shoulder in one movement and closed the locker. Glancing rapidly in both directions, there was still no sign of the elderly man. She didn't even try for Steve's backpack. She knew everything she needed would be in Emma's.

She looked around and found the women's restroom. She entered and went directly into the stall with a baby changer unit. She pulled everything out of the backpack. On top was a thick manila envelope full of papers. She quickly transferred it to her own backpack. She had to pull out all of Emma's clothes and personal items before she found the two parchment pieces stowed at the very bottom of the backpack.

She opened them up as quickly as she could—her hands were shaking. She recognized the first one—she already had a copy of it. But having the original would be valuable as well, so she stuffed both of them into her own pack.

She then replaced the other things in the order that she had found them. It took extra time, but she didn't want Emma to realize the parchments were gone—not yet anyhow.

With the backpack closed back up, she opened up the bathroom door. As she moved quickly down the hallway and turned the corner toward the lockers, she ran headlong into the elderly man.

"Oh!" he exclaimed as he bumped into her.

"I'm very sorry, brother," she apologized, glancing at the man's nametag. "Elder Manning," she added with a smile.

"No harm done," he said politely, smiling down at her. "Are you here for a tour?" he asked.

"Yes," she replied with another warm smile. "I've always wanted to see Winter Quarters," she added.

Brother Manning led her to the lockers, "You can store your backpacks in here. You know, security risks and all these days. Never heard the like of it in my day. We grew up in a small town in Utah and never even locked our doors!"

"I know," she added in a friendly voice, "Neither did my mom growing up. Could set something valuable down and come back hours later and still find it sitting right where ya left it." She had easily transitioned into a rural accent.

She stowed the backpacks in separate lockers, saying she didn't want to squish her stuff. The elderly guide led her throughout the visitors' center. She made sure to position herself so she could keep an eye on the door. She could see Steve and Emma, still outside with the elderly woman.

After 10 minutes of feigning interest, she saw Steve and Emma coming toward the door. "You know, Elder Manning," she said in a weak voice and leaning toward him for emphasis, "I'm not feeling so great. I think I might have the stomach flu. All of this backpacking and eating in the open—I think I've picked up something." She put her hand over her mouth and began to make retching motions.

Elder Manning didn't protest as she quickly headed back toward the bathroom. Once she was around the corner, she quickly opened the lockers, took both packs out and headed out the front door. She didn't look back as she quickly moved back through the trees and up to her vantage point on the hill.

She still needed the last clue and she hoped that Steve and Emma would find it. After 15 minutes, her patience was rewarded. Steve and Emma came out with Brother Manning in tow, and headed toward the cemetery.

She followed them with her binoculars. They were studying a paper they had with them, with Elder Manning pacing off steps and then gesturing to certain parts of the ground. *They're looking for something the Mormons buried,* she thought to herself. She set up her long-distance rifle and waited. Once they found it, she would make her final move.

Brother Manning had served at the visitors' center for over a year. He knew everything about it. When Steve and Emma had asked where to find certain burial plots, he knew right where to go. A surveyor by profession, he was skilled at measuring out distances. He knew how big the plots were and was able to walk off the distances.

He took them to each of the names they mentioned, explaining that the graves were unmarked.

But after visiting each one, they still had nothing else to go on. More visitors were arriving as the morning wore on, so Brother Manning went to start a tour in the visitors' center, leaving Steve and Emma out on the cemetery site.

"What do you think?' Steve asked Emma, glancing at the plot map and gazing at the nondescript land underneath and around them.

"I think it's here somewhere," Emma said, looking around. "I can almost feel it."

Steve could feel something as well. An urgency and also a growing sense of danger and alarm. Emma didn't seem to feel it. Maybe it was all of the years of his combat experience. He knew they were being watched. He knew trouble was coming. He glanced into the trees, but saw nothing. He turned behind them and checked once again. Nothing . . . nothing. There. He saw a glint in the trees at the top of a small hill.

He kept moving his head but kept his eyes on the same spot. He saw it again. He knew what it was. Someone was watching them with binoculars. He didn't want to alarm Emma, but he encouraged action by saying, "Maybe we should start to dig." He put himself between the hill and Emma, ensuring that he would be hit before her if something happened.

Emma scrunched up her face and replied, "I hate to grave dig. I can't think that Brigham would have wanted us to do that. Disturbing remains isn't really a Christian thing to do."

"Even if we have to do that, we can't do it now in broad daylight," Steve agreed with a sigh. "Digging up five graves is sure to be quickly noticed."

"Maybe it isn't here," Emma suggested. "Or long gone."

"No," Steve said shaking his head. "They wanted it to be found, just not in their day. They have been very careful so far to place the clues where they would be preserved."

"Then maybe it is here," Emma agreed, nodding her head. "No one would disturb a cemetery this large. I just remembered something I once read as well. The Saints had to abandon Winter Quarters earlier than they would have liked. The government put pressure on them because it was Indian land. They wanted to return the land to the Indians to pacify them. The Indians were stealing a lot of the Saints' cattle and other valuable goods. But Brigham knew Indians well. He knew that of all nationalities, Indians would preserve and protect burial grounds. I'm sure Brigham hoped as well one day that the church would be able to come back and regain the land."

"There's got to be a way then to know which plot," Emma said thoughtfully. "We have the clue, we just need to figure out what it is."

Something was nagging at the back of Steve's mind. It was something he had seen earlier that morning, but he couldn't quite focus on it. "Emma, let me see the plot map again," he requested.

Emma handed him the paper and he studied it closely. "Do you have a pen?" he asked.

"Yeah, but in my backpack back at the visitors' center," Emma replied. Steve stuck his hand firmly down into the dirt, extending his index finger deeply. He came out with mud on it, wet from the sprinklers that morning.

Emma leaned in closer to get a better look as he began to trace his finger from burial plot to burial plot of the five names. He finished at the top of the map.

"What is it?" Emma asked, glancing at it upside down.

"The one timeless way to find your destination that travelers have used from the beginning of time," Steve said with a broad smile, meeting Emma's gaze. He turned the map toward her so she could get a better view.

Emma followed the mud tracings, but didn't realize what she was seeing. "It's just a bunch of lines," she replied confused.

"That's because you weren't a boy scout," Steve teased and then added, "Nor a soldier. It's the Big Dipper, Emma."

"The Big Dipper," Emma echoed, gazing in wonder at Steve. "The Big Dipper was in Dr. Mangum's files."

"And it's also a symbol on the Salt Lake Temple," Steve added. "It points travelers to the North Star, which guides them home. I once got a merit badge in astronomy and the symbolism doesn't end there, Emma. The Big Dipper has seven stars and it has another name—The Plough."

"Plough . . ." Emma repeated. "That would indicate earth as well. Most ploughs don't dig very deep. They cut just below the surface."

Emma and Steve smiled at each other and Steve reached for Emma's hand and squeezed it. Emma squeezed it back and then asked, "So, where do we plow?"

"We find the North Star," Steve said, moving north and east of where they were standing. "If we follow this Big Dipper, it leads us to the one name that is off by itself. Right at the north end of the cemetery."

Ignoring the lingering pain in her ankle, Emma ran behind Steve. He didn't have to go far. "This is roughly where Brother Manning said it was." Steve dropped down on his hands and knees and began to probe the earth with his fingers. Emma dropped down and did the same. They moved in a systematic way, covering roughly 20 square feet of ground.

After coming up empty, Steve stood and said, "Emma, I need my shovel. I have my army shovel in my backpack back at the visitors' center. Let's run back and get it."

"My ankle is still tender," Emma replied. "You go ahead and get it and I'll wait here."

Steve hesitated. He knew someone was watching them, but so far, they had kept their distance. They hadn't found the clue yet, so he doubted they would make their move until they did find it.

"I'll be fine," Emma reassured him, rubbing her ankle. Running across to the northward plot hadn't been a good idea.

Steve glanced at the distance between their location and the visitors' center. If he sprinted, it would only be a few minutes. Whoever was watching them was far enough away that they couldn't reach Emma before he did.

"I don't want to leave you alone," Steve protested. "Why don't we walk slowly back together?" He was torn in his mind. If they both left this site, whoever was watching might come and search it while they were gone. Although they hadn't found anything, someone else might.

"I'll be fine," Emma said reassuringly.

"All right," Steve said reluctantly. "But I want you to move over by that group of trees and sit down."

"Why?" Emma asked, glancing around. "No one knows we're here, Steve."

Steve considered telling her about his feeling of being watched, but decided against it. Emma had been through so much already. He didn't want to worry her.

"Just humor an old soldier, Em, okay?" Steve asked helping her up and guiding her toward the trees. "I'll be right back—only a few minutes. Just sit down and wait for me and stay out of sight."

Before Emma could protest, Steve bolted off, running at top speed through the trees and down toward the visitors' center.

Emma sat, watching the spot where they felt the North Star was, and began to be a bit unsettled. *Why was Steve taking this precaution? Did he think they had already been found?* She glanced around nervously and jumped when she heard a dry twig snap. *I'm being paranoid*, she reassured herself and tried to calm down. She watched Steve run and once he was out of sight, she heard a clicking noise.

Chapter 36

"Hello, Emma," Carl said in a gruff voice.

Emma turned her head sharply, her pulse racing. She looked into the eyes of the man who had shot her back at Hill Cumorah. She glanced back toward where Steve had disappeared into the trees.

"Don't worry, he'll be back," Carl added in a mock smoothing tone. "And we'll be waiting for him."

Emma instantly began to pray silently that somehow they would get through this. That somehow Steve wouldn't come back and get shot. She couldn't bear it if anything happened to him.

"Where are the other clues you've already found?" Carl said menacingly. Emma turned and faced him. She noticed he was hiding behind one of the larger trees. Steve wouldn't see him as he came. Panic filled her mind and stomach.

"They are in the glove box in the rental car," she offered, hoping he would leave her and go to look.

"Nope," he answered with his voice growing impatient. "I've already checked the car. Try again."

Emma watched as he screwed on his silencer. Her mind raced for another idea, but in her panic-filled state, she couldn't think of anything. "They're in my backpack," she answered honestly with a sigh.

"And where's your backpack?" he asked through gritted teeth. Emma noticed he had gloves on. No fingerprints. No trace. Would anyone know what happened to her? Steve would, she thought. But would Steve survive this to tell anyone? No, she knew this could be the end of the road. If they found the last clue, they would both be dead instantly.

"At the visitors' center," she began, thinking if she talked enough, she might still be alive when Steve returned. "We didn't want to leave our packs. But the elderly couple who run the visitors' center said that it's church security policy now. They won't allow anyone to carry backpacks around the visitors' center or on the grounds. So I had to give it up. I put it in one of the lockers and so did Steve. Both of our packs are there. Everything we have, all of the clues, are in there."

Emma came to the end of her ramblings and saw a movement from the corner of her eye. She turned her head quickly and saw Steve running toward her at a full sprint. Emma's natural reaction was to call out to Steve to stop, but Carl intervened, "I'll shoot him if you call out."

Emma snapped her mouth closed. Fear and panic filled her eyes which she used to plead with Steve, hoping he would get the message. But he was in soldier mode and was scanning the area as he ran instead of looking at Emma. By the time he got close and saw her eyes, he stopped suddenly in his tracks.

"Emma, what is it, what's wrong?" he asked looking around rapidly.

Carl stepped from behind the tree with his gun focused on Steve. "Hello, Steve," he began. "So here we all are again." Carl noticed the army shovel in Steve's hands and added, "Doing a little digging?" When Steve didn't reply, but instead racked his brains to try and figure out a way to protect Emma, Carl added, "I've been watching you feeling around down there. I know you know where it is. I'll give you ten minutes to find what you're looking for. If you haven't found it, I will put a bullet in Emma here. I'll start with her arms and move inward. Her survival is up to you."

Steve began to protest and so Carl reached over and hit a button on his watch. "You're wasting time, Steve. You know I'll do it."

Steve saw the determined look in his eye and knew he would. He looked at Emma's scared face. There were now tears running down her cheeks. She tried to smile bravely, and it broke Steve's heart.

But he would take the ten minutes to try and figure out how to save Emma. He rushed back to the plot and began to dig. He hit the stopwatch button on his own watch to keep track of time.

1 minute. He furiously dug, not going too deep, but looking for something within a few inches of the surface.

2 minutes. The seconds were flying by on his watch. He glanced back up at Emma. Carl had moved closer and had the gun to Emma's head. Steve tried to focus despite his growing fears that Carl would indeed hurt Emma.

3 minutes. He dug and dug, using his hands to pull up the grass. The church, in characteristic style, had taken excellent care of the cemetery and the grass was thick and lush. He moved around, searching for the North Star. For something. Anything.

4 minutes. He continued digging and sweat broke out on his face and arms. It wasn't the physical activity—he was in excellent shape. It was the thought of Emma being hurt.

5 minutes. He had covered several feet of ground. He was moving further south as he went. Nothing. Nothing.

6 minutes. He kept digging but turned his focus on Emma. Should he rush the gunman? Another glance at the gun pointed at Emma's head told him that he couldn't. He would shoot her long before Steve could get there.

7 minutes. Panic filled him. He started to taste bile. Would he be responsible for Emma's death? He had ruined Kari's life. Would he ruin Emma's as well?

8 minutes. He abandoned the spot he was working on and moved north above his original digging location. He moved

left to right, not bothering to dig, but only prodded with his shovel, hoping to hit something.

9 minutes. He heard the hitman call out a one-minute warning. He flung the shovel into the earth again and again, madly trying, searching. Sweat began to pour down his face, stinging his eyes. His eyes kept furtively darting at the seconds rapidly scrolling through on his watch. He knew he had started his watch a few seconds after Carl's.

He heard a shot go off and he leapt up into action, running to Emma with a loud cry involuntarily coming from his chest and mouth. He would try to save her somehow. He would die trying to save her.

As he sprinted to her, his eyes struggled to comprehend what he was seeing and what he had heard. The hit man had a silencer on his gun, but the shot he had heard was from a rifle and was still echoing. He watched as Carl's body flung forward and collapsed into a heap on the ground.

Another shot rang out and Steve continued his sprint, trying to figure out where the second shot was coming from. Just as he reached Emma, who was crying in her sitting position, he saw her.

She was coming from behind Emma and had a long-range rifle in her hand. It was the same woman he had found bleeding to death in the Vermont visitors' center. It was the same woman he had originally seen at BYU. It was the accomplice.

He reached Emma and pulled her into a protective hug, scanning her body rapidly to look for blood. Emma's face was white and pale. Steve pulled Emma into a standing position and moved her behind him. He could still hear her crying.

He looked at the girl, but she didn't have the gun pointed at them. She still had it trained on Carl and shot him a third time. Steve watched his body twitch and knew he was dead. The girl walked up and smiled.

"Payback is sweet," she said, her eyes bright with fulfillment. "I've been wanting to kill Carl. It was all I could think about as I lay in that hospital bed."

Steve began to reach for his knife behind his back, but she instantly trained the gun on him. "Drop it, Steve."

Steve froze, assessing. He could throw the knife and hit her. But the gun might go off as well and as a long-range rifle, it could pass through his body and still hit Emma.

He finally pulled out the knife and threw it on the ground. "Now that's better," she said relaxing. "You should be happy to see me," she added, lowering her rifle slightly.

"Why's that?" he asked taking the bait.

"Because I owe you one," she explained simply. "You saved my life back in Vermont. Carl had left me for dead. I don't know why you saved me, but you did. It's the first time anyone has ever done anything like that for me. So I owe you."

Steve considered her words in amazement and replied, "Are you going to let us go?"

"Yes," she answered honestly. Steve could feel Emma relax behind him. But Steve stayed on alert—it wouldn't be that easy, he was sure of it. "After you find the last clue for me," she added. "You're close, aren't you? I've been watching you all morning. I saw Carl watching you as well and I was waiting for my chance. You saved my life and now I've saved yours. I just want the final clue and then I'll let you both go."

Emma, feeling braver, came out from behind Steve. "We don't know where it is exactly," she stated.

"Look, Emma. I'll be straight with you," she offered. "I don't want to hurt either of you anymore. I'm in this for the money and for professional advancement. If I don't get it from you, someone else will. And it will be someone like Carl. We need to end this. Right now. With the three of us. Just find the last clue and we all go home."

Emma stepped forward and pleaded, "This clue could embarrass our church. You can't want that to happen. Our leaders separated and hid this document to protect our church. We can't let you have it."

She raised the gun and pointed it back at Emma. Emma took a step backwards. "I really don't care about that, Emma.

195

Don't let my not killing you give you the wrong idea. I don't even believe in God. If there is one, then maybe He'll help you and your church out of this, but I'm not leaving here without the last clue."

She cocked her rifle to emphasize her point. Emma looked at Steve. He had dropped his shovel on his sprint to Emma. "Emma, I believe she is telling the truth. We have to find the last clue." He picked up his shovel and put his arm around Emma. "Let's keep looking."

Emma looked up at Steve with sad eyes. He nodded his head to encourage her. They walked back over to the burial plot and began to dig. Steve found it within a few minutes. There was a clunk as he drove his shovel down into the ground.

At first he thought it was a rock, but as he pulled away the earth, he saw a distinct metal star emerge about three inches underneath the ground. "Emma," he prompted, drawing her gaze over to the star. He glanced up, but the girl had moved closer to them and had the rifle still pointing at them. They would have to just hand over the clue. At least she didn't have the other ones, he reasoned. He had checked Emma's locker as well when he went back for the shovel since he had both keys. Her backpack was still there.

Emma moved over next to Steve and began to smooth out the earth away from the star. As she moved the earth, she realized the star was attached to something. Steve noticed as well and began to dig around the star. As he dug and Emma pulled away the dirt, they saw a rough, long wooden box emerge.

Emma's heart sank. While an hour before, she couldn't wait to find the last clue, now she dreaded finding it and handing it over to people who would use it to try to destroy the church. She sighed as Steve lifted the box out of the earth and set it on the ground next to her.

Steve looked at her and said, "Go ahead and open the box, Emma."

Emma lifted up the lid and found another box inside. She thought of Brigham's wisdom in trying to protect the document from water and other elements. As she opened the second box, she saw a rolled piece of deerskin in the bottom. She lifted it gently out, opened it and studied the parchment.

Reformed Egyptian characters were in neat rows across the page. Emma studied each one of them, wishing she knew the meaning. She went line by line, scanning, looking for the meaning. What could these innocent-looking characters hold that would damage God's church on earth?

"Hand it over, Emma," the girl ordered, interrupting Emma's thoughts.

Emma hesitated. Steve looked at her and a meaningful look passed between them. They had reached the end of the journey. But they had failed. Steve gently took the scroll and parchment and rolled it back up. He then stood and handed it to the girl.

She clutched it in her hand and started to back away, keeping the rifle pointed at Emma. "Thank you both," she said in an exhilarated tone. "You should be proud of yourselves. Not just anyone could have followed the trail and figured out everything. It was very impressive to watch." She continued to back away and when Steve took a step toward her, she fired off a warning shot. "Don't," she pleaded. "I want to keep my word on this. It's important to me that I pay you back for saving my life. Just let me go."

Steve, in answer to her request, put his arms around Emma and held her for at least five minutes. The birds began to sing again around them and when they turned to look, she was gone.

"At least we're alive," Steve said in a defeated voice.

"What does that matter?' Emma spat angrily. "We should have died trying to protect the secret."

"Emma, she doesn't have the other clues," Steve reassured. "I checked—your backpack is still locked away safely in the visitors' center.

"Well, at least that's something," Emma replied with a weak smile. "Let's clean up this mess and then head back to the visitors' center.

They worked quickly to put the box back in the earth and as Steve lowered it down into the ground he suddenly stopped. "Emma, there are some kind of markings on the back of the box," he said puzzled, feeling with his fingers. He pulled the box back out and turned it over. On the bottom were circular carvings, overlapping each other.

"They're moonstones," Emma exclaimed, feeling them with her fingers. "Brigham was quite the carpenter." She turned the box over to look at the engraving. "This carving is beautiful. They had such craftsmanship back then."

"What are moonstones?" Steve asked puzzled.

"It depicts the phases of the moon. They are also on the Salt Lake Temple. It represents birth to resurrection and also a journey from darkness into light," she explained. "Maybe Brigham is just letting us know this is the end of the journey."

"Yes, but why put it on the temple as well?" Steve asked hopefully.

"It could just be a coincidence," she said in a tired voice. Now that her adrenaline had returned to normal, she felt tired and exhausted.

"Just in case, I think we should head back to Salt Lake and take the box with us," Steve suggested.

"Yes, it's time to go home," Emma agreed. "We can at least try and get the second clue translated and see what this is all about. Hopefully, President Thompson has found someone by now whom we can trust to translate it." She thought again about Dr. Mangum, wishing he had lived long enough to complete the translation. As she thought about going home, she realized how empty her life would be at the university without Dr. Mangum there to watch over her.

Steve helped her up and they walked in silence back to the visitors' center. It was crowded now with visitors due to the summer season. They slipped through the crowd and made their way to the lockers. Steve unlocked the lockers and grabbed both their packs. They headed out to the car and Steve began to drive toward the airport, calling the jet pilot on their way to let him know they were ready to head back to Utah.

As Steve drove to the airport, Emma reached inside her backpack for a hair tie. She then closed her pack tightly with the cinch and snapped the buckle into place. She pulled back her hair and then leaned back in her car seat to rest. She was just drifting off to sleep when she bolted upright, her eyes wide and her back rigid, and began to furiously open her pack.

Steve, surprised at her sudden movement, swerved the car into the other lane a few inches while he watched her. He heard a car horn and immediately swerved back into their lane. "What is it, Emma," he asked, glancing over at her again, "What's wrong?"

Emma didn't answer, but began rapidly pulling everything out of her back. Dread filled Steve as he watched— he knew what she was looking for. Emma threw her clothes and personal things aside and looked at the bottom of her pack in disbelief. "They're gone," she said in a whisper. "Everything is gone."

Steve pulled over to the side of the road and began to sift through Emma's things, "Are you sure? Maybe they're in my pack." He then reached in the backseat on the floor for his pack.

"No, they were in mine," she said absently due to shock. "She took them. She took everything."

Steve, not wanting to believe it, went through his pack, but everything was as he left it, neatly packed in military style. He went through Emma's things again, his pulse racing. Nothing.

He looked over at Emma and saw tears running down her cheeks. He leaned over and wrapped his arms around her and held her.

"We failed," Emma continued in a whisper, just staring straight ahead out the front car windshield. "We failed to protect the document."

Steve could tell how hard this was for Emma. She was the type of person that had never failed at anything in her entire life. Steve, on the other hand, had a failed marriage to already adjust him to the idea. Still, deep down he still thought somehow this mission would help him redeem his past mistakes. And now he had failed yet again. Failed to protect the original artifact and now failed to protect the documents themselves.

As he held Emma, he realized at least he hadn't failed in protecting her. She was alive. But would she ever forgive him for their failure? Would she forgive herself?

"At least President Thompson has copies of the first two clues and we have the first translated already," Steve offered. "Once the second clue is translated, we will at least know what we're dealing with. The church can figure out how best to prepare for whatever criticism may come."

"That's little comfort, Steve," Emma replied bitterly.

Yes, Steve knew he was right. This would drive a wedge between them. He slowly released his arms from Emma and resumed his drive toward the airport.

Chapter 37

Preston had never seen RJ so excited. He was in his office when the call came. She had the full document and was on her way back to Atlanta. And she had taken care of Carl for good this time. Three bullets. She was much cheaper than Carl and RJ reveled in the cost savings.

"This is it, Preston," RJ shouted triumphantly, clenching his fists and shaking them in the general direction of Utah. "I've got those Mormons back on their heels now." For good measure, he pulled up SalesTeam's Web site and talked directly to the computer monitor. "Enjoy your success today, you delusional cult followers—because within a few days, you'll be history. No one will ever want to do business with you again. You'll lay off all of your people. You will be the laughing stock of the industry. You'll need all of your extra wives to console you then."

Preston thought about correcting RJ. He knew that Mormons no longer practiced polygamy and hadn't for around a century. But it was pointless. Preston subconsciously adjusted his tie. All of a sudden, it was feeling very tight around his neck.

"Preston, call an emergency board meeting for tonight," RJ barked, "I want to tell all of those blood-sucking idiots where they can go—in person! Trying to take away my company. *My* company, Preston. How *dare* they! They'll be changing their tune when our stock goes through the roof in the next few days. When we make our announcement."

"RJ," Preston tried to reason. "We don't even know what the document says yet. We should hold off and wait for the translation."

"Preston," RJ scolded. "You worry too much! You think this could be anything other than completely obliterating for the Mormon church? They separated the pieces and buried it. *Buried* it, Preston. Sounds pretty damning to me. No, we're going ahead. I'm sure of it."

Preston knew there was no way to stop him now. He had that determined glint in his eye.

"She will be here around 8:00 tonight," RJ continued, turning his full focus on Preston. He put both of his hands on Preston's shoulders and looked him square in the eye. "I want you here, Preston. I want you here when she comes. You've stood by me at a very difficult time, Preston. And I want you by my side as we go through our finest hour. As we embarrass and humiliate the Mormons and SalesTeam."

Preston managed a weak smile and then turned more practical. "Did you find someone to translate the document?" he asked, hoping that would delay things while he figured out what to do.

"Yes, and he's already here," RJ announced triumphantly. "I found him a few days ago. Bookish fella from Princeton. Expert in ancient Egyptian languages. He was pretty cheap as well, considering how much everything else has cost. Probably because he's on summer break. Flew him in two days ago. I've got him staying at the Marriott downtown. And I used my rewards points, Preston, so it's not even costing you a thing! Not that money will be of any consequence after we destroy SalesTeam. Their clients will come over in throngs to us, Preston. Maybe we should look at raising our prices, in anticipation of that. It will help us cover some of this overhead..."

Preston listened to RJ ramble on and on without really hearing him. Inwardly, he was trying to formulate a plan. Any plan. He didn't have much time.

RJ finally finished talking and took a business call. Preston slowly walked back to his office and closed the door, locking it. He looked at his immaculately kept desk. All of the folders on his desk were neatly stacked with computer-printed labels on them. The order around him betrayed the chaos in his mind.

He finally gave in and pulled out his mother's picture. This was his favorite one. She was standing in front of a building all dressed in white. He thought that she looked like an angel. She *was* an angel, he thought to himself, gently caressing the picture.

Memories came flooding back and he finally let them come. He remembered the day it all had started. It was the 4th of July. His mom had the day off from both of her jobs and Preston stayed close to her all day, not wanting to leave her side, even though he was a teenager by then. She was humming and singing around their trailer home as she tidied it up. They were alone together. All of his sisters were off living on their own by then. They were coming over later that night and bringing fireworks.

As Preston watched his mom, he noticed that she had a few gray hairs at the front and side of her head. She stooped a bit when she walked and he realized abruptly that she was getting older. "Momma," he offered, "When I get older, I'm going to work at a big company in Atlanta and earn lots of money. That way, you'll never have to work again." He stood up and put his arms around his mom affectionately. "I'll take care of you, Momma," he assured, emphasizing his point with a kiss.

His momma chuckled at that and replied, "As long as you're a good person, Pressie, and you stay close to God, then I'll always be proud of you. Money ain't everything, sweetheart. Being together and loving God, now those are the good things in life."

Preston glanced around at their rundown trailer and in his heart didn't agree. But he was happy to be around his momma, so he didn't say anything. He didn't want to spoil the day. It was so rare that they got to be together.

Just then, he heard a knock on their thin, trailer door. He protectively glanced out of the kitchen window to see who it was. There had been some trouble lately in the trailer park. Someone had been stabbed a few months ago. But what he saw wasn't what he expected at all. He saw two young boys, in white shirts and ties with nametags on, standing and smiling toward the door. He was just about to shout through the door and tell them to go away, when Preston's mom swung open the door and said a friendly hello.

"Good morning, ma'am," one of the young boys said. Preston sized him up. He had a long drawl and Preston recognized his voice as Texan. He didn't look much older than Preston's 16 years.

"You boys must be hot on a day like this," Preston's mom said kindly. "Ya'll come in and get in the cool. I just made some fresh lemonade."

They both smiled and accepted her invitation. Preston felt alarm bells going off in his head. What were two young boys doing in white shirts and ties? And in July? Maybe they were selling something. Well, they had come to the wrong neighborhood, Preston thought with a laugh. No one had money around here.

Preston's mom went into their small kitchen and poured out two generous glasses of lemonade, selecting her best glasses. It was a matched pair that Preston's sister had given her for Christmas last year.

"Now, what brings ya'll around today?" Preston's mother asked kindly, smiling at the two young boys. Preston moved closer—he wanted to hear this.

"We're sharing God's word, ma'am," the Texan drawled between gulps. "About how He still speaks to us today."

"Amen and praise the Lord," Preston's mom said softly in agreement. Preston's mom attended a Baptist church nearby. Preston went occasionally, but usually found an excuse not to go.

"Then you agree that man can still speak to God, so you do?" the other young man asked. Preston didn't recognize his accent and realized he was from far away. England or maybe Ireland. He wasn't quite sure.

"Why of course I do," Preston's mom answered warmly. "Didn't He go and tell me that you two boys would come and see me today?" Her smile was broad and sincere. The missionaries looked at each other in surprise.

Preston looked at his mom, but wasn't shocked. She was a deeply spiritual woman. Over the years, she had explained to Preston that she had seen her mother who was dead come to her and counsel her at critical times in her life. She had also heard God's voice counsel her as well.

Preston had tried to pray and hear God's voice as well, like his mother, but he never had. He felt warm when he prayed, but that was all. Over time, he realized how special his mom was and how much she relied on God to get her through each day.

But Preston, still feeling protective, asked, "God told you they were coming, Momma?"

"Yes, He did, Pressie, last night" she acknowledged sweetly. "And He said they had an important message for me and that I should listen. So I got up early this morning, cleaned my house and made some fresh lemonade for ya'll comin'."

The missionaries looked at each other again and then the Texan continued, "Well, ma'am, that's because we are His servants and we do have a special message for ya'll today. It's about a boy named Joseph Smith—"

"Joseph Smith?" Preston interrupted as he stood up. "You're *Mormons*!" he spat. On the few occasions where Preston did go to with his mother to church, he had heard their pastor comment on the Mormons. It wasn't complimentary. He also knew a boy at school who was a Mormon. Everyone picked on him and made fun of him. *Mormons*, Preston thought with disdain.

"Now, Preston," his mom interjected, "Stop being rude to our guests." He could hear a warning tone in his mother's voice and knew he had crossed the line. Why did these Mormons have to come and spoil his lovely day with his momma? "Now, young man, please continue and my son *won't* be interrupting you again." Preston sat down dejectedly next to his mother.

"Thank you ma'am," the Texas continued, glancing hesitantly at Preston and then said, "Yes, siree, we sure do get that reaction a lot, but Christ himself had a lot of opposition as well."

"Praise His name," Preston's mom agreed softly.

"Well, ma'am, as you know, there are a lot of churches out there," he continued with a smile. "And back in the 1800s, it wasn't much different. Joseph Smith was only 14 when he was trying to figure out which church to join. He went to lots of different congregations with his family, tryin' to decide. But he couldn't figure out which one was true, ma'am. So he was reading in the bible one night, James chapter 1 verse 5 and it said that if anyone needed an answer, they could ask of God, and He would answer their prayers."

Preston's mom stood up and for a second Preston thought she would have them leave, but she went into her room and came out with her worn copy of the Bible. The missionaries waited while she found the scripture.

Then the other missionary continued, "So Joseph decided to pray and ask God, so he did. He was dead serious about it, so he was. So he went into the woods near his house and began to earnestly pray to God, asking Him which church to join. And in answer to his prayers, he saw God and Jesus Christ." The missionary paused for a reaction, looking at Preston's mother.

"What did they look like?" she finally asked, deep in thought.

The missionary, who they later found to be from Northern Ireland, pulled out a flipchart and went through his illustrations. Finally finding the one he wanted, he turned it around and showed Preston's mom the artist's rendering.

She gazed at the picture for a full minute, silence filling the small trailer. Preston looked at his momma and could tell it was deeply affecting her. He looked at the picture as well and could feel, deep down, something stirring.

"Yes, sir, I do believe it," Preston's mom finally added, still not taking her eyes off of the picture.

The missionaries looked at each other again and then the missionary from Northern Ireland asked, "You believe it's true? You believe he saw God and Jesus Christ?"

"Yes, indeed I do, yes," she emphasized. "God loves all of us. If Joseph asked, God wouldn't ignore him."

"So you see, ma'am, Joseph did ask them which church to join," the Texan missionary continued. "And they told him none of 'em. That Christ's true church was no longer on the earth. But that it was time to bring it back—to restore it. So that's what they did. They restored Christ's true church, with the priesthood authority of Christ given to Joseph Smith by John the Baptist and Peter, James and John."

"Amen," she added, deep in thought.

The missionary from Northern Ireland pulled a book out of his backpack. Preston knew what it was—it was that Mormon bible he had heard about at school. "Joseph was also visited by an angel," he taught. "His name was Moroni. He was a prophet who lived here in America a long time ago, so he did. His ancestors were prompted by God to leave Jerusalem and travel here to America. This book is a record of their people from the time they left Jerusalem until they were almost all destroyed in America. It is another testament of Jesus Christ, so it is. And I know it's the word of God."

Preston's mom reached out her hand and took the book. She then reached into her pocket and pulled out some money. "How much do I owe ya'll for this?" she asked thoughtfully.

"Nothing, ma'am," the Texan drawled. "It's a gift. We'd like you to read it and we'd like to come back and visit you again in a few days to teach you some more."

Preston's mom held the book close to her chest. "I thank you kindly," she replied. "And I will read it."

The missionaries left then and Preston started in on his mom, "Mom, they're devil-worshipers, they're not even Christians. Don't let them back in the house."

"Now, Pressie," she replied with patience in her voice, "Of course they're not devil-worshipers. They're good boys and you can see that for yourself. Just because something's different, doesn't mean we have to be afraid of it."

"But, Momma," Preston continued, trying again, "Everyone knows Mormons ain't nothing but trouble. Please stay away from them, momma."

Preston's mother had been washing the lemonade glasses, but she stopped, turned toward Preston, took his hand with her wet, soapy hands and said, "Now, Pressie, that's enough. I'm a grown woman and know my own mind. God himself told me they were comin'. And I've been having more dreams about Momma. I feel this is important. I'm going to give it a chance. Besides, didn't you feel something while they were here?"

Preston hated lying to his mother, but he felt he needed to protect her. "No, I didn't," he said stubbornly, raising his chin in defiance.

"Well, now, Pressie, I did," she replied softly. "I felt something powerful. It's the hand of God and I'll not turn my back on Him." To emphasize her point, she finished doing the dishes and then picked up her copy of the Book of Mormon and went into her bedroom to read.

Preston saw her reading the Book of Mormon a lot over the next few weeks. Every spare minute when she was home, she would read. She seemed fascinated by the book. Preston even began to be curious himself and picked it up a couple of times when she was at work. But to him it just sounded like a bunch of religious language, like the Bible, and he wasn't interested.

The missionaries came back several times trying to visit his mother. He was happy to tell them that she was at work. They tried a couple more times, but their visits became less and less frequent. Preston was happy that it seemed it was all going to fizzle, until one day. That horrible, awful day.

He had come home from school and was puzzled to hear his mother in her bedroom when she was usually at work. He walked back and was shocked to see her lying in her bed. Her face was gray and withdrawn. Beads of sweat had formed on her face and she looked at Preston without even seeing him.

"Momma, Momma," he cried as he dropped his backpack on the floor and rushed to her bedside. "What is it, Momma? Are you okay?"

His mom didn't even acknowledge he was there. Preston reached over and grabbed her arm and then quickly pulled it back in shock. Her skin was hot and clammy. He stood up in desperation, trying to figure out what to do. His sisters would know. He went and dialed their home numbers, but knew they would be at work. He left a message, hoping they would somehow come home early. He didn't have their work numbers.

He thought of calling an ambulance, but they didn't have health insurance and he worried about the cost. He decided to run to the neighbors and see if anyone could help. He opened the door and sprinted toward the nearest trailer and ran headlong into the missionaries, knocking over the Texan.

His first reaction as he got up was anger, but it quickly melted away. "M-mm-my mom, she's very sick," he blurted out, tears forming in his eyes. "I . . . I don't know what to do. I just came home from school and found her like this."

The missionaries quickly went into the trailer with Preston following forlornly behind. He couldn't lose his momma. She was everything to him. His momma that worked so hard. His momma that always put everyone else first.

The tears were coming freely now and streaming down Preston's face. Panic filled his heart. Through his tears, he saw the missionaries stand very close to his mother's bed and put their hands on her head. One of them had a small container and dropped what looked like a drop of oil onto her head.

Preston began to be suspicious of what weird rite they were about to do, when he saw them both bow their heads and begin a prayer. Confused, he bowed his head as well and pleaded inwardly for God to save his mother.

He listened to the missionaries' prayer and as he did, he felt a warmth spreading through his body. He had never felt anything like that before. It started in his head and went down to his toes. He felt so peaceful and happy. He knew, somehow he knew, everything was going to be all right. He heard the missionary from Northern Ireland say, "In the name of Jesus Christ and according to your faith, rise, and be whole."

He opened his eyes and met his mother's gaze. Her eyes had opened and she smiled at Preston. He was then amazed as he watched his mother sit up and then stand up. She hugged both of the missionaries at once, and then came over and hugged Preston. He stood in disbelief, feeling her cool skin against his.

"Momma," Preston whispered into her ear, "Momma."

"Praise be to God," she responded to him. "In His name, I have been healed."

As Preston hugged his mom, he stared across the room at the two missionaries. They had bowed their head in thanks and then were smiling at his mom. Preston couldn't say anything—his amazement overwhelmed him.

They stayed all evening and taught his mom. She made them dinner and read scriptures from the Bible and the Book of Mormon with them. Preston just stood by mutely watching.

The things they were teaching her made sense. And it was clear that they had power to heal from God. He watched his mother all night—she was perfectly well. Better than well. She seemed to glow with happiness and radiate peace.

As the missionaries were leaving, he walked outside with them. They looked worried, thinking Preston would tell them not to come back, but Preston reached out his hand to both of them and shook it.

"Thank you both," he said earnestly, looking them in the eye. "You saved my mother's life."

A smile spread across the Texan's face, as wide as Texas itself, "We didn't save her. God did, Preston. We're just His servants."

Tears came to Preston's eyes and he nodded his head, not trusting himself to say any more. His mother was baptized the following week. Preston and his sisters were there and Preston again felt something during the baptismal ceremony. The same warmth returned and spread through his body.

As his mother came up out of the water, her face glowed and she praised God. She was so happy that day. The missionaries had taken her picture in her white baptismal clothes before the baptism and had given Preston and his mom a copy. She truly looked like an angel.

Preston had attended church with her a few times, but had politely declined the missionaries' invitation to be baptized. A year later, he was off to college and living his own life. But he never forgot what happened that day. And from that point on, he always treated Mormon missionaries, as well as any members he encountered, with kindness and respect.

His mother had pleaded with him to join as well as his sisters, but they never did. After his mother died, it seemed all in the past.

When he met Beth, he told her everything. Beth was a strong Christian, like his mother, and he loved that about her. But the Mormon church just seemed too restrictive to Preston, particularly paying a tithing on all his earnings. As Preston advanced in his career, he became obsessed with money.

The missionaries came to their home one day when the kids were little. He invited them in and had them stay for dinner, but when asked if they were interested in learning more, Preston politely declined again.

Preston's phone rang and it brought him back to reality. He didn't pick up and let it go to voicemail. He looked one more time at his mother's picture on her baptism day. He could almost hear her voice, pleading with him, to save the Mormons, just as they had saved her.

Ideas started to come to him and he reached over for his yellow legal notepad. He uncapped his expensive fountain pen and began to write. The ideas flowed freely and when he finished writing, he knew what he had to do.

Chapter 38

"Here's our girl!" RJ boomed as Callie walked into the room, clapping her on the shoulder. "I always knew you had talent, Callie. Yes, I did!"

Preston watched from the edge of the boardroom in amusement. He had never met the girl that RJ had hired as a backup on the Mormon project. She looked young and beautiful, but Preston could see an edge in her eyes.

The boardroom door opened and RJ's son, Riley, came through it. He was immaculately dressed in expensive clothes and looked annoyed to have been called in. "Riley, my son, glad you could come and be here for your dad's finest moment!" Preston wondered if RJ had been drinking in celebration. He hadn't seen him this giddy in years.

"Wouldn't miss it, dad," Riley replied in a fake voice and his eyes immediately went to Callie. "Hello again, Cal. Nice job." His eyes lingered on her and he instantly decided that he would ditch his date that night and take Callie out. She was looking good.

The door opened again and a bookish professor came through, looking nervous. "Professor Martin, come in, come in," RJ welcomed. Preston could see that RJ was in his element. He was finally going to achieve his goal to destroy the Mormons.

Callie, straight to the point, said as she patted her backpack, "Where's my final payment?"

"Now, my dear, let's see the document first. Preston has the money ready to wire to your usual account," RJ countered politely, still in a jovial mood. Callie looked at Preston and he nodded in confirmation.

Callie walked over to the board table and one by one took out the three pieces of parchment. The professor moved closer and as she unrolled them he urged, "Gently, gently." Silence filled the room while everyone stared at the three pieces. The professor sat down and lined up the edges, making a perfect match.

He then took out his notebook and began to scribble notes, mumbling to himself. RJ moved over to stand behind him, to watch the translation. Preston didn't move from his spot in the corner. Riley's eyes were glued to Callie and she leaned over and whispered in his ear. Riley had surprise in his eyes and whispered back, quickly glancing at his father.

But RJ's full attention was focused on Professor Martin and the translation. He was rapidly writing down words on his notepad. RJ leaned in closer and read aloud.

"Let...all...the...Saints....of....the...heavenly......Go d...listen....and...hear...His.......word...Let...not...their... hearts...be...closed...but...open....to...the...will...of...the .....Lord."

RJ began to pace the room in anticipation. He glanced over at Preston nervously. Preston returned his gaze with a reassuring smile.

"For....God...our...Father...loves...all....of...his...chi ldren...the...same...and...they...are...all...his...children. Therefore...let...the...authority...of...God...be... given...to...all...worthy...men...no...matter...what...their ...race...or...color...of...skin."

"What?" RJ exclaimed, clutching the professor by the shoulder. "What is it saying?"

Preston inwardly gave a sigh of relief and then walked over to RJ to explain, "It's saying their priesthood authority should be given to African Americans, to all men."

RJ stared at Preston with a puzzled expression. Preston continued, "They believe they have the priesthood of Christ, of God himself. The authority to act in his name. But from the time the church was founded, blacks didn't have the priesthood. It wasn't until 1978 that the church extended the priesthood authority to African American men. It's quite a controversial point for them."

RJ's eyes narrowed suspiciously, "Preston, how do you know so much about these Mormons?"

"As always, RJ I did some research when you began this project," Preston answered smoothly. "I wanted to know what we were up against, what challenges we might face, if indeed we did find some Mormon secret."

"But it doesn't make sense!" RJ barked. "This isn't a damning secret. Why would the Mormons try to hide this?" He then turned to the professor and shouted, "You must have translated it wrong, Professor."

The professor squirmed in his chair and did his best not to meet RJ's eyes. "I haven't finished the translation yet," he said in a mere whisper.

"That's, right, that's right," RJ boomed, grasping on to the idea. "Keep going—maybe there's something else." He then added menacingly, "There better be something else."

The professor turned his attention back to the document and began to scribble furiously.

"And...if...my...people...do...this...and...follow...my ...counsel...they...shall...be...blessed...for...generations ...to...come.　　　For...my....children...must...face... trials...if...they...are....to...be...worthy...to...live...in...m y...kingdom.　　　For...God...is...the...same....yesterday ....today...and...forever...Amen."

RJ finished reading it out loud and was silent for a minute. Preston could see his eyes roaming over the whole translation again, thinking.

"It *was* damning, RJ, *back then*" Preston interjected, trying to help him understand. "Based on my research, the

Mormons encountered severe opposition because they were different. The mobs burned their homes, beat them, murdered them and chased them from state to state. When Joseph Smith wrote this, African Americans were still slaves. Is there a date on it?" Preston asked the professor.

Professor Martin looked at the document again and said, "Yes, in the top corner. It says April 23, 1828."

"RJ," Preston continued, "This was long before Civil War days. African Americans were little more than property back then. If this revelation would have become public back then, it would have been one more thing for their enemies to use against them. The Mormon church leaders, Smith and Young, must have felt it wasn't the right time to make it public because of what they felt it might do to their people. So they didn't make it public, but hid enough clues for the document to be found. Maybe they hoped one day the church and the world would be ready for it and they hoped it would come to light then."

RJ considered Preston's words and then slammed down his fist on the boardroom table. The table shook and so did the professor. "This *isn't* what I wanted. This *isn't* what I needed. I need something that will *destroy* the Mormons!" RJ shouted, looking around the room for answers.

Riley looked at his dad in amusement, "Just change it, dad. Change it to say blacks aren't equal and that they will never have the priesthood, or whatever it was. That should be damning enough in our day and age."

Preston looked at Riley in alarm, "You can't forge a historic document."

"Why not?" RJ exclaimed. "I've done far worse, that's for sure." He then turned to the professor and said, "Professor, I want you to change the translation or change the original, I don't care. But it has to come out bad for the Mormons."

The professor looked nervously at RJ and then back at Preston. He then bravely stood up, gathered his briefcase and said, "I don't feel comfortable doing it." He then headed for the door, his eyes on the floor, hoping no one would stop him.

RJ shifted into his path to stop him. "Now, professor, it's not as bad as you think. Just tell us how to alter the document to make it say the opposite. I will do it myself. You just have to show me how." When the professor still hesitated, RJ added, "I will make it very worth your while, professor."

He hesitated. He had a penchant for gambling and he hadn't been doing very well lately. He had some huge debts that he was hiding from his family. He needed the money. "How much?" he asked looking RJ in the eye.

"Two hundred fifty thousand," RJ offered, not even glancing at Preston for approval.

"Agreed." The professor turned around and walked back over to the document. "It's actually quite simple really. There are two characters, one that describes blacks being equal and the other indicates they will receive the priesthood. If you place dots here and here," he pointed to the document at the symbols, "it will mean the opposite of what I stated."

RJ walked over to look at the document and where the professor was pointing. He reached into his pocket and was about to put the dots on the parchment when Preston interrupted, "RJ, don't do it."

RJ froze—Preston had never told him what to do before. He was shocked. He hesitated and turned to look at Preston.

"RJ, you can't just take a fountain pen and make dots on a historic document. Anyone who examines it will be able to tell that it's been altered," Preston explained, walking over to RJ. He then continued, "Let's make a photocopy of the document, add the dots then, make another copy, and we'll keep the originals locked up in our company safe. We then release the copies to the public tomorrow morning."

"What if someone asks to see the originals?" RJ asked. "To prove that it isn't a forgery?"

"Then we will let them examine either the top or bottom piece for authenticity, but not the middle. We will say we're not willing to let the entire document out into the open for security reasons," Preston explained.

To emphasize his point, Preston took out his checkbook and wrote out a check for the professor. "Professor, you'll remember that I had you sign a nondisclosure agreement for this. If you disclose any of this to anyone, we will be able to sue you for full damages," he emphasized.

"Not to mention that we have friends," RJ added. "Very dangerous friends." He glanced over at Callie and she smirked in response. Yes, she was now RJ's go-to person. She had finally made it.

Preston took the document over to the copy machine and carefully lined up the pages. He copied the document and then took it over to the professor. He felt more comfortable not marking the original, so he marked the photocopies with the two dots, being careful to do it in the exact place. Preston then photocopied the document again and instructed the professor to write out another translation, including the dots.

He paged his administrative assistant who was waiting at her desk. She was a notary public. He had her notarize the professor's translation and then sent her home. He then rolled up the originals into the deerskin coverings and walked over to an expensive armoire in the boardroom. He used his key to open the armoire and then rapidly dialed the combination of the safe, blocking everyone's view with his body. Only he and RJ knew the code. He put the documents inside the large safe and then spun the dial and relocked the armoire.

"Thank you, professor," he said, walking the professor out. "We appreciate your services." After he closed the board room door, he turned to look at RJ.

"I've just paid $250,000 for two dots," RJ snorted. "But, it was worth it. To destroy the Mormons? It was very worth it."

Callie was tired of waiting patiently and stepped forward, "RJ, I've delivered the document. I want my final payment."

"Yes, yes, of course, my dear," RJ agreed looking at Preston. Preston sat down at the boardroom table and opened up his laptop. He had the bank transfer information all set up and ready to go. He pressed the transfer button and Callie looked at her smartphone where she had her bank account info pulled up. She refreshed and confirmed receiving the money.

"Thank you, gentlemen," she said and she picked up her pack and slung it over her shoulder. "I feel like celebrating," she added, looking slyly in Riley's direction.

Riley picked up on the cue and replied earnestly, "Me, too. See ya, Dad. Good night, Preston."

RJ watched them leave and now alone with Preston, he walked over to the minibar and helped himself. He poured a large glass of whiskey. "Join me, Preston?" he asked jovially.

Preston smiled and walked over to the minibar. He wasn't a whiskey drinker, so he reached into the fridge and pulled out a bottle of champagne. "I've been saving this," Preston stated, "for a special occasion."

He uncorked the champagne bottle and poured himself and RJ a glass each. "A toast," he proposed, handing RJ his glass. "To you, RJ. For all you've done for me and for this company." RJ smiled, reveling in his success and heartily clinked glasses with Preston.

They talked late into the night about how to release the document. RJ wanted it to come directly from their company, but Preston advised that they release it in a more subtle way. In the end, they decided to send it to the NAACP through a third-party lawyer who wouldn't disclose their identity.

Later that night, Riley and Callie were having dinner together at an exclusive restaurant in Atlanta. Riley had always liked Callie—she was beautiful, but also intelligent and gritty. He liked the way she had come from the slums and was determined to make her way in the world by herself.

They were just finishing dessert when Callie leaned over the table and said softly, "I have something you might want."

Riley smiled, reached over to softly caress her hand and implied coyly, "I know you do."

But Callie surprised him and reached over for her backpack. She took out a manila folder and opened it up. "I didn't tell your dad about this—I was saving it for you," she said with a smile. "It's Dr. Mangum's research—his *secret* research."

"That's not what I want," Riley replied and then leaned over and whispered in her ear, "I want you."

But Callie was all business. "Later," she whispered back. "You're going to want this, I promise, Riley. I looked through all of it on the flight back. There are some pretty interesting things in here."

"Such as?" Riley asked in a very disinterested voice. Historic documents were just boring to him. He was much more interested in live and beautiful things such as Callie.

"I can tell you're not interested," Callie said and began to put the folder back into her backpack. "I'm sure your dad will be. I just gave you first offer because you helped me get in with your dad."

Riley thought about her words. It would be very nice to have one over on his dad, to have something he didn't have. It could be good leverage if he ever fell out of grace with him or needed money.

"All right," Riley answered, "I'm interested. How much?"

"There are a lot of documents in here and some of them are very valuable," Callie bartered.

Riley pulled away—this was the one thing he hated about Callie. Everything was money to her. Money meant nothing to Riley—it was just something he always had. Riley thought about how much he had and weighed up his offer.

"Your dad would give me a million for this," Callie started.

"My dad doesn't have a million left to give," Riley answered honestly, getting bored with the conversation. He turned his focus to the pretty server who came back to gather up their plates. Maybe he would go home with her instead of Callie.

"How about $500K," she countered, looking intently at Riley.

Riley inwardly laughed. She must think I actually have money, he thought to himself. He spent enough to give off the impression he did, but when it came to ready cash, he didn't have as much as people thought. "Check, please," he said to the waitress, giving her a dazzling smile. She was definitely looking more fun than Callie.

Callie went ahead and put the documents in her backpack and closed it. "I'll look for another buyer," she stated disappointed.

Riley looked back at her and gave his final offer, "50K," he said.

"Done," Callie said and then added, "But you take me home with you instead of the waitress." Callie had always liked Riley and she knew one day he would inherit his dad's money. It would be good to stay in his good graces, even though she could get a lot more for the documents elsewhere.

"Deal," Riley replied. He would have to sell one of his luxury cars, but it would be worth it.

Chapter 39

Preston was in the office early the next morning. He had his assistant cancel all of his meetings and he feverishly made all of the final arrangements. He made several calls to set things in motion. He knew this day was coming and had been preparing for over a week.

He then instructed his lawyer to leak the news about the document to the New York Times. Within a few hours, it was all over the news. The lawyer sent the photocopied document to the NAACP and the news was full of outrage over the document.

The Mormon church, of course, called for authentication of the document. Preston's lawyer scheduled the authentication, only disclosing the first piece of parchment, saying they feared for the document's safety. Preston had arranged for a third-party to authenticate the document. He testified that given the type of parchment, the handwriting and the ink used, that the document was indeed from 1828 and was Joseph Smith's handwriting. The lawyer then produced the notarized translation from Professor Martin. The Mormon church demanded the full document be released and that the translation be verified from another expert. But the attorney continued to find excuses not to release the document—to stall.

The board, pleased with the news and knowing it would hurt SalesTeam, unanimously apologized to RJ and reassured him of their full confidence. Clients began to call voicing their concerns about SalesTeam and discussions of transferring the business kept RJ sequestered in his office night and day.

The week played out exactly as Preston had hoped. RJ left early on Friday to celebrate and didn't come into the office as usual on Saturday. Preston used the day to finalize his plans.

When he came into the office on Sunday morning, all was quiet. He felt sad as he walked through the halls. He had been with the company a long time. He slowly cleaned out his desk and carried the boxes one by one to his car. Beth had offered to come and help him, but he wanted to be alone.

It took several hours to box everything up. He carefully emptied his office, cleaning his desk, keyboard and monitor. He then wiped his computer's hard drive, deleting all of the files. It felt cleansing to erase the past. Looking back at his years at SalesPro, he wasn't proud of everything he had done, but he was setting everything right in the end.

He called Beth around lunchtime to check on her progress. Beth had been packing for days. They had received an excellent offer on their home and Preston was pleased with the profit. He had sold all of their cars and he was carefully putting their money into various savings accounts that were well protected.

Beth sounded a bit teary on the phone. The kids were there helping her and they were all reminiscing the past. But Beth reassured him this was what she wanted and she was excited for their future together. Just before they hung up, she told Preston how proud she was of him.

He had several letters printed out on his desk. The first one was to his administrative assistant. She had been with him for eight years and was invaluable to him. In a day and age when administrative assistants were becoming obsolete, Preston fought to keep her. She was incredibly intelligent and routinely provided unique strategic input and ideas that were well above her pay grade. She had worked long hours without complaint, even though she was a single mom.

His letter was full of praise and thanks. He also included a letter of recommendation. She was a good woman and

Preston had tried to shield her from the unsavory parts of SalesPro, but there was a good chance she would be unhappy once he left. Preston wrote out a generous bonus check for her and sealed the envelope. He walked over to her desk and put the envelope under her keyboard with just the edge showing.

He then reviewed his letters for RJ. The first was a letter of resignation and he had a copy for the board as well. He thanked them for all of their years of support in his position and wished them well.

The second letter was more detailed and more personal:

Dear RJ,

First of all, I want to thank you for everything you have done for me. You gave me a chance early in my career and believed in me, something that not everyone in Atlanta would do for an African American professional at an executive level.

I have watched you work tirelessly to build this company and I know how much you love it. I have kept my promise and have helped you save SalesPro. I have also worked to save you, RJ. I'm sure at first you will be angry at what I've done, but it's the best for everyone and I have ensured that you will come out ahead because of it.

I am returning the original document to the Mormon church. It was wrong to try to destroy them and to falsify the document. Hate and anger are wrong and will only end up destroying you, RJ. My mother taught me that.

You see, my mother was a Mormon and was an incredible Christian woman. You never knew her—she died before I came here. But the Mormon church brought her a lot of peace and comfort. I honestly believe they are good people. Two of their missionaries saved my mother's life once. I owe them a life debt and hope it is repaid with this act.

But like I said, I haven't forgotten you, RJ. Over the years, I was in the position to do a few favors for some of our clients. One in particular fell on some hard times many years ago and I allowed them to delay their payments for almost a year. The cash relief was what they needed to make key investments and they went on to launch internationally shortly after that and become a market leader. A few years later, they were lured away by SalesTeam. I talked with the CEO this week, called in a return favor, and they are bringing their $50M program back to SalesPro.

I have ensured that SalesPro's stock has risen beyond expectations and your position as CEO is very secure.

By the time you read this tomorrow morning, the Mormon church will have the original document and will be issuing a press release to that effect, countering the false document. Since we released the document through our lawyer, he can claim confidentiality and he is prepared for the onslaught. He will simply state that he was never given full access to the document and was just making public his clients' claims.

It will not be traced back to you or to SalesPro. Dr. Martin is protected because he will just say he only saw the photocopy, not the original and since he is under NDA, he can't disclose who asked him to do the translation.

I am retiring and Beth and I are moving to a tropical location. I plan to work on my golf game and travel the world with Beth.

Thanks again for everything and I wish you and Riley all of the best.

Sincerely,

Preston Charles Montgomery

Preston carefully folded up the document and slid it into an envelope. He then walked across the marble floor over to the board room and opened the thick door. He looked at the expensive mahogany table and soft, leather chairs and thought about all of the long nights he had spent here with tempers raging. Suddenly, it all seemed so unimportant and all he wanted to do was get away with Beth.

Preston walked over to the armoire and carefully unlocked it. He dialed the combination of the safe and it clicked open. He slid out the deerskin scrolls and replaced them with the thick envelope. He locked the safe back up and spun the dial. He gently put the documents into his briefcase and locked it.

He walked back to his office, lost in thought. He took one last glance at his office and then firmly pulled the door closed. As he walked toward the elevator, he felt he was walking on air. All of the business burdens of the past years seemed to fall away with each step toward his new life. He had plenty of money to take care of Beth for the rest of his life. The kids were set.

He loosened his tie as he descended in the elevator. He would never wear a tie again, he vowed. It felt good to take it off. He had worn one too much of his life.

He thought about Beth and their life ahead. They had been like newlyweds again, staying up late each night, planning their future. They had purchased a beautiful, remodeled beach house on the North Shore of Oahu, Hawaii. They had stayed there three summers ago for two weeks as a family and had fallen in love with it. A wealthy California businessman owned it as an investment, but only went once a year and it was easy to convince him to sell it to them.

Beth loved the Pacific and they planned to start their world travels with visiting each island in Hawaii and then go to Fiji. From there, they would start circumnavigating the world, taking three or four big trips each year. Preston could see himself golfing two or three times each week and spending the rest of the time lying on the beach with Beth while she read.

The house had several guest rooms and the kids would come home and visit often. He and Beth would also visit them. He would reconnect with his kids and get to know them better. In five or seven years, he might even have some grandchildren.

It sounded wonderful and all of the sudden, he couldn't wait for his new life to begin.

His body was relaxed and happy as he exited the elevator and searched for his car keys in his pocket. He turned to the alarm panel in the lobby and was just punching in the numbers to set the alarm when he heard a noise.

He paused and turned to look. He saw RJ coming through the front door, putting his keys in his pocket. Panic filled Preston's mind and chest. RJ never came in the office on Sundays. He had been counting on that when he set everything up. He thought of his empty office upstairs and his briefcase suddenly felt heavy with the documents inside. He had planned everything meticulously, but he hadn't planned on this. If RJ went upstairs and realized what Preston was doing, he would try and stop him.

"Preston!" RJ said casually, walking toward him smiling. "What are you doing here?"

Preston's mind raced with options and he forced his face into a smile and tried to look relaxed. He had to get out of this building with the documents. And he preferably had to get RJ out as well. "You know me, I always work on Sundays," Preston answered casually, hearing a slight betraying tremor in his voice. He widened his smile to compensate and added, "But the question is, what are *you* doing here?"

RJ didn't seem to notice Preston's discomfort and replied, "I got so drunk last night that I forgot I have a presentation due to Microsoft by 8:00 tomorrow morning. Got to finish it up and get it out tonight."

Preston swallowed—he wouldn't be able to get RJ out of the office now. RJ lived by client deadlines. He wouldn't risk losing the business no matter what.

RJ added, "Why don't you stick around and give me a hand?" Preston thought he heard something in RJ's voice, but he couldn't be sure. He was probably being paranoid; his heart was racing.

"I wish I could," Preston said, shifting a step closer to the door. "But I promised Beth I would take her out to dinner tonight. She's been on at me about all of the late nights lately," he lied.

"Yes, it's been crazy this week," RJ replied, not moving to the elevator.

Preston could hear he was in one of his talkative moods, so he glanced at his watch. "Yeah, I'd better get going. We have reservations and you know how I hate to be late."

RJ seemed to consider Preston's words and then replied, "Well, you and Beth have a good time. You deserve it. I'll see you in the morning."

Preston relaxed as he saw RJ move toward the elevator. "Will do," he said and walked quickly toward the front door. As he left the building, he glanced back through the glass door to see RJ getting in the elevator. Once the doors closed, he sprinted for his car.

He pushed the unlock button on his remote from several feet away and threw his briefcase into the passenger seat. He slammed the gearbox into reverse and cringed as he heard the gears grind. He pushed his clutch down all of the way and awkwardly reversed. . He drove as fast as he could toward the airport and then dialed Beth's number.

Ring. Ring. Ring. "Hi, honey," Beth answered warmly, sounding out of breath.

"Beth, thank God you picked up," Preston said relieved, speaking rapidly. "Beth, meet me at the airport. I'm going straight there. Bring one of the boys and take a taxi so that he can take my car home."

"Preston, what's wrong? You sound awful. What's happened?" Beth said nervously.

"RJ came into the office, just now, Beth," Preston explained. Beth knew what that meant. They had talked at length about Preston's plans.

"Oh, no," she said in dismay and he heard her say something undetectable to one of their sons. "Does he know you have the documents?"

Preston hit his accelerator and ran through a very yellow light that was about to turn red. "No, I don't think so. But he was acting weird. At least I think he was. I don't know. I might be just paranoid."

Preston heard some confusion in the background while Beth was saying something urgently to their son. "Ok, Preston, we're on our way. John is calling for the taxi. We'll meet you at the airport. I'll meet you at the ticket counter."

"Tell John to hurry, Beth," Preston pleaded, glancing in his rearview mirror for anyone following. "We have to get through security before RJ finds out. We have to get on that plane with the documents."

Chapter 40

Emma looked at the clock on her desk. It said 9:05. She usually didn't work on a Sunday night, but she knew Steve was on patrol tonight and she hoped he would stop in and see her.

Things hadn't turned out like she hoped. When they arrived home in defeat, they had both gone back to their lives. She waited every day for Steve to call, but so far he hadn't.

They both felt terribly guilty about losing the document, no doubt. But she thought despite that, they would be able to continue to explore their relationship. She had felt that their relationship had gone beyond just a situational one, and she was surprised at Steve's distance. Surprised and hurt.

Of course things had gotten really ugly the day after they arrived home. An independent lawyer had gone public with the document. The church's worst fears were realized when the translation revealed that blacks weren't authorized to receive the priesthood and were not considered equals.

The church's PR department was working overtime to restate the church's current stance that all men should have the priesthood. They still challenged the authenticity of the document because the lawyer had only revealed the beginning of the document for testing and translation validation.

Nevertheless, it was a nightmare. Emma hadn't slept the night they arrived home. As she tossed and turned, she examined her actions, trying to think of what she would have done differently to save the documents, but she couldn't come up with anything.

She glanced down at the stack of papers she was trying to grade. She had looked at the top paper at least 10 times so far, but couldn't seem to focus. A fellow professor had covered her summer classes while she was gone, but now she was back, the work piled up quickly.

Emma finally shoved the papers aside and leaned back in her chair. She thought back to the past few weeks and focused her attention on all of those moments with Steve. He felt something for her—she was sure. So why was he avoiding her now?

Emma pulled out a small mirror that she kept in her office drawer and looked into it. She had put makeup on, wore one of her favorite outfits and had curled her hair, all just in case Steve stopped by.

Emma finally decided to take matters in her own hands. She would go find Steve and talk with him about what he was feeling. She locked her office and walked toward the lobby. She glanced over at the display cases. The university had replaced the glass and the artifacts were rearranged to cover up the space. There was now no visible sign that anything had happened.

The building felt empty. Part of it was because it was summer and fewer students were on campus. But the other part was the emptiness Emma felt because of Dr. Mangum's death. She felt it acutely now that she was back in the office every day. His office was just down the hall from hers and it felt strange and lonely without him.

She pushed through the front doors and walked out into the plaza area. She sauntered toward the sidewalk, rounding the corner of the building, looking both ways for Steve, trying to think of what to say as she went. But the campus was empty and all she could hear was the sound of crickets starting their nightly song.

She decided to sit down on a nearby bench and wait for Steve to pass by.

Steve stood in the shadows of the Maeser building. He had just checked the rear of the building and was coming around the front when he saw her. She was walking toward him, looking around. The sun was just setting and Steve knew she couldn't see him.

Part of him wanted to go to her, to hold her and comfort her. He was sure now that he loved Emma. Her strong determination, her intelligence and her courage were remarkable. But he had felt her pull away as they traveled home and it was better that he just leave things as they were.

He had failed so much in his life, no matter how hard he tried. He had failed at his first marriage with Kari. He had failed to keep his home together for Ari. He also felt he had failed as a soldier. There were so many that somehow made it work—why couldn't he? And now, he had failed to protect the church's secret. It was just too much.

Maybe he would never marry again, he thought. Maybe it was his lot to live his life in isolation so he didn't hurt anyone else.

He saw Emma walk over to a bench and sit down. The campus lights were just coming on and it gave Emma a soft glow in the twilight. She looked so sad that he almost went to her. She looked beautiful tonight.

He forced himself to stay put. She would find someone else. She was beautiful, intelligent and talented. Someone else deserved her more than he did, he surmised.

Just then, his cell phone began to vibrate. He looked at the number and paused. Out of state. He was going to let it go to voicemail, but something told him to answer it.

"Hello?" he answered quietly, moving deeper into the shadows of the building.

"Is this Steve Call?" the man with a deep voice asked.

"Yes," Steve answered hesitantly.

"There's a chance you can get your document back tonight," the voice continued. Steve's body went rigid and his heart started to race. "Be at the Salt Lake airport tonight at 11. Wait in the lobby. He will find you."

"Who is this?" Steve asked skeptically, wondering if it was a prank call. There had been a lot of publicity about the document in the past few days.

"I'm a lawyer for someone involved in taking the document. He wants it returned to your church. He doesn't feel good about what has happened. He is trying to make it right," the man explained.

"Ok, I'll be there," Steve said as he glanced back over to Emma and then added "with Dr. Worthington."

"If he doesn't show, then your document is gone forever," the man added. "He is taking great personal risk to do this."

"I understand," Steve added and heard the line go dead.

He paused only for a split-second and then began to run toward Emma at full speed. He saw her look up at him. Her first reaction was pleasure—her entire face broke out into a smile. The next emotion was confusion—why was Steve running toward her?

Steve arrived in seconds and Emma stood up to meet him. She thought he would embrace her, but instead he pulled her into a run. "Emma, c'mon, we've got to hurry," he said urgently, pulling her toward him.

"What's going on, Steve? Where are we going?" Emma asked in confusion.

"To the Salt Lake airport," Steve said. "I just got a tip that someone is trying to return the document to us. He will be at the airport at 11. We have to make sure we're on time."

Emma glanced at her watch while she ran—it said 9:30. Steve was pulling her toward the north end of campus where he had his car. "This way," Emma said, changing their direction. "My car is closer."

They turned and ran toward the faculty parking lot. Steve called Gary on his cell phone while they ran. "Gary, it's

232

me, Steve. I need someone to cover for me right now. We just got a tip that we might be able to get the document back tonight. I have to run to the Salt Lake airport to meet someone tonight."

"No problem," Gary replied. "Good luck and be careful," he added. Steve had spoken at length with Gary when he returned about their failed journey.

Emma was unlocking the car and getting in, "Emma, let me drive," he said authoritatively. Emma nodded her head and threw him the keys as she ran around to the passenger seat. Her heart was racing, but it wasn't just because of the document. She was happy to be back on the adventure with Steve. She had missed him desperately the past few days.

Steve wound his way through Provo and onto the freeway. He pushed the accelerator to the floor until he heard Emma's warning. "Steve, slow down, we have time. We don't want to get pulled over or get in an accident. We'll make it in time." To emphasize her point, she reached over and touched Steve's arm.

Steve slowed down, but still kept the needle around 75. He was anxious to redeem himself. Could it possibly work out? Was someone really trying to restore the document to them? Who? And why? In the back of his mind, he wondered if it was a trap. Was someone trying to silence Emma and himself? He shook off the thought. They didn't know who was behind this. Carl was dead and the girl had let them go. They had no idea whom she was working for. And besides, they had the document and had already gone public with it.

As they drove, Steve thought of trying to talk to Emma about their relationship, but decided against it. If this worked out and he was redeemed, then maybe, finally, he could move on with her.

But Emma sat uncomfortably in the silence. She finally ventured, "How have you been, Steve?"

Her words cut into Steve's heart. He could hear the hurt in them. He knew all about hurt women. He had heard that tone many times before.

"Good," he answered lamely. "How about you?"

"Fine," she said and then added bravely, "I've missed you, Steve."

Steve swallowed hard and felt his mouth go dry. She's better off without me, he reminded himself.

Emma waited for his reply that he missed her as well, but it didn't come. Tears sprang to her eyes and she tried to rapidly blink them away. "So that's it, Steve?" she asked in a shaky voice. "It was just a treasure hunt fling? You didn't really mean any of those things you said?"

Steve looked over at her tear-stained face and his resolve wavered. "Emma, I *did* mean those things I said. But I'm no good for you, Emma. I'm no good for anyone. It's better if you just find someone else. Someone better."

Emma felt relief flood her heart. He *did* love her. He just didn't feel he was good enough for her. "Steve, don't be silly," she said, reaching over for his hand. "I don't want anyone else. I want you."

"Emma, I'll just end up hurting you. I've already caused enough hurt. All of the people I killed in the wars. How much I hurt Kari and Ari. I don't want to hurt anyone else," Steve defended.

"I'm tough," Emma emphasized. "Remember, I was named after Emma Smith. Besides, the only way you can hurt me is to stop loving me. I couldn't bear that, Steve."

Steve thought about her words and then felt all of his internal resolve crumble. "Me, neither," Steve said honestly and snuck a glance at Emma. She smiled through her tears at him and he lifted her hand up to his mouth and kissed it.

Emma's heart melted and relief poured through her body. "All right, then, what's the plan?"

Steve recounted the entire phone conversation to her and then added, "It's almost a miracle—to think that someone else could be trying to help us."

"Maybe the Lord has provided a way out of this mess," Emma suggested. "He knew we did all we could to protect it."

"I hope so," Steve replied.

Chapter 41

RJ McAllister typed his password into his computer. It was his latest wife's name, although he was already losing interest in her. All she wanted to do was spend his money and she seemed very uninterested in him personally. Of course, it wasn't like that in the beginning. She doted on his every word, complained when he had to be out of town on business. Now, she looked annoyed when he approached her and was often out with friends when he arrived home from his business trips.

The stillness of the office bugged RJ. It was too quiet for him. He liked the steady hum of frantic activity in the office. He put some music on to drown out the silence. He worked for a half an hour, until something started nagging at his subconscious.

It was something about Preston. He paused typing and tried to figure out what seemed out of place. Preston always came into the office on Sundays—that was no surprise. The man was a workaholic. Not that RJ wasn't. But his constant composure and steady working ability irked RJ.

Composure. Yes, that's what was out of place. When he ran into Preston in the lobby, Preston clearly looked flustered. He had his tie off and RJ hadn't ever seen him with his tie off. And there was something about his mannerisms. They almost looked guilty.

RJ stood up and stretched, turning to look out of his spacious office window. The Atlanta streets were quiet with only the occasional car passing by. He saw a family walking by with young children—the dad and mom were swinging the youngest between them and he was squealing with delight.

He thought again of his failed marriages and children who despised him. He had no idea where he had gone wrong. He knew he worked too much and drank too much, but who didn't? They would complain a lot more if the company didn't do well and he ran out of money.

The company. RJ thought again about Preston. He slowly walked over to Preston's office and tried the door. It was locked. Preston always locked it because he didn't want any of the company employees accessing their financial statements. They always projected a positive, successful outlook to the employees, even when it was a lie.

He fished in his pocket for his ring of keys. He had a master key on his ring. He put it into the lock and pushed the door open.

Empty. He dropped his keys when he saw that the office had been cleaned out. The furniture sat empty, accusatory. RJ walked over to the desk, trying to make sense of what he was seeing. Preston, gone?

RJ pulled each desk drawer out, looking for answers. All of the office supplies and company files were neatly organized and in place. Everything was there except for Preston's personal things. His laptop sat docked by his monitor.

Maybe he had gone over the edge with this Mormon thing, RJ thought to himself. Preston had principles and didn't like to get into the unsavory parts of the business. RJ understood that. But to just walk out the door without saying a word?

RJ headed back to his office and stopped when he reached the boardroom door. *He wouldn't have*, he thought to himself. *Not Preston, not after all of these years*. But Preston's guilty behavior in the lobby convinced him otherwise. RJ threw open the boardroom door, the loud sound echoing throughout the empty office. He unlocked the armoire and dialed the combination to the safe, roughly yanking the door open. His sharp intake of breath confirmed the truth—the Mormon documents were gone.

He saw a single white envelope sitting in the safe. He pulled it out and growled when he saw Preston's handwriting on the front. He plunged his hand into his pocket to retrieve his cell phone. Callie would take care of Preston for him. He tried her phone and threw his cell against the wall when the voicemail came on. *How dare she not answer him!* he thought angrily. He then tried Riley's phone, but he didn't pick up either. *Worthless boy*, he thought again. He started to have a searing headache.

He ripped open the letter, hoping Preston would indicate where he had gone so he could stop him. When he saw the words, "return the document to the Mormons," he swore long and loud. He scoffed when he read that Preston had called in a favor to bring back a large client. It wasn't about the money. It was never about the money for him. It was about power and control. It was about destroying the company and the people he hated so much.

He stopped reading when he read "tropical location." Preston was headed for the airport—that much was certain. He would take care of this himself. He went back into his office and pulled out a gun from his bottom drawer. He made sure it was loaded and had plenty of bullets. Preston was a traitor and he would pay for it.

He ran as quickly as he could to his car. His heavy girth slowed him down and he was out of breath, but he pushed himself on and on. He finally got to the car and proceeded to the airport, running through every red light, swerving to avoid collisions. He glanced at his expensive Rolex watch. Preston had almost an hour head start. But he didn't have Beth with him yet. That would slow him down.

He watched for Preston's car on the freeway and hoped as he got closer to the airport that he would find him. It would be difficult to stop them inside of the airport, if not impossible. He drove his car faster and faster, reaching 100 mph and even higher. As he came into the airport, he saw a silvery haired African American woman getting out of a taxi as he passed.

Beth! He slammed on his brakes and cut off a car coming up behind him to get to the curb. He opened his car door wide, nearly hitting another car. He ran toward Beth, but she had already gone into the airport. He heard an airport security guard shouting at him that he couldn't leave his car, but he ignored him. He had to stop them.

As the automatic doors swung wide for him, he glanced around the airport. Beth was walking quickly, but he could still catch her before she reached the escalators. He ran through the airport, roughly dodging people, and when he came up to Beth, he grabbed her roughly by the arm. She had just stepped onto the escalator. With his other hand, RJ felt his gun in his pants pocket.

Beth cried out in pain at the sharp grasp and turned to look at RJ in alarm.

"Hello, Bethy," RJ scowled as he whispered in her ear. "Going somewhere?"

The escalator moved slowly upward and Beth looked around frantically for help. She was between levels and couldn't see much up above yet. She knew Preston was waiting for her at the security entrance. Once they made it through there, RJ wouldn't be able to get in. They only allowed ticketed passengers into security.

Beth didn't respond and so RJ added in her ear, "I've got a gun, Beth. I will kill you. I will kill you and Preston for this. This is the ultimate betrayal. Preston, after all of these years. After everything I've done for him. Now, trying to help the Mormons. I'll kill you both before I'll let that document leave."

Beth felt faint, but she forced herself to concentrate. She knew enough about RJ to know he would do it. Preston had carefully shielded her, but Atlanta's upper crust was a small community and word got around. As the escalator lifted her higher, she turned her head away from RJ and saw Preston standing at the entrance to security. She also saw a security guard standing within a few feet of Preston. They just had to get through security, she reminded herself.

As they reached the top of the escalator, RJ tightened his grip on her. "Stop right here, Beth," he commanded into her ear.

Preston was scanning the airport for Beth and smiled when he saw her. But his smile dropped instantly when he saw that RJ was standing next to her. He looked around and saw a security officer standing to his right, but he was talking to someone. He saw the pale look on Beth's face and the fear in her eyes.

Fear gripped his heart and the briefcase suddenly felt heavy in his hand. He knew what RJ wanted. But what if he gave it to him? Yes, he would let them leave, but he would probably send someone after them. They would always be looking over their shoulders—waiting for someone to come and silence them forever.

But he couldn't walk away and leave Beth either. Maybe he would try and reason with RJ he thought or offer him money. But Preston dismissed the idea when he saw the wild look in RJ's eyes. He had seen it before and it was never a good outcome for the offender.

RJ pushed Beth forward two steps and then stopped. It was clear he wanted to make a trade. Preston stepped forward one step and then stopped when he saw Beth clearly shake her head. He could see the determination in her eyes. She didn't want him to make the trade. He froze, feeling helpless, praying to God for the first time in a long time that He would somehow spare Beth.

Beth then turned to RJ fully and faced him. "RJ you *know* this is wrong. You *know* you have to let us go. I'm going to walk away now, RJ. You've been good to us and I don't want you killed or see you go to jail. I'm going to walk over to Preston and we're going to get on that plane. If you try to stop me, I will scream. There is a security guard right there. If you pull out your gun, he will shoot you, no questions asked. You have to let us go, RJ. It's over. It's all over."

With that Beth turned and faced Preston, smiling reassuringly. He returned her gaze with a look of fear and worry. She pulled away from RJ. At first he held strong, but she looked back at him silently, meeting his angry gaze. She stared at him unflinchingly and then turned again and used all of her strength to pull out of his grasp. The security guard had noticed them and was looking at them intently. RJ noticed that as well and released his grasp.

Beth kept her face focused on Preston and forced her legs to move forward, step and after step. She waited for a gun to go off and could imagine the searing pain she would feel as the bullet entered her back. Step. Step. She then saw Preston smile as she got closer and she knew they had won. He reached out and enveloped her in his arms protectively. He heard a sound and looked up in time to see RJ running toward them. Preston swiftly moved Beth to the security line and produced their tickets. The attendant quickly examined them and waved them through. As they walked over to the security scanners, Preston turned to look back. Beth grabbed his arm and said, "Preston, don't look back. Just keep walking. Just keep moving."

It wasn't until they were through security that they risked a glance backwards. They saw RJ standing at the head of the security line, looking dejected, tired and old. As he guided Beth toward their terminal, he stopped her once they were out of RJ's sight. "Beth, you were amazing. So courageous. How did you know he wouldn't shoot you?"

"I didn't," Beth replied and Preston could feel her body shaking slightly. "But your mother was standing beside you at the security entrance. She was smiling at me and beckoning me to come."

Preston looked at her and blinked back tears. "My mother?" he asked in amazement.

"Yes," Beth replied earnestly, taking both of Preston's hands in hers. "She was there guiding me. When you hugged me, I heard her say that she loves you."

Preston broke down and cried and Beth held him for several minutes while the swarm of travelers moved around them headed to their gates. They then slowly walked to the terminal together, hand in hand, toward their new life.

Chapter 42

Steve paced the floor, glancing around. Emma was sitting, trying not to bite her nail. They both glanced around the airport lobby, waiting anxiously. Steve looked at his watch for the hundredth time. It said 11:10.

"Maybe this person isn't coming," Emma suggested sadly. She gave in and bit her nail to ease her stress.

"The contact did say that he was doing this at great personal risk," Steve said. "Maybe he didn't make it."

Emma sighed and leaned her head onto her fist. "Come sit by me," she softly requested and patted the seat next to her.

"I can't," Steve replied with a half-smile. "Too keyed up."

They waited in silence for the next ten minutes while Steve continued to scan the crowd. He finally saw a group coming down the escalators and he perked up. He gently tapped Emma's shoe with his and nodded toward the group. Emma looked up and watched them one by one, but no one approached them.

As they all left the airport, Steve finally slumped down beside Emma. "It's 11:30," he said sadly. "Maybe this was all some kind of a prank."

"At least we tried," Emma said. "Let's wait another few minutes just in case." Steve nodded, but could feel the exhaustion replacing the adrenaline that he had felt.

The seconds on his watch continued to speed by and he finally turned to Emma at 11:45 and said, "Let's go. He's not—."

Just then, they heard a gentle voice behind them with a strong Southern accent, "Excuse me, but are you Steve and Emma?"

Steve jumped up and turned around while Emma did the same. "Yes, yes, we are," Steve replied, scanning the area and assessing the African American couple standing in front of them. They were both in their early 60s, good-looking, well dressed, very relaxed. They looked happy, although a bit tired.

The man reached out his hand, "I'm Preston Montgomery," he said in a friendly voice. Steve reached out and shook his hand. He had a firm grip. "This is my wife, Beth." After they all shook hands, Preston looked around the airport and seeing that it was empty, opened his briefcase.

Emma gasped when she saw the three rolled documents. She reached over and squeezed Steve's hands. Preston gently handed the documents over to Steve and Emma and they secured them in Steve's backpack.

"My deepest apologies," Preston said sincerely, meeting both Emma and then Steve's gaze. "And please pass that on to your church. These shouldn't have ever been stolen. They are your church's property and I am returning them to you. I also want to inform you that the translation was altered. The original had the opposite meaning. Your church can go public tomorrow with the document and the true translation."

Emma looked at Steve in amazement and then back at Preston and Beth. She could see kindness in Beth's eyes and smiled.

"Why were they taken in the first place?" Steve said. "Was it another church?"

"No," Preston answered, "It wasn't about religion at all. It was all to do with big business and getting ahead. But I ask you, as a personal favor, to just let it go. You have the documents back. Leave it at that. Don't try to find out who is behind this. I would greatly appreciate it. We must all just move on." He then reached over to hold his wife's hand and added, "We're headed to Hawaii. We're retiring there. Our plane leaves in about an hour. We're just here on a layover."

Emma suddenly thought of Dr. Mangum's papers. "There was something else stolen. It was a manila envelope full of research notes and papers. Do you have that as well?" she asked plaintively, glancing hopefully toward his briefcase.

Preston glanced at his wife in confusion and then answered, "I'm sorry. I wasn't aware that anything else was taken. This is all I have."

Steve could see the disappointment on Emma's face, so he put his arm around her. "This is great. Thank you so much for returning them to us and for letting us know the truth about the translation."

"Why are you doing it?" Emma asked curiously. "Why are you helping us?"

"Because the Mormon church once saved my mother's life," Preston explained with a smile. "And because my mother was a Mormon." Beth leaned over and put her head and Preston's shoulder. "Well, we best be on our way. Beth here has waited long enough for our retirement."

"Thank you again," Emma said and she impulsively reached up and hugged Preston. He smiled in surprise and hugged her back.

Steve and Emma watched as they walked hand in hand back toward the escalator, ascending until they disappeared from sight.

Steve threw his backpack over his arm and then said, "How about we get hotel rooms downtown so we can go straight to Temple Square tomorrow morning and give the documents to President Thompson?"

Emma nodded in agreement. She wanted to see this through and get the originals into the church's hands. Then maybe she and Steve could celebrate together.

They drove into town and decided to splurge and stay at the Grand America hotel to celebrate the turn of events. They also thought security would be better there, just in case someone was still coming after them.

They checked into their rooms and Emma got ready for bed, but she just stared at the ceiling. She tossed and turned all night, dreaming of Carl coming back to life and trying to get the documents again.

But she knew Steve was sleeping with them in his bed. They weren't taking any chances. They had the adjoining door open and she could hear Steve occasionally toss and turn and eventually cry out in his sleep. He was still having nightmares about the war.

When the clock beside Emma's bed finally displayed 6:00 a.m., she couldn't wait any longer and picked up her cell phone and dialed President Thompson's assistant. She explained that they had been given the documents and they wanted to get them into the church's hands immediately.

She and Steve were dressed by 7:00 and drove to Temple Square. The assistant had told them to enter through the garage entrance, so they drove down under Temple Square and parked. So much had happened since they had been here a few weeks ago. Several security guards approached them and they went through the usual security procedures. Steve stayed close to the backpack though and didn't let it out of his sight.

As they sat and waited for President Thompson, Steve studied a painting in his office. He had seen it before. It was of President Washington, holding the reins of his horse and kneeling in the cold snow in prayer. Steve had always liked that painting. There was probably chaos all around them and yet President Washington had taken time to pray. And that prayer had helped them win an impossible war.

Images of his tours of duty started to flit through his mind which focused on the young private from New Jersey. Rico was a tough, Hispanic kid, barely out of high school. He had always distanced himself from the group. Steve had tried several times to help him out, to talk with him, but he stayed closed off.

He was very handy with a knife and Steve knew it was from growing up on the streets. One day, Steve asked him to show him some of his moves and Rico finally opened up a little. A few days later, they were in a firefight together. They thought there were only a few insurgents ahead of them, but soon they were surrounded. Steve watched as each of the soldiers around him was shot, except for Rico. He had a keen sense of survival and had known the safest place to hunker down.

Steve had already accepted that he was going to die. But somehow he felt peaceful. As he continued to fight off the attackers, he began to wonder what heaven was like. He thought about everything that he had learned in church growing up. He thought about his grandparents who had passed away while he was in college. He had always heard that you had family meet you. He liked that. He had always been close to his grandpa and started to feel excited to see him again.

His thoughts were interrupted by Rico. In a scared voice, he asked, "Hey, Mormon, do you believe in God?"

Steve looked over at him and could see terror all over his face. Steve smiled encouragingly, shot an approaching attacker and then looked back at Rico. "Yes, I do," Steve answered steadily and then waited.

Rico seemed to process that and then, lifting his chin, answered defiantly, "I don't."

Steve could see so much in his young eyes. Fear. Anger. Hatred. It was easy to see that he had grown up in a very difficult situation. Steve didn't respond. He just waited.

Two more attackers rushed them and shot Rico in the shoulder. Steve shot them both and one of them fell on top of Steve. He shot him again and then pushed him away. He tried to think back and count how many they had killed. Fifteen? Twenty? How many of them were there? And where were their reinforcements?

He kept his gun pointing toward the noise he could hear and with his other hand, he leaned over, grabbed a medical pad out of his backpack and pressed it firmly into Rico's shoulder.

Steve glanced up at the sky. The sun was low and it would be dark soon. He doubted he would make it to see the dawn. He looked over at Rico who was surprisingly calm. Most young kids were pretty freaked out the first time they were shot. Steve had been shot in the leg and the arm, but both were just flesh wounds and he had quickly recovered.

Rico saw Steve watching him and said simply, "I've been shot lots worse before."

The chaos surrounding them started to subside and Steve risked a glance around. He could see about ten of them, gathered together, talking and gesturing toward the hill where Steve and Rico were hiding. Steve glanced at his watch—the fight had been going for four hours so far.

"Do you believe in heaven?" Rico asked so softly that Steve almost didn't hear him. He looked over at Rico and saw he was staring up into the sky.

"Yes," Steve answered again and then added, "And I also believe that we existed before this life. In a pre-existence, as spirits, before we were born."

Rico seemed to consider his words and then added, "And what about hell?"

Steve could see fear and worry creeping across his face. He was sweating now and looked to be in a lot of pain.

When Steve didn't respond, Rico's eyes flung wide open and he demanded of Steve, "What about hell? Is it for people like me? Murderers? Cheaters? Liars?"

Steve still didn't respond. He wasn't sure what Rico's life was like growing up, but he had a pretty good idea. It was easy to tell in the military. Living in such close quarters and relying on each other for survival exposed people's personalities, character and backgrounds pretty quickly.

"Yes, mi amigo, if there is a hell, I'm going there. And so are you," he spat angrily.

Steve looked over at him in surprise. Rico read the look on his face and said, "Yes, I've killed lots of people. And not just here in the war. At home, too. But there are other wars at home. They are just as real. How many people have you killed, Mormon?"

Steve's gut wrenched and he started to feel sick. He could see at least seven men he had just killed lying strewn on the field in front of him. How many others? Too many. He tried not to think about it. He tried to be the machine they wanted. But as he looked at the dead bodies in front of him, he wondered about them. Were they married? Did they have children? Who would cry for them tonight when they heard the news?

Steve fought through his emotions and grasped on to what he knew deep down was true, "War is different. God knows that." He tried to focus on that and push away the self-condemning thoughts that were coming into his mind.

"Then maybe I will go to heaven after all," Rico softly said, wistfully looking up at the sky.

All of a sudden, Steve could see a picture in his head. He could see a grenade at the bottom of a nearby pack. He could see himself throwing it at the group and running with Rico to safety. He could see it all happening in his head and knew that was their way out. He had thought they were out of grenades.

Steve looked over at Rico and said, "God has just showed me how we're going to get out of this." Rico looked at Steve in surprise and watched as Steve crawled over to a nearby pack and fished down into it and pulled out a grenade. Steve then crawled back over and tried to glance around them. This would only work if they weren't surrounded anymore. He couldn't see anyone else, but there was a good chance they were still there.

He looked over at the group of attackers and saw they were still discussing something. Now was the time. He would just have to trust the inspiration God had given him and go for it. "I'm going to throw this grenade and then we're making a run for it," Steve explained, helping Rico roll over into a flat position. "After I throw the grenade, I'll pull you up. Put your arm around me and I'll support you as we run."

Steve was just about to pull the pin when he felt Rico's hand on his arm. "Wait," he said urgently. Steve looked up at him questioning. But Rico's eyes were closed and Steve could see his lips moving and slightly hear some Spanish. He was praying.

Steve smiled and said a quick prayer as well and then pulled the pin and threw the grenade. He watched as it sailed toward the group of fighters and, seeing that it hit its mark, he pulled Rico's arm around his shoulder and then began to run toward their camp. Steve kept waiting for a bullet to sharply enter his back, but none came. He ran as fast as he could while supporting Rico. The further they ran, the more Rico leaned on Steve and then eventually dropped to the ground. He had passed out and blood was oozing from his shoulder.

Steve picked him up and slung him over his shoulder, trying to keep the wound pressed against his body. He ran for what felt like miles and then saw some American troops patrolling up ahead. He called to them and collapsed in front of them.

He felt Emma's hand on his arm and gently shook his head, brushing away the past. He wondered when he would stop thinking about the war, if ever. He looked over at Emma and smiled.

"You okay?" Emma asked softly, looking at him with concern.

"Yeah, just war memories," he said, nodding his head toward the painting of Washington. Emma's hand on his arm felt cooling and soothing. He reached over and held her hand and squeezed it gently.

They waited for a few minutes and then Emma added, "That painting makes me think of how ironic everything is."

"What do you mean?" Steve said, glancing at it again and then back at Emma.

"Washington fought for our independence, so that we could have, among other things, religious freedom. And yet, when our church was restored, the early members of our church were hated and persecuted for having a different

248

religious viewpoint," she explained looking sad. "They constantly appealed to the law and the constitution to uphold their rights and instead they were pushed from state to state, stripped of their lands and property, beaten, raped and murdered. All because they believed in a different religious viewpoint. It wasn't until we arrived in Utah, in a barren land that no one else wanted, that we found safety."

Steve thought back to those times. It was one thing to be a soldier in a war, but another to constantly have to protect your home and family. He thought about Kari and Ari. Thought about having to defend their very lives.

Emma broke into his thoughts by saying, "I'm pretty amazed actually. Joseph and Brigham constantly sought government support and redress and didn't receive it. They could have easily become a bitter people. When they arrived in Utah, they could have naturally become dissidents from the U.S. And yet they didn't. Instead they taught forgiveness and patience. They insisted on civic duty and loyalty to America. It's—."

Just then, President Thompson walked into the office with a huge smile on his face. "Hello, Steve and Emma! I hear your trip has been blessed." He came up and shook both of their hands and then instead of sitting in the chair at his desk, he pulled one up beside them to be closer.

Steve stood up and gently lifted out the parchment scrolls from his backpack and walked over to a nearby table. "May I?" he asked, pointing toward the table.

President Thompson and Emma stood up and walked over to the table and watched as Steve gently unrolled the scrolls. Emma helped Steve put them into order and hold them in place while President Thompson examined them.

"Fascinating," President Thompson said, examining the scrolls.

Steve and Emma recounted their journey and where they had found each piece of parchment. President Thompson listened intently. Steve then described the phone call and the late-night airport meeting with Preston. Emma also explained that the published translation was false and that it actually meant the opposite.

President Thompson listened with keen interest, and then replied, "What a remarkable journey. You have both completed a great service to the church. All of the members, worldwide, thank you." He then added with a slightly mischievous smile, "I can't wait to meet Joseph and Brigham one day in the next life. That's quite a trail they left for us. Ingenious. Now, I'm quite anxious to read this document for myself. With a pure translation."

Steve and Emma looked up in surprise. "You know the Reformed Egyptian language?" Emma asked in surprise.

President Thompson smiled and then replied, "No, but let's walk over to the temple and I'll show you something. Something that I've been hoping to get to do before I pass on to the next life."

Intrigued, Emma and Steve followed President Thompson out of his office and were surprised when he headed for the outside door instead of the elevator that led down to the secure, underground passageway.

Steve, fearing for the document's safety asked, "Wouldn't it be safer if we go to the temple underground?" But President Thompson, documents in hand just smiled and pushed on the outside door. "We are quite safe here," he reassured. "Besides, it is such a beautiful morning!"

And it was. As they walked down the steps and headed across the plaza toward Temple Square, the morning was clear and bright. Steve, ever the soldier though, constantly surveyed the landscape as they walked the block west. His heart raced as he waited, at any minute, for someone to jump out of the bushes and try to recover the document. He listened as the city began to wake up and cars started to pass by—were any of them stopping? Did he hear any frantic footsteps running toward them?

But as they walked, he could only hear the birds singing in the trees. Emma and President Thompson were happily chatting about the history of the temple, completely unconcerned with any impending danger. Still, Steve watched and waited, scanning the area constantly.

They finally arrived at the temple. Steve had always loved the design of the Salt Lake Temple. It looked like a castle and a fortress, all at the same time. He had heard growing up that the architect, Truman O. Angell, had traveled to Europe to gain inspiration and receive training. Despite the early Utah settlers' poverty, they had slowly built a magnificent granite temple, taking 40 years to finish it. Steve looked in admiration at the craftsmanship of the stone cutting and the metal working.

While there had been many desperate, gut-wrenching hours in the war, there had also been a lot of boredom. Steve had picked up the habit of carving wood in his spare time. But his creations were rough and rudimentary. He was amazed to think that the stone masons could produce such incredible creations from such an unyielding medium as granite.

President Thompson handed Emma the scrolls and then headed up the steps of the temple. Emma and Steve stopped. They had never seen anyone enter the temple this way. Traditionally, temple patrons went through the north entrance, a modern entrance. But President Thompson walked right up to the large western door, extracted an old key from his pocket and unlocked the door. The door swung open easily and President Thompson turned to look at Emma and Steve.

"Are you two coming?" he asked kindly with a glint in his eye as he put his key back in his pocket.

Emma and Steve walked up the steps with Steve giving the temple grounds one last look, but except for a few business people starting to walk across the plaza to work, the area was quiet.

Once inside the temple, President Thompson locked the heavy, outer door and then proceeded down the hallway. Steve looked around curiously—he had never been inside the Salt Lake Temple.

They passed a curving banister and Steve again marveled at the woodworking. President Thompson led them around the corner and down another long hallway. As they walked, they passed a few temple workers and they looked beautiful in their all-white clothing. Emma always thought it looked as if the temple was full of angels.

They finally arrived at a closed door. Emma tried to get her bearings and realized they were now in the northwest corner of the temple. President Thompson again took out his keys and unlocked the door that was marked with the moniker, First Presidency's Office.

They entered the office and it was decorated in the same style and taste as President Thompson's office that they had just left. President Thompson relocked the door and then gestured for both Emma and Steve to take a seat.

He took a seat as well and then looked at them both earnestly and said, "This office has been occupied by every president of the church since the temple was dedicated. Here we sit and ponder the Lord's will and how to lead His people to Him in a world that is ever decaying morally. But He has not left us without guidance. We have the scriptures. We have prayer and revelation and we have tools that he has left here on earth to help us."

At the word "tool," Emma perked up and looked at Steve with excitement in her eyes. "You mean the Urim and Thummim?" she asked enthusiastically.

President Thompson smiled in answer and said. "When I was called into the First Presidency, President Allen, my predecessor, took me into his trust, which I now take both of you into. You have both proven yourselves worthy of this knowledge. It has been a custom in the church to carry and protect church artifacts and once in a safe location, to secure these objects in the cornerstones of our temples."

President Thompson then stood up and walked around the desk, "May I?" he asked Emma, reaching for the parchment scrolls. Emma gently handed them back to President Thompson and then helped him as he unrolled them on his desk. They used paperweights and office accessories to secure the edges.

He then looked at them both solemnly and said, "As you know, when Joseph found the gold plates containing the ancient record of the people here in America in the stone box on the Hill Cumorah, there was also a breastplate, two bows and two stones, which when put together is the Urim and Thummim. Our Father in Heaven has provided the Urim and Thummim to prophets since Old Testament times to aid in translation and revelation. Most members assume that when Joseph had completed the translation of the Book of Mormon that he returned the Urim and Thummim back to the angel Moroni when he returned for the gold plates. But they have remained here on earth, as long as they were protected. Brigham brought it across the plains. Although Brigham died before the Salt Lake temple was completed in 1892, he passed them to President Taylor who then conferred them to President Woodruff, who dedicated the temple."

Emma couldn't wait any longer and asked, "Were they kept in the southeast cornerstone? Placed there at the dedication?" Without waiting for an answer, Emma turned to Steve and explained, "There is a record stone located at the base of the wall in the southeast corner. It's made of firestone from Red Butte Canyon and the stone has a one-square-foot cavity that contains such records, books, and papers. The cavity is covered with a sandstone slab."

President Thompson smiled at Emma's enthusiasm and confirmed her account, "Yes, there is a record stone in the southeast corner, but it was too public of a place to secure the Urim and Thummim. However, there was another record stone here in the temple." He studied Emma's face to see if she already knew, but her face only showed surprise.

He continued with a rueful smile, "The second record stone is much harder to access, as I've found out this past week. It is the capstone ball on which Moroni stands. When they laid the capstone, at the temple dedication, they placed music, scriptures, publications and pictures in it. But President Woodruff also placed the Urim and Thummim in there. What better place to hide such a sacred object? High above the ground at the top of the temple and sealed in a granite ball."

Steve looked in amazement at President Thompson and then back at Emma. "I didn't even know there were any record stones," he said, "Especially in the capstone. How did you access it?"

"Well, I knew the Urim and Thummim was there, President Allen told me of it long ago," he replied. "But we haven't needed it—until now. I must admit, it was exciting for me, an old man, to have my own adventure this week, trying to figure out how to access the capstone. When you sent me the first copy of the document, I knew I needed a pure translation. So I began to come to the temple early each morning, looking for a way to access it. As far as I know, it hasn't been disturbed since 1893."

President Thompson then stood up and said, "I think the rest is best told by showing. Will you both follow me?"

Steve and Emma followed President Thompson out of his office, which he then turned and locked to protect the document. As they walked toward an elevator, they saw more and more people in the temple. Several stopped to greet President Thompson and Emma was amazed at his kindness and patience as he briefly stopped and talked with each one of them.

They finally made it to an elevator and President Thompson took out a key and turned it into a lock on the elevator panel. It then popped open a small door which had a keypad on it and he punched in the code. The elevator began to ascend and Emma noticed that it went past all of the illuminated lights. They could only tell their floor progression by a quiet sounding of a bell as they passed each floor.

The elevator finally slowed and the doors opened to an empty hallway. Emma noticed as they followed President Thompson that this part of the temple was older and hadn't been remodeled over the years as the main rooms had. As they walked past a few windows, Emma realized they were now on what appeared to be the top floor of the temple. As they headed toward the east side, President Thompson finally stopped in front of a door right in the center of the east hallway. He slowly prodded the lock, but it was old and it took a few tries. He finally got the door open and they stepped inside a small, empty room. But in the middle of the room, there was a beautifully carved winding staircase ascending up through the ceiling.

Steve and Emma followed President Thompson up the stairs. It was very narrow and tight and seemed to go on forever. President Thompson stopped a couple of times to catch his breath, as did Emma. They finally arrived at a landing. The passageway was becoming very narrow and it was cramped as they all stood on the landing. The landing also had an old wooden ladder stretching up toward the ceiling.

"Steve, if you wouldn't mind," President Thompson said, slowly moving the ladder into position. "I'm getting a bit old for this part."

Steve looked up toward the ceiling and saw a small door, like an attic opening. He gently tried to lift it, but it was heavy, so he steadied himself on the ladder and then pushed again. The door gave way and he moved it up and over to the side.

President Thompson then pulled a small pocket flashlight from his suit coat pocket and passed it up to Steve. "It's in the box with the moonstones," he instructed.

Steve turned on the flashlight and stepped up higher on the ladder. His head was now in the entrance and he coughed as dust swirled around him.

"Are you okay?" Emma asked in a worried tone.

"Yeah," Steve replied. "It's just a bit musty up here." Steve swung the light around the small space. It was only several feet in diameter and was filled with objects on all sides of him. He examined each object with the light. It was an amazing journey back into time. The old books and photographs had long been waiting for a visitor.

Not seeing the moonstone box, he slowly twisted his body around to look behind him. There he saw what looked like an original copy of the Book of Mormon laying on top of an old wooden box. He gently lifted the Book of Mormon copy off the box and set it to the side. He then picked up the box. It was heavier than he thought and he had to steady himself on the ladder.

It took all of his strength to heft the box and keep his balance on the ladder. He descended step by step, feeling Emma steady his legs as he came down. Once down, he handed the box to President Thompson. It was covered in dust, but intricately carved.

As Steve headed back up the ladder to close the attic covering, he paused. "Is it all right if Emma comes and has a look?" he asked President Thompson.

"Of course," he replied, smiling encouragingly at Emma and nodded toward the ladder.

Steve came down and then helped Emma up the ladder. She moved swiftly, excited to see the contents of the record stone. Steve heard her gasp as she entered the opening and heard her commenting on each of the contents. Emma could have probably stayed up there for hours, but she remembered that they now had the Urim and Thummim, and she was excited to see it used, so she finally descended the ladder.

Steve noticed there were tears on her face as she came down. Seeing the insides of the record stone was a dream come true for her as a historian.

"Steve, if you would please carry the moonstone box for us," President Thompson said, handing it over. They then all began their slow, swirling descent back down the spiral staircase into the room and from there, they headed back into the hallway with President Thompson locking the door behind them.

Emma and Steve looked at each other as they passed the elevators they had just come up in. But President Thompson continued walking down the long southern hallway and then along the western. They finally came to another room which he unlocked. Inside was another spiral stairway, but this time it descended. "Now that we have the Urim and Thummim, it's best if we don't run into anyone," he explained with a smile. "So it's more stairs I'm afraid."

They slowly wound their way down the stairwell for several flights. Just when they were all feeling dizzy, they arrived in a small backroom which was the size of a closet. President Thompson unlocked the door and Emma and Steve realized they were now back in the First Presidency's temple office.

Exhausted from the exertion, President Thompson lowered himself in his desk chair and took out a handkerchief to wipe the sweat from his face. The journey through the temple had been hard on Emma and she was still young. She was amazed to think that President Thompson, as an 80-year-old-man, could do it. Emma saw a jug of water on a sideboard and went to pour him a glass.

"Thank you, my dear," he said gratefully, gulping down the water. Once he recovered, he stood up and walked over to Steve. He gently tried to open the box, but seeing it was locked, he returned to his desk drawer. He pulled out a small, miniature key and unlocked the box.

Emma moved closer to get a better look. On top was a metal plate that had fabric strips attached to it. President Thompson lifted the breastplate out of the box and Emma helped him put the fabric straps over his shoulders. Emma then looked back inside the box. She saw two long, thin, bow-shaped metal strips. She could see where they attached onto the breastplate and so she went ahead and connected them.

The last two items in the box were the stones themselves. Emma was fascinated by this part. These "seer stones" were actual translation devices. Emma couldn't wait to see them in action.

President Thompson gently lifted the stones out of the box one by one and put them into a resting place at the end of each bow. As he touched the stones, they seemed to generate some type of power source and started to glow. He then adjusted the bows slightly, so that the stones were now right in front of his eyes. Satisfied that everything was in place, he turned toward the document.

"Emma, will you please act as my scribe?" President Thompson asked, inclining his head toward a notepad and pen. Emma picked them up and sat down, ready for his dictation, feeling the magnitude of the moment as she was about to witness a pure translation through the power of God and she was acting as scribe for a prophet of God.

She and Steve watched as he momentarily closed his eyes and then as he opened them, they heard him take a sharp intake of breath and then he smiled.

Emma wanted so much to ask if she could have a look through the stones, but knew it would be inappropriate. President Thompson was the Lord's chosen prophet and it was his right and duty to be a seer.

President Thompson began to speak in a clear, strong voice as he read the translation that he could see through the Urim and Thummim. He didn't hesitate and moved through the document so rapidly that Emma had to write quickly to keep up with him.

He soon finished and seemed reluctant to put the Urim and Thummim away, wanting more to translate. When he detached the stones, they went dark, losing their power source. "Remarkable," he muttered with a smile as he unassembled the breastplate and bows and gently put them back into the box.

Emma read over the translation. It was very close to the previously published version, with a few significant changes and it did indeed mean the opposite. The revelation, given to Joseph in 1828 said:

> Let all the Saints of the most high God listen and hear His word. Let not their hearts be hardened, but open to the will of the Lord.
>
> For God our Father loves all of His children equally and they are all His spiritually begotten children. Therefore, let the priesthood of God be given to all worthy men no matter what their race or color of skin.
>
> And if my people do this and follow my instructions, they shall be blessed for generations to come. For my children must face opposition if they are

to be worthy to live in my kingdom. For God is the same yesterday, today and forever. Amen.

"Everything is starting to make sense now," President Thompson commented. "While researching a subject many years ago, I came across one of Joseph Smith's papers. It was a letter to Brigham Young and it talked about several revelations that had not been made public. Joseph was explaining to Brigham that even though the Lord had revealed them to Joseph, he had also been warned that the time to make them public was not yet here. It was when they were in Nauvoo and he knew his time was short. He wanted to make sure the revelations were not made public after his death. Brigham must have had the responsibility to hide them before they headed west."

Steve considered President Thompson's words and then asked, "Why would the Lord wait so long to re-reveal this revelation to President Kimball in 1978?"

"I think because He knew the world wasn't ready to accept it yet," President Thompson replied, sitting down in his chair. Emma noticed that he appeared to be physically exhausted from the translation. "You both are born in a wonderful time and age. We as a society have come so far in our progression and acceptance of all races. It is a glorious age. But I have lived a long time, and know that the world wasn't ready for it before then. Black rights almost destroyed America twice. First, during the Civil War and again in the 60s. It was a difficult subject and one that I'm pleased to say has now been resolved."

"There are several accounts of blacks receiving the priesthood authority back in the 1830s," Emma added. "Maybe it was because Joseph had received this revelation."

"Yes," President Thompson replied, "And Brigham, back in the 1850s said that 'the time would come when blacks would have the privilege of all we have the privilege of and more.' They knew it was an eternal principle."

"But didn't Brigham also say something about how blacks would never have the priesthood?" Steve asked, confused.

"He's reputed to have said that," Emma explained. "But it was reported in the newspaper, not in any church documentation, and many believe he was misquoted since his own personal papers said they would someday."

"Yes, I personally think it had a lot more to do with slavery issues, than with race. Can you imagine if the early members of the church gave slaves the priesthood? It would have created chaos to have slaves with the priesthood authority exerting leadership over white people," President Thompson mused.

"It obviously would have caused a lot of additional persecution for the early church," Emma conceded.

"Looking back over the history of the gospel in all ages," President Thompson explained, "I think the Lord understands that we need to grow and develop as a people. For example, in Old Testament times, the priesthood authority was only given to one of the twelve tribes—the tribe of Levi. And in Jesus' time, the gospel was only preached to the Jews. After Jesus' resurrection, the Lord expanded the gospel to go to the Gentiles."

"I also think He considers the sustainability of the church here on earth," he continued. "Giving blacks the priesthood would have created severe political challenges for the church. Already seen as leaning toward the abolitionist side, the church received intense persecution in Missouri because of that. He understood that given the prevailing social situation, it was not possible for blacks to have the priesthood. As our society developed and progressed, we then became ready to accept it. More than ready. I have read that President Kimball pleaded with the Lord, for several days, to lift the ban. The church was starting to experience persecution *because* of the ban. That showed the Lord that society was ready. It was finally time."

Steve considered his words and added, "I really admire those men of African descent who joined the church pre-1980s, in spite of the ban. They must have been incredible, humble individuals. It was a great day for the church when President Kimball made the announcement. I was just a small boy, but I remember how happy everyone was when we heard about it."

President Thompson leaned forward in his chair and added, "The Lord will have a humble people. We have been persecuted for so much over the years. The early Christians were no different. Who are we to dictate to the Lord how He should run His church? I have often pondered some of the eternal principals of the gospel. For example, I am quite relieved that we do not have the burden of living the law of polygamy at this time. Yet, we know that it is an eternal principal. Abraham, David—many of the great prophets of the Old Testament were polygamous and it was approved by the Lord. It was a great test for Joseph, Brigham and many of the early leaders and members of the church to live the law. It is distasteful for us as individuals and as a society."

He continued, "The government had passed an unconstitutional anti-polygamy law—unconstitutional because the constitution allows us freedom of religion. The members of the church were so persecuted by the government back in President Taylor's time, that the government imprisoned over 10,000 LDS men and many leaders had to go into hiding. They confiscated church property and threatened to take over the church's temples in Utah. It was then, on the brink of financial and physical destruction, that President Woodruff pleaded with the Lord for polygamy to cease and He finally consented. It was a great relief throughout the Church and the Manifesto was unanimously and instantly approved."

President Thompson then stood up and locked the box. "Well, I thank you both for everything you have done. I shall arrange for a certified translation to be published throughout the world. Your mission is complete. I will keep the document as well as the Urim and Thummim in the secure vaults of the church."

He then paused, as if listening to something and then came around the desk and took both Emma and Steve by the hand. He looked intently into Steve's eyes and said, "Steve, I promise you peace and give you the knowledge that the Lord loves you. He accepts your military service. You can forgive yourself of your past. He wants you to now look to your future."

He then turned to Emma and looked intently into her eyes as well, "Emma, I promise you that you shall be a wife and a mother in Zion here upon this earth. And I bless you with the ability to forgive and reconcile with your mother."

Both Steve and Emma looked at each other. President Thompson didn't know how they felt about those issues. Very few people did. But the Lord did. They both felt a deep and lasting peace enter their bodies as well as relief—their mission was complete and they had succeeded. President Thompson then escorted them to the outer door of the temple and hugged both of them. "Until the next time that the church needs your service," he added with a smile.

Steve and Emma walked silently together as they crossed the plaza. The area was now crowded with business people rushing from building to building. Tourists from all over the world were mingling in the plaza as well. As they walked, Steve felt lighter and more peaceful than he had felt in a long time. He could feel a healing happening in his soul and he reached over and held Emma's hand, stopping her in her tracks.

"I love you, Emma," he said in a rush of words, with a smile. He could feel his confidence returning and he began to think of the rest of his life instead of dwelling on the past.

Emma smiled and leaned up on tiptoes to kiss Steve. They kissed for several minutes, with the whole world passing by them. When Emma finally pulled away and looked up into Steve's eyes, he said with a wry smile, "Will you go out with me tonight?"

Emma pushed her way into his arms and said with a sigh, "I thought you'd never ask."

Chapter 43

He waited outside her townhouse in a dark, rented car. He knew her habits and expected her home from work at any moment. He needed to catch her by surprise. It was the only way she would see him.

He glanced over at the manila envelope sitting in the passenger seat. Part of him was still torn. But he was tired of following in his dad's footsteps. He knew he had deeply wronged her and somehow it bothered him.

He had used a lot of women over the years, but there was something about her. Something so young and innocent—he didn't encounter that very often anymore. She had wholeheartedly fallen for his scam and he knew she had been deeply in love with him.

Love didn't mean much to him. In his world growing up, Riley had only know the philosophy of use or be used. His father, who only kept him around because he was useful, had quickly discarded his mother when she was no longer useful to him. Women were disposable to RJ.

Most women that he had been with were looking to use him as well. All of Atlanta knew who he was and they thought they knew how much money he had. It was more about how much money he spent, than how much he actually had, Riley thought ruefully.

Preston, of all people, had foiled his dad's plan. They hadn't seen that coming. But then, they hadn't known about

Preston's mom. He had hidden that well. Riley wondered if RJ would go after Preston and his wife. Riley hoped he wouldn't. He had always liked Preston.

Now that RJ's plan was destroyed, Riley had begun to think of Staci again. He had purchased the manila folder from Callie at first to use it as leverage with his dad. He had thoroughly looked through the folder, but it didn't mean much to him. Most of the notes were concerning church doctrine or historical sites and he wasn't very familiar with those aspects of the Mormon church.

But he couldn't get the look on Staci's face out of his head. She hated him—he could tell when he ran into her at her parents' house. And it was that hatred that bothered him. Staci was beautiful and intelligent. Most of the girls he was with were beautiful, but lacked the character and intelligence that Staci had.

He found himself replaying their time together. He remembered all of their dates. His favorite was when they would drive up Provo canyon and build a fire and roast marshmallows together. She had just finished an astronomy class and she would point out the various constellations to him. He had grown up in the city which made looking at stars nearly impossible. He loved to look up at the star-studded sky in the canyon and listen to Staci explain the history of the constellations to him.

It was then that he began to wonder if there was something to religion. His father and mother had never been church-going people, so he wasn't as an adult either. But as he gazed up at the stars with Staci, he could believe that there was something else out there. Something that he didn't understand. But he could feel it.

Staci had told him of the Mormon's belief that there were numerous other planets like ours with civilizations just like ours. He began to feel miniscule in a vast universe full of possibilities.

His thoughts were interrupted by the sound of an approaching car. He watched as Staci pulled up to her condo.

She looked good, as always. Riley loved how she was a no-nonsense, low maintenance kind of girl. She wore little makeup and dressed in jeans and cotton t-shirts. Yet he found her more alluring than a lot of the models he had dated. There was something so genuine and real about her. He found himself still wanting her. It had been frustrating for him—their chastity standards. Staci explained her commitment to remain a virgin until her marriage and to have complete fidelity after her marriage.

He had pushed that resolve on several occasions, but she had remained firm. He admired her all the more for it. He had never met a woman he couldn't conquer. It bewitched him.

If he was being honest with himself, he knew that he had fallen in love with her. He had even begged his dad to cancel the project, wanting to spare Staci and her family. But RJ was relentless.

Riley had started to hope there was nothing to find. They had targeted her and her dad because Dr. Mangum was renowned for his church history research. But Riley had quizzed both of them for months without any hint of a secret or scandal potential. Riley had broken up with her then, saying she wasn't being open enough with him about the intricacies of the Mormon church. But really, Riley had hoped there truly wasn't something and as he left, he hoped it meant Staci and her family would be spared from further onslaught.

But Staci had called him after the breakup and pleaded with him to come back. He tried to use all of his resolve to not go back, even though he knew his dad wanted him to. But he knew by then that he was in love with Staci, and he couldn't make himself stay away.

There was still a part of him that wanted to walk away from his old life, join the Mormon church, and marry Staci. But he knew deep down inside he wouldn't be able to stick to it. Their Word of Wisdom revelation, or health code, dictated no coffee or tea, no alcohol, no drugs. He couldn't live that way. Not even for Staci.

He watched as she went inside and closed the door. Riley took a deep breath, gathering his courage. He reached for the door handle and then paused. He reconsidered for a slight second about returning the documents. But he pushed the door open and blocked the thoughts of money and power out of his head.

The walk from his car to Staci's door was long and he almost turned around several times. Then he stood on the steps, just waiting. It took all of his self-control to reach over and ring the doorbell.

He could hear her footsteps, so he lifted the manila envelope up and held it in front of him as a peace offering. Otherwise, she would slam the door in his face and that would be it.

Staci opened the door with her natural smile which quickly faded when she recognized Riley. She slammed the door and tears sprung to her eyes. She didn't think she would ever see Riley again. What was he doing here? It was bad enough to find him trying to break into her parents' house after her dad died. But the parchment had been recovered by the church. She had seen the articles on it in the newspaper.

It was then that the manila envelope registered in her mind. Riley had been holding it. It looked like the one she had found in her parents' house. It was her dad's research. Riley must be here to blackmail me or try to get some money, she thought angrily.

But she really wanted her dad's research back, so she swung the door open angrily and folded her hands defensively in front of her.

"What do you want, Riley?" she demanded, trying to control her anger. She wanted to hit him again.

He lowered the envelope and attempted a smile, "To return this to you and your family." To prove his point, he extended the envelope in her direction.

"What do you want for it?" Staci asked mistrustfully, trying to think how much money her family might be able to scrape up for it. It wouldn't be much.

"May I come in?" Riley asked plaintively.

Staci hesitated. She didn't want him in her condo, but she wanted her dad's documents back even more. "Yes," she answered curtly and then went and sat down in her favorite chair, but instead of sinking into it as she usually did, she sat rigidly upright.

Riley stepped into the living room and then gently closed the door. "Thank you," he said politely. When Staci said nothing, he asked again, "May I sit down?"

Staci had forgotten his Southern manners. She used to find them very charming. Now, they just seemed to amplify his manipulative personality. "Yes," she repeated, still annoyed.

He sat on the couch on the end closest to her and leaned forward. "How have you been, Staci?" he asked genuinely, searching her eyes.

"What business is it of yours, how I've been," she spat. "Get to the point, Riley. What do you want?"

He sighed. Her hatred was evident. He handed her the envelope. "I'm sorry we took this. I went to great lengths to get this back for you. I wanted to return it to you and your family. Ya'll showed me nothing but kindness and I repaid it with theft and dishonesty. I'm sorry, Staci. Honestly."

Staci looked at his extended hand and snatched the envelope away before he could change his mind. She yanked it open and pulled out the documents. It was, indeed, her dad's research.

She waited for him to say something, but he just waited. She stuffed the papers back into the manila envelope and finally grunted a half-hearted, "thank you." She couldn't meet his eyes. She could feel her heart breaking yet again. *When would she finally get over this man?* she demanded of herself. It didn't help that he kept showing up. And it didn't help that he was well-dressed, polite and incredibly handsome.

She finally met his gaze and there were tears in her eyes. She blinked them back rapidly, angry at herself that she couldn't control them.

Riley felt his own heart breaking as well. He reached over and took her hand gently, but she quickly pulled hers away and her crying increased. He felt like a heel, like a dog. He rarely saw the effects of his dirty work for his dad. But he wanted to see it with Staci. He wanted to punish himself for hurting someone so innocent.

"Staci," he said, his voice catching in his throat and he realized he was about to cry as well. "I'm so sorry. So very sorry. For everything." He reached out for her hand again and this time she didn't pull away, so he stood up and pulled her into his arms. She felt so natural in his arms and he held her tightly. He wanted to protect her from the evil world he lived in. He wanted to go back in time and not betray her. He gently caressed her hair and he could feel the tears rolling down his cheeks.

It had been so long since he'd cried. He couldn't remember the last time. But it felt good. Here with Staci, it felt good. He felt a warmth when he was around Staci. He felt the possibility of being a better man. He felt so far away from his wicked, wasteful lifestyle. Part of him didn't want to ever leave her side.

He could feel her body wracking with sobs and he held her even tighter. He then leaned over and whispered in her ear, "I love you, Staci. I've never loved anyone before. But I truly love you. Please, please forgive me."

He kissed her then and could taste both of their salty tears on her lips. He kissed her gently at first, but as she clung to him, he kissed her harder and deeper. He crushed her body up against his. He wanted her so much. He always had. He wanted to be her first time. He would be gentle and considerate. He wanted to make her feel incredible—to give her that.

He laid her down on the couch and they kissed passionately for several minutes, but when Riley's hands started to move around on her body, she pushed him away. "Don't," she said softly, sitting up, pushing her hair away from her face and wiping away the tears.

"I won't hurt you," Riley said softly, wrapping his arms around her. "I will be very gentle."

"It's not that, Riley, and you know it," Staci said sadly. "You *know* how I feel about premarital sex. I'm committed to wait. And I'm not going to break that—for you, or anyone. And then, as her head started to clear she added, "*Especially* not for you. You'd just be gone in the morning."

Her comment stung him deeply, but he couldn't argue with her. He wanted it to be different. He wanted to think he would be different with her. But he didn't know for sure. Even if he did marry her, he knew he couldn't join the Mormon church nor live up to their standards. He loved her enough to know that he wasn't good for her. He would only continue to bring her sorrow and disappointment.

"I wish things could be different," Riley said, running a hand through his hair and standing up. "I want to be with you, Staci. More than I have anyone else. I don't know what that means. But I do. That's why I came back. That's why I returned your dad's papers."

"It wouldn't work," Staci said flatly, not looking up at him. "We both know it."

Riley could see that her mind was made up, so he turned to go, but then turned back and asked. "So do you?" he asked softly in an earnest voice.

"What?" Staci asked in a tired voice, meeting his gaze.

"Do you forgive me?" he asked, searching her face.

Staci stood up and took a step toward him, "I will try. But you can't keep coming back. I need time to heal. Seeing you every few months isn't helping that." She opened up the door and then said directly, "Goodbye, Riley. And don't come back."

"Goodbye, Staci," he said and leaned in for one more kiss. He could see the hurt deep in her eyes as he pulled away. It bore into his memory and as he walked back to the car, he wanted to turn around, go back and promise her that he would live up to her lifestyle.

But he made himself get in the car. He knew himself well enough to know that he couldn't do it. He wouldn't make it as a Mormon. It was impossible for him. And he would only end up hurting her more than he already had.

He looked back up at her doorway as he started the car, but she had already closed the door. He drove through Provo's streets and headed toward the freeway. As he drove, he was lost in thought. He considered turning around several times. He couldn't believe the strong attraction he had for Staci. He had never wanted to be in a long-term relationship with anyone before. But he knew what she wanted and he just couldn't do it.

He arrived at the airport and mechanically went through the process of returning his rental car and checking in at the airport. He stood at the gate, still wanting to go back to her, to figure out a way to make it work. He waited for the last call and then forced himself to get on the airplane.

He was no good and he knew it. Yes, he had returned her father's papers to her, but there was one thing he hadn't told her. He had kept one of them. Callie had made him pay extra, just for that one paper. And he knew it was worth it. The rest of the papers were just gibberish to him. But he knew what this one meant. He knew how much it was worth. And he just couldn't give that up.

He had the paper folded up in his pocket the whole time. He had decided if she agreed to be with him, he would give it to her as a present, to show his commitment to her. But she had rejected him, so he kept it in his pocket.

As the airplane engines roared to life, he buckled himself into his first class seat. An attractive flight attendant smiled warmly at him, handing him a newspaper. But instead of pursuing conversation with her, he just thanked her for the newspaper and opened it up to distract himself. It was too soon after seeing Staci to return to his old ways. He would at least wait until he arrived home in Atlanta.

Chapter 44

Emma glanced at the clock on the wall. It was 11:30 p.m. and she had no hope of leaving before midnight. She sighed and looked at the pile of papers stacked up on both sides of her. Fall semester was underway and she had a full load of classes now that she was back. And to her surprise, she had also been named dean of religion upon her return.

She was the first female dean of religion in the history of BYU. She was warmly congratulated by her colleagues who took her out to lunch to celebrate. Yet as she looked around the table at lunch, she felt humble by the tremendous scholars around her.

She was so young as well. The youngest dean in history. But upon arriving home, her work finding the lost revelation was heavily publicized and she and Steve became local heroes in Utah.

So with her duties as dean, as well as her teaching workload, she was swamped. She and Steve had gone out every other weekend since they arrived home, on the weekends he didn't have Ari. He had really missed Ari on their journey and reveled in the opportunity to spend more time with her.

But with Steve working nights and her working days, they didn't get to see each other much during the week. She found her mind wandering to think of Steve instead of grading papers.

So far their dates had been typical first dates. They had gone miniature golfing, gone out for dinner, taken drives up Provo Canyon to look at the leaves changing color. They asked each other endless questions about their likes and dislikes, who their first kiss was, food they hated—things like that.

It sometimes seemed silly to Emma. They had been through a lot together and knew each other already on a much deeper level. But neither of them wanted to rush things, especially with Steve being divorced.

Emma hadn't even met Ari yet. Part of her wondered why. Did that mean Steve wasn't as serious about her as she was about him? But another part knew that he loved Ari deeply and just didn't want to introduce someone in her life unless it was someone he was going to marry.

Emma tried to focus on the paper in front of her, but the words just kept going fuzzy. She stood up and stretched, trying to refocus her mind. She was just about to sit down when she heard a sound just outside her door.

Her body immediately tensed and she checked to make sure the door was locked. She realized with a start that she had forgotten to lock it. She had been in her office since 6:00 and the building was still full of students walking through or studying. The hours had flown by and it was late now. She reached over and quickly locked the door, straining to hear into the hallway.

Her heart raced as she heard footsteps. She had worried that someone might come after them. She knew Steve worried about it as well. That's why he had arranged to work nights on the same nights that she worked late. He wanted to be around in case she needed him.

But tonight wasn't one of those nights. It was a Friday night and he had Ari tonight. He would be home asleep with Ari.

She heard another noise and frantically searched her purse for her cell phone. She dialed Steve's number and prayed he would pick up. Ring. Ring. Ring. It finally went to voicemail.

She knew no one else would be in the building. None of her colleagues worked this late, especially on a Friday night. They would all have gone to their kids' football or soccer games, or on a date with their husbands or wives and would now be snugly curled up in bed together.

She tried Steve's number again, but he still didn't pick up. Panicked, she thought of calling 911, but hesitated. What if she was wrong? What if she had imagined the noise? It would look really silly to have the campus and Provo police surrounding the empty building with her alone in it.

She put her ear up against the door and listened. The footsteps were gone and she couldn't hear anything. She watched the clock and waited. 5 minutes. 10 minutes. She tried Steve's number again, but still nothing.

It was now after midnight and she knew she couldn't stay in her office forever. She had to know what she was up against so she could make a judgment call on whether to notify the police.

Her cell phone gripped tightly in her hand, she gently eased the lock open. Nothing. She summoned all of her courage and pushed down on the door lock, trying to do it silently. She cracked the door open about a half an inch and looked out. The hallway was empty. She listened again for a few more minutes, but all her ears found was silence. She gathered up her purse and got out her car keys. She would make a dash from the building to her car in the parking lot. That was, *if* she made it out of the building.

Her entire body on alert, she pulled the door open a few more inches and pushed her head through the opening, glancing in both directions down the hallway. What she saw puzzled her. There, lying in the middle of the hallway was a red rose.

Confused, but still scared, she opened the door farther and looked down the hallway at the rose. She saw another one at the end of the hallway, where it curved toward the lobby.

Her first thought was of Steve. Had he left her the rose? But it didn't make sense. Steve was home with Ari and he hadn't picked up his cell phone.

Maybe it was a trap. They knew she had locked her office, so they needed to lure her out. She hesitated and listened, but still couldn't hear anything. She went back into her office and locked the door again. She would ask one of the campus police to come by, just in case. She dialed the police number and asked if they could have someone come by and escort her to her car. They confirmed that someone would be there within five minutes.

She waited, still with her ear pressed against the locked door. Everything was quiet. After a few minutes, she heard approaching footsteps and almost jumped when she heard a loud knock on the door.

"Professor Worthington, it's Sam," she heard the young police officer call. "I'm here to escort you to your car."

She recognized his voice—she had met him one night when Steve was off duty, so she opened the door. He was a thin, redhead, freckle-faced kid and Emma wondered who would be protecting whom. But he had a gun, so she gathered up her papers and followed him out into the hallway.

"Working late, huh?" Sam asked conversationally.

Emma could hear a lilt in his voice, almost as if he was mocking her. Yes, she was probably being foolish, she thought to herself. But she had been through enough danger lately. She didn't want to be in any more. "Yes, probably too late," Emma said self-depreciatingly. "I don't like walking out to the parking lot alone."

Sam smiled and nodded and as they came around the corner, he stopped. Emma could see a trail of red roses leading all of the way down the hallway. At the end of the trail was a smiling Steve.

"I told you she would be freaked out, Steve," Sam said laughing as he walked toward Steve.

Emma just stopped in her tracks and said accusingly, "Steve! What are you doing? Why haven't you picked up your phone!"

Steve walked toward her and said, "Man, kill a guy for trying to do something romantic," he teased. "Thanks, Sam. I can protect her from here on out. That is, protect her from *myself.*"

Sam laughed and headed out the door with the smug reply, "Have fun you two."

Steve laughed again when he saw the upset look on Emma's face. "Emma, I was just trying to surprise you!" he said smiling.

"Well, you did!" Emma shouted. "You nearly gave me a heart attack! I thought someone was out for revenge." She playfully hit him on the shoulder when he got close enough, but he just pulled her into his arms for a kiss.

"Ah, no, you're still in trouble," she said leaning stubbornly away from his kiss. "I thought you had Ari tonight. I thought you were home in bed. And why didn't you pick up your phone? You could have let me know if was just you out here."

Steve reached out and held her hand and replied, "That would have spoiled the surprise. I didn't know you were going to freak out and call the police."

Emma finally relaxed enough to laugh at herself, "Well, do you blame me? We've been through a lot lately. Hearing footsteps outside of my office door at midnight and when everything started here as well."

Steve smiled and slyly replied, "That's right, we met right here in this hallway for the first time."

Emma smiled back and said sarcastically, "Yeah, and you held a gun to my head. Very romantic." Emma had been grading papers late that night as well. She thought back to the past few months. Her whole life had changed and all because of Steve.

"You were pretty cool under pressure," Steve whispered in her ear and then added playfully, "more so than tonight."

She pushed him playfully and then said, "So you still haven't answered my question. I thought you had Ari tonight."

"Kari called and said she had the stomach flu and wanted to keep her at home," Steve replied sadly. "So I thought I would work on a special surprise. I had the roses on the doorstep of your condo, but when you didn't come home, I resorted to Plan B and came here."

He then pulled her gently down the hallway and into the lobby area. "Besides, Plan B is so much better than Plan A," he said in a soft voice into her ear. She looked into the common room area and saw that Steve had put a tablecloth over one of the study tables and had long candles that were lit. He had slices of cheesecake on plates.

Emma smiled at his thoughtfulness and leaned over to kiss him on the cheek. "This *is* very romantic," she agreed. "I'm sorry I didn't come home earlier. I would have if I had known. I haven't been very effective at grading papers in the last few hours. I'm just been sitting here thinking of you, missing you."

Steve pulled her into his arms and held her. He felt Emma's body relax and he kissed her on top of the head. "You haven't even seen the best part," he added. He pulled a remote control out of his pocket and pushed play. An iPod in a docking station began playing one of Emma's favorite slow songs. "May I have this dance?" he whispered in her ear.

Emma nodded and realized she was about to cry. Steve heard her sniffle and lifted her chin up so he could look at her face. "Happy cry or sad cry?" he asked.

"Happy-that-I'm-not-going-to-get-killed-tonight cry," she said, smiling through the tears. "And happy-that-I- have-you cry," she added sincerely. Steve kissed her again and then resumed the dance. He slowly guided her over to the table and after the song ended, Steve pulled back Emma's chair and helped her sit down.

She felt like a teenager again, fluttering with excitement. And she realized it was a small miracle. She and Steve had been through so much both apart and together. It was so great to be here, together. For everything to have come full circle.

They ate their cheesecake and talked late into the night. Emma noticed Steve had started to become a bit nervous. She finally asked, "What's wrong?"

Steve hesitated and then said, "I have something very serious to ask you. I've been wanting to ask you all week, but I've been waiting for the right time."

Emma's heart fluttered and she wondered if he was about to ask her to marry him. She leaned forward in her chair in anticipation.

"Yes?" she prompted with an encouraging smile.

Steve gathered his courage and then said, "Will you have dinner with me and Ari next weekend?"

Emma felt deflated. "That's it?" she blurted out.

Steve turned red and embarrassed and said, "What do you mean?"

"I thought you were going to ask me to marry you!" Emma said disappointedly.

Steve searched her face and then said, "I don't want to take things too fast. But this is a big thing for me, having you now in Ari's life. I would only ask that with someone who I'm very serious about, Emma."

Emma still felt disappointment, but she tried to cover it. "I know," she reassured him. "And I'd love to have dinner with you and Ari. I've been looking forward to meeting her."

But Steve could see the disappointment on her face and he knew he had blown it. "Ok, I will let you know when she's feeling better and I'll cook you both dinner," he said.

The mood was gone, so Emma helped Steve clean up. As she picked up the rose trail leading to her office, she pricked her finger on one of the roses. It was nothing compared to the prick she had felt in her heart.

Chapter 45

Steve didn't sleep well that night. He knew he had blown it. The truth was, he wanted to ask Emma to marry him, but he was still afraid. He knew he had waited too long as well to have her meet Ari. He didn't know why he was holding back.

He finally got up and drove around, thinking. He ended up at a park near Ari's house. He knew Kari jogged there each morning. He went and sat on a park bench and waited. The sun was just coming up when he heard Kari come around the corner. She was toward the end of her workout and she was heavily sweating.

She looked at Steve in surprise and stopped, running in place. "Steve, what are you doing here?" she asked, panting, checking her pulse.

"Can we talk?" he asked sincerely, looking up at Kari hopefully.

Kari hesitated. She wanted to finish her run and get back to the house to see how Ari was doing this morning, but there was something in Steve's face that made her give in. "All right," she agreed, sitting down beside him on the bench.

Steve was quiet for a few minutes, trying to figure out how to start. He finally looked at Kari and said, "I've met someone and I think I want to marry her."

Kari looked at Steve and could see dark circles underneath his eyes and the worry on his face. "That's great, Steve," she responded with enthusiasm. "I'm really happy for you." She realized she genuinely meant it. She had found happiness with her second husband, Brian. Steve deserved that much as well. He didn't respond and so she asked, "*Are you happy?*"

"Yes," Steve replied, almost sadly, "Happier than I've been since before I went on my first tour of duty."

"So what's the problem then?" Kari asked, getting straight to the point. She flexed her leg muscles while she waited, hoping to get back to her run soon.

"I don't want to be a bad husband again," Steve answered honestly as he focused on the ground, "Like I was with you."

Kari thought about that for a minute. Yes, she had punished him for years for being a "bad husband." But as the years had gone on and she found happiness with Brian, she knew deep down that a lot of their problems were her fault as well. She had just wanted to blame Steve and he was already punishing himself, so it made it easy to focus on him.

She finally sighed and put her hand on Steve's back. "Steve, you weren't a bad husband," she assured. "In fact, looking back, you did a lot to try and save our marriage. More than I was willing to do. You were just an absent husband. And I just didn't have it in me to be a military wife."

Steve thought about her words, but didn't reply, nor look up from the ground.

Kari could see he still wasn't convinced, so she added, "Steve, I'm a lot older now and I can see that I made a lot of mistakes, too. I wasn't supportive. I was selfish. I wasn't as strong as I could have been. You were doing a brave thing, serving our country. I'm sure you went through some horrible things. But I could only think of myself. I know it's not an excuse, but I'm pretty sure I had post-partum depression after Ari was born. I've looked back on photographs of myself and I'm frowning in every single one of them. Everything was overwhelming to me. I couldn't cope."

"I should have been there for you," Steve offered sincerely. "I should have helped you through it."

Kari smiled and continued, "If I would have known what it was at the time, I could have gotten some help from my doctor. I just didn't know. She was my first baby."

At the word baby, Steve tensed. He thought about letting it drop, but he needed to say it. He forced the words out. "I'm sorry I wasn't there for you when you lost our son," he said, tears coming to his eyes. He looked into Kari's eyes and saw that she had them, too.

Kari nodded, not able to speak. She finally said, "It was s-so hard."

Steve put his arm around Kari and pulled her into a half hug. Their heads touched and they both watched as their tears fell down onto the sidewalk.

"Sometimes I dream about him," Steve whispered. He hadn't even told Emma that yet. It was just too painful. "I dream about all of us standing together, with him and Ari. In my dreams, he looks like a miniature version of your dad."

Kari smiled and thought about that. "He would be three years old now," she said sadly.

They sat in silence for a few minutes and then Kari reached over and took Steve's hand and pulled back to look into his eyes. "I forgive you, Steve," she answered honestly. "And please forgive me as well. It just didn't work out with us. But I'm happy now with Brian. I truly am. And you deserve that as well. If you love this girl, marry her, and have a wonderful life together. Ari will love her, too."

Steve stood up and pulled Kari into a hug and felt years of failure and frustration falling off of him. Forgiveness was such a powerful thing. He felt so grateful to finally see the Kari he had fallen in love with—the kind, happy Kari. He knew now that he could move on. He knew that he and Kari would be even better co-parents with Ari as well.

"Thank you, Kari," he whispered into her ear. "It means so much to me."

"Why don't you come back to the house with me," Kari said generously. "Ari should be up by now and if she's feeling better, she can come home with you. She slept all night, so I'm thinking the stomach flu is over. She told me she was really sad that she couldn't see you last night."

Steve smiled and walked back to the house with Kari and found Brian cooking breakfast in the kitchen and Ari sitting at the table.

"How's my girl?" Steve asked brightly, glad to see Ari up and around.

"Daddy!" Ari screamed in delight and came running toward him. "I missed you!"

Steve scooped Ari up in his arms and swung her around. He then pulled her into a hug and whispered, "I missed you, too, Aribuggyboo."

He took a deep breath and inhaled. He loved that first-of-the-morning smell of Ari. He could still smell the strawberry-scented shampoo that Kari used on her hair the night before.

"How are you feeling, honey?" Steve asked, holding Ari back so he could look at her face.

"Daddy, Brian is making chocolate chip pancakes!" Ari squealed.

Kari and Brian laughed at that. "I'll take that as a yes, that you're feeling lots better, pumpkin," Steve replied with a smile.

Brian flipped a pancake and then asked, "Stay for breakfast, Steve?"

Steve once again admired Brian. He had always reached out the olive branch to Steve over the years. He tried to include him as much as possible. Steve was glad Kari had found a guy like Brian to remarry.

But in the past, Steve had always politely declined. It had been too hard to witness Kari and Brian's little happy family up close. Steve suddenly didn't feel that way anymore. He felt his talk with Kari that morning was healing his heart. "I'd love to," he brightly responded.

Brian looked surprised and looked at Kari for an explanation, but Kari just smiled. "And guess, what, Ari?" she asked.

"What?" Ari asked with big eyes.

"After you eat your pancakes, you get to go home with Daddy!" Kari added warmly. "And he has someone very special for you to meet."

Ari looked at Steve with big eyes, "Is it President Thompson?" she asked.

Steve laughed and said, "Well, maybe another time, but this is someone else. Her name is Emma. And she's my girlfriend." It felt good to say it out loud. It felt like everything was falling into place just as it should.

"Ooo, Daddy!" Ari commented with a smile, "You have a girlfriend?"

"Yes," Steve replied. "And we're going to make her dinner tonight." Steve knew how much Ari loved to help him cook. It usually ended up as a big mess, but he loved it anyway.

"Are we going to make chocolate chip cookies?" Ari asked brightly.

"Sure," Steve replied. "But we'd better make some other food, too, okay?"

"Okay, Daddy," she agreed, nodding her head seriously.

"Now, let's have some of Brian's chocolate chip pancakes!" Steve said, setting Ari back down at the table.

They ate companionably together and Steve could see this was their future. They were all a big family together—Ari, Kari, Brian and himself. He hoped Emma as well. They would all work together to raise Ari and hopefully they would have other children.

Kari and Brian asked Steve about his adventure. They had read about it in the paper. He recounted all except the scariest parts. It felt good to share his life with Kari and Brian. He talked a lot about Emma and even told them about the previous night.

"Daddy," Ari offered, "If you hurt her feelings then you should say you're sorry.

"I know," Steve answered with a smile. "I will."

"We could make her a sorry card with my crayons," Ari suggested. "I even have some glitter glue!"

Steve couldn't resist the offer and agreed. He followed Ari into her bedroom and together they spent the next hour making a card for Emma. Steve then helped Ari pack her weekend bag and he carried her out to the car.

"Tummy still okay?" he asked her as he buckled her into her car seat.

"Yes, Daddy," Ari nodded, her curls bobbing.

"How about we take Emma's card to her right now?" Steve asked.

"Yes," Ari answered solemnly, "We should, daddy."

Steve drove right over to Emma's townhouse and looked at the time. It was almost 9 and he thought Emma would be up, despite the late night. Just in case, he gently knocked on the door.

After a minute, Emma came to the door. She was still in her sweats and had her hair in a ponytail. She looked surprised to see Steve and then glanced down at Ari.

"Emma, this is my daughter, Ari," Steve introduced. "And Ari, this is my girlfriend, Emma."

Emma smiled at Ari and then got down on her knees to meet Ari at eye level. "Hello, Arianna," Emma said kindly. "I'm so happy to meet you."

Ari smiled and replied directly, "My daddy is sorry and we made you this card!" She then produced the card from behind her back and shoved it excitedly in Emma's face.

Emma leaned back in surprise, almost falling over. "Well, thank you, Ari!" She took the card and looked at it, her heart melting. She impulsively pulled Ari into a hug and added, "I especially like the glitter. Did you do that part?"

"Uh-huh," Ari replied nodding her head and then looked up pointedly at Steve. "But Daddy wrote the sorry part."

Emma smiled and then stood up to meet Steve's gaze. He reached over and took her hand and said, "I *am* sorry, Emma."

"It's okay," Emma offered with a half-smile. "You're cheating though. Coming to ask forgiveness with such a cute little girl and a glitter card."

Steve smiled and squeezed her hand as he laughed, "I know, but I just don't want to lose you." He then pulled her hand up to his lips and kissed it.

Emma studied his face. Something was different. Steve had changed somehow since last night. He seemed more relaxed. More confident. Less troubled. "Why don't you two come on in," Emma offered, guiding Ari into her townhouse. "And, Ari, come into the kitchen with me. I have a surprise for you."

Steve watched them disappear into the kitchen. He was happy to see how at ease Emma and Ari were with each other. Emma seemed a natural with her. He heard Ari's squeal of delight in the kitchen, so he followed them in to see what was happening.

"I bought this a few weeks ago, for when I met you," Emma said. "I thought we could do it together."

Ari saw Steve walk into the room, so she said, "Look, Daddy, Emma and I are going to make necklaces together." Ari was holding a necklace-making kit. It was the perfect gift. She loved girlie things and Emma had nailed it perfectly picking something they could do together.

"How about we do them right now?" Emma suggested, looking at Ari and then Steve.

Ari heartily agreed and Steve watched as Emma and Ari opened the box and dumped out the contents. Tiny squares had individual letters on them as well other shapes like stars, hearts and rainbows.

Steve sat down with them at the table and watched his two girls together. He felt warm and happy inside, seeing them together. Emma was already a natural mom.

"Ari, what's your favorite color?" Emma was asking Ari as she held out the different string colors.

"Pink!" Ari answered brightly, carefully selecting all of the heart-shaped squares. She then slowly picked out the letters for her name.

Emma helped Ari thread the small blocks onto the string, putting a heart block between each letter of her name. They then made a bracelet using all of the rainbow blocks and made the words, I Love You.

"Daddy, aren't you going to make a necklace?" Ari asked plaintively.

Steve laughed and thought again how lucky he was to have Ari. "Okay," Steve agreed and then an idea came to his mind. Emma was busy focusing on Ari, so he quickly put together a necklace for Emma.

When they were all finished, Ari said, "Let's see your necklace, Daddy."

Steve slipped it into his pocket. "I made one for Emma, but I'm going to wait and give it to her tonight. Emma, will you come and have dinner with Ari and me tonight? Ari is going to help me cook, aren't you, sweetie?"

"Uh-huh," Ari nodded brightly, looking at Emma, "And we're going to make chocolate chip cookies."

Steve stood up and helped Emma clean the table. "Depending on how the cooking goes, that might be all we're having for dinner," he whispered to Emma.

She smiled and looked over at him. He stopped cleaning for a minute and reached over to gently kiss Emma. Suddenly, everything he wanted in the whole world was right here. He wanted every day to be like this, together with his girls. He couldn't wait for tonight—to finally ask Emma to marry him.

"Well, Ari, we'd better head out," Steve said, thinking of all the things he needed to do before tonight. "We've got to go shopping so we can make dinner for Emma tonight."

Emma carefully tied on Ari's necklace and bracelet. Ari hugged Emma and then said, "Thank you, Emma, for the fun play date."

Steve and Emma smiled and looked at each other. Steve thought how beautiful Emma looked, even in sweats and with a ponytail. He pulled her close into a hug and whispered in her ear, "I love you."

She held on to him tightly and then whispered back, "I love you, too, Steve."

Steve cupped her face in his hands and kissed her gently several times.

"C'mon, Daddy," Ari pleaded impatiently. "Let's go make cookies."

Steve smiled at Emma and said, "We'll see you tonight. How about 6?"

Emma nodded her agreement and waved as they left.

Emma had spent all day getting pampered. She had gone to the hairdressers and had even splurged and had her nails done. She then went shopping and bought herself a new outfit. She could feel her life was about to change—forever and for the better.

She could see the change in Steve that morning and knew he had come to terms with his past. She hoped that meant he was ready to move on with his future.

She arrived at Steve's house right at 6. Ari was dressed up in a black, velvet dress with a black bow in her curly hair. She answered the door and hugged Emma. Emma was amazed by her warmth and immediate acceptance. She is at a good age to have someone new come into her life, Emma thought. She knew it could have been different had Ari been older.

Ari led her into Steve's living room where Emma could see a candlelight table set up in the living room. She started to head toward the kitchen when Steve intercepted her. He was dressed in his best suit, but still had a *Kiss the Cook* apron around his neck.

"Hello, Em," he said, giving her a quick kiss. When Emma tried to move with him into the kitchen, he stopped her. "Take my word for it—you *don't* want to go in there." He smiled and then whispered, "I had *a lot* of help making dinner."

"Ah," Emma said knowingly smiling at Steve and then Ari.

Steve then guided Emma over to the table and pulled out her chair for her and seated her. He then said, "C'mon, Ari, let's get the food." Ari happily skipped into the kitchen, holding Steve's hand.

Emma happily soaked up the atmosphere. Steve had put on soft music and there was a bowl full of red roses on the table. The candles were glowing and Emma felt content with happiness. She felt at ease now that Steve had introduced Ari in her life. It meant that they had a future together.

She reflected on how much her life had changed over the past few months. She had thought she would never marry nor have children. Now she hoped to marry Steve and if so, she would become an instant parent.

"Careful, careful," Emma heard Steve instruct Ari. She was walking in with a bowl of salad with Steve crouched behind her, steadying her hands on the heavy bowl. She made it to the table without spilling and Steve gently lifted the bowl from Ari's hands and placed it on the table.

He then pulled back Ari's chair to seat her. "No, Daddy," she said in a determined voice. "I want to help you serve *everything*."

Emma smiled knowingly at Steve who was trying to hide his impatience. "All right, darlin', c'mon."

Serving took several minutes as Ari carried in each and every item with Steve helping her balance the heavier things. They finally had everything on the table and they stopped to bow their heads in prayer to offer thanks and ask for a blessing on the food.

As they began to eat, Emma found herself staring at Steve. He looked so handsome in his suit and tie. She watched him with Ari and knew he was an incredible father. She felt so lucky as she watched him during dinner, so lucky that he loved *her*. She asked Ari lots of questions as well, so that she could get to know her better.

After they had eaten dinner, Ari scampered off to the kitchen to bring in the chocolate chip cookies. Emma smiled as she saw some of them were two inches in diameter and some were six. She would have to remember as a parent that everything didn't have to be precise.

As they finished dessert, Steve then asked Ari if she wanted to dance and Emma watched happily as Ari's face glowed with delight as she danced with Steve. Emma could tell that they did this all of the time together. Ari naturally placed her shoes on top of Steve's shoes and they danced around the room together.

After a few songs, Steve said to Ari, "Now it's Emma's turn. But it's also time for you to go to bed. Let's go get your jammies on. Say goodnight to Emma."

Emma knelt down and met Ari's hug. "Goodnight, Ari," she said with a smile. "Sweet dreams."

"Bye-bye, Emma," Ari replied and then happily skipped off to her room with Steve.

While Steve was off with Ari, Emma took the chance to glance in the kitchen. It was a disaster. Flour was scattered all over the countertops and on the floor. Dishes were piled up in the sink. Egg shells were strewn across the countertops. Typically a neat freak, Emma smiled and thought about how life changed as you had kids. Making dinner together was much more about being together than being efficient and clean. Emma admired Steve's priorities.

"Now, now," Steve said, pulling Emma away from the kitchen. "You weren't supposed to look in there."

She smiled at him in reply as Steve pulled her into a dance. He then added softly, looking into her eyes, "I wanted tonight to be perfect."

Emma sighed with contentment and replied, "It *is* perfect." She sank closer toward his chest as they danced and he held her tightly as they swayed to the music.

Midway through the third song, they heard Ari's voice, "Daddy, I need a drink." Steve and Emma smiled at each other knowingly. She was too excited to go to bed.

Steve stopped dancing and walked over to Ari, "Now young lady, you know I put a drink of water by your bed."

Ari smiled sheepishly and said, "Oh yeah, I forgot."

"Uh-huh," Steve said knowingly. "Now c'mon, back to bed." Emma watched as Steve walked her back to her bedroom. She could then hear Steve reading her another story, trying to settle her down for the night.

Emma studied pictures in the living room. Steve had several pictures of her as a baby, and then a few each year until the current year. He also had a picture of his family growing up. Emma looked forward to meeting them.

Steve finally re-emerged from Ari's room and said, "I had to rub her back forever, but she finally fell asleep."

Emma smiled at Steve. It felt so domestic, putting Ari to bed and then being alone together. It felt like they were already married.

"Now that she's finally asleep . . ." Steve said, nuzzling Emma's neck and pulling her down to sit on the couch together.

Emma smiled happily and relaxed, feeling the warmth spread throughout her body. He kissed her neck and then moved up toward her earlobes. Emma closed her eyes and felt Steve tug gently on her ear with his teeth.

He then whispered in her ear, "Emma, I love you. I want every night to be like this. I want to be with you every day, every minute."

"Me, too," she whispered back contentedly.

Steve then pulled back and studied Emma's face. He smiled and then reached into his suit coat pocket. He gave Emma the necklace that he had made earlier with Ari.

Emma smiled and looked at the necklace. Steve had spelled out the words Will You Marry Me.

Tears came to Emma's eyes and she happily nodded yes, not trusting herself to speak. The tears ran over her eyelids as she tried to blink them away and they rolled down her cheeks. Steve gently kissed her tears away and then kissed her lips, at first softly and then more insistently. They kissed again and again, locked in a tight embrace. Emma didn't want him to ever stop.

Steve finally slowed and then said in her ear, "How about we get married tomorrow? I don't know how long I can wait."

Emma smiled and said, "Me neither. Let's get married as soon as possible."

They started to talk wedding plans. They both wanted to get married in the Salt Lake temple. Emma could already see them kneeling across from each other, their hands clasped together on the soft, padded altar, looking into the mirrors on either side of the room that created an eternal reflection. Their family and friends would encircle them around the room and would watch as they were pronounced husband and wife not just for this life, but for all eternity as well.

Emma finally couldn't stand it anymore and said, "Now, let's go clean up the kitchen together."

Steve smiled, knowing her compulsively clean nature and replied as he pulled her up off the couch, "Hey, I told you not to look."

Emma smiled back and then held hands as they walked into the kitchen together.

Chapter 46

RJ sat at his home office desk, surrounded by piles of bills. He had let his personal life slide during his crusade to destroy the Mormons. And while he was absent, his soon-to-be-ex-wife had been racking up a considerable amount of bills. Shopping trips to New York. Weekend getaways with friends to Paris. Regular visits to the liposuction doctor.

He hadn't even seen his wife for several weeks now. She was always out when he came home from work. He couldn't face being in the office anymore, so he had uncharacteristically taken a few weeks off.

It was Preston's betrayal that was hardest for him. At first all he could feel was anger. He had even met with Callie several times to discuss how to take out Preston. But in the end, RJ couldn't do it. Preston had been his only friend for over a decade. Even though he had saved the Mormons, he had saved RJ financially as well.

He had to admit it—he admired Preston and always had. Preston always had his life so together. While RJ had nothing but chaos. A string of failed marriages. Children who either used or hated him. Multiple failed investments.

RJ stood up and stretched. He felt so tired these days. It had been deflating, watching the Mormons become vindicated. It had been all over the news with several prominent individuals commenting positively about the Mormons.

It had made him sick.

He walked around the house, searching for something, even though he didn't know what. He went room to room, wandering aimlessly. The house was clean—he had a maid come in every day and she also cooked breakfast for him. But it was cluttery. RJ had a passion to possess things, and impulsively bought obscure items as he traveled. He looked at the elephant statue he had purchased in San Francisco, the weird art mosaic in New York, the surfboard signed by a championship surfer in Hawaii. He had wanted an eclectic collection, but here, in his house, it just looked bizarre.

He had been in Preston's house numerous times. Beth always warmly invited him to join them for holiday dinners. When he was between marriages, he always accepted and brought Riley with him. Preston's home was everything that RJ's wasn't. Manicured was the word that came to mind. Everything was neat and tidy. His art collection flowed from room to room. It had even been commented on by local experts.

Preston and Beth were renowned for their generous charitable contributions and Beth didn't stop at just writing out a check. She was always on-site to help the homeless, the sick and the needy.

RJ wondered if he had found someone like Beth how his life might have been different. But RJ knew the differences didn't stop there. Preston had principles and had worked tirelessly over the past decade to keep RJ out of jail.

RJ wandered toward the conservatory at the back of the house. This had been his second wife's idea. She had wanted to bring more sunlight into their mansion, so RJ had added a conservatory on the back to please her.

But there wasn't any sunlight today. Rain streaked down the windows and RJ heard a clap of thunder outside. He watched the rain for a few minutes and then headed back to his study. He was just starting to pay the bills when he heard a noise in the hallway.

"Hi, Dad," RJ heard coming from the entryway. It was Riley's voice. He had a key and always just let himself in.

"Hello, son," RJ said in a mellow voice as Riley came through the office door.

Riley was running a hand through his hair, trying to get the water off. "It's sure coming down out there," he said. Riley took off his jacket and flung it over the nearest couch and sat down.

When his dad didn't respond, but continued to examine the bills he was paying, Riley studied his dad's face. He looked older now, less confident, even defeated. It stunned Riley a bit. He had always thought of his dad as a formidable force that was hell-bent on getting his own way with everything.

Watching him now, he just looked like a tired, old man.

It unnerved Riley a bit. Trying to spark some of his bluster, he said, "So how are things at the office, Dad?"

RJ continued to write out checks and didn't look up. "I haven't been in for a few weeks. Needed a break."

Riley started to feel alarmed. His dad had never taken more than a week off in his whole life. Usually it was just a day here and there at the insistence of whatever wife he had at the time.

RJ paused writing, seemed to think of something, and looked up at Riley. "How's your mother?"

Riley was stunned. RJ never asked about his mom. They had been divorced for a long time. "She's painting again," Riley finally offered, studying RJ's face carefully. "She's hoping to do an exhibit in the spring."

RJ thought about that and smiled. "She always loved to paint. When we first met, I would sneak away from work to meet her at her art studio. I used to stand behind her and watch her painting emerge from the canvas, like magic."

Now Riley was really alarmed. He couldn't remember a time when his dad had said something positive about his mom. "Dad, are you feeling all right?" he ventured.

"Yes, of course I am," RJ said, a hint of impatience in his voice but then he admitted, "Just a little tired lately."

Riley studied his face. It looked a bit pale, but then, his dad didn't get out of the office much to enjoy the sunshine or go on vacation.

RJ was studying Riley as well. He looked so much like his mother. RJ hadn't ever admitted to anyone, not even himself, that he wished he hadn't divorced her. Of all his ex-wives, she was his favorite. She had loved him before he had any money. They had fallen in love as students. He remembered those years fondly, going on dates and always sharing a dinner since they couldn't afford anything else.

She had grown up in a wealthy family though and as the years had gone on, she had wanted more than their shabby apartment. He began to push himself very hard at work and eventually made the gutsy move to start his own business. He worked around the clock to ensure success and wealth for her.

But the long hours took their toll and they easily grew apart. She began to see her old friends and hang out with Atlanta's elite and from that point, they never recovered. He had taken her and Riley on a vacation to the Caribbean, to try and salvage things. But by that point, she was no longer interested.

Still, she stayed with RJ. He thought just for the money, but looking back, he wondered if she had hoped things would change. He recalled several of their fights where she pleaded with him not to work so much.

He had an affair soon after that and divorced her so he could make room for wife number two. But looking back, he realized he had been trying to fill the gap that she had left all of those years ago.

He realized, deep down, that money was the problem. Maybe they would have been happy living in their two-bedroom apartment if neither of them were obsessed with getting more money. And it was never enough. They always spent more than they earned and constantly needed more and more.

Now RJ had money. Lots of it. But he had an empty house and a string of ex-wives and alimony and child support payments.

Riley had decided to save the paper he had folded in his pocket until the right moment. He was waiting to use it when his dad was ready to disinherit him or cut off his allowance. But this was much worse. Seeing his dad defeated like this and only a shadow of the blustery, aggressive person that he usually was. It unnerved Riley.

"Dad, I have a present for you," Riley said, reaching into his pocket and pulling out the folded paper.

RJ looked up in surprise. Riley was all about taking—very rarely about giving. Maybe there was hope for the boy yet, he thought. RJ took the offered paper and slowly unfolded it, looking at Riley's face and then down at the paper.

It took him a few minutes to understand what was on the paper. He studied the handmade drawing and read some of the comments written at the side. And then slowly, it dawned on him what he held in his hands.

He looked up at Riley and saw the pleading look of wanting approval. It was subtle, but he hadn't gotten so far in business without being able to read people. RJ's face broke out into a huge smile and he impulsively pulled Riley into a hug.

"Well, done, my boy!" he boomed, feeling infused with his old enthusiasm, patting Riley heartily on the back. "Where did you get this?"

Riley smiled, basking finally in his dad's approval. "I have my sources," he said slyly, grinning from ear to ear.

"You're a chip off the old block, Riley, my boy!" RJ continued. "We'll get those Mormons now. Let's see 'em try to get out of this one! I've got to get dressed and get to the office. We've got so much to do. And you'll be there. Right by my side, son, when we take them down once and for all."

A mental picture of Staci flashed in front of Riley's face, but he pushed it away. Staci had rejected him. He owed this to his father. His father had taken care of him his whole life. It was time for Riley to step up and do something for his dad now.

The years seemed to melt off of his dad. His face exuded excitement and he was rambling on about how he would destroy the Mormons. In his giddy state, he turned to Riley and said, "Son, you wait right here while I get dressed and then we'll head into the office together. We'll get you an office right next to mine . . ."

He was still rambling as he literally ran up the steps, taking them two at a time. Riley watched him in amazement. He couldn't believe the complete transformation from a tired, old man to a vibrant, driven, younger man.

But as his dad neared the top, he suddenly stopped. Riley watched as his dad bent over slightly and turned. RJ was clutching his chest and his eyes were filled with alarm. Riley realized his dad was having a heart attack and rushed up the stairs, taking them two at a time himself.

He got to his dad just as he fell backwards onto the landing. His dad was clutching his chest with one arm and the paper Riley had just given him with the other. Riley pulled his cell phone out of his pocket and dialed 911.

As he answered the dispatcher's questions, he watched his dad's face in agony and shock. He finally had his moment. They were going to destroy the Mormons together. But years of neglect and hard living had finally taken its toll on RJ.

Minutes felt like hours as Riley waited for the ambulance and EMTs. He finally heard a knock on the door and was just about to go answer it when he heard his dad whisper his name. He turned to look at his dad, who was trying to tell him something.

He leaned down closer to his dad to listen and he felt his dad shove the paper back into his hands. His dad's voice was barely audible as he said, "If I don't make it . . ." He paused, gathering his strength. "If I don't make it," he said a little louder, "Then you have to finish it. For me."

Riley looked at his dad's pleading yet insistent face. "Promise me . . ." his dad demanded with both his words and his eyes.

Riley could hear the paramedics pounding on the door again. He thought of Staci one more time and then realized this may well be his dad's last request. Riley took the paper from his dad and put it into his pocket and met his steady gaze. "I promise."

About the Author

It all started in 5th Grade when Lisa's mom bought her a Nancy Drew book and Lisa discovered she had an insatiable love of books.

Lisa graduated from Brigham Young University with a Bachelor of Arts Degree in English. She met her husband Glenn in Northern Ireland while studying abroad with BYU in London. She is a professional proposal and technical writer.

Lisa and Glenn have two wonderful children, Gavin and Sienna. They love traveling together and can be found most days at a soccer field.

www.ingramcontent.com/pod-product-compliance
Lightning Source LLC
Chambersburg PA
CBHW071254170626
46809CB00001B/221